Poet to Poet
Shelley Selected by Kat

Percy Bysshe Shelley (1792–1822) is best known for such shorter lyrics as 'Ode to the West Wind' and 'To a Skylark'. But his major works, strongly influenced by neo-platonism, are *Prometheus Unbound*, *Epipsychidion*, *Adonais* and his prose work, *A Defence of Poetry*.

Kathleen Raine was born in 1908. She studied at Girton College, Cambridge, where she later became a Fellow. Her first book of verse was *Stone and Flower* (1943). Her collected poems were published in 1956, since when she has published several volumes of verse, of which *The Lost Country* (1971) won the W. H. Smith Award for 1972. She carried out intensive scholarly work for many years on William Blake and delivered the Andrew Mellon lectures in Washington in 1962, which were later published as *William Blake and Traditional Mythology*. A selection of her poems is published in *Penguin Modern Poets 17*, together with selections by W. S. Graham and David Gascoyne.

SHELLEY

Selected by

Kathleen Raine

Penguin Books

Penguin Books Ltd, Harmondsworth,
Middlesex, England
Penguin Books Inc., 7110 Ambassador Road,
Baltimore, Maryland 21207, U.S.A.
Penguin Books Australia Ltd, Ringwood,
Victoria, Australia
Penguin Books Canada Ltd, 41 Steelcase Road
West, Markham, Ontario, Canada

First published, 1973

Made and printed in Great Britain by
Richard Clay (The Chaucer Press) Ltd
Bungay, Suffolk
Set in Monotype Ehrhardt

Contents

Introduction

'I am young and ye are very old' were the words of Elihu whose counsel brought comfort to Job where his friends had failed. Blake's well-known figure of Elihu seems to capture the very spirit of that 'new age' heralded by the American and French revolutions of which Shelley seems the type and embodiment. The new impulse the world felt at that time was a rise of youth, and the spirit of youth, against all the senile and rigid institutions of 'Aged Ignorance'; a reversal of the archetype of aged wisdom and youthful folly whose power, both for good and ill, we continue to experience. Those 'Notable Characters of the French Revolution' (to use the title of a book by Mary Shelley's mother, Mary Wollstonecraft) were most of them in their early twenties; the history of that time, both the best and the worst, was the work of young men; we should now call them 'students'.

Shelley's is the poetry of youth; 'But there is a spirit in man: and the inspiration of the Almighty giveth them understanding.' Of that spirit of God-given inspiration – expressed more often perhaps in music than in poetry – Shelley is the supreme poet. We do not think of the music of Mozart and Schubert as immature but as 'pure', flowing from some source whose unknown springs are not to be found in the world of experience. It is easy to say that youth is not always inspired and that Shelley's own life is a record of rash and ill-considered acts of whose consequence his elders could have warned him. But that brief life and early death (before his thirtieth birthday) seems a type and symbol of his age. His pursuit of perfection, with its trail of disaster in the lives of others and in his own, leaves us nevertheless wondering whether Shelley or the world was wrong.

Youth has a wisdom of its own which time and the world can only confuse and obscure; the vision of an ideal order and beauty imprinted in our nature like the memory of a pre-existent state, which we recognize in all those images of Paradisal perfection artists of the Platonic tradition – the 'inspired', be they musicians, painters or poets – have perennially depicted. In his art, if not in his life, Shelley was able to soar, to give expression to those dreams and visions which, continually broken by reality, are inextinguishable in the human spirit.

Inspiration, of the kind claimed for, or by, such poets, from Plato to Yeats, at one time scoffed at by fashionable positivists, seems again, as we learn more of the human psyche, credible. There are regions of the mind which seem possessed of knowledge beyond anything we may have acquired by study or experience; and this 'other mind' tells always of an immortal beauty, a mode of being which we can only long for and attempt to realize, or turn away from because such longing is too painful in this world necessity compels us to call real.

The young read Shelley because he writes of the world and of human beings as these seem to those in love; but his scope and depth stand the test of time and learning. That those in love see the world more truly, more fully, we doubt only when we are not ourselves in that state of expanded awareness. C. S. Lewis, in the best criticism of Shelley's poetry known to me, has hard words to say on 'imposters who claim to be disenchanted and are really unenchanted: mere "natural" men who have never risen so high as to be in danger of the generous illusions they claim to have escaped from . . . We need to be on our guard against such people. They talk like sages who have passed through the half-truths of humanitarian benevolence, aristocratic honour, or romantic passion, while in fact they are clods who have never yet advanced so far.' Happily the younger generation of 1972 are recovering the courage of their feelings; so much more reliable, as a rule, than their convictions. To respond to Shelley's invitation to ecstasy is to be lifted on wings like those Plato fabled grow on the shoulders of lovers. Those who cannot so respond can barely claim ever to have experienced poetry in its fulness, as the language of the awakened human spirit. C. S. Lewis (to return again to his defence of Shelley) wrote,

> Some anti-romantic repudiations of such poetry rest, perhaps, on a misunderstanding. It might be true, as the materialists must hold, that there is no possible way by which men can arrive at such felicity; or again, as Mr Eliot and I believe, that there is one Way, and only one, and that Shelley has missed it. But while we discuss these things, the romantic poet has added meaning to the word Felicity itself. Whatever the result of our debate, we had better attend to his discovery lest we remain more ignorant than we need have been of the very thing about which we debated.*

C. S. Lewis is defending Shelley against T. S. Eliot's anti-romantic strictures. He shares with Eliot the Christian view of man as a 'fallen' being in his nature and not merely in his circumstances. Shelley, a Platonist, believed that the soul is in its essential nature incorruptible, and that all evil results from a 'descent' into the material world. The Christian realization of 'original sin' belongs to the wisdom of bitter experience; but if the Christian view is, in terms of the living of a life in this world, the more realistic doctrine, it yet remains true that in the very idea of a 'fall' from some original perfection the Platonic view of the soul's nature is implicit. Shelley was anti-Christian not as Marxists and other sorts of materialists are, but as a Platonist who saw in

*C. S. Lewis, 'Shelley, Dryden, and Mr Eliot', *Selected Literary Essays*, ed. W. Hooper, Cambridge University Press, 1969, p. 208.

Christianity a distortion of a more ancient and universal knowledge. He believed – with much justification, and so did Blake, a Christian – that the 'God' of Christianity had become a moral tyrant, the projection of that human spirit of judgement and condemnation which Blake unhesitatingly calls 'Satan the Selfhood'. The sense of guilt implanted by this kind of moral Christianity seemed to Shelley (again as to Blake) at once the fruit of cruelty and its cause. C. S. Lewis defends Shelley against the facile charge of having no understanding of evil; quoting from *The Cenci* lines remarkable, on the contrary, for the modern penetration of the introspective mind of the man who sees the evil in himself, at once appalled and fascinated, as he becomes more deeply involved in, more deeply committed to, his lower nature. 'To know how bad we are, in the condition of nature, is an excellent recipe for becoming much worse'; so Lewis comments on the psychology of that powerful and still shocking play. When the soul outsoars this world of good and evil and as Shelley's successor, Yeats (also a Platonist), was to write:

> . . . learns at last that it is self-delighting,
> Self-appeasing, self-affrighting,
> And that its own sweet will is Heaven's will*

– then only will humanity discover its true lineaments.

For Shelley did believe that the true human lineaments are noble and beautiful beyond anything seen or conceived by the 'pestilence-stricken multitudes'. If Shelley's student politics are for the most part a projection of his own revolt against a remarkably intolerant father, and the means by which he hoped to see humanity made perfect by the mere overthrow of all 'tyrants' naïvely over-simple, not so his vision of what our humanity might be, and essentially is. The intuition of Apocatastasis – the return of all things to some

*W. B. Yeats, 'Prayer for my Daughter', *Collected Poems*, Macmillan, 1950, p. 214.

original perfection – is world-wide and age-old. In Platonic terms it is expressed in the myth of a Golden Age, periodically renewed in the revolutions of the Great Year of history. The Holy City of St John's Apocalypse is a theme already present in Plato, which has continued, as Blake's New Jerusalem, as the Byzantium both of Constantine and of Yeats, throughout European thought. It is abroad among a new generation who speak of their new 'Age of Aquarius'. Of this vision of transformation *Prometheus Unbound* is the supreme expression; a poem whose sustained greatness both of imaginative thought and of poetic form makes the ancient Aeschylean drama (again I quote from C. S. Lewis) seem 'merely embryonic'.

It has of course often been pointed out that the notion that the eighteenth-century 'Augustan' poets are in any sense truly 'classical' in thought or versification is mistaken. The name 'romantic' has, conversely, obscured the real and profound indebtedness of Coleridge, Blake, and – above all – Shelley to the Greek poets and philosophers. All these poets were in their several ways and degrees participants in the Greek Revival; Keats more especially in its visual and mythological aspect; Blake and Coleridge in the Neoplatonic philosophy and the aesthetics of Plotinus, revived at that time through the translations and writings of Thomas Taylor, 'the English Pagan'; and Shelley in both the Greek philosophy and the Greek literary works both lyrical and dramatic, which he read with ease in the original, and from which he has left several fine translations.

Shelley possessed Taylor's Plato and could very well have met 'the modern Pletho'. Mary Shelley's mother, Mary Wollstonecraft, had at one time been a lodger in Taylor's household; and his friend Thomas Love Peacock was an enthusiastic disciple and friend of Taylor (who is the 'Mr Mystic' of *Melincourt* even as Shelley is the 'Skythrop' of

Nightmare Abbey). Taylor wished to see and hoped to inaugurate a revival of the 'true religion' (the Platonic theology) and wrote of Christianity with the scorn of Gibbon. But unlike Gibbon he was what would later in the nineteenth century have been called a theosophist; he believed not too little for Christian orthodoxy, but a great deal too much:

> With respect to true philosophy, you must be sensible that all modern sects are in a state of barbarous ignorance: for Materialism, with its attendant Sensuality, have darkened the eyes of *many*, with the mists of error; and are continually strengthening its corporeal tie. And can any thing more effectually dissipate this increasing gloom than discourses composed by so sublime a genius, pregnant with the most profound conceptions, and everywhere full of intellectual light? Can any thing so thoroughly destroy the phantom of false enthusiasm, as establishing the real object of the true? Let us then boldly enlist ourselves under the banners of Plotinus, and, by his assistance vigorously repel the encroachments of error, plunge her dominions into the abyss of forgetfulness, and disperse the darkness of her baneful night. For, indeed, there never was a period which required so much philosophic exertion; or such vehement contribution from the lovers of Truth.*

So also thought Shelley; and I believe his debt to Taylor and the Greek revival is deeper than his debt to his tiresome father-in-law Godwin, whose debts he was for ever paying. If Shelley the student activist was inspired by Godwin, Shelley the poet was inspired by Plato and Plotinus.

As a pamphleteer and propagandist Shelley was no match for those clerical 'black-coated gentlemen' of Oxford whom Taylor – for whom Academic erudition was merely the instrument of philosophy – also scorned. But in his poetry Platonism is informed with imaginative life, clothed in beauty,

*'Concerning the Beautiful' (1787), Footnote II. See *Thomas Taylor the Platonist: Selected Writings*, ed. K. Raine and G. M. Harper, Routledge & Kegan Paul, 1969, p. 159.

activated by passion. Indeed Shelley more than any other of the Romantic poets (even Coleridge himself) restored to English poetry an intellectual scope, content and context comparable with that of the Athenian drama; and this, united with a purity and depth of feeling unsurpassed.

For we find in Shelley's poetry not only Plato's philosophy but his theology likewise. Shelley's 'spirit of Earth' is Plato's immortal and happy 'god', guardian-spirit of the single life of the planet as a whole, in which all creatures, from the elemental to the animate, and man himself, participate. It is not possible to see in the spirits and daemons of *Prometheus* mere poetic apparatus; for Shelley all things are spiritually animate: there are informing and guardian-spirits of cloud and river, of all living things; and the human mind itself is visited by impulses, thoughts and intuitions which may truly be called spiritual guides and guardians since they do not originate in the mind of any poor human individual, but belong to some greater order which sustains us in body and soul. All these ideas, all these agencies may be traced to the Orphic theology and, if not to Plato himself, to some one or other of those Neoplatonic philosophers Taylor had translated, but whose writings of course Shelley could, and undoubtedly did, read for himself in the original Greek.

A Christian objection constantly hurled at Shelley (but not by C. S. Lewis) is 'pantheism', whatever that means. But it can be equally objected (and Shelley doubtless strongly felt this objection) that Christian theology, by placing God outside his creation, has deprived 'nature' of spiritual life, and prepared the way for that scientific secularization and profanation of the universe from whose deadly results we now suffer. For the Platonic theology, all things have within and above them a spiritual dimension, a 'soul'; and are, in their various degrees, under the protection of the mundane and supermundane gods. For Shelley, as for Blake, 'everything that lives is holy'; not only in a general but in a very precise way not fully to be understood without some understanding of the Platonic theology which is the highly organized framework of Shelley's 'pantheism'. His 'atheism' too is Platonic; for Plato calls the Supreme spirit not a 'god' but the Good, and the One; altogether higher than the Demiurge or world-creator, or those hierarchies of lesser 'gods' whose operations are restricted to some part within the whole. A similar conception underlies the Tree of God of Jewish Cabbala; for the *Ain Soph* both is, and is not, 'God'; and so of course in Indian philosophy both Hindu and Buddhist.

Shelley has been blamed for what is in truth his supreme poetic gift – the lyrical ease, the fluency, the seemingly effortless eloquence of his language pouring itself out in perfect verse. There have been great poets – Yeats is one – the perfection of whose verse is the fruit of labour. But every true poet knows that his best lines, his best poems are those which seem divinely 'given', inspired, as Plato in the *Ion* describes it, by his 'Muse', or, as we should now say, the Unconscious or something of the kind – Elihu's 'inspiration of the Almighty'. Shelley's notebooks have somewhat the appearance of musical scores. It is as if whole poems came to him, or the forms of whole poems, with lines and phrases here and there, to be filled out by revision, as Mozart or Beethoven might fill in the orchestration of concerto or symphony. Almost one may speak of the 'orchestration' of that great symphony *Prometheus Unbound*, and yet music and meaning are born together, inseparably one. Such inspiration is only given to poets who, like Coleridge, like Milton, or Shelley himself, are deeply read in literature and intimately familiar with the forms of verse. I do not remember when it was that critics began to describe a poem as 'the words on the page'; a definition which would rule out Homer and Aeschylus. Yet I doubt whether even the critics memorize 'words on the page'. I hope not, for it is a fact that whereas we may read a poem with the eye we experience it with the ear – a test which quickly reveals weaknesses which 'words on the page' may conceal. Shelley's work is for the ear, and comes as near to music as poetry ever may, not only in its euphony but by that miraculous evocation of deep understanding which we receive from the greatest music.

Shelley is, above all, a poet of ideas. True, he can describe natural appearances (and especially those Turner-esque effects of light and cloud and water so characteristic of his vision) which the nineteenth century, and many critics even to the present day, tended to see as the proper themes of poetry. But with the Greeks this was not so; how rare are passages of description in the Greek tragedies, those expressions of the human mind struggling to discover its own inner laws and forms! There is in Shelley's poetry that same pressure, that urgency of human self-discovery. His love-poems, occasional only as arising out of some immediate situation, some event in the poet's life, tend to become, like *Epipsychidion*, as philosophic as the discourse of Diotima. Nor is there in this any forcing and strain; for Shelley love is full of profound insights and perceptions both of mind and heart. It is not *Epipsychidion* which exceeds the bounds of the theme of love: any lesser or merely carnal treatment does not come within sight of those frontiers.

Nor with Shelley is natural description given merely for its own sake. When he is describing the onrush of the West Wind he is speaking also of the Spirit that 'bloweth where it listeth'; when he describes the sky reflected in a forest pool he is speaking of heaven reflected on earth, eternity in time; or in the skylark's song discerns the very springs of poetic inspiration. And yet one may read such descriptions of cloud or wind or moonlight merely as description and find them exact in their beauty. Yet Shelley was himself aware at all times of the traditional language of analogy which he employs continually and with the ease of a mind that did in truth see the earth as the vesture of a living god. His symbols are not, as in Blake, as sometimes in Yeats, 'arbitrary, harsh, and difficult'; they are gathered up with the speed of thought from the natural world which was for him the mirror in which he saw reflected the spiritual forms of an intelligible order.

It was Eliot who saw in Shelley the one poet of his century 'who could even have begun to follow' Dante's footsteps; and saw in his latest work (presumably, above all, in the *Triumph of Life*) the influence of Dante. C. S. Lewis, commenting on this concession from Eliot, claims for Shelley that 'Shelley and Milton are, each, the half of Dante'; and he then attempts to describe (as to one who does not know Dante) what he means by this:

> You know the massive quality of Milton, the sense that every word is being held in place by a gigantic pressure, so that there is an architectural sublime in every verse whether the matter be sublime at the moment or not. You know also the air and fire of Shelley, the very antithesis of Miltonic solidity, the untrammelled, reckless speed through pellucid spaces which makes us imagine while we are reading him that we have somehow left our bodies behind.

Dante's poetry, he concludes, is 'as bright and piercing and aereal as the one, yet as weighty, as pregnant, as lapidary as the other'; but to be half of Dante 'is fame enough for any poet'.* Mary Shelley, who knew him best, wrote of him in the preface to the volume of his posthumous poems (published in 1824) which she had prepared:

> His life was spent in the contemplation of Nature, in arduous study, or in acts of kindness and affection. He was an elegant

*C. S. Lewis, op. cit.

scholar and a profound metaphysician; without possessing much scientific knowledge, he was unrivalled in the justness and extent of his observations on natural objects; he knew every plant by its name, and was familiar with the history and habits of every production of the earth; he could interpret without a fault each appearance in the sky: and the varied phenomena of heaven and earth filled him with a deep emotion.

It is useless to speculate on the possible future greatness, had he lived, of a poet whose death seems so much a part of his life as to be no accident. He strove to live, in time, according to the laws of eternity; only to be drowned in that 'Unfathomable sea, whose waves are years', ancient and universal symbol of the material world to whose laws Shelley was never reconciled. Blake would have understood him; he wrote:

> Many Persons, such as Paine & Voltaire, with some of the Ancient Greeks, say: 'we will not converse concerning Good & Evil; we will live in Paradise & Liberty.' You may do so in Spirit, but not in the Mortal Body as you pretend, till after the Last Judgment; for in Paradise they have no Corporeal & Mortal Body – that originated with the Fall & was call'd Death & cannot be removed but by a Last Judgment; while we are in the world of Mortality we Must Suffer. The Whole Creation Groans to be deliver'd; there will always be as many Hypocrites born as Honest Men, & they will always have superior Power in Mortal Things. You cannot have Liberty in this World without what you call Moral Virtue, & you cannot have Moral Virtue without the Slavery of that half of the Human Race who hate what you call Moral Virtue.*

I regret that space does not allow the inclusion in this volume of *The Cenci*; of that exuberant early poem *The Daemon of the World*, with its cosmic fantasy; or the fragment

*William Blake, 'A Vision of the Last Judgment', *Complete Writings*, ed. Keynes, Oxford University Press, 1966.

Prince Athanase that Yeats loved; verbally below Shelley's best level, but, for the two archetypal figures of the scholar-prince and his aged philosopher-mentor, so memorable. Without regret I have omitted *Laon and Cythna* (later revised and renamed *The Revolt of Islam*), and a great deal of occasional political verse by Shelley the student activist in which the inspirers had no hand. Many short, familiar anthology lyrics and fragments seemed to me, on re-reading, to be endeared more by habit than merit. Shelley is not at his best in short poems; he needs the sweep, the orchestration, the dithyrambic choric speed and movement not to be generated in a few lines. Nor is it within the scope of this selection to include any of Shelley's prose-writings; those fine descriptive letters from Italy to Thomas Love Peacock; his *Defence of Poetry*; his magnificent translation of Plato's *Banquet*; all of which reveal other sides of Shelley's mind, scarcely less remarkable in its discursive than in its imaginative energy.

KATHLEEN RAINE

Alastor; or, The Spirit of Solitude

Preface

The poem entitled 'Alastor' may be considered as allegorical of one of the most interesting situations of the human mind. It represents a youth of uncorrupted feelings and adventurous genius led forth by an imagination inflamed and purified through familiarity with all that is excellent and majestic, to the contemplation of the universe. He drinks deep of the fountains of knowledge, and is still insatiate. The magnificence and beauty of the external world sinks profoundly into the frame of his conceptions, and affords to their modifications a variety not to be exhausted. So long as it is possible for his desires to point towards objects thus infinite and unmeasured, he is joyous, and tranquil, and self-possessed. But the period arrives when these objects cease to suffice. His mind is at length suddenly awakened and thirsts for intercourse with an intelligence similar to itself. He images to himself the Being whom he loves. Conversant with speculations of the sublimest and most perfect natures, the vision in which he embodies his own imaginations unites all of wonderful, or wise, or beautiful, which the poet, the philosopher, or the lover could depicture. The intellectual faculties, the imagination, the functions of sense, have their respective requisitions on the sympathy of corresponding powers in other human beings. The Poet is represented as uniting these requisitions, and attaching them to a single image. He seeks in vain for a prototype of his conception. Blasted by his disappointment, he descends to an untimely grave.

The picture is not barren of instruction to actual men. The

Poet's self-centred seclusion was avenged by the furies of an irresistible passion pursuing him to speedy ruin. But that Power which strikes the luminaries of the world with sudden darkness and extinction, by awakening them to too exquisite a perception of its influences, dooms to a slow and poisonous decay those meaner spirits that dare to abjure its dominion. Their destiny is more abject and inglorious as their delinquency is more contemptible and pernicious. They who, deluded by no generous error, instigated by no sacred thirst of doubtful knowledge, duped by no illustrious superstition, loving nothing on this earth, and cherishing no hopes beyond, yet keep aloof from sympathies with their kind, rejoicing neither in human joy nor mourning with human grief; these, and such as they, have their apportioned curse. They languish, because none feel with them their common nature. They are morally dead. They are neither friends, nor lovers, nor fathers, nor citizens of the world, nor benefactors of their country. Among those who attempt to exist without human sympathy, the pure and tender-hearted perish through the intensity and passion of their search after its communities, when the vacancy of their spirit suddenly makes itself felt. All else, selfish, blind, and torpid, are those unforeseeing multitudes who constitute, together with their own, the lasting misery and loneliness of the world. Those who love not their fellow-beings, live unfruitful lives, and prepare for their old age a miserable grave.

'The good die first,
And those whose hearts are dry as summer dust,
Burn to the socket!'

December 14, 1815.

Nondum amabam, et amare amabam, quaerebam quid
amarem, amans amare.* – *Confess. St August.*

Earth, ocean, air, beloved brotherhood!
If our great Mother has imbued my soul
With aught of natural piety to feel
Your love, and recompense the boon with mine;
If dewy morn, and odorous noon, and even,
With sunset and its gorgeous ministers,
And solemn midnight's tingling silentness;
If autumn's hollow sighs in the sere wood,
And winter robing with pure snow and crowns
Of starry ice the grey grass and bare boughs;
If spring's voluptuous pantings when she breathes
Her first sweet kisses, have been dear to me;
If no bright bird, insect, or gentle beast
I consciously have injured, but still loved
And cherished these my kindred; then forgive
This boast, beloved brethren, and withdraw
No portion of your wonted favour now!

Mother of this unfathomable world!
Favour my solemn song, for I have loved
Thee ever, and thee only; I have watched
Thy shadow, and the darkness of thy steps,
And my heart ever gazes on the depth
Of thy deep mysteries. I have made my bed
In charnels and on coffins, where black death
Keeps record of the trophies won from thee,
Hoping to still these obstinate questionings
Of thee and thine, by forcing some lone ghost
Thy messenger, to render up the tale
Of what we are. In lone and silent hours,

*'I was not yet in love, but I was in love with love. I sought something to love, since I was in love with loving.'

When night makes a weird sound of its own stillness,
Like an inspired and desperate alchymist
Staking his very life on some dark hope,
Have I mixed awful talk and asking looks
With my most innocent love, until strange tears
Uniting with those breathless kisses, made
Such magic as compels the charmed night
To render up thy charge: . . . and, though ne'er yet
Thou hast unveil'd thy inmost sanctuary,
Enough from incommunicable dream,
And twilight phantasms, and deep noonday thought,
Has shone within me, that serenely now
And moveless, as a long-forgotten lyre
Suspended in the solitary dome
Of some mysterious and deserted fane,
I wait thy breath, Great Parent, that my strain
May modulate with murmurs of the air,
And motions of the forests and the sea,
And voice of living beings, and woven hymns
Of night and day, and the deep heart of man.

There was a Poet whose untimely tomb
No human hands with pious reverence reared,
But the charmed eddies of autumnal winds
Built o'er his mouldering bones a pyramid
Of mouldering leaves in the waste wilderness: –
A lovely youth, – no mourning maiden decked
With weeping flowers, or votive cypress wreath,
The lone couch of his everlasting sleep: –
Gentle, and brave, and generous, – no lorn bard
Breathed o'er his dark fate one melodious sigh:
He lived, he died, he sung, in solitude.
Strangers have wept to hear his passionate notes,
And virgins, as unknown he past, have pined

And wasted for fond love of his wild eyes.
The fire of those soft orbs has ceased to burn,
And Silence, too enamoured of that voice,
Locks its mute music in her rugged cell.

By solemn vision, and bright silver dream,
His infancy was nurtured. Every sight
And sound from the vast earth and ambient air,
Sent to his heart its choicest impulses.
The fountains of divine philosophy
Fled not his thirsting lips, and all of great,
Or good, or lovely, which the sacred past
In truth or fable consecrates, he felt
And knew. When early youth had past, he left
His cold fireside and alienated home
To seek strange truths in undiscovered lands.
Many a wide waste and tangled wilderness
Has lured his fearless steps; and he has bought
With his sweet voice and eyes, from savage men,
His rest and food. Nature's most secret steps
He like her shadow has pursued, where'er
The red volcano overcanopies
Its fields of snow and pinnacles of ice
With burning smoke, or where bitumen lakes
On black bare pointed islets ever beat
With sluggish surge, or where the secret caves
Rugged and dark, winding among the springs
Of fire and poison, inaccessible
To avarice or pride, their starry domes
Of diamond and of gold expand above
Numberless and immeasurable halls,
Frequent with crystal column, and clear shrines
Of pearl, and thrones radiant with chrysolite.
Nor had that scene of ampler majesty

Than gems or gold, the varying roof of heaven
And the green earth lost in his heart its claims
To love and wonder; he would linger long
In lonesome vales, making the wild his home,
Until the doves and squirrels would partake
From his innocuous hand his bloodless food,
Lured by the gentle meaning of his looks,
And the wild antelope, that starts whene'er
The dry leaf rustles in the brake, suspend
Her timid steps to gaze upon a form
More graceful than her own.
His wandering step
Obedient to high thoughts, has visited
The awful ruins of the days of old:
Athens, and Tyre, and Balbec, and the waste
Where stood Jerusalem, the fallen towers
Of Babylon, the eternal pyramids,
Memphis and Thebes, and whatsoe'er of strange
Sculptured on alabaster obelisk,
Or jasper tomb, or mutilated sphynx,
Dark Aethiopia in her desert hills
Conceals. Among the ruined temples there,
Stupendous columns, and wild images
Of more than man, where marble daemons watch
The Zodiac's brazen mystery, and dead men
Hang their mute thoughts on the mute walls around,
He lingered, poring on memorials
Of the world's youth, through the long burning day
Gazed on those speechless shapes, nor, when the moon
Filled the mysterious halls with floating shades
Suspended he that task, but ever gazed
And gazed, till meaning on his vacant mind
Flashed like strong inspiration, and he saw
The thrilling secrets of the birth of time.

Meanwhile an Arab maiden brought his food,
Her daily portion, from her father's tent,
And spread her matting for his couch, and stole
From duties and repose to tend his steps: –
Enamoured, yet not daring for deep awe
To speak her love: – and watched his nightly sleep,
Sleepless herself, to gaze upon his lips
Parted in slumber, whence the regular breath
Of innocent dreams arose: then, when red morn
Made paler the pale moon, to her cold home
Wildered, and wan, and panting, she returned.

The Poet wandering on, through Arabie
And Persia, and the wild Carmanian waste,
And o'er the aërial mountains which pour down
Indus and Oxus from their icy caves,
In joy and exultation held his way;
Till in the vale of Cashmire, far within
Its loneliest dell, where odorous plants entwine
Beneath the hollow rocks a natural bower,
Beside a sparkling rivulet he stretched
His languid limbs. A vision on his sleep
There came, a dream of hopes that never yet
Had flushed his cheek. He dreamed a veiled maid
Sate near him, talking in low solemn tones.
Her voice was like the voice of his own soul
Heard in the calm of thought; its music long,
Like woven sounds of streams and breezes, held
His inmost sense suspended in its web
Of many-coloured woof and shifting hues.
Knowledge and truth and virtue were her theme,
And lofty hopes of divine liberty,
Thoughts the most dear to him, and poesy,
Herself a poet. Soon the solemn mood

Of her pure mind kindled through all her frame
A permeating fire: wild numbers then
She raised, with voice stifled in tremulous sobs
Subdued by its own pathos: her fair hands
Were bare alone, sweeping from some strange harp
Strange symphony, and in their branching veins
The eloquent blood told an ineffable tale.
The beating of her heart was heard to fill
The pauses of her music, and her breath
Tumultuously accorded with those fits
Of intermitted song. Sudden she rose,
As if her heart impatiently endured
Its bursting burthen: at the sound he turned,
And saw by the warm light of their own life
Her glowing limbs beneath the sinuous veil
Of woven wind, her outspread arms now bare,
Her dark locks floating in the breath of night,
Her beamy bending eyes, her parted lips
Outstretched, and pale, and quivering eagerly.
His strong heart sunk and sickened with excess
Of love. He reared his shuddering limbs and quelled
His gasping breath, and spread his arms to meet
Her panting bosom: . . . she drew back a while,
Then, yielding to the irresistible joy,
With frantic gesture and short breathless cry
Folded his frame in her dissolving arms.
Now blackness veiled his dizzy eyes, and night
Involved and swallowed up the vision; sleep,
Like a dark flood suspended in its course,
Rolled back its impulse on his vacant brain.

Roused by the shock he started from his trance –
The cold white light of morning, the blue moon
Low in the west, the clear and garish hills,

The distinct valley and the vacant woods,
Spread round him where he stood. Whither have fled
The hues of heaven that canopied his bower
Of yesternight? The sounds that soothed his sleep,
The mystery and the majesty of Earth,
The joy, the exultation? His wan eyes
Gaze on the empty scene as vacantly
As ocean's moon looks on the moon in heaven.
The spirit of sweet human love has sent
A vision to the sleep of him who spurned
Her choicest gifts. He eagerly pursues
Beyond the realms of dream that fleeting shade;
He overleaps the bounds. Alas! alas!
Were limbs, and breath, and being intertwined
Thus treacherously? Lost, lost, forever lost,
In the wide pathless desert of dim sleep,
That beautiful shape! Does the dark gate of death
Conduct to thy mysterious paradise,
O Sleep? Does the bright arch of rainbow clouds,
And pendant mountains seen in the calm lake,
Lead only to a black and watery depth,
While death's blue vault, with loathliest vapours hung,
Where every shade which the foul grave exhales
Hides its dead eye from the detested day,
Conduct, O Sleep, to thy delightful realms?
This doubt with sudden tide flowed on his heart,
The insatiate hope which it awakened, stung
His brain even like despair.

While daylight held
The sky, the Poet kept mute conference
With his still soul. At night the passion came,
Like the fierce fiend of a distempered dream,
And shook him from his rest, and led him forth
Into the darkness. – As an eagle grasped

In folds of the green serpent, feels her breast
Burn with the poison, and precipitates
Through night and day, tempest, and calm, and cloud,
Frantic with dizzying anguish, her blind flight
O'er the wide aëry wilderness: thus driven
By the bright shadow of that lovely dream,
Beneath the cold glare of the desolate night,
Through tangled swamps and deep precipitous dells,
Startling with careless step the moonlight snake,
He fled. Red morning dawned upon his flight,
Shedding the mockery of its vital hues
Upon his cheek of death. He wandered on
Till vast Aornos seen from Petra's steep
Hung o'er the low horizon like a cloud;
Through Balk, and where the desolated tombs
Of Parthian kings scatter to every wind
Their wasting dust, wildly he wandered on,
Day after day, a weary waste of hours,
Bearing within his life the brooding care
That ever fed on its decaying flame.
And now his limbs were lean; his scattered hair
Sered by the autumn of strange suffering
Sung dirges in the wind; his listless hand
Hung like dead bone within its withered skin;
Life, and the lustre that consumed it, shone
As in a furnace burning secretly
From his dark eyes alone. The cottagers,
Who ministered with human charity
His human wants, beheld with wondering awe
Their fleeting visitant. The mountaineer,
Encountering on some dizzy precipice
That spectral form, deemed that the Spirit of wind
With lightning eyes, and eager breath, and feet
Disturbing not the drifted snow, had paused

In its career: the infant would conceal
His troubled visage in his mother's robe
In terror at the glare of those wild eyes,
To remember their strange light in many a dream
Of after-times; but youthful maidens, taught
By nature, would interpret half the woe
That wasted him, would call him with false names
Brother, and friend, would press his pallid hand
At parting, and watch, dim through tears, the path
Of his departure from their father's door.

At length upon the lone Chorasmian shore
He paused, a wide and melancholy waste
Of putrid marshes. A strong impulse urged
His steps to the sea-shore. A swan was there,
Beside a sluggish stream among the reeds.
It rose as he approached, and with strong wings
Scaling the upward sky, bent its bright course
High over the immeasurable main.
His eyes pursued its flight. – 'Thou hast a home,
Beautiful bird; thou voyagest to thine home,
Where thy sweet mate will twine her downy neck
With thine, and welcome thy return with eyes
Bright in the lustre of their own fond joy.
And what am I that I should linger here,
With voice far sweeter than thy dying notes,
Spirit more vast than thine, frame more attuned
To beauty, wasting these surpassing powers
In the deaf air, to the blind earth, and heaven
That echoes not my thoughts?' A gloomy smile
Of desperate hope wrinkled his quivering lips.
For sleep, he knew, kept most relentlessly
Its precious charge, and silent death exposed,
Faithless perhaps as sleep, a shadowy lure,
With doubtful smile mocking its own strange charms.

Startled by his own thoughts he looked around.
There was no fair fiend near him, not a sight
Or sound of awe but in his own deep mind.
A little shallop floating near the shore
Caught the impatient wandering of his gaze.
It had been long abandoned, for its sides
Gaped wide with many a rift, and its frail joints
Swayed with the undulations of the tide.
A restless impulse urged him to embark
And meet lone Death on the drear ocean's waste;
For well he knew that mighty Shadow loves
The slimy caverns of the populous deep.

The day was fair and sunny, sea and sky
Drank its inspiring radiance, and the wind
Swept strongly from the shore, blackening the waves.
Following his eager soul, the wanderer
Leaped in the boat, he spread his cloak aloft
On the bare mast, and took his lonely seat,
And felt the boat speed o'er the tranquil sea
Like a torn cloud before the hurricane.

As one that in a silver vision floats
Obedient to the sweep of odorous winds
Upon resplendent clouds, so rapidly
Along the dark and ruffled waters fled
The straining boat. – A whirlwind swept it on,
With fierce gusts and precipitating force,
Through the white ridges of the chafed sea.
The waves arose. Higher and higher still
Their fierce necks writhed beneath the tempest's scourge
Like serpents struggling in a vulture's grasp.
Calm and rejoicing in the fearful war
Of wave ruining on wave, and blast on blast

Descending, and black flood on whirlpool driven
With dark obliterating course, he sate:
As if their genii were the ministers
Appointed to conduct him to the light
Of those beloved eyes, the Poet sate
Holding the steady helm. Evening came on,
The beams of sunset hung their rainbow hues
High 'mid the shifting domes of sheeted spray
That canopied his path o'er the waste deep;
Twilight, ascending slowly from the east,
Entwin'd in duskier wreaths her braided locks
O'er the fair front and radiant eyes of day;
Night followed, clad with stars. On every side
More horribly the multitudinous streams
Of ocean's mountainous waste to mutual war
Rushed in dark tumult thundering, as to mock
The calm and spangled sky. The little boat
Still fled before the storm; still fled, like foam
Down the steep cataract of a wintry river;
Now pausing on the edge of the riven wave;
Now leaving far behind the bursting mass
That fell, convulsing ocean. Safely fled –
As if that frail and wasted human form,
Had been an elemental god.
At midnight
The moon arose: and lo! the ethereal cliffs
Of Caucasus, whose icy summits shone
Among the stars like sunlight, and around
Whose cavern'd base the whirlpools and the waves
Bursting and eddying irresistibly
Rage and resound for ever. – Who shall save? –
The boat fled on, – the boiling torrent drove, –
The crags closed round with black and jagged arms,
The shattered mountain overhung the sea,

And faster still, beyond all human speed,
Suspended on the sweep of the smooth wave,
The little boat was driven. A cavern there
Yawned, and amid its slant and winding depths
Ingulphed the rushing sea. The boat fled on
With unrelaxing speed. – 'Vision and Love!'
The Poet cried aloud, 'I have beheld
The path of thy departure. Sleep and death
Shall not divide us long!'

The boat pursued
The windings of the cavern. Daylight shone
At length upon that gloomy river's flow;
Now, where the fiercest war among the waves
Is calm, on the unfathomable stream
The boat moved slowly. Where the mountain, riven,
Exposed those black depths to the azure sky,
Ere yet the flood's enormous volume fell
Even to the base of Caucasus, with sound
That shook the everlasting rocks, the mass
Filled with one whirlpool all that ample chasm;
Stair above stair the eddying waters rose,
Circling immeasurably fast, and laved
With alternating dash the knarled roots
Of mighty trees, that stretched their giant arms
In darkness over it. I' the midst was left,
Reflecting, yet distorting every cloud,
A pool of treacherous and tremendous calm.
Seized by the sway of the ascending stream,
With dizzy swiftness, round, and round, and round,
Ridge after ridge the straining boat arose,
Till on the verge of the extremest curve,
Where, through an opening of the rocky bank,
The waters overflow, and a smooth spot
Of glassy quiet mid those battling tides

Is left, the boat paused shuddering. – Shall it sink
Down the abyss? Shall the reverting stress
Of that resistless gulph embosom it?
Now shall it fall? – A wandering stream of wind,
Breathed from the west, has caught the expanded sail,
And, lo! with gentle motion, between banks
Of mossy slope, and on a placid stream,
Beneath a woven grove it sails, and, hark!
The ghastly torrent mingles its far roar,
With the breeze murmuring in the musical woods.
Where the embowering trees recede, and leave
A little space of green expanse, the cove
Is closed by meeting banks, whose yellow flowers
For ever gaze on their own drooping eyes,
Reflected in the crystal calm. The wave
Of the boat's motion marred their pensive task,
Which nought but vagrant bird, or wanton wind,
Or falling spear-grass, or their own decay
Had e'er disturbed before. The Poet longed
To deck with their bright hues his withered hair,
But on his heart its solitude returned,
And he forbore. Not the strong impulse hid
In those flushed cheeks, bent eyes, and shadowy frame
Had yet performed its ministry: it hung
Upon his life, as lightning in a cloud
Gleams, hovering ere it vanish, ere the floods
Of night close over it.
The noonday sun
Now shone upon the forest, one vast mass
Of mingling shade, whose brown magnificence
A narrow vale embosoms. There, huge caves,
Scooped in the dark base of their aëry rocks
Mocking its moans, respond and roar for ever.
The meeting boughs and implicated leaves

Wove twilight o'er the Poet's path, as led
By love, or dream, or god, or mightier Death,
He sought in Nature's dearest haunt, some bank,
Her cradle, and his sepulchre. More dark
And dark the shades accumulate. The oak,
Expanding its immense and knotty arms,
Embraces the light beech. The pyramids
Of the tall cedar overarching, frame
Most solemn domes within, and far below,
Like clouds suspended in an emerald sky.
The ash and the acacia floating hang
Tremulous and pale. Like restless serpents, clothed
In rainbow and in fire, the parasites,
Starred with ten thousand blossoms, flow around
The grey trunks, and, as gamesome infants' eyes,
With gentle meanings, and most innocent wiles,
Fold their beams round the hearts of those that love,
These twine their tendrils with the wedded boughs
Uniting their close union; the woven leaves
Make net-work of the dark blue light of day,
And the night's noontide clearness, mutable
As shapes in the weird clouds. Soft mossy lawns
Beneath these canopies extend their swells,
Fragrant with perfumed herbs, and eyed with blooms
Minute yet beautiful. One darkest glen
Sends from its woods of musk-rose, twined with jasmine,
A soul-dissolving odour, to invite
To some more lovely mystery. Through the dell,
Silence and Twilight here, twin-sisters, keep
Their noonday watch, and sail among the shades,
Like vaporous shapes half seen; beyond, a well,
Dark, gleaming, and of most translucent wave,
Images all the woven boughs above,
And each depending leaf, and every speck

Of azure sky, darting between their chasms;
Nor aught else in the liquid mirror laves
Its portraiture, but some inconstant star
Between one foliaged lattice twinkling fair,
Or, painted bird, sleeping beneath the moon,
Or gorgeous insect floating motionless,
Unconscious of the day, ere yet his wings
Have spread their glories to the gaze of noon.

Hither the Poet came. His eyes beheld
Their own wan light through the reflected lines
Of his thin hair, distinct in the dark depth
Of that still fountain; as the human heart,
Gazing in dreams over the gloomy grave,
Sees its own treacherous likeness there. He heard
The motion of the leaves, the grass that sprung
Startled and glanced and trembled even to feel
An unaccustomed presence, and the sound
Of the sweet brook that from the secret springs
Of that dark fountain rose. A Spirit seemed
To stand beside him – clothed in no bright robes
Of shadowy silver or enshrining light,
Borrowed from aught the visible world affords
Of grace, or majesty, or mystery; –
But, undulating woods, and silent well,
And leaping rivulet, and evening gloom
Now deepening the dark shades, for speech assuming
Held commune with him, as if he and it
Were all that was, – only . . . when his regard
Was raised by intense pensiveness, . . . two eyes,
Two starry eyes, hung in the gloom of thought,
And seemed with their serene and azure smiles
To beckon him.

Obedient to the light
That shone within his soul, he went, pursuing
The windings of the dell. – The rivulet
Wanton and wild, through many a green ravine
Beneath the forest flowed. Sometimes it fell
Among the moss with hollow harmony
Dark and profound. Now on the polished stones
It danced; like childhood laughing as it went;
Then, through the plain in tranquil wanderings crept,
Reflecting every herb and drooping bud
That overhung its quietness. – 'O stream!
Whose source is inaccessibly profound,
Whither do thy mysterious waters tend?
Thou imagest my life. Thy darksome stillness,
Thy dazzling waves, thy loud and hollow gulphs,
Thy searchless fountain, and invisible course
Have each their type in me: and the wide sky,
And measureless ocean may declare as soon
What oozy cavern or what wandering cloud
Contains thy waters, as the universe
Tell where these living thoughts reside, when stretched
Upon thy flowers my bloodless limbs shall waste
I' the passing wind!'
Beside the grassy shore
Of the small stream he went; he did impress
On the green moss his tremulous step, that caught
Strong shuddering from his burning limbs. As one
Roused by some joyous madness from the couch
Of fever, he did move; yet, not like him,
Forgetful of the grave, where, when the flame
Of his frail exultation shall be spent,
He must descend. With rapid steps he went
Beneath the shade of trees, beside the flow
Of the wild babbling rivulet; and now

The forest's solemn canopies were changed
For the uniform and lightsome evening sky.
Grey rocks did peep from the spare moss, and stemmed
The struggling brook: tall spires of windlestrae
Threw their thin shadows down the rugged slope,
And nought but knarled roots of antient pines
Branchless and blasted, clenched with grasping roots
The unwilling soil. A gradual change was here,
Yet ghastly. For, as fast years flow away,
The smooth brow gathers, and the hair grows thin
And white, and where irradiate dewy eyes
Had shone, gleam stony orbs: – so from his steps
Bright flowers departed, and the beautiful shade
Of the green groves, with all their odorous winds
And musical motions. Calm, he still pursued
The stream, that with a larger volume now
Rolled through the labyrinthine dell; and there
Fretted a path through its descending curves
With its wintry speed. On every side now rose
Rocks, which, in unimaginable forms,
Lifted their black and barren pinnacles
In the light of evening, and its precipice
Obscuring the ravine, disclosed above,
Mid toppling stones, black gulphs and yawning caves,
Whose windings gave ten thousand various tongues
To the loud stream. Lo! where the pass expands
Its stony jaws, the abrupt mountain breaks,
And seems, with its accumulated crags,
To overhang the world: for wide expand
Beneath the wan stars and descending moon
Islanded seas, blue mountains, mighty streams,
Dim tracts and vast, robed in the lustrous gloom
Of leaden-coloured even, and fiery hills
Mingling their flames with twilight, on the verge

Of the remote horizon. The near scene,
In naked and severe simplicity,
Made contrast with the universe. A pine,
Rock-rooted, stretched athwart the vacancy
Its swinging boughs, to each inconstant blast
Yielding one only response, at each pause
In most familiar cadence, with the howl
The thunder and the hiss of homeless streams
Mingling its solemn song, whilst the broad river,
Foaming and hurrying o'er its rugged path,
Fell into that immeasurable void
Scattering its waters to the passing winds.

Yet the grey precipice and solemn pine
And torrent, were not all; – one silent nook
Was there. Even on the edge of that vast mountain,
Upheld by knotty roots and fallen rocks,
It overlooked in its serenity
The dark earth, and the bending vault of stars.
It was a tranquil spot, that seemed to smile
Even in the lap of horror. Ivy clasped
The fissured stones with its entwining arms,
And did embower with leaves for ever green,
And berries dark, the smooth and even space
Of its inviolated floor, and here
The children of the autumnal whirlwind bore,
In wanton sport, those bright leaves, whose decay,
Red, yellow, or etherially pale,
Rivals the pride of summer. 'Tis the haunt
Of every gentle wind, whose breath can teach
The wilds to love tranquillity. One step,
One human step alone, has ever broken
The stillness of its solitude: – one voice
Alone inspired its echoes; – even that voice

Which hither came, floating among the winds,
And led the loveliest among human forms
To make their wild haunts the depository
Of all the grace and beauty that endued
Its motions, render up its majesty,
Scatter its music on the unfeeling storm,
And to the damp leaves and blue cavern mould,
Nurses of rainbow flowers and branching moss,
Commit the colours of that varying cheek,
That snowy breast, those dark and drooping eyes.

The dim and horned moon hung low, and poured
A sea of lustre on the horizon's verge
That overflowed its mountains. Yellow mist
Filled the unbounded atmosphere, and drank
Wan moonlight even to fulness: not a star
Shone, not a sound was heard; the very winds,
Danger's grim playmates, on that precipice
Slept, clasped in his embrace. – O, storm of death!
Whose sightless speed divides this sullen night:
And thou, colossal Skeleton, that, still
Guiding its irresistible career
In thy devasting omnipotence
Art king of this frail world, from the red field
Of slaughter, from the reeking hospital,
The patriot's sacred couch, the snowy bed
Of innocence, the scaffold and the throne,
A mighty voice invokes thee. Ruin calls
His brother Death. A rare and regal prey
He hath prepared, prowling around the world;
Glutted with which thou mayst repose, and men
Go to their graves like flowers or creeping worms,
Nor ever more offer at thy dark shrine
The unheeded tribute of a broken heart.

When on the threshold of the green recess
The wanderer's footsteps fell, he knew that death
Was on him. Yet a little, ere it fled,
Did he resign his high and holy soul
To images of the majestic past,
That paused within his passive being now,
Like winds that bear sweet music, when they breathe
Through some dim latticed chamber. He did place
His pale lean hand upon the rugged trunk
Of the old pine. Upon an ivied stone
Reclined his languid head, his limbs did rest,
Diffused and motionless, on the smooth brink
Of that obscurest chasm; – and thus he lay,
Surrendering to their final impulses
The hovering powers of life. Hope and despair,
The torturers, slept; no mortal pain or fear
Marred his repose, the influxes of sense,
And his own being unalloyed by pain,
Yet feebler and more feeble, calmly fed
The stream of thought, till he lay breathing there
At peace, and faintly smiling: – his last sight
Was the great moon, which o'er the western line
Of the wide world her mighty horn suspended,
With whose dun beams inwoven darkness seemed
To mingle. Now upon the jagged hills
It rests, and still as the divided frame
Of the vast meteor sunk, the Poet's blood,
That ever beat in mystic sympathy
With nature's ebb and flow, grew feebler still:
And when two lessening points of light alone
Gleamed through the darkness, the alternate gasp
Of his faint respiration scarce did stir
The stagnate night: – till the minutest ray
Was quenched, the pulse yet lingered in his heart.

It paused – it fluttered. But when heaven remained
Utterly black, the murky shades involved
An image, silent, cold, and motionless,
As their own voiceless earth and vacant air.
Even as a vapour fed with golden beams
That ministered on sunlight, ere the west
Eclipses it, was now that wonderous frame –
No sense, no motion, no divinity –
A fragile lute, on whose harmonious strings
The breath of heaven did wander – a bright stream
Once fed with many-voiced waves – a dream
Of youth, which night and time have quenched for ever,
Still, dark, and dry, and unremembered now.
  O, for Medea's wondrous alchemy,
Which wheresoe'er it fell made the earth gleam
With bright flowers, and the wintry boughs exhale
From vernal blooms fresh fragrance! O, that God,
Profuse of poisons, would concede the chalice
Which but one living man has drained, who now,
Vessel of deathless wrath, a slave that feels
No proud exemption in the blighting curse
He bears, over the world wanders for ever,
Lone as incarnate death! O, that the dream
Of dark magician in his visioned cave,
Raking the cinders of a crucible
For life and power, even when his feeble hand
Shakes in its last decay, were the true law
Of this so lovely world! But thou art fled
Like some frail exhalation; which the dawn
Robes in its golden beams, – ah! thou hast fled!
The brave, the gentle, and the beautiful,
The child of grace and genius. Heartless things
Are done and said i' the world, and many worms
And beasts and men live on, and mighty Earth

From sea and mountain, city and wilderness,
In vesper low or joyous orison,
Lifts still its solemn voice: – but thou art fled –
Thou canst no longer know or love the shapes
Of this phantasmal scene, who have to thee
Been purest ministers, who are, alas!
Now thou art not. Upon those pallid lips
So sweet even in their silence, on those eyes
That image sleep in death, upon that form
Yet safe from the worm's outrage, let no tear
Be shed – not even in thought. Nor, when those hues
Are gone, and those divinest lineaments,
Worn by the senseless wind, shall live alone
In the frail pauses of this simple strain,
Let not high verse, mourning the memory
Of that which is no more, or painting's woe
Or sculpture, speak in feeble imagery
Their own cold powers. Art and eloquence,
And all the shews o' the world are frail and vain
To weep a loss that turns their lights to shade.
It is a woe too 'deep for tears', when all
Is reft at once, when some surpassing Spirit,
Whose light adorned the world around it, leaves
Those who remain behind, not sobs or groans,
The passionate tumult of a clinging hope;
But pale despair and cold tranquillity,
Nature's vast frame, the web of human things,
Birth and the grave, that are not as they were.

Mutability

We are as clouds that veil the midnight moon;
   How restlessly they speed, and gleam, and quiver,
Streaking the darkness radiantly! – yet soon
   Night closes round, and they are lost for ever:

Or like forgotten lyres, whose dissonant strings
   Give various response to each varying blast,
To whose frail frame no second motion brings
   One mood or modulation like the last.

We rest. – A dream has power to poison sleep;
   We rise. – One wandering thought pollutes the day;
We feel, conceive or reason, laugh or weep;
   Embrace fond woe, or cast our cares away:

It is the same! – For, be it joy or sorrow,
   The path of its departure still is free:
Man's yesterday may ne'er be like his morrow;
   Nought may endure but Mutability.

Hymn to Intellectual Beauty

I

The awful shadow of some unseen Power
  Floats tho' unseen amongst us, – visiting
  This various world with as inconstant wing
As summer winds that creep from flower to flower, –
Like moonbeams that behind some piny mountain shower,
    It visits with inconstant glance
    Each human heart and countenance;
Like hues and harmonies of evening, –
    Like clouds in starlight widely spread, –
    Like memory of music fled, –
    Like aught that for its grace may be
Dear, and yet dearer for its mystery.

II

Spirit of BEAUTY, that dost consecrate
  With thine own hues all thou dost shine upon
  Of human thought or form, – where art thou gone?
Why dost thou pass away and leave our state,
This dim vast vale of tears, vacant and desolate?
    Ask why the sunlight not for ever
    Weaves rainbows o'er yon mountain river,
Why aught should fail and fade that once is shewn,
    Why fear and dream and death and birth
    Cast on the daylight of this earth
    Such gloom, – why man has such a scope
For love and hate, despondency and hope?

III

No voice from some sublimer world hath ever
  To sage or poet these responses given –
  Therefore the names of Demon, Ghost, and Heaven
Remain the records of their vain endeavour,
Frail spells – whose uttered charm might not avail to sever,
    From all we hear and all we see,
    Doubt, chance, and mutability.
Thy light alone – like mist o'er mountains driven,
    Or music by the night wind sent,
    Thro' strings of some still instrument,
    Or moonlight on a midnight stream,
Gives grace and truth to life's unquiet dream.

IV

Love, Hope, and Self-esteem, like clouds depart
  And come, for some uncertain moments lent.
  Man were immortal, and omnipotent,
Didst thou, unknown and awful as thou art,
Keep with thy glorious train firm state within his heart.
    Thou messenger of sympathies,
    That wax and wane in lovers' eyes –
Thou – that to human thought art nourishment,
    Like darkness to a dying flame!
    Depart not as thy shadow came,
    Depart not – lest the grave should be,
Like life and fear, a dark reality.

V

While yet a boy I sought for ghosts, and sped
  Thro' many a listening chamber, cave and ruin,
  And starlight wood, with fearful steps pursuing
Hopes of high talk with the departed dead.

I called on poisonous names with which our youth is fed,
    I was not heard – I saw them not –
    When musing deeply on the lot
Of life, at that sweet time when winds are wooing
    All vital things that wake to bring
    News of birds and blossoming, –
    Sudden, thy shadow fell on me;
I shrieked, and clasped my hands in extacy!

VI

I vowed that I would dedicate my powers
  To thee and thine – have I not kept the vow?
  With beating heart and streaming eyes, even now
I call the phantoms of a thousand hours
Each from his voiceless grave: they have in visioned bowers
    Of studious zeal or love's delight
    Outwatched with me the envious night –
They know that never joy illumed my brow
    Unlinked with hope that thou wouldst free
    This world from its dark slavery,
    That thou – O awful LOVELINESS,
Wouldst give whate'er these words cannot express.

VII

The day becomes more solemn and serene
  When noon is past – there is a harmony
  In autumn, and a lustre in its sky,
Which thro' the summer is not heard or seen,
As if it could not be, as if it had not been!
        Thus let thy power, which like the truth
        Of nature on my passive youth

Descended, to my onward life supply
    Its calm – to one who worships thee,
    And every form containing thee,
    Whom, SPIRIT fair, thy spells did bind
To fear himself, and love all human kind.

Mont Blanc

Lines Written in the Vale of Chamouni

I

The everlasting universe of things
Flows through the mind, and rolls its rapid waves,
Now dark – now glittering – now reflecting gloom –
Now lending splendour, where from secret springs
The source of human thought its tribute brings
Of waters, – with a sound but half its own,
Such as a feeble brook will oft assume
In the wild woods, among the mountains lone,
Where waterfalls around it leap for ever,
Where woods and winds contend, and a vast river
Over its rocks ceaselessly bursts and raves.

II

Thus thou, Ravine of Arve – dark, deep Ravine –
Thou many-coloured, many-voiced vale,
Over whose pines, and crags, and caverns sail
Fast cloud shadows and sunbeams: awful scene,
Where Power in likeness of the Arve comes down
From the ice gulphs that gird his secret throne,
Bursting through these dark mountains like the flame
Of lightning thro' the tempest; – thou dost lie,
Thy giant brood of pines around thee clinging,
Children of elder time, in whose devotion
The chainless winds still come and ever came

To drink their odours, and their mighty swinging
To hear – an old and solemn harmony;
Thine earthly rainbows stretched across the sweep
Of the ethereal waterfall, whose veil
Robes some unsculptured image; the strange sleep
Which when the voices of the desart fail
Wraps all in its own deep eternity; –
Thy caverns echoing to the Arve's commotion,
A loud, lone sound no other sound can tame;
Thou art pervaded with that ceaseless motion,
Thou art the path of that unresting sound –
Dizzy Ravine! and when I gaze on thee
I seem as in a trance sublime and strange
To muse on my own separate phantasy,
My own, my human mind, which passively
Now renders and receives fast influencings,
Holding an unremitting interchange
With the clear universe of things around;
One legion of wild thoughts, whose wandering wings
Now float above thy darkness, and now rest
Where that or thou art no unbidden guest,
In the still cave of the witch Poesy,
Seeking among the shadows that pass by
Ghosts of all things that are, some shade of thee,
Some phantom, some faint image; till the breast
From which they fled recalls them, thou art there!

III

Some say that gleams of a remoter world
Visit the soul in sleep, – that death is slumber,
And that its shapes the busy thoughts outnumber
Of those who wake and live. – I look on high;
Has some unknown omnipotence unfurled

The veil of life and death? or do I lie
In dream, and does the mightier world of sleep
Spread far around and inaccessibly
Its circles? For the very spirit fails,
Driven like a homeless cloud from steep to steep
That vanishes among the viewless gales!
Far, far above, piercing the infinite sky,
Mont Blanc appears, – still, snowy, and serene –
Its subject mountains their unearthly forms
Pile around it, ice and rock; broad vales between
Of frozen floods, unfathomable deeps,
Blue as the overhanging heaven, that spread
And wind among the accumulated steeps;
A desart peopled by the storms alone,
Save when the eagle brings some hunter's bone,
And the wolf tracks her there – how hideously
Its shapes are heaped around! rude, bare, and high,
Ghastly, and scarred, and riven. – Is this the scene
Where the old Earthquake-daemon taught her young
Ruin? Were these their toys? or did a sea
Of fire, envelope once this silent snow?
None can reply – all seems eternal now.
The wilderness has a mysterious tongue
Which teaches awful doubt, or faith so mild,
So solemn, so serene, that man may be,
But for such faith, with nature reconciled;
Thou hast a voice, great Mountain, to repeal
Large codes of fraud and woe; not understood
By all, but which the wise, and great, and good
Interpret, or make felt, or deeply feel.

IV

The fields, the lakes, the forests, and the streams,
Ocean, and all the living things that dwell
Within the daedal earth; lightning, and rain,
Earthquake, and fiery flood, and hurricane,
The torpor of the year when feeble dreams
Visit the hidden buds, or dreamless sleep
Holds every future leaf and flower; – the bound
With which from that detested trance they leap;
The works and ways of man, their death and birth,
And that of him and all that his may be;
All things that move and breathe with toil and sound
Are born and die; revolve, subside and swell.
Power dwells apart in its tranquillity
Remote, serene, and inaccessible:
And *this*, the naked countenance of earth,
On which I gaze, even these primaeval mountains
Teach the adverting mind. The glaciers creep
Like snakes that watch their prey, from their far fountains,
Slow rolling on; there, many a precipice,
Frost and the Sun in scorn of mortal power
Have piled: dome, pyramid, and pinnacle,
A city of death, distinct with many a tower
And wall impregnable of beaming ice.
Yet not a city, but a flood of ruin
Is there, that from the boundaries of the sky
Rolls its perpetual stream; vast pines are strewing
Its destined path, or in the mangled soil
Branchless and shattered stand; the rocks, drawn down
From yon remotest waste, have overthrown
The limits of the dead and living world,
Never to be reclaimed. The dwelling-place

Of insects, beasts, and birds, becomes its spoil,
Their food and their retreat for ever gone,
So much of life and joy is lost. The race
Of man flies far in dread; his work and dwelling
Vanish, like smoke before the tempest's stream,
And their place is not known. Below, vast caves
Shine in the rushing torrent's restless gleam,
Which from those secret chasms in tumult welling
Meet in the vale, and one majestic River,
The breath and blood of distant lands, for ever
Rolls its loud waters to the ocean waves,
Breathes its swift vapours to the circling air.

V

Mont Blanc yet gleams on high: – the power is there,
The still and solemn power of many sights,
And many sounds, and much of life and death.
In the calm darkness of the moonless nights,
In the lone glare of day, the snows descend
Upon that Mountain; none beholds them there,
Nor when the flakes burn in the sinking sun,
Or the star-beams dart through them: – Winds contend
Silently there, and heap the snow with breath
Rapid and strong, but silently! Its home
The voiceless lightning in these solitudes
Keeps innocently, and like vapour broods
Over the snow. The secret strength of things
Which governs thought, and to the infinite dome
Of heaven is as a law, inhabits thee!
And what were thou, and earth, and stars, and sea,
If to the human mind's imaginings
Silence and solitude were vacancy?

July 23, 1816

Ozymandias

I met a traveller from an antique land
Who said: Two vast and trunkless legs of stone
Stand in the desart. Near them, on the sand,
Half sunk, a shattered visage lies, whose frown,
And wrinkled lip, and sneer of cold command,
Tell that its sculptor well those passions read
Which yet survive, stamped on these lifeless things,
The hand that mocked them, and the heart that fed:
And on the pedestal these words appear:
'My name is Ozymandias, king of kings:
Look on my works, ye Mighty, and despair!'
Nothing beside remains. Round the decay
Of that colossal wreck, boundless and bare
The lone and level sands stretch far away.

To One Singing

My spirit like a charmèd bark doth swim
  Upon the liquid waves of thy sweet singing,
Far far away into the regions dim
  Of rapture – as a boat, with swift sails winging
Its way adown some many-winding river,
Speeds through dark forests o'er the waters swinging . . .

Julian and Maddalo

A Conversation

Preface

The meadows with fresh streams, the bees with thyme,
The goats with the green leaves of budding Spring,
Are saturated not – nor Love with tears. – Virgil's *Gallus*.

Count Maddalo is a Venetian nobleman of antient family and of great fortune, who, without mixing much in the society of his countrymen, resides chiefly at his magnificent palace in that city. He is a person of the most consummate genius, and capable, if he would direct his energies to such an end, of becoming the redeemer of his degraded country. But it is his weakness to be proud: he derives, from a comparison of his own extraordinary mind with the dwarfish intellects that surround him, an intense apprehension of the nothingness of human life. His passions and his powers are incomparably greater than those of other men; and, instead of the latter having been employed in curbing the former, they have mutually lent each other strength. His ambition preys upon itself, for want of objects which it can consider worthy of exertion. I say that Maddalo is proud, because I can find no other word to express the concentered and impatient feelings which consume him; but it is on his own hopes and affections only that he seems to trample, for in social life no human being can be more gentle, patient, and unassuming than Maddalo. He is cheerful, frank, and witty. His more serious conversation is a sort of intoxication; men are held by it as by a spell. He has travelled much; and there is an inexpressible charm in his relation of his adventures in different countries.

Julian is an Englishman of good family, passionately

attached to those philosophical notions which assert the power of man over his own mind, and the immense improvements of which, by the extinction of certain moral superstitions, human society may be yet susceptible. Without concealing the evil in the world, he is for ever speculating how good may be made superior. He is a complete infidel, and a scoffer at all things reputed holy; and Maddalo takes a wicked pleasure in drawing out his taunts against religion. What Maddalo thinks on these matters is not exactly known. Julian, in spite of his heterodox opinions, is conjectured by his friends to possess some good qualities. How far this is possible the pious reader will determine. Julian is rather serious.

Of the Maniac I can give no information. He seems, by his own account, to have been disappointed in love. He was evidently a very cultivated and amiable person when in his right senses. His story, told at length, might be like many other stories of the same kind: the unconnected exclamations of his agony will perhaps be found a sufficient comment for the text of every heart.

I rode one evening with Count Maddalo
Upon the bank of land which breaks the flow
Of Adria towards Venice: a bare strand
Of hillocks, heaped from ever-shifting sand,
Matted with thistles and amphibious weeds,
Such as from earth's embrace the salt ooze breeds,
Is this; an uninhabited sea-side,
Which the lone fisher, when his nets are dried,
Abandons; and no other object breaks
The waste, but one dwarf tree and some few stakes
Broken and unrepaired, and the tide makes
A narrow space of level sand thereon,
Where 'twas our wont to ride while day went down.

This ride was my delight. I love all waste
And solitary places; where we taste
The pleasure of believing what we see
Is boundless, as we wish our souls to be:
And such was this wide ocean, and this shore
More barren than its billows; and yet more
Than all, with a remembered friend I love
To ride as then I rode; – for the winds drove
The living spray along the sunny air
Into our faces; the blue heavens were bare,
Stripped to their depths by the awakening north;
And, from the waves, sound like delight broke forth
Harmonizing with solitude, and sent
Into our hearts aërial merriment.
So, as we rode, we talked; and the swift thought,
Winging itself with laughter, lingered not,
But flew from brain to brain, – such glee was ours,
Charged with light memories of remembered hours,
None slow enough for sadness: till we came
Homeward, which always makes the spirit tame.
This day had been cheerful but cold, and now
The sun was sinking, and the wind also.
Our talk grew somewhat serious, as may be
Talk interrupted with such raillery
As mocks itself, because it cannot scorn
The thoughts it would extinguish: – 'twas forlorn,
Yet pleasing, such as once, so poets tell,
The devils held within the dales of Hell
Concerning God, freewill and destiny:
Of all that earth has been or yet may be,
All that vain men imagine or believe,
Or hope can paint or suffering may achieve,
We descanted, and I (for ever still
Is it not wise to make the best of ill?)

Argued against despondency, but pride
Made my companion take the darker side.
The sense that he was greater than his kind
Had struck, methinks, his eagle spirit blind
By gazing on its own exceeding light.
Meanwhile the sun paused ere it should alight,
Over the horizon of the mountains; – Oh
How beautiful is sunset, when the glow
Of Heaven descends upon a land like thee,
Thou Paradise of exiles, Italy!
Thy mountains, seas and vineyards and the towers
Of cities they encircle! – it was ours
To stand on thee, beholding it; and then
Just where we had dismounted the Count's men
Were waiting for us with the gondola. –
As those who pause on some delightful way
Tho' bent on pleasant pilgrimage, we stood
Looking upon the evening, and the flood
Which lay between the city and the shore
Paved with the image of the sky . . . the hoar
And aery Alps towards the North appeared
Thro' mist, an heaven-sustaining bulwark reared
Between the East and West; and half the sky
Was roofed with clouds of rich emblazonry
Dark purple at the zenith, which still grew
Down the steep West into a wondrous hue
Brighter than burning gold, even to the rent
Where the swift sun yet paused in his descent
Among the many folded hills: they were
Those famous Euganean hills, which bear
As seen from Lido thro' the harbour piles
The likeness of a clump of peaked isles –
And then – as if the Earth and Sea had been
Dissolved into one lake of fire, were seen

Those mountains towering as from waves of flame
Around the vaporous sun, from which there came
The inmost purple spirit of light, and made
Their very peaks transparent. 'Ere it fade,'
Said my companion 'I will show you soon
A better station' – so, o'er the lagune
We glided; and from that funereal bark
I leaned, and saw the city, and could mark
How from their many isles in evening's gleam
Its temples and its palaces did seem
Like fabrics of enchantment piled to Heaven.
I was about to speak, when – 'We are even
'Now at the point I meant,' said Maddalo
And bade the gondolieri cease to row.
'Look, Julian, on the west, and listen well
'If you hear not a deep and heavy bell.'
I looked, and saw between us and the sun
A building on an island; such a one
As age to age might add, for uses vile,
A windowless, deformed and dreary pile
And on the top an open tower, where hung
A bell, which in the radiance swayed and swung;
We could just hear its hoarse and iron tongue:
The broad sun sunk behind it, and it tolled
In strong and black relief. – 'What we behold
'Shall be the madhouse and its belfry tower,'
Said Maddalo, 'and ever at this hour
'Those who may cross the water, hear that bell
'Which calls the maniacs each one from his cell
'To vespers.' – 'As much skill as need to pray
'In thanks or hope for their dark lot have they
'To their stern maker,' I replied. 'O ho!
'You talk as in years past,' said Maddalo,
''Tis strange men change not. You were ever still

'Among Christ's flock a perilous infidel,
'A wolf for the meek lambs – if you can't swim
'Beware of Providence.' I looked on him,
But the gay smile had faded in his eye.
'And such,' – he cried, 'is our mortality,
'And this must be the emblem and the sign
'Of what should be eternal and divine! –
'And like that black and dreary bell, the soul,
'Hung in a heaven-illumined tower, must toll
'Our thoughts and our desires to meet below
'Round the rent heart and pray – as madmen do
'For what? they know not, till the night of death
'As sunset that strange vision, severeth
'Our memory from itself, and us from all
'We sought and yet were baffled.' I recall
The sense of what he said, altho' I mar
The force of his expressions. The broad star
Of day meanwhile had sunk behind the hill,
And the black bell became invisible
And the red tower looked grey, and all between
The churches, ships and palaces were seen
Huddled in gloom; – into the purple sea
The orange hues of heaven sunk silently.
We hardly spoke, and soon the gondola
Conveyed me to my lodgings by the way.
The following morn was rainy, cold and dim:
Ere Maddalo arose, I called on him,
And whilst I waited with his child I played;
A lovelier toy sweet Nature never made,
A serious, subtle, wild, yet gentle being,
Graceful without design and unforeseeing,
With eyes – Oh speak not of her eyes! – which seem
Twin mirrors of Italian Heaven, yet gleam
With such deep meaning, as we never see

But in the human countenance: with me
She was a special favourite: I had nursed
Her fine and feeble limbs when she came first
To this bleak world; and she yet seemed to know
On second sight her antient playfellow
Less changed than she was by six months or so;
For after her first shyness was worn out
We sate there, rolling billiard balls about
When the Count entered – Salutations past –
'The words you spoke last night might well have cast
'A darkness on my spirit – if man be
'The passive thing you say, I should not see
'Much harm in the religions and old saws
'(Tho' *I* may never own such leaden laws)
'Which break a teachless nature to the yoke –
'Mine is another faith' – thus much I spoke
And noting he replied not, added: 'See
'This lovely child, blithe, innocent and free;
'She spends a happy time with little care,
'While we to such sick thoughts subjected are
'As came on you last night – it is our will
'That thus enchains us to permitted ill –
'We might be otherwise – we might be all
'We dream of, happy, high, majestical.
'Where is the love, beauty and truth we seek
'But in our mind? and if we were not weak
'Should we be less in deed than in desire?'
'Aye, if we were not weak – and we aspire
'How vainly to be strong!' said Maddalo:
'You talk Utopia.' 'It remains to know'
I then rejoined, 'and those who try may find
'How strong the chains are which our spirit bind;
'Brittle perchance as straw . . . We are assured
'Much may be conquered, much may be endured,

'Of what degrades and crushes us. We know
'That we have power over ourselves to do
'And suffer – what, we know not till we try;
'But something nobler than to live and die –
'So taught those kings of old philosophy
'Who reigned, before Religion made men blind;
'And those who suffer with their suffering kind
'Yet feel their faith, religion.' 'My dear friend'
Said Maddalo, 'my judgement will not bend
'To your opinion, tho' I think you might
'Make such a system refutation-tight
'As far as words go. I knew one like you
'Who to this city came some months ago
'With whom I argued in this sort, and he
'Is now gone mad, – and so he answered me, –
'Poor fellow! but if you would like to go
'We'll visit him, and his wild talk will shew
'How vain are such aspiring theories.'
'I hope to prove the induction otherwise
'And that a want of that true theory, still
'Which seeks a "soul of goodness" in things ill
'Or in himself or others has thus bowed
'His being – there are some by nature proud,
'Who patient in all else demand but this:
'To love and be beloved with gentleness;
'And being scorned, what wonder if they die
'Some living death? this is not destiny
'But man's own wilful ill.'
As thus I spoke
Servants announced the gondola, and we
Through the fast-falling rain and high-wrought sea
Sailed to the island where the madhouse stands.
We disembarked. The clap of tortured hands,
Fierce yells and howlings and lamentings keen

And laughter where complaint had merrier been,
Moans, shrieks, and curses, and blaspheming prayers
Accosted us. We climbed the oozy stairs
Into an old court yard. I heard on high,
Then, fragments of most touching melody
But looking up saw not the singer there –
Through the black bars in the tempestuous air
I saw, like weeds on a wrecked palace growing,
Long tangled locks flung wildly forth, and flowing,
Of those who on a sudden were beguiled
Into strange silence, and looked forth and smiled
Hearing sweet sounds. – Then I: 'Methinks there were
'A cure of these with patience and kind care,
'If music can thus move. . . . but what is he
'Whom we seek here?' 'Of his sad history
'I know but this,' said Maddalo, 'he came
'To Venice a dejected man, and fame
'Said he was wealthy, or he had been so;
'Some thought the loss of fortune wrought him woe;
'But he was ever talking in such sort
'As you do – far more sadly – he seemed hurt,
'Even as a man with his peculiar wrong
'To hear but of the oppression of the strong,
'Or those absurd deceits (I think with you
'In some respects you know) which carry through
'The excellent imposters of this earth
'When they outface detection – he had worth,
'Poor fellow! but a humourist in his way' –
'Alas, what drove him mad?' 'I cannot say;
'A lady came with him from France, and when
'She left him and returned, he wandered then
'About yon lonely isles of desert sand
'Till he grew wild – he had no cash or land
'Remaining, – the police had brought him here –

'Some fancy took him and he would not bear
'Removal; so I fitted up for him
'Those rooms beside the sea, to please his whim
'And sent him busts and books and urns for flowers
'Which had adorned his life in happier hours,
'And instruments of music – you may guess
'A stranger could do little more or less
'For one so gentle and unfortunate,
'And those are his sweet strains which charm the weight
'From madmen's chains, and make this Hell appear
'A heaven of sacred silence, hushed to hear.' –
'Nay, this was kind of you – he had no claim
'As the world says' – 'None – but the very same
'Which I on all mankind were I as he
'Fallen to such deep reverse; – his melody
'Is interrupted – now we hear the din
'Of madmen, shriek on shriek again begin;
'Let us now visit him; after this strain
'He ever communes with himself again,
'And sees nor hears not any.' Having said
These words we called the keeper, and he led
To an apartment opening on the sea –
There the poor wretch was sitting mournfully
Near a piano, his pale fingers twined
One with the other, and the ooze and wind
Rushed thro' an open casement, and did sway
His hair, and starred it with the brackish spray;
His head was leaning on a music book,
And he was muttering, and his lean limbs shook;
His lips were pressed against a folded leaf
In hue too beautiful for health, and grief
Smiled in their motions as they lay apart –
As one who wrought from his own fervid heart
The eloquence of passion, soon he raised

His sad meek face and eyes lustrous and glazed
And spoke – sometimes as one who wrote and thought
His words might move some heart that heeded not
If sent to distant lands: and then as one
Reproaching deeds never to be undone
With wondering self-compassion; then his speech
Was lost in grief, and then his words came each
Unmodulated, cold, expressionless;
But that from one jarred accent you might guess
It was despair made them so uniform:
And all the while the loud and gusty storm
Hissed thro' the window, and we stood behind
Stealing his accents from the envious wind
Unseen. I yet remember what he said
Distinctly: such impression his words made.

'Month after month' he cried 'to bear this load
And as a jade urged by the whip and goad
To drag life on, which like a heavy chain
Lengthens behind with many a link of pain! –
And not to speak my grief – O not to dare
To give a human voice to my despair,
But live and move, and wretched thing! smile on
As if I never went aside to groan
And wear this mask of falsehood even to those
Who are most dear – not for my own repose –
Alas no scorn or pain or hate could be
So heavy as that falshood is to me –
But that I cannot bear more altered faces
Than needs must be, more changed and cold embraces,
More misery dissappointment and mistrust
To own me for their father . . . Would the dust
Were covered in upon my body now!
That the life ceased to toil within my brow!

And then these thoughts would at the least be fled;
Let us not fear such pain can vex the dead.

'What Power delights to torture us? I know
That to myself I do not wholly owe
What now I suffer, tho' in part I may.
Alas none strewed sweet flowers upon the way
Where wandering heedlessly, I met pale Pain
My shadow, which will leave me not again –
If I have erred, there was no joy in error,
But pain and insult and unrest and terror;
I have not as some do, bought penitence
With pleasure, and a dark yet sweet offence,
For then, – if love and tenderness and truth
Had overlived hope's momentary youth
My creed should have redeemed me from repenting,
But loathed scorn and outrage unrelenting
Met love excited by far other seeming
Until the end was gained . . . as one from dreaming
Of sweetest peace, I woke, and found my state
Such as it is. –
'O Thou, my spirit's mate
Who, for thou art compassionate and wise,
Wouldst pity me from thy most gentle eyes
If this sad writing thou shouldst ever see –
My secret groans must be unheard by thee,
Thou wouldst weep tears bitter as blood to know
Thy lost friend's incommunicable woe.

'Ye few by whom my nature has been weighed
In friendship, let me not that name degrade
By placing on your hearts the secret load
Which crushes mine to dust. There is one road
To peace and that is truth, which follow ye!

Love sometimes leads astray to misery.
Yet think not tho' subdued – and I may well
Say that I am subdued – that the full Hell
Within me would infect the untainted breast
Of sacred nature with its own unrest;
As some perverted beings think to find
In scorn or hate a medicine for the mind
Which scorn or hate have wounded – O how vain
The dagger heals not but may rend again . . .
Believe that I am ever still the same
In creed as in resolve, and what may tame
My heart, must leave the understanding free
Or all would sink in this keen agony –
Nor dream that I will join the vulgar cry,
Or with my silence sanction tyranny,
Or seek a moment's shelter from my pain
In any madness which the world calls gain;
Ambition or revenge or thoughts as stern
As those which make me what I am, or turn
To avarice or misanthropy or lust . . .
Heap on me soon O grave, thy welcome dust!
Till then the dungeon may demand its prey,
And poverty and shame may meet and say –
Halting beside me on the public way –
"That love-devoted youth is our's – let's sit
Beside him – he may live some six months yet."
Or the red scaffold, as our country bends
May ask some willing victim, or ye friends
May fall under some sorrow which this heart
Or hand may share or vanquish or avert;
I am prepared – in truth with no proud joy –
To do or suffer aught, as when a boy
I did devote to justice and to love
My nature, worthless now! . . .

'I must remove
A veil from my pent mind. 'Tis torn aside!
O, pallid as death's dedicated bride,
Thou mockery which art sitting by my side,
Am I not wan like thee? at the grave's call
I haste, invited to thy wedding-ball
To greet the ghastly paramour, for whom
Thou hast deserted me . . . and made the tomb
Thy bridal bed . . . but I beside your feet
Will lie and watch ye from my winding sheet –
Thus . . . wide awake tho' dead . . . yet stay, O stay,
Go not so soon – I know not what I say –
Hear but my reasons . . . I am mad I fear,
My fancy is o'erwrought . . . thou are not here . . .
Pale art thou, 'tis most true . . . but thou art gone,
Thy work is finished . . . I am left alone! –
. . . .

'Nay was it I who wooed thee to this breast
Which, like a serpent, thou envenomest
As in repayment of the warmth it lent?
Didst thou not seek me for thine own content?
Did not thy love awaken mine? I thought
That thou wert she who said "You kiss me not
Ever, I fear you do not love me now" –
In truth I loved even to my overthrow
Her, who would fain forget these words: but they
Cling to her mind and cannot pass away.
. . . .

'You say that I am proud – that when I speak
My lip is tortured with the wrongs which break
The spirit it expresses . . . Never one
Humbled himself before, as I have done!
Even the instinctive worm on which we tread
Turns, tho' it wound not – then with prostrate head

Sinks in the dust and writhes like me – and dies?
No: wears a living death of agonies!
As the slow shadows of the pointed grass
Mark the eternal periods, his pangs pass
Slow, ever-moving, – making moments be
As mine seem – each an immortality!

. . . .

'That you had never seen me – never heard
My voice, and more than all had ne'er endured
The deep pollution of my loathed embrace –
That your eyes ne'er had lied love in my face –
That, like some maniac monk, I had torn out
The nerves of manhood by their bleeding root
With mine own quivering fingers, so that ne'er
Our hearts had for a moment mingled there
To disunite in horror – these were not
With thee, like some suppressed and hideous thought
Which flits athwart our musings, but can find
No rest within a pure and gentle mind . . .
Thou sealedst them with many a bare broad word
And searedst my memory o'er them, – for I heard
And can forget not . . . they were ministered
One after one, those curses. Mix them up
Like self-destroying poisons in one cup
And they will make one blessing which thou ne'er
Didst imprecate for, on me, – death.

. . . .

'It were
A cruel punishment for one most cruel,
If such can love, to make that love the fuel
Of the mind's hell; hate, scorn, remorse, despair:
But *me* – whose heart a stranger's tear might wear
As water-drops the sandy fountain-stone,
Who loved and pitied all things, and could moan

For woes which others hear not, and could see
The absent with the glance of phantasy,
And with the poor and trampled sit and weep
Following the captive to his dungeon deep;
Me – who am as a nerve o'er which do creep
The else unfelt oppressions of this earth
And was to thee the flame upon thy hearth
When all beside was cold – that thou on me
Shouldst rain these plagues of blistering agony –
Such curses are from lips once eloquent
With love's too partial praise – let none relent
Who intend deeds too dreadful for a name
Henceforth, if an example for the same
They seek . . . for thou on me lookedst so, and so –
And didst speak thus . . and thus . . . I live to shew
How much men bear and die not!

. . . .

'Thou wilt tell
With the grimace of hate how horrible
It was to meet my love when thine grew less;
Thou wilt admire how I could e'er address
Such features to love's work . . . this taunt, tho' true,
(For indeed Nature nor in form nor hue
Bestowed on me her choicest workmanship)
Shall not be thy defence . . . for since thy lip
Met mine first, years long past, since thine eye kindled
With soft fire under mine, I have not dwindled
Nor changed in mind or body, or in aught
But as love changes what it loveth not
After long years and many trials.

'How vain
Are words! I thought never to speak again
Not even in secret, – not to my own heart –
But from my lips the unwilling accents start

And from my pen the words flow as I write
Dazzling my eyes with scalding tears . . . my sight
Is dim to see that charactered in vain
On this unfeeling leaf which burns the brain
And eats into it . . . blotting all things fair
And wise and good which time had written there.

'Those who inflict must suffer, for they see
The work of their own hearts, and this must be
Our chastisement or recompense – O child!
I would that thine were like to be more mild
For both our wretched sakes . . . for thine the most
Who feelest already all that thou hast lost
Without the power to wish it thine again;
And as slow years pass, a funereal train
Each with the ghost of some lost hope or friend
Following it like its shadow, wilt thou bend
No thought on my dead memory?

. . . .

'Alas, love,
Fear me not . . . against thee I would not move
A finger in despite. Do I not live
That thou mayst have less bitter cause to grieve?
I give thee tears for scorn and love for hate;
And that thy lot may be less desolate
Than his on whom thou tramplest, I refrain
From that sweet sleep which medicines all pain.
Then, when thou speakest of me, never say
"He could forgive not." Here I cast away
All human passions, all revenge, all pride;
I think, speak, act no ill; I do but hide
Under these words, like embers, every spark
Of that which has consumed me – quick and dark
The grave is yawning . . . as its roof shall cover

My limbs with dust and worms under and over
So let Oblivion hide this grief . . . the air
Closes upon my accents, as despair
Upon my heart – let death upon despair!'

He ceased, and overcome leant back awhile
Then rising, with a melancholy smile
Went to a sofa, and lay down, and slept
A heavy sleep, and in his dreams he wept
And muttered some familiar name, and we
Wept without shame in his society.
I think I never was impressed so much;
The man who were not, must have lacked a touch
Of human nature . . . then we lingered not,
Although our argument was quite forgot
But calling the attendants, went to dine
At Maddalo's; yet neither cheer nor wine
Could give us spirits, for we talked of him
And nothing else, till daylight made stars dim;
And we agreed his was some dreadful ill
Wrought on him boldly, yet unspeakable,
By a dear friend; some deadly change in love
Of one vowed deeply which he dreamed not of;
For whose sake he it seemed had fixed a blot
Of falshood on his mind which flourished not
But in the light of all-beholding truth;
And having stamped this canker on his youth
She had abandoned him – and how much more
Might be his woe, we guessed not – he had store
Of friends and fortune once, as we could guess
From his nice habits and his gentleness;
These were now lost . . . it were a grief indeed
If he had changed one unsustaining reed
For all that such a man might else adorn.

The colours of his mind seemed yet unworn;
For the wild language of his grief was high
Such as in measure were called poetry;
And I remember one remark which then
Maddalo made. He said: 'Most wretched men
Are cradled into poetry by wrong,
They learn in suffering what they teach in song.'

If I had been an unconnected man
I, from this moment, should have formed some plan
Never to leave sweet Venice, – for to me
It was delight to ride by the lone sea;
And then, the town is silent – one may write
Or read in gondolas by day or night,
Having the little brazen lamp alight,
Unseen, uninterrupted; books are there,
Pictures, and casts from all those statues fair
Which were twin-born with poetry, and all
We seek in towns, with little to recall
Regrets for the green country. I might sit
In Maddalo's great palace, and his wit
And subtle talk would cheer the winter night
And make me know myself, and the firelight
Would flash upon our faces, till the day
Might dawn and make me wonder at my stay:
But I had friends in London too: the chief
Attraction here, was that I sought relief
From the deep tenderness that maniac wrought
Within me – 'twas perhaps an idle thought –
But I imagined that if day by day
I watched him, and but seldom went away,
And studied all the beatings of his heart
With zeal, as men study some stubborn art
For their own good, and could by patience find

An entrance to the caverns of his mind,
I might reclaim him from his dark estate:
In friendships I had been most fortunate –
Yet never saw I one whom I would call
More willingly my friend; and this was all
Accomplished not; such dreams of baseless good
Oft come and go in crowds and solitude
And leave no trace – but what I now designed
Made for long years impression on my mind.
The following morning urged by my affairs
I left bright Venice.
After many years
And many changes I returned; the name
Of Venice, and it's aspect was the same;
But Maddalo was travelling far away
Among the mountains of Armenia.
His dog was dead. His child had now become
A woman; such as it has been my doom
To meet with few, a wonder of this earth
Where there is little of transcendant worth,
Like one of Shakespeare's women: kindly she
And with a manner beyond courtesy
Received her father's friend; and when I asked
Of the lorn maniac, she her memory tasked
And told as she had heard the mournful tale.
'That the poor sufferer's health began to fail
'Two years from my departure, but that then
'The lady who had left him, came again.
'Her mien had been imperious, but she now
'Looked meek – perhaps remorse had brought her low.
'Her coming made him better, and they stayed
'Together at my father's – for I played
'As I remember with the lady's shawl –
'I might be six years old – but after all

'She left him' . . . 'Why, her heart must have been tough:
'How did it end?' 'And was not this enough?
'They met – they parted' – 'Child, is there no more?'
'Something within that interval which bore
'The stamp of *why* they parted, *how* they met:
'Yet if thine aged eyes disdain to wet
'Those wrinkled cheeks with youth's remembered tears,
'Ask me no more, but let the silent years
'Be closed and cered over their memory
'As yon mute marble where their corpses lie.'
I urged and questioned still, she told me how
All happened – but the cold world shall not know.

Sonnet

Lift not the painted veil which those who live
Call Life: though unreal shapes be pictured there,
And it but mimic all we would believe
With colours idly spread, – behind, lurk Fear
And Hope, twin destinies; who ever weave
The shadows, which the world calls substance, there.
I knew one who had lifted it – he sought,
For his lost heart was tender, things to love,
But found them not, alas! nor was there aught
The world contains, the which he could approve.
Through the unheeding many he did move,
A splendour among shadows, a bright blot
Upon this gloomy scene, a Spirit that strove
For truth, and like the Preacher found it not.

Lines Written among the Euganean Hills

October, 1818

Many a green isle needs must be
In the deep wide sea of misery,
Or the mariner, worn and wan,
Never thus could voyage on
Day and night, and night and day,
Drifting on his dreary way,
With the solid darkness black
Closing round his vessel's track;
Whilst above the sunless sky,
Big with clouds, hangs heavily,
And behind the tempest fleet
Hurries on with lightning feet,
Riving sail, and cord, and plank,
Till the ship has almost drank
Death from the o'er-brimming deep;
And sinks down, down, like that sleep
When the dreamer seems to be
Weltering through eternity;
And the dim low line before
Of a dark and distant shore
Still recedes, as ever still
Longing with divided will,
But no power to seek or shun,
He is ever drifted on
O'er the unreposing wave
To the haven of the grave.
What, if there no friends will greet;
What, if there no heart will meet

His with love's impatient beat;
Wander wheresoe'er he may,
Can he dream before that day
To find refuge from distress
In friendship's smile, in love's caress?
Then 'twill wreak him little woe
Whether such there be or no:
Senseless is the breast, and cold,
Which relenting love would fold;
Bloodless are the veins and chill
Which the pulse of pain did fill;
Every little living nerve
That from bitter words did swerve
Round the tortured lips and brow,
Are like sapless leaflets now
Frozen upon December's bough.

On the beach of a northern sea
Which tempests shake eternally,
As once the wretch there lay to sleep,
Lies a solitary heap,
One white skull and seven dry bones,
On the margin of the stones,
Where a few grey rushes stand,
Boundaries of the sea and land:
Nor is heard one voice of wail
But the sea-mews, as they sail
O'er the billows of the gale;
Or the whirlwind up and down
Howling, like a slaughtered town,
When a king in glory rides
Through the pomp of fratricides:
Those unburied bones around
There is many a mournful sound;

There is no lament for him,
Like a sunless vapour, dim,
Who once clothed with life and thought
What now moves nor murmurs not.

Aye, many flowering islands lie
In the waters of wide Agony:
To such a one this morn was led,
My bark by soft winds piloted:
'Mid the mountains Euganean
I stood listening to the paean,
With which the legioned rooks did hail
The sun's uprise majestical;
Gathering round with wings all hoar,
Thro' the dewy mist they soar
Like grey shades, till th' eastern heaven
Bursts, and then, as clouds of even,
Flecked with fire and azure, lie
In the unfathomable sky,
So their plumes of purple grain,
Starred with drops of golden rain,
Gleam above the sunlight woods,
As in silent multitudes
On the morning's fitful gale
Thro' the broken mist they sail,
And the vapours cloven and gleaming
Follow down the dark steep streaming,
Till all is bright, and clear, and still,
Round the solitary hill.

Beneath is spread like a green sea
The waveless plain of Lombardy,
Bounded by the vaporous air,
Islanded by cities fair;

Underneath day's azure eyes
Ocean's nursling, Venice lies,
A peopled labyrinth of walls,
Amphitrite's destined halls,
Which her hoary sire now paves
With his blue and beaming waves.
Lo! the sun upsprings behind,
Broad, red, radiant, half reclined
On the level quivering line
Of the waters chrystalline;
And before that chasm of light,
As within a furnace bright,
Column, tower, and dome, and spire,
Shine like obelisks of fire,
Pointing with inconstant motion
From the altar of dark ocean
To the sapphire-tinted skies;
As the flames of sacrifice
From the marble shrines did rise,
As to pierce the dome of gold
Where Apollo spoke of old.

Sun-girt City, thou hast been
Ocean's child, and then his queen;
Now is come a darker day,
And thou soon must be his prey,
If the power that raised thee here
Hallow so thy watery bier.
A less drear ruin then than now,
With thy conquest-branded brow
Stooping to the slave of slaves
From thy throne, among the waves
Wilt thou be, when the sea-mew
Flies, as once before it flew,

O'er thine isles depopulate,
And all is in its antient state,
Save where many a palace gate
With green sea-flowers overgrown
Like a rock of ocean's own,
Topples o'er the abandoned sea
As the tides change sullenly.
The fisher on his watery way,
Wandering at the close of day,
Will spread his sail and seize his oar
Till he pass the gloomy shore,
Lest thy dead should, from their sleep
Bursting o'er the starlight deep,
Lead a rapid masque of death
O'er the waters of his path.

Those who alone thy towers behold
Quivering through aerial gold,
As I now behold them here,
Would imagine not they were
Sepulchres, where human forms,
Like pollution-nourished worms
To the corpse of greatness cling,
Murdered, and now mouldering:
But if Freedom should awake
In her omnipotence, and shake
From the Celtic Anarch's hold
All the keys of dungeons cold,
Where a hundred cities lie
Chained like thee, ingloriously,
Thou and all thy sister band
Might adorn this sunny land,
Twining memories of old time
With new virtues more sublime;

If not, perish thou and they,
Clouds which stain truth's rising day
By her sun consumed away,
Earth can spare ye: while like flowers,
In the waste of years and hours,
From your dust new nations spring
With more kindly blossoming.

Perish – let there only be
Floating o'er thy hearthless sea,
As the garment of thy sky
Clothes the world immortally,
One remembrance, more sublime
Than the tattered pall of time,
Which scarce hides thy visage wan; –
That a tempest-cleaving Swan
Of the songs of Albion,
Driven from his ancestral streams
By the might of evil dreams,
Found a nest in thee; and Ocean
Welcomed him with such emotion
That its joy grew his, and sprung
From his lips like music flung
O'er a mighty thunder-fit
Chastening terror: – what though yet
Poesy's unfailing River,
Which thro' Albion winds for ever
Lashing with melodious wave
Many a sacred Poet's grave,
Mourn its latest nursling fled?
What though thou with all thy dead
Scarce can for this fame repay
Aught thine own? oh, rather say
Though thy sins and slaveries foul

Overcloud a sunlike soul?
As a ghost of Homer clings
Round Scamander's wasting springs;
As divinest Shakespeare's might
Fills Avon and the world with light
Like omniscient power which he
Imaged 'mid mortality;
As the love from Petrarch's urn,
Yet amid yon hills doth burn,
A quenchless lamp by which the heart
Sees things unearthly; – so thou art
Mighty spirit – so shall be
The City that did refuge thee.

Lo, the sun floats up the sky
Like thought-winged Liberty,
Till the universal light
Seems to level plain and height;
From the sea a mist has spread,
And the beams of morn lie dead
On the towers of Venice now,
Like its glory long ago.
By the skirts of that grey cloud
Many-domed Padua proud
Stands, a peopled solitude,
'Mid the harvest shining plain,
Where the peasant heaps his grain
In the garner of his foe,
And the milk-white oxen slow
With the purple vintage strain,
Heaped upon the creaking wain,
That the brutal Celt may swill
Drunken sleep with savage will;
And the sickle to the sword

Lies unchanged, though many a lord,
Like a weed whose shade is poison,
Overgrows this region's foizon,
Sheaves of whom are ripe to come
To destruction's harvest home:
Men must reap the things they sow,
Force from force must ever flow,
Or worse; but 'tis a bitter woe
That love or reason cannot change
The despot's rage, the slave's revenge.

Padua, thou within whose walls
Those mute guests at festivals,
Son and Mother, Death and Sin,
Played at dice for Ezzelin,
Till Death cried, 'I win, I win!'
And Sin cursed to lose the wager,
But Death promised, to assuage her,
That he would petition for
Her to be made Vice-Emperor,
When the destined years were o'er,
Over all between the Po
And the eastern Alpine snow,
Under the mighty Austrian.
Sin smiled so as Sin only can,
And since that time, aye, long before,
Both have ruled from shore to shore,
That incestuous pair, who follow
Tyrants as the sun the swallow,
As Repentance follows Crime,
And as changes follow Time.

In thine halls the lamp of learning,
Padua, now no more is burning;

Like a meteor, whose wild way
Is lost over the grave of day,
It gleams betrayed and to betray:
Once remotest nations came
To adore that sacred flame,
When it lit not many a hearth
On this cold and gloomy earth:
Now new fires from antique light
Spring beneath the wide world's might;
But their spark lies dead in thee,
Trampled out by tyranny.
As the Norway woodman quells,
In the depth of piny dells,
One light flame among the brakes,
While the boundless forest shakes,
And its mighty trunks are torn
By the fire thus lowly born:
The spark beneath his feet is dead,
He starts to see the flames it fed
Howling through the darkened sky
With a myriad tongues victoriously,
And sinks down in fear: so thou,
O tyranny, beholdest now
Light around thee, and thou hearest
The loud flames ascend, and fearest:
Grovel on the earth: aye, hide
In the dust thy purple pride!

Noon descends around me now:
'Tis the noon of autumn's glow,
When a soft and purple mist
Like a vaporous amethyst,
Or an air-dissolved star
Mingling light and fragrance, far

From the curved horizon's bound
To the point of heaven's profound,
Fills the overflowing sky;
And the plains that silent lie
Underneath, the leaves unsodden
Where the infant frost has trodden
With his morning-winged feet,
Whose bright print is gleaming yet;
And the red and golden vines,
Piercing with their trellised lines
The rough, dark-skirted wilderness;
The dun and bladed grass no less,
Pointing from this hoary tower
In the windless air; the flower
Glimmering at my feet; the line
Of the olive-sandalled Apennine
In the south dimly islanded;
And the Alps, whose snows are spread
High between the clouds and sun;
And of living things each one;
And my spirit which so long
Darkened this swift stream of song,
Interpenetrated lie
By the glory of the sky:
Be it love, light, harmony,
Odour, or the soul of all
Which from heaven like dew doth fall,
Or the mind which feeds this verse
Peopling the lone universe.

Noon descends, and after noon
Autumn's evening meets me soon,
Leading the infantine moon,
And that one star, which to her

Almost seems to minister
Half the crimson light she brings
From the sunset's radiant springs:
And the soft dreams of the morn,
(Which like winged winds had borne
To that silent isle, which lies
'Mid remembered agonies,
The frail bark of this lone being)
Pass, to other sufferers fleeing,
And its antient pilot, Pain,
Sits beside the helm again.

Other flowering isles must be
In the sea of life and agony:
Other spirits float and flee
O'er that gulph: even now, perhaps,
On some rock the wild wave wraps,
With folded wings they waiting sit
For my bark, to pilot it
To some calm and blooming cove,
Where for me, and those I love,
May a windless bower be built,
Far from passion, pain, and guilt,
In a dell 'mid lawny hills,
Which the wild sea-murmur fills,
And soft sunshine, and the sound
Of old forests echoing round,
And the light and smell divine
Of all flowers that breathe and shine:
We may live so happy there,
That the spirits of the air,
Envying us, may even entice
To our healing paradise
The polluting multitude;

But their rage would be subdued
By that clime divine and calm,
And the winds whose wings rain balm
On the uplifted soul, and leaves
Under which the bright sea heaves;
While each breathless interval
In their whisperings musical
The inspired soul supplies
With its own deep melodies,
And, the love which heals all strife
Circling, like the breath of life,
All things in that sweet abode
With its own mild brotherhood:
They, not it would change; and soon
Every sprite beneath the moon
Would repent its envy vain,
And the earth grow young again.

Prometheus Unbound

A Lyrical Drama
in Four Acts

*Audisne haec Amphiarae, sub terram abdite?**

Preface

The Greek tragic writers, in selecting as their subject any portion of their national history or mythology, employed in their treatment of it a certain arbitrary discretion. They by no means conceived themselves bound to adhere to the common interpretation or to imitate in story as in title their rivals and predecessors. Such a system would have amounted to a resignation of those claims to preference over their competitors which incited the composition. The Agamemnonian story was exhibited in the Athenian theatre with as many variations as dramas.

I have presumed to employ a similar licence. The 'Prometheus Unbound' of Aeschylus supposed the reconciliation of Jupiter with his victim as the price of the disclosure of the danger threatened to his empire by the consummation of his marriage with Thetis. Thetis, according to this view of the subject, was given in marriage to Peleus, and Prometheus, by the permission of Jupiter, delivered from his captivity by

*'Hearest thou these things, Amphiaraus, hidden away beneath the earth?' (This line was inscribed by Shelley on the title page of the first edition of *Prometheus Unbound*, London 1820.)

Amphiaraus, a seer, deceived by his wife Eriphyte, unwillingly took part in the war of the Seven against Thebes, in the course of which he was swallowed up in a cleft in the earth with his chariot by Zeus.

Hercules. Had I framed my story on this model, I should have done no more than have attempted to restore the lost drama of Aeschylus; an ambition which, if my preference to this mode of treating the subject had incited me to cherish, the recollection of the high comparison such an attempt would challenge might well abate. But, in truth, I was averse from a catastrophe so feeble as that of reconciling the Champion with the Oppressor of mankind. The moral interest of the fable, which is so powerfully sustained by the sufferings and endurance of Prometheus, would be annihilated if we could conceive of him as unsaying his high language and quailing before his successful and perfidious adversary. The only imaginary being resembling in any degree Prometheus, is Satan; and Prometheus is, in my judgement, a more poetical character than Satan, because, in addition to courage, and majesty, and firm and patient opposition to omnipotent force, he is susceptible of being described as exempt from the taints of ambition, envy, revenge, and a desire for personal aggrandisement, which, in the Hero of Paradise Lost, interfere with the interest. The character of Satan engenders in the mind a pernicious casuistry which leads us to weigh his faults with his wrongs, and to excuse the former because the latter exceed all measure. In the minds of those who consider that magnificent fiction with a religious feeling it engenders something worse. But Prometheus is, as it were, the type of the highest perfection of moral and intellectual nature, impelled by the purest and the truest motives to the best and noblest ends.

This Poem was chiefly written upon the mountainous ruins of the Baths of Caracalla, among the flowery glades, and thickets of odoriferous blossoming trees, which are extended in ever winding labyrinths upon its immense platforms and dizzy arches suspended in the air. The bright blue sky of Rome, and the effect of the vigorous awakening spring in that divinest climate, and the new life with which it drenches the spirits even to intoxication, were the inspiration of this drama.

The imagery which I have employed will be found, in many instances, to have been drawn from the operations of the human mind, or from those external actions by which they are expressed. This is unusual in modern poetry, although Dante and Shakspeare are full of instances of the same kind: Dante indeed more than any other poet, and with greater success. But the Greek poets, as writers to whom no resource of awakening the sympathy of their contemporaries was unknown, were in the habitual use of this power; and it is the study of their works, (since a higher merit would probably be denied me,) to which I am willing that my readers should impute this singularity.

One word is due in candour to the degree in which the study of contemporary writings may have tinged my composition, for such has been a topic of censure with regard to poems far more popular, and indeed more deservedly popular, than mine. It is impossible that any one who inhabits the same age with such writers as those who stand in the foremost ranks of our own, can conscientiously assure himself that his language and tone of thought may not have been modified by the study of the production of those extraordinary intellects. It is true that, not the spirit of their genius, but the forms in which it has manifested itself, are due less to the peculiarities of their own minds than to the peculiarity of the moral and intellectual condition of the minds among which they have been produced. Thus a number of writers possess the form, whilst they want the spirit of those whom, it is alleged, they imitate; because the former is the endowment of the age in which they live, and the latter must be the uncommunicated lightning of their own mind.

The peculiar style of intense and comprehensive imagery which distinguishes the modern literature of England, has not been, as a general power, the product of the imitation of any particular writer. The mass of capabilities remains at every period materially the same; the circumstances which awaken it to action perpetually change. If England were divided into forty republics, each equal in population and extent to Athens, there is no reason to suppose but that, under institutions not more perfect than those of Athens, each would produce philosophers and poets equal to those who (if we except Shakspeare) have never been surpassed. We owe the great writers of the golden age of our literature to that fervid awakening of the public mind which shook to dust the oldest and most oppressive form of the Christian religion. We owe Milton to the progress and developement of the same spirit: the sacred Milton was, let it ever be remembered, a republican, and a bold inquirer into morals and religion. The great writers of our own age are, we have reason to suppose, the companions and forerunners of some unimagined change in our social condition or the opinions which cement it. The cloud of mind is discharging its collected lightning, and the equilibrium between institutions and opinions is now restoring, or is about to be restored.

As to imitation, poetry is a mimetic art. It creates, but it creates by combination and representation. Poetical abstractions are beautiful and new, not because the portions of which they are composed had no previous existence in the mind of man or in nature, but because the whole produced by their combination has some intelligible and beautiful analogy with those sources of emotion and thought, and with the contemporary condition of them: one great poet is a masterpiece of nature which another not only ought to study but must study. He might as wisely and as easily determine that his mind should no longer be the mirror of all that is lovely in the visible universe, as exclude from his contemplation the beautiful which exists in the writings of a great contemporary.

The pretence of doing it would be a presumption in any but the greatest; the effect, even in him, would be strained, unnatural, and ineffectual. A poet is the combined product of such internal powers as modify the nature of others; and of such external influences as excite and sustain these powers; he is not one, but both. Every man's mind is, in this respect, modified by all the objects of nature and art; by every word and every suggestion which he ever admitted to act upon his consciousness; it is the mirror upon which all forms are reflected, and in which they compose one form. Poets, not otherwise than philosophers, painters, sculptors, and musicians, are, in one sense, the creators, and, in another, the creations, of their age. From this subjection the loftiest do not escape. There is a similarity between Homer and Hesiod, between Aeschylus and Euripides, between Virgil and Horace, between Dante and Petrarch, between Shakspeare and Fletcher, between Dryden and Pope; each has a generic resemblance under which their specific distinctions are arranged. If this similarity be the result of imitation, I am willing to confess that I have imitated.

Let this opportunity be conceded to me of acknowledging that I have, what a Scotch philosopher characteristically terms, 'a passion for reforming the world:' what passion incited him to write and publish his book, he omits to explain. For my part I had rather be damned with Plato and Lord Bacon, than go to Heaven with Paley and Malthus. But it is a mistake to suppose that I dedicate my poetical compositions solely to the direct enforcement of reform, or that I consider them in any degree as containing a reasoned system on the theory of human life. Didactic poetry is my abhorrence; nothing can be equally well expressed in prose that is not tedious and supererogatory in verse. My purpose has hitherto been simply to familiarize the highly refined imagination of the more select classes of poetical readers with beautiful idealisms of moral excellence; aware that until the mind can love, and admire, and trust, and hope, and endure, reasoned principles of moral conduct are seeds cast upon the highway of life which the unconscious passenger tramples into dust, although they would bear the harvest of his happiness. Should I live to accomplish what I purpose, that is, produce a systematical history of what appear to me to be the genuine elements of human society, let not the advocates of injustice and superstition flatter themselves that I should take Aeschylus rather than Plato as my model.

The having spoken of myself with unaffected freedom will need little apology with the candid; and let the uncandid consider that they injure me less than their own hearts and minds by misrepresentation. Whatever talents a person may possess to amuse and instruct others, be they ever so inconsiderable, he is yet bound to exert them: if his attempt be ineffectual, let the punishment of an unaccomplished purpose have been sufficient; let none trouble themselves to heap the dust of oblivion upon his efforts; the pile they raise will betray his grave which might otherwise have been unknown.

Dramatis Personae

PROMETHEUS. APOLLO.
DEMOGORGON. MERCURY. HERCULES.
THE PHANTASM OF JUPITER.
THE SPIRIT OF THE EARTH.
THE SPIRIT OF THE MOON.
SPIRITS OF THE HOURS.
JUPITER. ASIA
THE EARTH. PANTHEA } Oceanides.
OCEAN. IONE
SPIRITS. ECHOES. FAUNS. FURIES.

Act I

SCENE. *A Ravine of Icy Rocks in the Indian Caucasus.* PROMETHEUS *is discovered bound to the Precipice.* PANTHEA *and* IONE *are seated at his Feet. Time, Night. During the Scene, Morning slowly breaks.*

PROMETHEUS: Monarch of Gods and Daemons, and all Spirits
But One, who throng those bright and rolling worlds
Which Thou and I alone of living things
Behold with sleepless eyes! regard this Earth
Made multitudinous with thy slaves, whom thou
Requitest for knee-worship, prayer, and praise,
And toil, and hecatombs of broken hearts,
With fear and self-contempt and barren hope.
Whilst me, who am thy foe, eyeless in hate,
Hast thou made reign and triumph, to thy scorn,
O'er mine own misery and thy vain revenge.
Three thousand years of sleep-unsheltered hours,
And moments aye divided by keen pangs
Till they seemed years, torture and solitude,
Scorn and despair, – these are mine empire.
More glorious far than that which thou surveyest
From thine unenvied throne, O, Mighty God!
Almighty, had I deigned to share the shame
Of thine ill tyranny, and hung not here
Nailed to this wall of eagle-baffling mountain,
Black, wintry, dead, unmeasured; without herb,
Insect, or beast, or shape, or sound of life.
Ah me! alas, pain, pain ever, for ever!

No change, no pause, no hope! Yet I endure.
I ask the Earth, have not the mountains felt?

I ask yon Heaven, the all-beholding Sun,
Has it not seen? The Sea, in storm or calm,
Heaven's ever-changing Shadow, spread below,
Have its deaf waves not heard my agony?
Ah me! alas, pain, pain, ever, for ever!

The crawling glaciers pierce me with the spears
Of their moon-freezing chrystals, the bright chains
Eat with their burning cold into my bones.
Heaven's winged hound, polluting from thy lips
His beak in poison not his own, tears up
My heart; and shapeless sights come wandering by,
The ghastly people of the realm of dream,
Mocking me: and the Earthquake-fiends are charged
To wrench the rivets from my quivering wounds
When the rocks split and close again behind:
While from their loud abysses howling throng
The genii of the storm, urging the rage
Of whirlwind, and afflict me with keen hail.
And yet to me welcome is day and night,
Whether one breaks the hoar frost of the morn,
Or starry, dim, and slow, the other climbs
The leaden-coloured east; for then they lead
The wingless, crawling hours, one among whom
– As some dark Priest hales the reluctant victim –
Shall drag thee, cruel King, to kiss the blood
From these pale feet, which then might trample thee
If they disdained not such a prostrate slave.
Disdain! Ah no! I pity thee. What ruin
Will hunt thee undefended thro' wide Heaven!
How will thy soul, cloven to its depth with terror,
Gape like a hell within! I speak in grief,
Not exultation, for I hate no more,
As then ere misery made me wise. The curse

Once breathed on thee I would recall. Ye Mountains,
Whose many-voiced Echoes, through the mist
Of cataracts, flung the thunder of that spell!
Ye icy Springs, stagnant with wrinkling frost,
Which vibrated to hear me, and then crept
Shuddering thro' India! Thou serenest Air,
Thro' which the Sun walks burning without beams!
And ye swift Whirlwinds, who on poised wings
Hung mute and moveless o'er yon hushed abyss,
As thunder, louder than your own, made rock
The orbed world! If then my words had power,
Though I am changed so that aught evil wish
Is dead within; although no memory be
Of what is hate, let them not lose it now!
What was that curse? for ye all heard me speak.

FIRST VOICE *(from the mountains)*:

Thrice three hundred thousand years
O'er the Earthquake's couch we stood:
Oft, as men convulsed with fears,
We trembled in our multitude.

SECOND VOICE *(from the springs)*:

Thunder-bolts had parched our water,
We had been stained with bitter blood,
And had run mute, 'mid shrieks of slaughter,
Thro' a city and a solitude.

THIRD VOICE *(from the air)*:

I had clothed, since Earth uprose,
Its wastes in colours not their own,
And oft had my serene repose
Been cloven by many a rending groan.

FOURTH VOICE *(from the whirlwinds)*:

We had soared beneath these mountains
  Unresting ages; nor had thunder,
Nor yon volcano's flaming fountains,
  Nor any power above or under
  Ever made us mute with wonder.

FIRST VOICE:

But never bowed our snowy crest
As at the voice of thine unrest.

SECOND VOICE:

Never such a sound before
To the Indian waves we bore.
A pilot asleep on the howling sea
Leaped up from the deck in agony,
And heard, and cried, 'Ah, woe is me!'
And died as mad as the wild waves be.

THIRD VOICE:

By such dread words from Earth to Heaven
My still realm was never riven:
When its wound was closed, there stood
Darkness o'er the day like blood.

FOURTH VOICE:

And we shrank back: for dreams of ruin
To frozen caves our flight pursuing
Made us keep silence – thus – and thus –
Though silence is as hell to us.

THE EARTH: The tongueless Caverns of the craggy hills
Cried, 'Misery!' then; the hollow Heaven replied,
'Misery!' And the Ocean's purple waves,

Climbing the land, howled to the lashing winds,
And the pale nations heard it, 'Misery!'

PROMETHEUS: I heard a sound of voices: not the voice
Which I gave forth. Mother, thy sons and thou
Scorn him, without whose all-enduring will
Beneath the fierce omnipotence of Jove,
Both they and thou had vanished, like thin mist
Unrolled on the morning wind. Know ye not me,
The Titan? He who made his agony
The barrier to your else all-conquering foe?
Oh, rock-embosomed lawns, and snow-fed streams,
Now seen athwart frore vapours, deep below,
Through whose o'ershadowing woods I wandered once
With Asia, drinking life from her loved eyes;
Why scorns the spirit which informs ye, now
To commune with me? me alone, who check'd,
As one who checks a fiend-drawn charioteer,
The falsehood and the force of him who reigns
Supreme, and with the groans of pining slaves
Fills your dim glens and liquid wildernesses:
Why answer ye not, still? Brethren!

THE EARTH: They dare not.

PROMETHEUS: Who dares? for I would hear that curse again.
Ha, what an awful whisper rises up!
'Tis scarce like sound: it tingles thro' the frame
As lightning tingles, hovering ere it strike.
Speak, Spirit! from thine inorganic voice
I only know that thou art moving near
And love. How cursed I him?

THE EARTH: How canst thou hear
Who knowest not the language of the dead?

PROMETHEUS: Thou art a living spirit; speak as they.

THE EARTH: I dare not speak like life, lest Heaven's fell King
Should hear, and link me to some wheel of pain

More torturing than the one whereon I roll.
Subtle thou art and good, and tho' the Gods
Hear not this voice, yet thou art more than God
Being wise and kind: earnestly hearken now.
PROMETHEUS: Obscurely thro' my brain, like shadows dim,
Sweep awful thoughts, rapid and thick. I feel
Faint, like one mingled in entwining love;
Yet 'tis not pleasure.
THE EARTH: No, thou canst not hear:
Thou art immortal, and this tongue is known
Only to those who die.
PROMETHEUS: And what art thou,
O, melancholy Voice?
THE EARTH: I am the Earth,
Thy mother; she within whose stony veins,
To the last fibre of the loftiest tree
Whose thin leaves trembled in the frozen air,
Joy ran, as blood within a living frame,
When thou didst from her bosom, like a cloud
Of glory, arise, a spirit of keen joy!
And at thy voice her pining sons uplifted
Their prostrate brows from the polluting dust,
And our almighty Tyrant with fierce dread
Grew pale, until his thunder chained thee here.
Then, see those million worlds which burn and roll
Around us: their inhabitants beheld
My sphered light wane in wide Heaven; the sea
Was lifted by strange tempest, and new fire
From earthquake-rifted mountains of bright snow
Shook its portentous hair beneath Heaven's frown;
Lightning and Inundation vexed the plains;
Blue thistles bloomed in cities; foodless toads
Within voluptuous chambers panting crawled:
When Plague had fallen on man, and beast, and worm,

And Famine; and black blight on herb and tree;
And in the corn, and vines, and meadow-grass,
Teemed ineradicable poisonous weeds
Draining their growth, for my wan breast was dry
With grief; and the thin air, my breath, was stained
With the contagion of a mother's hate
Breathed on her child's destroyer; aye, I heard
Thy curse, the which, if thou rememberest not,
Yet my innumerable seas and streams,
Mountains, and caves and winds, and yon wide air,
And the inarticulate people of the dead,
Preserve, a treasured spell. We meditate
In secret joy and hope those dreadful words
But dare not speak them.

PROMETHEUS: Venerable mother!
All else who live and suffer take from thee
Some comfort; flowers, and fruits, and happy sounds,
And love, though fleeting; these may not be mine.
But mine own words, I pray, deny me not.

THE EARTH: They shall be told. Ere Babylon was dust,
The Magus Zoroaster, my dead child,
Met his own image walking in the garden.
That apparition, sole of men, he saw.
For know there are two worlds of life and death:
One that which thou beholdest; but the other
Is underneath the grave, where do inhabit
The shadows of all forms that think and live
Till death unite them and they part no more;
Dreams and the light imaginings of men,
And all that faith creates or love desires,
Terrible, strange, sublime and beauteous shapes.
There thou art, and dost hang, a writhing shade,
'Mid whirlwind-peopled mountains; all the gods
Are there, and all the powers of nameless worlds,

Vast, sceptred phantoms; heroes, men, and beasts;
And Demogorgon, a tremendous gloom;
And he, the supreme Tyrant, on his throne
Of burning gold. Son, one of these shall utter
The curse which all remember. Call at will
Thine own ghost, or the ghost of Jupiter,
Hades or Typhon, or what mightier Gods
From all-prolific Evil, since thy ruin
Have sprung, and trampled on my prostrate sons.
Ask, and they must reply: so the revenge
Of the Supreme may sweep thro' vacant shades,
As rainy wind thro' the abandoned gate
Of a fallen palace.

PROMETHEUS: Mother, let not aught
Of that which may be evil, pass again
My lips, or those of aught resembling me.
Phantasm of Jupiter, arise, appear!

IONE:

My wings are folded o'er mine ears:
My wings are crossed o'er mine eyes:
Yet thro' their silver shade appears,
And thro' their lulling plumes arise,
A Shape, a throng of sounds;
May it be no ill to thee
O thou of many wounds!
Near whom, for our sweet sister's sake,
Ever thus we watch and wake.

PANTHEA:

The sound is of whirlwind underground,
Earthquake, and fire, and mountains cloven;
The shape is awful like the sound,
Clothed in dark purple, star-inwoven.

A sceptre of pale gold
To stay steps proud, o'er the slow cloud
His veined hand doth hold.
Cruel he looks, but calm and strong,
Like one who does, not suffers wrong.

PHANTASM OF JUPITER: Why have the secret powers of this strange world
Driven me, a frail and empty phantom, hither
On direst storms? What unaccustomed sounds
Are hovering on my lips, unlike the voice
With which our pallid race hold ghastly talk
In darkness? And, proud sufferer, who art thou?
PROMETHEUS: Tremendous Image, as thou art must be
He whom thou shadowest forth. I am his foe,
The Titan. Speak the words which I would hear,
Although no thought inform thine empty voice.
THE EARTH: Listen! And tho' your echoes must be mute,
Grey mountains, and old woods, and haunted springs,
Prophetic caves, and isle-surrounding streams,
Rejoice to hear what yet ye cannot speak.
PHANTASM: A spirit seizes me and speaks within:
It tears me as fire tears a thunder-cloud.
PANTHEA: See, how he lifts his mighty looks, the Heaven
Darkens above.
IONE: He speaks! O shelter me!
PROMETHEUS: I see the curse on gestures proud and cold,
And looks of firm defiance, and calm hate,
And such despair as mocks itself with smiles,
Written as on a scroll: yet speak: Oh, speak!

PHANTASM:

Fiend, I defy thee! with a calm, fixed mind,
All that thou canst inflict I bid thee do;

Foul Tyrant both of Gods and Human-kind,
  One only being shalt thou not subdue.
Rain then thy plagues upon me here,
Ghastly disease, and frenzying fear;
And let alternate frost and fire
Eat into me, and be thine ire
Lightning, and cutting hail, and legioned forms
Of furies, driving by upon the wounding storms.

Aye, do thy worst. Thou art omnipotent.
  O'er all things but thyself I gave thee power,
And my own will. Be thy swift mischiefs sent
  To blast mankind, from yon ethereal tower.
Let thy malignant spirit move
In darkness over those I love:
On me and mine I imprecate
The utmost torture of thy hate;
And thus devote to sleepless agony,
This undeclining head while thou must reign on high.

But thou, who art the God and Lord: O, thou,
  Who fillest with thy soul this world of woe,
To whom all things of Earth and Heaven do bow
  In fear and worship: all-prevailing foe!
I curse thee! let a sufferer's curse
Clasp thee, his torturer, like remorse;
'Till thine Infinity shall be
A robe of envenomed agony;
And thine Omnipotence a crown of pain,
To cling like burning gold round thy dissolving brain.

Heap on thy soul, by virtue of this Curse,
  Ill deeds, then be thou damned, beholding good;
Both infinite as is the universe,
  And thou, and thy self-torturing solitude.

An awful image of calm power
Though now thou sittest, let the hour
Come, when thou must appear to be
That which thou art internally.
And after many a false and fruitless crime
Scorn track thy lagging fall thro' boundless space and time.

PROMETHEUS: Were these my words, O, Parent?
THE EARTH: They were thine.
PROMETHEUS: It doth repent me: words are quick and vain;
Grief for awhile is blind and so was mine.
I wish no living thing to suffer pain.

THE EARTH:

Misery, Oh misery to me,
That Jove at length should vanquish thee.
Wail, howl aloud, Land and Sea,
The Earth's rent heart shall answer ye.
Howl, Spirits of the living and the dead,
Your refuge, your defence lies fallen and vanquished.

FIRST ECHO:

Lies fallen and vanquished!

SECOND ECHO:

Fallen and vanquished!

IONE:

Fear not: 'tis but some passing spasm,
The Titan is unvanquished still.
But see, where thro' the azure chasm
Of yon forked and snowy hill
Trampling the slant winds on high
With golden-sandalled feet, that glow

Under plumes of purple dye,
Like rose-ensanguined ivory,
  A Shape comes now,
Stretching on high from his right hand
A serpent-cinctured wand.

PANTHEA: 'Tis Jove's world-wandering herald, Mercury.

IONE:

And who are those with hydra tresses
  And iron wings that climb the wind,
Whom the frowning God represses
  Like vapours steaming up behind,
Clanging loud, an endless crowd –

PANTHEA:

  These are Jove's tempest-walking hounds,
Whom he gluts with groans and blood,
When charioted on sulphurous cloud
  He bursts Heaven's bounds.

IONE:

  Are they now led, from the thin dead
  On new pangs to be fed?

PANTHEA: The Titan looks as ever, firm, not proud.
FIRST FURY: Ha! I scent life!
SECOND FURY: Let me but look into his eyes!
THIRD FURY: The hope of torturing him smells like a heap
  Of corpses, to a death-bird after battle.
FIRST FURY: Darest thou delay, O Herald! take cheer, Hounds
  Of Hell: what if the Son of Maia soon

Should make us food and sport – who can please long
The Omnipotent?
MERCURY: Back to your towers of iron,
And gnash, beside the streams of fire and wail,
Your foodless teeth. Geryon, arise! and Gorgon,
Chimaera, and thou Sphinx, subtlest of fiends
Who ministered to Thebes Heaven's poisoned wine,
Unnatural love, and more unnatural hate:
These shall perform your task.
FIRST FURY: Oh, mercy! mercy!
We die with our desire: drive us not back!
MERCURY: Crouch then in silence.
Awful Sufferer
To thee unwilling, most unwillingly
I come, by the great Father's will driven down,
To execute a doom of new revenge.
Alas! I pity thee, and hate myself
That I can do no more: aye from thy sight
Returning, for a season, heaven seems hell,
So thy worn form pursues me night and day,
Smiling reproach. Wise art thou, firm and good,
But vainly wouldst stand forth alone in strife
Against the Omnipotent; as yon clear lamps
That measure and divide the weary years
From which there is no refuge, long have taught
And long must teach. Even now thy Torturer arms
With the strange might of unimagined pains
The powers who scheme slow agonies in Hell,
And my commission is to lead them here,
Or what more subtle, foul, or savage fiends
People the abyss, and leave them to their task.
Be it not so! there is a secret known
To thee, and to none else of living things,
Which may transfer the sceptre of wide Heaven,

The fear of which perplexes the Supreme:
Clothe it in words, and bid it clasp his throne
In intercession; bend thy soul in prayer,
And like a suppliant in some gorgeous fane,
Let the will kneel within thy haughty heart:
For benefits and meek submission tame
The fiercest and the mightiest.

PROMETHEUS: Evil minds
Change good to their own nature. I gave all
He has; and in return he chains me here
Years, ages, night and day: whether the Sun
Split my parched skin, or in the moony night
The chrystal-winged snow cling round my hair:
Whilst my beloved race is trampled down
By his thought-executing ministers.
Such is the tyrants' recompense: 'tis just:
He who is evil can receive no good;
And for a world bestowed, or a friend lost,
He can feel hate, shame; not gratitude:
He but requites me for his own misdeed.
Kindness to such is keen reproach, which breaks
With bitter stings the light sleep of Revenge.
Submission, thou dost know I cannot try:
For what submission but that fatal word,
The death-seal of mankind's captivity,
Like the Sicilian's hair-suspended sword,
Which trembles o'er his crown, would he accept,
Or could I yield? Which yet I will not yield.
Let others flatter Crime, where it sits throned
In brief Omnipotence: secure are they:
For Justice, when triumphant, will weep down
Pity, not punishment, on her own wrongs,
Too much avenged by those who err. I wait,
Enduring thus, the retributive hour

Which since we spake is even nearer now.
But hark, the hell-hounds clamour: fear delay:
Behold! Heaven lowers under thy Father's frown.

MERCURY: Oh, that we might be spared: I to inflict
And thou to suffer! Once more answer me:
Thou knowest not the period of Jove's power?

PROMETHEUS: I know but this, that it must come.

MERCURY: Alas!
Thou canst not count thy years to come of pain?

PROMETHEUS: They last while Jove must reign: nor more, nor less
Do I desire or fear.

MERCURY: Yet pause, and plunge
Into Eternity, where recorded time,
Even all that we imagine, age on age,
Seems but a point, and the reluctant mind
Flags wearily in its unending flight,
Till it sink, dizzy, blind, lost, shelterless;
Perchance it has not numbered the slow years
Which thou must spend in torture, unreprieved?

PROMETHEUS: Perchance no thought can count them, yet they pass.

MERCURY: If thou might'st dwell among the Gods the while
Lapped in voluptuous joy?

PROMETHEUS: I would not quit
This bleak ravine, these unrepentant pains.

MERCURY: Alas! I wonder at, yet pity thee.

PROMETHEUS: Pity the self-despising slaves of Heaven,
Not me, within whose mind sits peace serene,
As light in the sun, throned: how vain is talk!
Call up the fiends.

IONE: O, sister, look! White fire
Has cloven to the roots yon huge snow-loaded cedar;
How fearfully God's thunder howls behind!

MERCURY: I must obey his words and thine: alas!
Most heavily remorse hangs at my heart!
PANTHEA: See where the child of Heaven, with winged feet,
Runs down the slanted sunlight of the dawn.
IONE: Dear sister, close thy plumes over thine eyes
Lest thou behold and die: they come: they come
Blackening the birth of day with countless wings,
And hollow underneath, like death.
FIRST FURY: Prometheus!
SECOND FURY: Immortal Titan!
THIRD FURY: Champion of Heaven's slaves!
PROMETHEUS: He whom some dreadful voice invokes is here,
Prometheus, the chained Titan. Horrible forms,
What and who are ye? Never yet there came
Phantasms so foul thro' monster-teeming Hell
From the all-miscreative brain of Jove;
Whilst I behold such execrable shapes,
Methinks I grow like what I contemplate,
And laugh and stare in loathsome sympathy.
FIRST FURY: We are the ministers of pain, and fear,
And disappointment, and mistrust, and hate,
And clinging crime; and as lean dogs pursue
Thro' wood and lake some struck and sobbing fawn,
We track all things that weep, and bleed, and live,
When the great King betrays them to our will.
PROMETHEUS: Oh! many fearful natures in one name.
I know ye; and these lakes and echoes know
The darkness and the clangour of your wings.
But why more hideous than your loathed selves
Gather ye up in legions from the deep?
SECOND FURY: We knew not that: Sisters, rejoice, rejoice!
PROMETHEUS: Can aught exult in its deformity?
SECOND FURY: The beauty of delight makes lovers glad,

Gazing on one another: so are we.
As from the rose which the pale priestess kneels
To gather for her festal crown of flowers
The aerial crimson falls, flushing her cheek,
So from our victim's destined agony
The shade which is our form invests us round,
Else we are shapeless as our mother Night.

PROMETHEUS: I laugh your power, and his who sent you here,
To lowest scorn. Pour forth the cup of pain.

FIRST FURY: Thou thinkest we will rend thee bone from bone,
And nerve from nerve, working like fire within?

PROMETHEUS: Pain is my element, as hate is thine;
Ye rend me now: I care not.

SECOND FURY: Dost imagine
We will but laugh into thy lidless eyes?

PROMETHEUS: I weigh not what ye do, but what ye suffer,
Being evil. Cruel was the power which called
You, or aught else so wretched, into light.

THIRD FURY: Thou think'st we will live thro' thee, one by one,
Like animal life, and tho' we can obscure not
The soul which burns within, that we will dwell
Beside it, like a vain loud multitude
Vexing the self-content of wisest men:
That we will be dread thought beneath thy brain,
And foul desire round thine astonished heart,
And blood within thy labyrinthine veins
Crawling like agony?

PROMETHEUS: Why, ye are thus now;
Yet am I king over myself, and rule
The torturing and conflicting throngs within,
As Jove rules you when Hell grows mutinous.

CHORUS OF FURIES:

From the ends of the earth, from the ends of the earth,
Where the night has its grave and the morning its birth,
Come, come, come!
Oh, ye who shake hills with the scream of your mirth,
When cities sink howling in ruin; and ye
Who with wingless footsteps trample the sea,
And close upon Shipwreck and Famine's track,
Sit chattering with joy on the foodless wreck;
Come, come, come!
Leave the bed, low, cold, and red,
Strewed beneath a nation dead;
Leave the hatred, as in ashes
Fire is left for future burning;
It will burst in bloodier flashes
When ye stir it, soon returning:
Leave the self-contempt implanted
In young spirits, sense-enchanted,
Misery's yet unkindled fuel:
Leave Hell's secrets half unchanted
To the maniac dreamer; cruel
More than ye can be with hate
Is he with fear.
Come, come, come!
We are steaming up from Hell's wide gate
And we burthen the blasts of the atmosphere,
But vainly we toil till ye come here.

IONE: Sister, I hear the thunder of new wings.

PANTHEA: These solid mountains quiver with the sound
Even as the tremulous air: their shadows make
The space within my plumes more black than night.

FIRST FURY:

Your call was as a winged car
Driven on whirlwinds fast and far;
It rapt us from red gulphs of war.

SECOND FURY:

From wide cities, famine-wasted;

THIRD FURY:

Groans half heard, and blood untasted;

FOURTH FURY:

Kingly conclaves stern and cold,
Where blood with gold is bought and sold;

FIFTH FURY:

From the furnace, white and hot,
In which –

A FURY:

Speak not: whisper not:
I know all that ye would tell,
But to speak might break the spell
Which must bend the Invincible,
The stern of thought;
He yet defies the deepest power of Hell.

A FURY:

Tear the veil!

ANOTHER FURY:

It is torn.

CHORUS:

The pale stars of the morn
Shine on a misery, dire to be borne.
Dost thou faint, mighty Titan? We laugh thee to scorn.
Dost thou boast the clear knowledge thou waken'dst for
man?
Then was kindled within him a thirst which outran
Those perishing waters; a thirst of fierce fever,
Hope, love, doubt, desire, which consume him for ever.
One came forth of gentle worth
Smiling on the sanguine earth;
His words outlived him, like swift poison
Withering up truth, peace, and pity.
Look! where round the wide horizon
Many a million-peopled city
Vomits smoke in the bright air.
Hark that outcry of despair!
'Tis his mild and gentle ghost
Wailing for the faith he kindled:
Look again, the flames almost
To a glow-worm's lamp have dwindled:
The survivors round the embers
Gather in dread.
Joy, joy, joy!
Past ages crowd on thee, but each one remembers.
And the future is dark, and the present is spread
Like a pillow of thorns for thy slumberless head.

SEMICHORUS I:

Drops of bloody agony flow
From his white and quivering brow.
Grant a little respite now:
See a disenchanted nation
Springs like day from desolation;

To truth its state is dedicate,
And Freedom leads it forth, her mate;
A legioned band of linked brothers
Whom Love calls children –

SEMICHORUS II:

'Tis another's:
See how kindred murder kin:
'Tis the vintage-time for death and sin:
Blood, like new wine, bubbles within:
'Till Despair smothers
The struggling world, which slaves and tyrants win.
[*All the* FURIES *vanish, except one.*]

IONE: Hark, sister! what a low yet dreadful groan
Quite unsuppressed is tearing up the heart
Of the good Titan, as storms tear the deep,
And beasts hear the sea moan in inland caves.
Darest thou observe how the fiends torture him?

PANTHEA: Alas! I looked forth twice, but will no more.

IONE: What didst thou see?

PANTHEA: A woeful sight: a youth
With patient looks nailed to a crucifix.

IONE: What next?

PANTHEA: The heaven around, the earth below
Was peopled with thick shapes of human death,
All horrible, and wrought by human hands,
And some appeared the work of human hearts,
For men were slowly killed by frowns and smiles:
And other sights too foul to speak and live
Were wandering by. Let us not tempt worse fear
By looking forth: those groans are grief enough.

FURY: Behold an emblem: those who do endure
Deep wrongs for man, and scorn, and chains, but heap
Thousandfold torment on themselves and him.

PROMETHEUS: Remit the anguish of that lighted stare;
Close those wan lips; let that thorn-wounded brow
Stream not with blood; it mingles with thy tears!
Fix, fix those tortured orbs in peace and death,
So thy sick throes shake not that crucifix,
So those pale fingers play not with thy gore.
O, horrible! Thy name I will not speak,
It hath become a curse. I see, I see
The wise, the mild, the lofty, and the just,
Whom thy slaves hate for being like to thee,
Some hunted by foul lies from their heart's home,
An early-chosen, late-lamented home;
As hooded ounces cling to the driven hind:
Some linked to corpses in unwholesome cells:
Some – Hear I not the multitude laugh loud? –
Impaled in lingering fire: and mighty realms
Float by my feet, like sea-uprooted isles,
Whose sons are kneaded down in common blood
By the red light of their own burning homes.
FURY: Blood thou canst see, and fire; and canst hear groans;
Worse things, unheard, unseen, remain behind.
PROMETHEUS: Worse?
FURY: In each human heart terror survives
The ravin it has gorged: the loftiest fear
All that they would disdain to think were true:
Hypocrisy and custom make their minds
The fanes of many a worship, now outworn.
They dare not devise good for man's estate,
And yet they know not that they do not dare.
The good want power, but to weep barren tears.
The powerful goodness want: worse need for them.
The wise want love; and those who love want wisdom;
And all best things are thus confused to ill.
Many are strong and rich, and would be just,

But live among their suffering fellow-men
As if none felt: they know not what they do.
PROMETHEUS: Thy words are like a cloud of winged snakes;
And yet I pity those they torture not.
FURY: Thou pitiest them? I speak no more! [*Vanishes.*]
PROMETHEUS: Ah woe!
Ah woe! Alas! pain, pain ever, for ever!
I close my tearless eyes, but see more clear
Thy works within my woe-illumed mind,
Thou subtle tyrant! Peace is in the grave.
The grave hides all things beautiful and good:
I am a God and cannot find it there,
Nor would I seek it: for, though dread revenge,
This is defeat, fierce king, not victory.
The sights with which thou torturest gird my soul
With new endurance, till the hour arrives
When they shall be no types of things which are.
PANTHEA: Alas! what sawest thou more?
PROMETHEUS: There are two woes;
To speak, and to behold; thou spare me one.
Names are there, Nature's sacred watch-words, they
Were borne aloft in bright emblazonry;
The nations thronged around, and cried aloud,
As with one voice, Truth, liberty, and love!
Suddenly fierce confusion fell from heaven
Among them: there was strife, deceit, and fear:
Tyrants rushed in, and did divide the spoil.
This was the shadow of the truth I saw.
THE EARTH: I felt thy torture, son, with such mixed joy
As pain and virtue give. To cheer thy state
I bid ascend those subtle and fair spirits,
Whose homes are the dim caves of human thought,
And who inhabit, as birds wing the wind,
Its world-surrounding ether: they behold

Beyond that twilight realm, as in a glass,
The future: may they speak comfort to thee!
PANTHEA: Look, sister, where a troop of spirits gather,
Like flocks of clouds in spring's delightful weather,
Thronging in the blue air!
IONE: And see! more come,
Like fountain-vapours when the winds are dumb,
That climb up the ravine in scattered lines.
And, hark! is it the music of the pines?
Is it the lake? Is it the waterfall?
PANTHEA: 'Tis something sadder, sweeter far than all.

CHORUS OF SPIRITS:

From unremembered ages we
Gentle guides and guardians be
Of heaven-oppressed mortality;
And we breathe, and sicken not,
The atmosphere of human thought:
Be it dim, and dank, and grey,
Like a storm-extinguished day,
Travelled o'er by dying gleams;
Be it bright as all between
Cloudless skies and windless streams,
Silent, liquid, and serene;
As the birds within the wind,
As the fish within the wave,
As the thoughts of man's own mind
Float thro' all above the grave;
We make there our liquid lair,
Voyaging cloudlike and unpent
Thro' the boundless element:
Thence we bear the prophecy
Which begins and ends in thee!

IONE: More yet come, one by one: the air around them
Looks radiant as the air around a star.

FIRST SPIRIT:
On a battle-trumpet's blast
I fled hither, fast, fast, fast,
'Mid the darkness upward cast.
From the dust of creeds outworn,
From the tyrant's banner torn,
Gathering 'round me, onward borne,
There was mingled many a cry –
Freedom! Hope! Death! Victory!
Till they faded thro' the sky;
And one sound, above, around,
One sound beneath, around, above,
Was moving; 'twas the soul of Love;
'Twas the hope, the prophecy,
Which begins and ends in thee.

SECOND SPIRIT:
A rainbow's arch stood on the sea,
Which rocked beneath, immoveably;
And the triumphant storm did flee,
Like a conqueror, swift and proud,
Between with many a captive cloud,
A shapeless, dark and rapid crowd,
Each by lightning riven in half:
I heard the thunder hoarsely laugh:
Mighty fleets were strewn like chaff
And spread beneath a hell of death
O'er the white waters. I alit
On a great ship lightning-split,
And speeded hither on the sigh
Of one who gave an enemy
His plank, then plunged aside to die.

THIRD SPIRIT:

I sate beside a sage's bed,
And the lamp was burning red
Near the book where he had fed,
When a Dream with plumes of flame
To his pillow hovering came,
And I knew it was the same
Which had kindled long ago
Pity, eloquence, and woe;
And the world awhile below
Wore the shade, its lustre made.
It has borne me here as fleet
As Desire's lightning feet:
I must ride it back ere morrow,
Or the sage will wake in sorrow.

FOURTH SPIRIT:

On a poet's lips I slept
Dreaming like a love-adept
In the sound his breathing kept;
Nor seeks nor finds he mortal blisses,
But feeds on the aerial kisses
Of shapes that haunt thought's wildernesses.
He will watch from dawn to gloom
The lake-reflected sun illume
The yellow bees in the ivy-bloom,
Nor heed nor see, what things they be;
But from these create he can
Forms more real than living man,
Nurslings of immortality!
One of these awakened me,
And I sped to succour thee.

IONE:

Behold'st thou not two shapes from the east and west
Come, as two doves to one beloved nest,
Twin nurslings of the all-sustaining air
On swift still wings glide down the atmosphere?
And hark! their sweet, sad voices! 'tis despair
Mingled with love and then dissolved in sound.

PANTHEA: Canst thou speak, sister? all my words are drowned.

IONE: Their beauty gives me voice, See how they float
On their sustaining wings of skiey grain,
Orange and azure deepening into gold:
Their soft smiles light the air like a star's fire.

CHORUS OF SPIRITS:

Hast thou beheld the form of Love?

FIFTH SPIRIT:

As over wide dominions
I sped, like some swift cloud that wings the wide air's wildernesses,
That planet-crested shape swept by on lightning-braided pinions,
Scattering the liquid joy of life from his ambrosial tresses;
His footsteps paved the world with light; but as I past 'twas fading,
And hollow Ruin yawned behind: great sages bound in madness,
And headless patriots, and pale youths who perished, unupbraiding,
Gleamed in the night. I wandered o'er, till thou, O King of sadness,
Turned by thy smile the worst I saw to recollected gladness.

SIXTH SPIRIT:

Ah, sister! Desolation is a delicate thing:
  It walks not on the earth, it floats not on the air,
But treads with lulling footstep, and fans with silent wing
  The tender hopes which in their hearts the best and gentlest bear;
Who, soothed to false repose by the fanning plumes above
  And the music-stirring motion of its soft and busy feet,
Dream visions of aerial joy, and call the monster, Love,
  And wake, and find the shadow Pain, as he whom now we greet.

CHORUS:

Tho' Ruin now Love's shadow be,
Following him, destroyingly,
  On Death's white and winged steed,
Which the fleetest cannot flee,
  Trampling down both flower and weed,
Man and beast, and foul and fair,
Like a tempest thro' the air;
Thou shalt quell this horseman grim,
Woundless though in heart or limb.

PROMETHEUS: Spirits! how know ye this shall be?

CHORUS:

  In the atmosphere we breathe,
As buds grow red when the snow-storms flee,
  From spring gathering up beneath,
Whose mild winds shake the elder brake,
And the wandering herdsmen know
That the white-thorn soon will blow;

Wisdom, Justice, Love, and Peace,
When they struggle to increase,
Are to us as soft winds be
To shepherd boys, the prophecy
Which begins and ends in thee.

IONE: Where are the Spirits fled?
PANTHEA: Only a sense
Remains of them, like the omnipotence
Of music, when the inspired voice and lute
Languish, ere yet the responses are mute,
Which thro' the deep and labyrinthine soul,
Like echoes thro' long caverns, wind and roll.
PROMETHEUS: How fair these air-born shapes! and yet I feel
Most vain all hope but love; and thou art far,
Asia! who, when my being overflowed,
Wert like a golden chalice to bright wine
Which else had sunk into the thirsty dust.
All things are still: alas! how heavily
This quiet morning weighs upon my heart;
Tho' I should dream I could even sleep with grief
If slumber were denied not. I would fain
Be what it is my destiny to be,
The saviour and the strength of suffering man,
Or sink into the original gulph of things:
There is no agony, and no solace left;
Earth can console, Heaven can torment no more.
PANTHEA: Hast thou forgotten one who watches thee
The cold dark night, and never sleeps but when
The shadow of thy spirit falls on her?
PROMETHEUS: I said all hope was vain but love: thou lovest.
PANTHEA: Deeply in truth; but the eastern star looks white,
And Asia waits in that far Indian vale
The scene of her sad exile; rugged once

And desolate and frozen, like this ravine;
But now invested with fair flowers and herbs,
And haunted by sweet airs and sounds, which flow
Among the woods and waters, from the ether
Of her transforming presence, which would fade
If it were mingled not with thine. Farewell!

END OF THE FIRST ACT

Act II

SCENE I. *Morning. A lovely Vale in the Indian Caucasus.*
ASIA *alone.*

ASIA: From all the blasts of heaven thou hast descended:
Yes, like a spirit, like a thought, which makes
Unwonted tears throng to the horny eyes,
And beatings haunt the desolated heart,
Which should have learnt repose: thou hast descended
Cradled in tempests; thou dost wake, O Spring!
O child of many winds! As suddenly
Thou comest as the memory of a dream,
Which now is sad because it hath been sweet;
Like genius, or like joy which riseth up
As from the earth, clothing with golden clouds
The desert of our life.
This is the season, this the day, the hour;
At sunrise thou shouldst come, sweet sister mine,
Too long desired, too long delaying, come!
How like death-worms the wingless moments crawl!
The point of one white star is quivering still
Deep in the orange light of widening morn
Beyond the purple mountains: thro' a chasm
Of wind-divided mist the darker lake
Reflects it: now it wanes: it gleams again
As the waves fade, and as the burning threads

Of woven cloud unravel in pale air:
'Tis lost! and thro' yon peaks of cloudlike snow
The roseate sun-light quivers: hear I not
The Aeolian music of her sea-green plumes
Winnowing the crimson dawn?
[PANTHEA *enters*.] I feel, I see
Those eyes which burn thro' smiles that fade in tears,
Like stars half quenched in mists of silver dew.
Beloved and most beautiful, who wearest
The shadow of that soul by which I live,
How late thou art! the sphered sun had climbed
The sea; my heart was sick with hope, before
The printless air felt thy belated plumes.

PANTHEA: Pardon, great Sister! but my wings were faint
With the delight of a remembered dream,
As are the noon-tide plumes of summer winds
Satiate with sweet flowers. I was wont to sleep
Peacefully, and awake refreshed and calm
Before the sacred Titan's fall, and thy
Unhappy love, had made, thro' use and pity,
Both love and woe familiar to my heart
As they had grown to thine: erewhile I slept
Under the glaucous caverns of old Ocean
Within dim bowers of green and purple moss,
Our young Ione's soft and milky arms
Locked then, as now, behind my dark, moist hair,
While my shut eyes and cheek were pressed within
The folded depth of her life-breathing bosom:
But not as now, since I am made the wind
Which fails beneath the music that I bear
Of thy most wordless converse; since dissolved
Into the sense with which love talks, my rest
Was troubled and yet sweet; my waking hours
Too full of care and pain.

ASIA: Lift up thine eyes,
And let me read thy dream.
PANTHEA: As I have said
With our sea-sister at his feet I slept.
The mountain mists, condensing at our voice
Under the moon, had spread their snowy flakes,
From the keen ice shielding our linked sleep.
Then two dreams came. One, I remember not,
But in the other his pale wound-worn limbs
Fell from Prometheus, and the azure night
Grew radiant with the glory of that form
Which lives unchanged within, and his voice fell
Like music which makes giddy the dim brain,
Faint with intoxication of keen joy:
'Sister of her whose footsteps pave the world
'With loveliness – more fair than aught but her,
'Whose shadow thou art – lift thine eyes on me.'
I lifted them: the overpowering light
Of that immortal shape was shadowed o'er
By love; which, from his soft and flowing limbs,
And passion-parted lips, and keen, faint eyes,
Steamed forth like vaporous fire; an atmosphere
Which wrapt me in its all-dissolving power,
As the warm ether of the morning sun
Wraps ere it drinks some cloud of wandering dew.
I saw not, heard not, moved not, only felt
His presence flow and mingle thro' my blood
Till it became his life, and his grew mine,
And I was thus absorb'd, until it past,
And like the vapours when the sun sinks down,
Gathering again in drops upon the pines,
And tremulous as they, in the deep night
My being was condensed; and as the rays
Of thought were slowly gathered, I could hear

His voice, whose accents lingered ere they died
Like footsteps of weak melody: thy name
Among the many sounds alone I heard
Of what might be articulate; tho' still
I listened thro' the night when sound was none.
Ione wakened then, and said to me:
'Canst thou divine what troubles me to-night?
'I always knew what I desired before,
'Nor ever found delight to wish in vain.
'But now I cannot tell thee what I seek;
'I know not; something sweet, since it is sweet
'Even to desire, it is thy sport, false sister;
'Thou hast discovered some enchantment old,
'Whose spells have stolen my spirit as I slept
'And mingled it with thine: for when just now
'We kissed, I felt within thy parted lips
'The sweet air that sustained me, and the warmth
'Of the life-blood, for loss of which I faint,
'Quivered between our intertwining arms.'
I answered not, for the Eastern star grew pale,
But fled to thee.

ASIA: Thou speakest, but thy words
Are as the air: I feel them not: Oh, lift
Thine eyes, that I may read his written soul!

PANTHEA: I lift them tho' they droop beneath the load
Of that they would express: what canst thou see
But thine own fairest shadow imaged there?

ASIA: Thine eyes are like the deep, blue, boundless heaven
Contracted to two circles underneath
Their long, fine lashes; dark, far, measureless,
Orb within orb, and line thro' line inwoven.

PANTHEA: Why lookest thou as if a spirit past?

ASIA: There is a change: beyond their inmost depth
I see a shade, a shape: 'tis He, arrayed

In the soft light of his own smiles, which spread
Like radiance from the cloud-surrounded moon.
Prometheus, it is thine! depart not yet!
Say not those smiles that we shall meet again
Within that bright pavilion which their beams
Shall build o'er the waste world? The dream is told.
What shape is that between us? Its rude hair
Roughens the wind that lifts it, its regard
Is wild and quick, yet 'tis a thing of air
For thro' its grey robe gleams the golden dew
Whose stars the noon has quench'd not.

DREAM: Follow! Follow!

PANTHEA: It is mine other dream.

ASIA: It disappears.

PANTHEA: It passes now into my mind. Methought
As we sate here, the flower-infolding buds
Burst on yon lightning-blasted almond-tree,
When swift from the white Scythian wilderness
A wind swept forth wrinkling the Earth with frost:
I looked, and all the blossoms were blown down;
But on each leaf was stamped, as the blue bells
Of Hyacinth tell Apollo's written grief,
O, FOLLOW, FOLLOW!

ASIA: As you speak, your words
Fill, pause by pause, my own forgotten sleep
With shapes. Methought among these lawns together
We wandered, underneath the young grey dawn,
And multitudes of dense white fleecy clouds
Were wandering in thick flocks along the mountains
Shepherded by the slow, unwilling wind;
And the white dew on the new bladed grass,
Just piercing the dark earth, hung silently;
And there was more which I remember not:
But on the shadows of the moving clouds,

Athwart the purple mountain slope, was written
FOLLOW, O, FOLLOW! As they vanished by,
And on each herb, from which Heaven's dew had fallen,
The like was stamped, as with a withering fire,
A wind arose among the pines; it shook
The clinging music from their boughs, and then
Low, sweet, faint sounds, like the farewell of ghosts,
Were heard: OH, FOLLOW, FOLLOW, FOLLOW ME!
And then I said: 'Panthea, look on me.'
But in the depth of those beloved eyes
Still I saw, FOLLOW, FOLLOW!

ECHO: Follow! follow!

PANTHEA: The crags, this clear spring morning, mock our voices
As they were spirit-tongued.

ASIA: It is some being
Around the crags. What fine clear sounds! O, list!

ECHOES [*unseen*]:
Echoes we: listen!
We cannot stay:
As dew-stars glisten
Then fade away –
Child of Ocean!

ASIA: Hark! Spirits speak. The liquid responses
Of their aerial tongues yet sound.

PANTHEA: I hear.

ECHOES:

O, follow, follow,
As our voice recedeth
Thro' the caverns hollow,
Where the forest spreadeth;

[*more distant*]

O, follow, follow!
Thro' the caverns hollow,
As the song floats thou pursue,
Where the wild bee never flew,
Thro' the noontide darkness deep,
By the odour-breathing sleep
Of faint night flowers, and the waves
At the fountain-lighted caves,
While our music, wild and sweet,
Mocks thy gently falling feet,
Child of Ocean!

ASIA: Shall we pursue the sound? It grows more faint
And distant.

PANTHEA: List! the strain floats nearer now.

ECHOES:

In the world unknown
Sleeps a voice unspoken;
By thy step alone
Can its rest be broken;
Child of Ocean!

ASIA: How the notes sink upon the ebbing wind!

ECHOES:

O, follow, follow!
Thro' the caverns hollow,
As the song floats thou pursue,
By the woodland noon-tide dew;
By the forests, lakes, and fountains
Thro' the many-folded mountains;
To the rents, and gulphs, and chasms,
Where the Earth reposed from spasms,

On the day when He and thou
Parted, to commingle now;
Child of Ocean!

ASIA: Come, sweet Panthea, link thy hand in mine,
And follow, ere the voices fade away.

SCENE II. *A Forest, intermingled with Rocks and Caverns.* ASIA *and* PANTHEA *pass into it. Two young Fauns are sitting on a Rock listening.*

SEMICHORUS I OF SPIRITS:

The path thro' which that lovely twain
Have past, by cedar, pine, and yew,
And each dark tree that ever grew,
Is curtained out from Heaven's wide blue;
Nor sun, nor moon, nor wind, nor rain,
Can pierce its interwoven bowers,
Nor aught, save where some cloud of dew,
Drifted along the earth-creeping breeze,
Between the trunks of the hoar trees,
Hangs each a pearl in the pale flowers
Of the green laurel, blown anew;
And bends, and then fades silently.
One frail and fair anemone:
Or when some star of many a one
That climbs and wanders thro' steep night,
Has found the cleft thro' which alone
Beams fall from high those depths upon
Ere it is borne away, away,
By the swift Heavens that cannot stay,
It scatters drops of golden light,
Like lines of rain that ne'er unite:
And the gloom divine is all around;
And underneath is the mossy ground.

SEMICHORUS II:

There the voluptuous nightingales,
  Are awake thro' all the broad noon-day.
When one with bliss or sadness fails,
    And thro' the windless ivy-boughs,
  Sick with sweet love, droops dying away
On its mate's music-panting bosom;
Another from the swinging blossom,
    Watching to catch the languid close
  Of the last strain, then lifts on high
  The wings of the weak melody,
'Till some new strain of feeling bear
  The song, and all the woods are mute;
When there is heard thro' the dim air
The rush of wings, and rising there
  Like many a lake-surrounded flute,
Sounds overflow the listener's brain
So sweet, that joy is almost pain.

SEMICHORUS I:

There those enchanted eddies play
  Of echoes, music-tongued, which draw,
  By Demogorgon's mighty law,
  With melting rapture, or sweet awe,
All spirits on that secret way;
  As inland boats are driven to Ocean
Down streams made strong with mountain-thaw:
    And first there comes a gentle sound
    To those in talk or slumber bound,
  And wakes the destined. – Soft emotion
Attracts, impels them: those who saw
  Say from the breathing earth behind
  There steams a plume-uplifting wind

Which drives them on their path, while they
Believe their own swift wings and feet
The sweet desires within obey:
And so they float upon their way,
Until, still sweet, but loud and strong,
The storm of sound is driven along,
Sucked up and hurrying: as they fleet
Behind, its gathering billows meet
And to the fatal mountain bear
Like clouds amid the yielding air.

FIRST FAUN: Canst thou imagine where those spirits live
Which make such delicate music in the woods?
We haunt within the least frequented caves
And closest coverts, and we know these wilds,
Yet never meet them, tho' we hear them oft:
Where may they hide themselves?
SECOND FAUN: 'Tis hard to tell:
I have heard those more skilled in spirits say,
The bubbles, which the enchantment of the sun
Sucks from the pale faint water-flowers that pave
The oozy bottom of clear lakes and pools,
Are the pavilions where such dwell, and float
Under the green and golden atmosphere
Which noon-tide kindles thro' the woven leaves;
And when these burst, and the thin fiery air,
The which they breathed within those lucent domes,
Ascends to flow like meteors thro' the night,
They ride on them, and rein their headlong speed,
And bow their burning crests, and glide in fire
Under the waters of the earth again.
FIRST FAUN: If such live thus, have others other lives,
Under pink blossoms or within the bells
Of meadow flowers, or folded violets deep,

Or on their dying odours, when they die,
Or in the sunlight of the sphered dew?
SECOND FAUN: Aye, many more which we may well divine.
But, should we stay to speak, noontide would come,
And thwart Silenus find his goats undrawn,
And grudge to sing those wise and lovely songs
Of fate, and chance, and God, and Chaos old,
And Love, and the chained Titan's woful doom,
And how he shall be loosed, and make the earth
One brotherhood: delightful strains which cheer
Our solitary twilights, and which charm
To silence the unenvying nightingales.

SCENE III. *A Pinnacle of Rock among Mountains.* ASIA *and* PANTHEA.

PANTHEA: Hither the sound has borne us – to the realm
Of Demogorgon, and the mighty portal,
Like a volcano's meteor-breathing chasm,
Whence the oracular vapour is hurled up
Which lonely men drink wandering in their youth,
And call truth, virtue, love, genius, or joy,
That maddening wine of life, whose dregs they drain
To deep intoxication; and uplift,
Like Maenads who cry loud, Evoe! Evoe!
The voice which is contagion to the world.
ASIA: Fit throne for such a Power! Magnificent!
How glorious art thou, Earth! And if thou be
The shadow of some spirit lovelier still,
Though evil stain its work, and it should be
Like its creation, weak yet beautiful,
I could fall down and worship that and thee.
Even now my heart adoreth: Wonderful!
Look, sister, ere the vapour dim thy brain:

Beneath is a wide plain of billowy mist,
As a lake, paving in the morning sky,
With azure waves which burst in silver light,
Some Indian vale. Behold it, rolling on
Under the curdling winds, and islanding
The peak whereon we stand, midway, around,
Encinctured by the dark and blooming forests,
Dim twilight-lawns, and stream-illumed caves,
And wind-enchanted shapes of wandering mist;
And far on high the keen sky-cleaving mountains
From icy spires of sun-like radiance fling
The dawn, as lifted Ocean's dazzling spray,
From some Atlantic islet scattered up,
Spangles the wind with lamp-like water-drops.
The vale is girdled with their walls, a howl
Of cataracts from their thaw-cloven ravines
Satiates the listening wind, continuous, vast,
Awful as silence. Hark! the rushing snow!
The sun-awakened avalanche! whose mass,
Thrice sifted by the storm, had gathered there
Flake after flake, in heaven-defying minds
As thought by thought is piled, till some great truth
Is loosened, and the nations echo round,
Shaken to their roots, as do the mountains now.

PANTHEA: Look how the gusty sea of mist is breaking
In crimson foam, even at our feet! It rises
As Ocean at the enchantment of the moon
Round foodless men wrecked on some oozy isle.

ASIA: The fragments of the cloud are scattered up;
The wind that lifts them disentwines my hair;
Its billows now sweep o'er mine eyes; my brain
Grows dizzy; see'st thou shapes within the mist?

PANTHEA: A countenance with beckoning smiles: there burns

An azure fire within its golden locks!
Another and another: hark! they speak!

SONG OF SPIRITS:

To the deep, to the deep,
Down, down!
Through the shade of sleep,
Through the cloudy strife
Of Death and of Life;
Through the veil and the bar
Of things which seem and are
Even to the steps of the remotest throne,
Down, down!

While the sound whirls around,
Down, down!
As the fawn draws the hound,
As the lightning the vapour,
As a weak moth the taper;
Death, despair; love, sorrow;
Time both; today, tomorrow;
As steel obeys the spirit of the stone,
Down, down.

Through the grey, void abysm,
Down, down!
Where the air is no prism,
And the moon and stars are not,
And the cavern-crags wear not
The radiance of Heaven,
Nor the gloom to Earth given,
Where there is one pervading, one alone.
Down, down!

In the depth of the deep
Down, down!
Like veiled lightning asleep,
Like the spark nursed in embers,
The last look Love remembers,
Like a diamond, which shines
On the dark wealth of mines,
A spell is treasur'd but for thee alone.
Down, down!

We have bound thee, we guide thee;
Down, down!
With the bright form beside thee;
Resist not the weakness,
Such strength is in meekness
That the Eternal, the Immortal,
Must unloose through life's portal
The snake-like Doom coiled underneath his throne
By that alone.

SCENE IV. *The Cave of Demogorgon.* ASIA *and* PANTHEA.

PANTHEA: What veiled form sits on that ebon throne?
ASIA: The veil has fallen.
PANTHEA: I see a mighty darkness
Filling the seat of power, and rays of gloom
Dart round, as light from the meridian sun,
Ungazed upon and shapeless; neither limb,
Nor form, nor outline; yet we feel it is
A living Spirit.
DEMOGORGON: Ask what thou wouldst know.
ASIA: What canst thou tell?
DEMOGORGON: All things thou dar'st demand.
ASIA: Who made the living world?

DEMOGORGON: God.
ASIA: Who made all
That it contains? thought, passion, reason, will,
Imagination?
DEMOGORGON: God: Almighty God.
ASIA: Who made that sense which, when the winds of spring
In rarest visitation, or the voice
Of one beloved heard in youth alone,
Fills the faint eyes with falling tears which dim
The radiant looks of unbewailing flowers,
And leaves this peopled earth a solitude
When it returns no more?
DEMOGORGON: Merciful God.
ASIA: And who made terror, madness, crime, remorse,
Which from the links of the great chain of things,
To every thought within the mind of man
Sway and drag heavily, and each one reels
Under the load towards the pit of death;
Abandoned hope, and love that turns to hate;
And self-contempt, bitterer to drink than blood;
Pain, whose unheeded and familiar speech
Is howling, and keen shrieks, day after day:
And Hell, or the sharp fear of Hell?
DEMOGORGON: He reigns.
ASIA: Utter his name: a world pining in pain
Asks but his name: curses shall drag him down.
DEMOGORGON: He reigns.
ASIA: I feel, I know it: who?
DEMOGORGON: He reigns.
ASIA: Who reigns? There was the Heaven and Earth at first,
And Light and Love; then Saturn, from whose throne
Time fell, an envious shadow: such the state
Of the earth's primal spirits beneath his sway,
As the calm joy of flowers and living leaves

Before the wind or sun has withered them
And semivital worms; but he refused
The birthright of their being, knowledge, power,
The skill which wields the elements, the thought
Which pierces this dim universe like light,
Self-empire, and the majesty of love;
For thirst of which they fainted. Then Prometheus
Gave wisdom, which is strength, to Jupiter,
And with this law alone, 'Let man be free,'
Clothed him with the dominion of wide Heaven.
To know nor faith, nor love, nor law; to be
Omnipotent but friendless is to reign;
And Jove now reigned; for on the race of man
First famine, and then toil, and then disease,
Strife, wounds, and ghastly death unseen before,
Fell; and the unseasonable seasons drove
With alternating shafts of frost and fire,
Their shelterless, pale tribes to mountain caves:
And in their desert hearts fierce wants he sent,
And mad disquietudes, and shadows idle
Of unreal good, which levied mutual war,
So ruining the lair, wherein they raged.
Prometheus saw, and waked the legioned hopes
Which sleep within folded Elysian flowers,
Nepenthe, Moly, Amaranth, fadeless blooms,
That they might hide with thin and rainbow wings
The shape of Death; and Love he sent to bind
The disunited tendrils of that vine
Which bears the wine of life, the human heart;
And he tamed fire which, like some beast of prey,
Most terrible, but lovely, played beneath
The frown of man; and tortured to his will
Iron and gold, the slaves and signs of power,
And gems and poisons, and all subtlest forms

Hidden beneath the mountains and the waves.
He gave man speech, and speech created thought,
Which is the measure of the universe;
And Science struck the thrones of earth and heaven,
Which shook, but fell not; and the harmonious mind
Poured itself forth in all-prophetic song;
And music lifted up the listening spirit
Until it walked, exempt from mortal care,
Godlike, o'er the clear billows of sweet sound;
And human hands first mimicked and then mocked,
With moulded limbs more lovely than its own,
The human form, till marble grew divine;
And mothers, gazing, drank the love men see
Reflected in their race, behold, and perish.
He told the hidden power of herbs and springs,
And Disease drank and slept. Death grew like sleep.
He taught the implicated orbits woven
Of the wide-wandering stars; and how the sun
Changes his lair, and by what secret spell
The pale moon is transformed, when her broad eye
Gazes not on the interlunar sea:
He taught to rule, as life directed the limbs,
The tempest-winged chariots of the Ocean,
And the Celt knew the Indian. Cities then
Were built, and through their snow-like columns flowed
The warm winds, and the azure aether shone,
And the blue sea and shadowy hills were seen.
Such, the alleviations of his state,
Prometheus gave to man, for which he hangs
Withering in destined pain: but who rains down
Evil, the immedicable plague, which, while
Man looks on his creation like a God
And sees that it is glorious, drives him on
The wreck of his own will, the scorn of earth,

The outcast, the abandoned, the alone?
Not Jove; while yet his frown shook Heaven, aye when
His adversary from adamantine chains
Cursed him, he trembled like a slave. Declare
Who is his master? Is he too a slave?

DEMOGORGON: All spirits are enslaved which serve things evil:
Thou knowest if Jupiter be such or no.

ASIA: Whom called'st thou God?

DEMOGORGON: I spoke but as ye speak,
For Jove is the supreme of living things.

ASIA: Who is the master of the slave?

DEMOGORGON: If the abysm
Could vomit forth its secrets . . . But a voice
Is wanting, the deep truth is imageless;
For what would it avail to bid thee gaze
On the revolving world? What to bid speak
Fate, Time, Occasion, Chance and Change? To these
All things are subject but eternal Love.

ASIA: So much I asked before, and my heart gave
The response thou hast given; and of such truths
Each to itself must be the oracle.
One more demand; and do thou answer me
As my own soul would answer, did it know
That which I ask. Prometheus shall arise
Henceforth the sun of this rejoicing world:
When shall the destined hour arrive?

DEMOGORGON: Behold!

ASIA: The rocks are cloven, and through the purple night
I see cars drawn by rainbow-winged steeds
Which trample the dim winds: in each there stands
A wild-eyed charioteer urging their flight.
Some look behind, as fiends pursued them there,
And yet I see no shapes but the keen stars:

Others, with burning eyes, lean forth, and drink
With eager lips the wind of their own speed,
As if the thing they loved fled on before,
And now, even now, they clasped it. Their bright locks
Stream like a comet's flashing hair: they all
Sweep onward.

DEMOGORGON: These are the immortal Hours,
Of whom thou didst demand. One waits for thee.

ASIA: A spirit with a dreadful countenance
Checks its dark chariot by the craggy gulph.
Unlike thy brethren, ghastly charioteer,
Who art thou? Whither wouldst thou bear me? Speak!

SPIRIT: I am the shadow of a destiny
More dread than is my aspect: ere yon planet
Has set, the darkness which ascends with me
Shall wrap in lasting night heaven's kingless throne.

ASIA: What meanest thou?

PANTHEA: That terrible shadow floats
Up from its throne, as may the lurid smoke
Of earthquake-ruined cities o'er the sea.
Lo! it ascends the car; the coursers fly
Terrified: watch its path among the stars
Blackening the night!

ASIA: Thus I am answered: strange!

PANTHEA: See, near the verge, another chariot stays;
An ivory shell inlaid with crimson fire,
Which comes and goes within its sculptured rim
Of delicate strange tracery; the young spirit
That guides it has the dove-like eyes of hope;
How its soft smiles attract the soul! as light
Lures winged insects thro' the lampless air.

SPIRIT:

My coursers are fed with the lightning,
  They drink of the whirlwind's stream,
And when the red morning is bright'ning
  They bathe in the fresh sunbeam;
  They have strength for their swiftness I deem,
Then ascend with me, daughter of Ocean.

I desire: and their speed makes night kindle;
  I fear: they outstrip the Typhoon;
Ere the cloud piled on Atlas can dwindle
  We encircle the earth and the moon:
  We shall rest from long labours at noon:
Then ascend with me, daughter of Ocean.

SCENE V. *The Car pauses within a Cloud on the top of a snowy Mountain.* ASIA, PANTHEA, *and the* SPIRIT OF THE HOUR.

SPIRIT:

On the brink of the night and the morning
  My coursers are wont to respire;
But the Earth has just whispered a warning
  That their flight must be swifter than fire:
  They shall drink the hot speed of desire!

ASIA: Thou breathest on their nostrils, but my breath
  Would give them swifter speed.

SPIRIT: Alas! it could not.

PANTHEA: Oh Spirit! pause, and tell whence is the light
  Which fills this cloud? the sun is yet unrisen.

SPIRIT: The sun will rise not until noon. Apollo
  Is held in heaven by wonder; and the light
  Which fills this vapour, as the aerial hue
  Of fountain-gazing roses fills the water,
  Flows from the mighty sister.

PANTHEA: Yes, I feel –

ASIA: What is it with thee, sister? Thou art pale.
PANTHEA: How thou art changed! I dare not look on thee;
I feel but see thee not. I scarce endure
The radiance of thy beauty. Some good change
Is working in the elements, which suffer
Thy presence thus unveiled. The Nereids tell
That on the day when the clear hyaline
Was cloven at thine uprise, and thou didst stand
Within a veined shell, which floated on
Over the calm floor of the crystal sea,
Among the Aegean isles, and by the shores
Which bear thy name; love, like the atmosphere
Of the sun's fire filling the living world,
Burst from thee, and illumined earth and heaven
And the deep ocean and the sunless caves
And all that dwells within them; till grief cast
Eclipse upon the soul from which it came:
Such art thou now; nor is it I alone,
Thy sister, thy companion, thine own chosen one,
But the whole world which seeks thy sympathy.
Hearest thou not sounds i' the air which speak the love
Of all articulate beings? Feelest thou not
The inanimate winds enamoured of thee? List!
[*Music*.]
ASIA: Thy words are sweeter than aught else but his
Whose echoes they are: yet all love is sweet,
Given or returned. Common as light is love.
And its familiar voice wearies not ever.
Like the wide heaven, the all-sustaining air,
It makes the reptile equal to the God:
They who inspire it most are fortunate,
As I am now; but those who feel it most
Are happier still, after long sufferings,
As I shall soon become.

PANTHEA: List! Spirits speak.

VOICE IN THE AIR [*singing*]:

Life of Life! thy lips enkindle
 With their love the breath between them;
And thy smiles before they dwindle
 Make the cold air fire; then screen them
In those looks, where whoso gazes
Faints, entangled in their mazes.

Child of Light! thy limbs are burning
 Thro' the vest which seems to hide them;
As the radiant lines of morning
 Thro' the clouds ere they divide them;
And this atmosphere divinest
Shrouds thee wheresoe'er thou shinest.

Fair are others; none beholds thee,
 But thy voice sounds low and tender
Like the fairest, for it folds thee
 From the sight, that liquid splendour,
And all feel, yet see thee never,
As I feel now, lost for ever!

Lamp of Earth! where'er thou movest
 Its dim shapes are clad with brightness
And the souls of whom thou lovest
 Walk upon the winds with lightness,
Till they fail, as I am failing,
Dizzy, lost, yet unbewailing!

ASIA:

My soul is an enchanted boat,
Which, like a sleeping swan, doth float

Upon the silver waves of thy sweet singing;
  And thine doth like an angel sit
  Beside the helm conducting it,
Whilst all the winds with melody are ringing.
  It seems to float ever, for ever,
  Upon that many-winding river,
  Between mountains, woods, abysses,
  A paradise of wildernesses!
Till, like one in slumber bound,
Borne to the ocean, I float down, around,
Into a sea profound, of ever-spreading sound:

  Meanwhile thy spirit lifts its pinions
  In music's most serene dominions;
Catching the winds that fan that happy heaven.
  And we sail on, away, afar,
  Without a course, without a star,
But, by the instinct of sweet music driven;
  Till through Elysian garden islets
By thee, most beautiful of pilots,
  Where never mortal pinnace glided,
  The boat of my desire is guided:
Realms where the air we breathe is love,
Which in the winds and on the waves doth move,
Harmonizing this earth with what we feel above.

  We have pass'd Age's icy caves,
  And Manhood's dark and tossing waves,
And Youth's smooth ocean, smiling to betray:
  Beyond the glassy gulphs we flee
  Of shadow-peopled Infancy,
Through Death and Birth, to a diviner day;
  A paradise of vaulted bowers,
  Lit by downward-gazing flowers,

And watery paths that wind between
Wildernesses calm and green,
Peopled by shapes too bright to see,
And rest, having beheld; somewhat like thee;
Which walk upon the sea, and chaunt melodiously!

END OF THE SECOND ACT

Act III

SCENE I. *Heaven.* JUPITER *on his Throne;* THETIS *and the other Deities assembled.*

JUPITER: Ye congregated powers of heaven, who share
The glory and the strength of him ye serve,
Rejoice! henceforth I am omnipotent.
All else had been subdued to me; alone
The soul of man, like unextinguished fire,
Yet burns towards heaven with fierce reproach, and doubt,
And lamentation, and reluctant prayer,
Hurling up insurrection, which might make
Our antique empire insecure, though built
On eldest faith, and hell's coeval, fear;
And tho' my curses thro' the pendulous air,
Like snow on herbless peaks, fall flake by flake,
And cling to it; tho' under my wrath's night
It climbs the crags of life, step after step,
Which wound it, as ice wounds unsandalled feet
It yet remains supreme o'er misery,
Aspiring, unrepressed, yet soon to fall:
Even now have I begotten a strange wonder,
That fatal child, the terror of the earth,
Who waits but till the destined hour arrive,
Bearing from Demogorgon's vacant throne
The dreadful might of ever-living limbs
Which clothed that awful spirit unbeheld,

To redescend, and trample out the spark.
Pour forth heaven's wine, Idaean Ganymede,
And let it fill the Daedal cups like fire,
And from the flower-inwoven soil divine
Ye all-triumphant harmonies arise,
As dew from earth under the twilight stars:
Drink! be the nectar circling thro' your veins
The soul of joy, ye ever-living Gods,
Till exultation burst in one wide voice
Like music from Elysian winds.
And thou
Ascend beside me, veiled in the light
Of the desire which makes thee one with me,
Thetis, bright image of eternity!
When thou didst cry, 'Insufferable might!
'God! Spare me! I sustain not the quick flames,
'The penetrating presence; all my being,
'Like him whom the Numidian seps did thaw
'Into a dew with poison, is dissolved,
'Sinking thro' its foundations:' even then
Two mighty spirits, mingling, made a third
Mightier than either, which, unbodied now,
Between us floats, felt, although unbeheld,
Waiting the incarnation, which ascends,
(Hear ye the thunder of the fiery wheels
Griding the winds?) from Demogorgon's throne.
Victory! victory! Feel'st thou not, O world,
The earthquake of his chariot thundering up
Olympus?

[*The Car of the Hour arrives.* DEMOGORGON *descends and moves towards the Throne of* JUPITER.]

Awful shape, what art thou? Speak!

DEMOGORGON: Eternity. Demand no direr name.
Descend, and follow me down the abyss.

I am thy child, as thou wert Saturn's child;
Mightier than thee: and we must dwell together
Henceforth in darkness. Lift thy lightnings not.
The tyranny of heaven none may retain,
Or reassume, or hold, succeeding thee:
Yet if thou wilt, as 'tis the destiny
Of trodden worms to writhe till they are dead,
Put forth thy might.

JUPITER: Detested prodigy!
Even thus beneath the deep Titanian prisons
I trample thee! thou lingerest?
Mercy! mercy!
No pity, no release, no respite! Oh,
That thou wouldst make mine enemy my judge,
Even where he hangs, seared by my long revenge,
On Caucasus! he would not doom me thus.
Gentle, and just, and dreadless, is he not
The monarch of the world? What then art thou?
No refuge! no appeal!
Sink with me then,
We two will sink on the wide waves of ruin,
Even as a vulture and a snake outspent
Drop, twisted in inextricable fight,
Into a shoreless sea. Let hell unlock
Its mounded oceans of tempestuous fire,
And whelm on them into the bottomless void
This desolated world, and thee, and me,
The conqueror and the conquered, and the wreck
Of that for which they combated.
Ai! Ai!
The elements obey me not. I sink
Dizzily down, ever, for ever, down.
And, like a cloud, mine enemy above
Darkens my fall with victory! Ai, Ai!

SCENE II. *The Mouth of a great River in the Island Atlantis.* OCEAN *is discovered reclining near the Shore;* APOLLO *stands beside him.*

OCEAN: He fell, thou sayest, beneath his conqueror's frown?
APOLLO: Aye, when the strife was ended which made dim
  The orb I rule, and shook the solid stars,
  The terrors of his eye illumined heaven
  With sanguine light, through the thick ragged skirts
  Of the victorious darkness, as he fell:
  Like the last glare of day's red agony,
  Which, from a rent among the fiery clouds,
  Burns far along the tempest-wrinkled deep.
OCEAN: He sunk to the abyss? To the dark void?
APOLLO: An eagle so caught in some bursting cloud
  On Caucasus, his thunder-baffled wings
  Entangled in the whirlwind, and his eyes
  Which gazed on the undazzling sun, now blinded
  By the white lightning, while the ponderous hail
  Beats on his struggling form, which sinks at length
  Prone, and the aerial ice clings over it.
OCEAN: Henceforth the fields of Heaven-reflecting sea
  Which are my realm, will heave, unstain'd with blood,
  Beneath the uplifting winds, like plains of corn
  Swayed by the summer air; my streams will flow
  Round many-peopled continents, and round
  Fortunate isles; and from their glassy thrones
  Blue Proteus and his humid nymphs shall mark
  The shadow of fair ships, as mortals see
  The floating bark of the light-laden moon
  With that white star, its sightless pilot's crest,
  Borne down the rapid sunset's ebbing sea;
  Tracking their path no more by blood and groans,
  And desolation, and the mingled voice

Of slavery and command; but by the light
Of wave-reflected flowers, and floating odours,
And music soft, and mild, free, gentle voices,
That sweetest music, such as spirits love.

APOLLO: And I shall gaze not on the deeds which make
My mind obscure with sorrow, as eclipse
Darkens the sphere I guide; but list, I hear
The small, clear, silver lute of the young Spirit
That sits i' the morning star.

OCEAN: Thou must away;
Thy steeds will pause at even, till when farewell:
The loud deep calls me home even now to feed it
With azure calm out of the emerald urns
Which stand for ever full beside my throne.
Behold the Nereids under the green sea,
Their wavering limbs borne on the wind-like stream,
Their white arms lifted o'er their streaming hair
With garlands pied and starry sea-flower crowns,
Hastening to grace their mighty sister's joy.
[*A sound of waves is heard.*]
It is the unpastured sea hungering for calm.
Peace, monster; I come now. Farewell.

APOLLO: Farewell.

SCENE III. *Caucasus.* PROMETHEUS, HERCULES, IONE, *the* EARTH, SPIRITS, ASIA, *and* PANTHEA, *borne in the Car with the* SPIRIT OF THE HOUR. HERCULES *unbinds* PROMETHEUS, *who descends.*

HERCULES: Most glorious among spirits, thus doth strength
To wisdom, courage, and long-suffering love,
And thee, who art the form they animate,
Minister like a slave.

PROMETHEUS: Thy gentle words
Are sweeter even than freedom long desired
And long delayed.
Asia, thou light of life,
Shadow of beauty unbeheld: and ye,
Fair sister nymphs, who made long years of pain
Sweet to remember, thro' your love and care:
Henceforth we will not part. There is a cave,
All overgrown with trailing odorous plants,
Which curtain out the day with leaves and flowers,
And paved with veined emerald, and a fountain
Leaps in the midst with an awakening sound.
From its curved roof the mountain's frozen tears
Like snow, or silver, or long diamond spires,
Hang downward, raining forth a doubtful light:
And there is heard the ever-moving air,
Whispering without from tree to tree, and birds,
And bees; and all around are mossy seats,
And the rough walls are clothed with long soft grass;
A simple dwelling, which shall be our own;
Where we will sit and talk of time and change,
As the world ebbs and flows, ourselves unchanged.
What can hide man from mutability?
And if ye sigh, then I will smile; and thou,
Ione, shalt chaunt fragments of sea-music,
Until I weep, when ye shall smile away
The tears she brought, which yet were sweet to shed.
We will entangle buds and flowers and beams
Which twinkle on the fountain's brim, and make
Strange combinations out of common things,
Like human babes in their brief innocence;
And we will search, with looks and words of love,
For hidden thoughts, each lovelier than the last,
Our unexhausted spirits; and like lutes

Touched by the skill of the enamoured wind,
Weave harmonies divine, yet ever new,
From difference sweet where discord cannot be;
And hither come, sped on the charmed winds,
Which meet from all the points of heaven, as bees
From every flower aerial Enna feeds,
At their known island-homes in Himera,
The echoes of the human world, which tell
Of the low voice of love, almost unheard,
And dove-eyed pity's murmured pain, and music,
Itself the echo of the heart, and all
That tempers or improves man's life, now free;
And lovely apparitions, dim at first,
Then radiant, as the mind, arising bright
From the embrace of beauty, whence the forms
Of which these are the phantoms, casts on them
The gathered rays which are reality
Shall visit us, the progeny immortal
Of Painting, Sculpture, and rapt Poesy,
And arts, tho' unimagined, yet to be.
The wandering voices and the shadows these
Of all that man becomes, the mediators
Of that best worship love, by him and us
Given and returned; swift shapes and sounds, which
  grow
More fair and soft as man grows wise and kind,
And, veil by veil, evil and error fall:
Such virtue has the cave and place around. [*Turning to the*
  SPIRIT OF THE HOUR.]
For thee, fair Spirit, one toil remains. Ione,
Give her that curved shell, which Proteus old
Made Asia's nuptial boon, breathing within it
A voice to be accomplished, and which thou
Didst hide in grass under the hollow rock.

IONE: Thou most desired Hour, more loved and lovely
  Than all thy sisters, this is the mystic shell;
  See the pale azure fading into silver
  Lining it with a soft yet glowing light:
  Looks it not like lulled music sleeping there?
SPIRIT: It seems in truth the fairest shell of Ocean:
  Its sound must be at once both sweet and strange.
PROMETHEUS: Go, borne over the cities of mankind
  On whirlwind-footed coursers: once again
  Outspeed the sun around the orbed world;
  And as thy chariot cleaves the kindling air,
  Thou breathe into the many-folded shell,
  Loosening its mighty music; it shall be
  As thunder mingled with clear echoes: then
  Return; and thou shalt dwell beside our cave.
  And thou, O, Mother Earth! –
THE EARTH: I hear, I feel;
  Thy lips are on me, and their touch runs down
  Even to the adamantine central gloom
  Along these marble nerves; 'tis life, 'tis joy,
  And thro' my withered, old, and icy frame
  The warmth of an immortal youth shoots down
  Circling. Henceforth the many children fair
  Folded in my sustaining arms; all plants,
  And creeping forms, and insects rainbow-winged,
  And birds, and beasts, and fish, and human shapes,
  Which drew disease and pain from my wan bosom,
  Draining the poison of despair, shall take
  And interchange sweet nutriment; to me
  Shall they become like sister-antelopes
  By one fair dam, snow-white and swift as wind
  Nursed among lilies near a brimming stream.
  The dew-mists of my sunless sleep shall float
  Under the stars like balm: night-folded flowers

Shall suck unwithering hues in their repose:
And men and beasts in happy dreams shall gather
Strength for the coming day, and all its joy:
And death shall be the last embrace of her
Who takes the life she gave, even as a mother
Folding her child, says, 'Leave me not again.'

ASIA: Oh, mother! wherefore speak the name of death?
Cease they to love, and move, and breathe, and speak,
Who die?

THE EARTH: It would avail not to reply:
Thou art immortal, and this tongue is known
But to the uncommunicating dead.
Death is the veil which those who live call life:
They sleep, and it is lifted: and meanwhile
In mild variety the seasons mild
With rainbow-skirted showers, and odorous winds,
And long blue meteors cleansing the dull night,
And the life-kindling shafts of the keen sun's
All-piercing bow, and the dew-mingled rain
Of the calm moonbeams, a soft influence mild,
Shall clothe the forests and the fields, aye, even
The crag-built deserts of the barren deep,
With ever-living leaves, and fruits, and flowers.
And thou! There is a cavern where my spirit
Was panted forth in anguish whilst thy pain
Made my heart mad, and those who did inhale it
Became mad too, and built a temple there,
And spoke, and were oracular, and lured
The erring nations round to mutual war,
And faithless faith, such as Jove kept with thee;
Which breath now rises, as amongst tall weeds
A violet's exhalation, and it fills
With a serener light and crimson air
Intense, yet soft, the rocks and woods around;

It feeds the quick growth of the serpent vine,
And the dark linked ivy tangling wild,
And budding, blown, or odour-faded blooms
Which star the winds with points of coloured light,
As they rain thro' them, and bright golden globes
Of fruit, suspended in their own green heaven,
And thro' their veined leaves and amber stems
The flowers whose purple and translucid bowls
Stand ever mantling with aerial dew,
The drink of spirits: and it circles round,
Like the soft waving wings of noonday dreams,
Inspiring calm and happy thoughts, like mine,
Now thou art thus restored. This cave is thine.
Arise! Appear!

[*A* SPIRIT *rises in the likeness of a winged child.*]

This is my torch-bearer;
Who let his lamp out in old time with gazing
On eyes from which he kindled it anew
With love, which is as fire, sweet daughter mine,
For such is that within thine own. Run, wayward,
And guide this company beyond the peak
Of Bacchic Nysa, Maenad-haunted mountain,
And beyond Indus and its tribute rivers,
Trampling the torrent streams and glassy lakes
With feet unwet, unwearied, undelaying,
And up the green ravine, across the vale,
Beside the windless and crystalline pool,
Where ever lies, on unerasing waves,
The image of a temple, built above,
Distinct with column, arch, and architrave,
And palm-like capital, and over-wrought,
And populous with most living imagery,
Praxitelean shapes, whose marble smiles
Fill the hushed air with everlasting love.

It is deserted now, but once it bore
Thy name, Prometheus; there the emulous youths
Bore to thy honour through the divine gloom
The lamp which was thine emblem; even as those
Who bear the untransmitted torch of hope
Into the grave, across the night of life,
As thou hast borne it most triumphantly
To this far goal of Time. Depart, farewell.
Beside that temple is the destined cave.

SCENE IV. *A Forest. In the Background a Cave.* PROMETHEUS, ASIA, PANTHEA, IONE, *and the* SPIRIT OF THE EARTH.

IONE: Sister, it is not earthly: how it glides
Under the leaves! how on its head there burns
A light, like a green star, whose emerald beams
Are twined with its fair hair! how, as it moves,
The splendour drops in flakes upon the grass!
Knowest thou it?

PANTHEA: It is the delicate spirit
That guides the earth thro' heaven. From afar
The populous constellations call that light
The loveliest of the planets; and sometimes
It floats along the spray of the salt sea,
Or makes its chariot of a foggy cloud,
Or walks thro' fields or cities while men sleep,
Or o'er the mountain tops, or down the rivers,
Or thro' the green waste wilderness, as now,
Wondering at all it sees. Before Jove reigned
It loved our sister Asia, and it came
Each leisure hour to drink the liquid light
Out of her eyes, for which it said it thirsted
As one bit by a dipsas, and with her

It made its childish confidence, and told her
All it had known or seen, for it saw much,
Yet idly reasoned what it saw; and called her,
For whence it sprung it knew not, nor do I,
Mother, dear mother.

THE SPIRIT OF THE EARTH [*running to* ASIA]: Mother, dearest mother;
May I then talk with thee as I was wont?
May I then hide my eyes in thy soft arms,
After thy looks have made them tired of joy?
May I then play beside thee the long noons,
When work is none in the bright silent air?

ASIA: I love thee, gentlest being, and henceforth
Can cherish thee unenvied: speak, I pray:
Thy simple talk once solaced, now delights.

SPIRIT OF THE EARTH: Mother, I am grown wiser, though a child
Cannot be wise like thee, within this day;
And happier too; happier and wiser both.
Thou knowest that toads, and snakes, and loathly worms,
And venomous and malicious beasts, and boughs
That bore ill berries in the woods, were ever
An hindrance to my walks o'er the green world:
And that, among the haunts of humankind,
Hard-featured men, or with proud, angry looks,
Or cold, staid gait, or false and hollow smiles,
Or the dull sneer of self-loved ignorance,
Or other such foul masks, with which ill thoughts
Hide that fair being whom we spirits call man;
And women too, ugliest of all things evil,
(Tho' fair, even in a world where thou art fair,
When good and kind, free and sincere like thee,)
When false or frowning made me sick at heart
To pass them, tho' they slept, and I unseen.

Well, my path lately lay thro' a great city
Into the woody hills surrounding it:
A sentinel was sleeping at the gate:
When there was heard a sound, so loud, it shook
The towers amid the moonlight, yet more sweet
Than any voice but thine, sweetest of all;
A long, long sound, as it would never end:
And all the inhabitants leapt suddenly
Out of their rest, and gathered in the streets,
Looking in wonder up to Heaven, while yet
The music pealed along. I hid myself
Within a fountain in the public square,
Where I lay like the reflex of the moon
Seen in a wave under green leaves; and soon
Those ugly human shapes and visages
Of which I spoke as having wrought me pain,
Past floating thro' the air, and fading still
Into the winds that scattered them; and those
From whom they past seemed mild and lovely forms
After some foul disguise had fallen, and all
Were somewhat changed, and after brief surprise
And greetings of delighted wonder, all
Went to their sleep again: and when the dawn
Came, would'st thou think that toads, and snakes, and
  efts,
Could e'er be beautiful? yet so they were,
And that with little change of shape or hue:
All things had put their evil nature off:
I cannot tell my joy, when o'er a lake
Upon a drooping bough with night-shade twined,
I saw two azure halcyons clinging downward
And thinning one bright bunch of amber berries,
With quick long beaks, and in the deep there lay
Those lovely forms imaged as in a sky;

So, with my thoughts full of these happy changes,
We meet again, the happiest change of all.
ASIA: And never will we part, till thy chaste sister
Who guides the frozen and inconstant moon
Will look on thy more warm and equal light
Till her heart thaw like flakes of April snow
And love thee.
SPIRIT OF THE EARTH: What; as Asia loves Prometheus?
ASIA: Peace, wanton, thou art yet not old enough.
Think ye by gazing on each other's eyes
To multiply your lovely selves, and fill
With sphered fires the interlunar air?
SPIRIT OF THE EARTH: Nay, mother, while my sister trims her lamp
'Tis hard I should go darkling.
ASIA: Listen; look!
[*The* SPIRIT OF THE HOUR *enters.*]
PROMETHEUS: We feel what thou hast heard and seen: yet speak.
SPIRIT OF THE HOUR: Soon as the sound had ceased whose thunder filled
The abysses of the sky and the wide earth,
There was a change: the impalpable thin air
And the all-circling sunlight were transformed
As if the sense of love dissolved in them
Had folded itself round the sphered world.
My vision then grew clear, and I could see
Into the mysteries of the universe:
Dizzy as with delight I floated down,
Winnowing the lightsome air with languid plumes,
My coursers sought their birth-place in the sun,
Where they henceforth will live exempt from toil
Pasturing flowers of vegetable fire;
And where my moonlike car will stand within

A temple, gazed upon by Phidian forms
Of thee, and Asia, and the Earth, and me,
And you fair nymphs looking the love we feel;
In memory of the tidings it has borne;
Beneath a dome fretted with graven flowers,
Poised on twelve columns of resplendent stone,
And open to the bright and liquid sky.
Yoked to it by an amphisbenic snake
The likeness of those winged steeds will mock
The flight from which they find repose. Alas,
Whither has wandered now my partial tongue
When all remains untold which ye would hear?
As I have said I floated to the earth:
It was, as it is still, the pain of bliss
To move, to breathe, to be; I wandering went
Among the haunts and dwellings of mankind,
And first was disappointed not to see
Such mighty change as I had felt within
Expressed in outward things; but soon I looked,
And behold, thrones were kingless, and men walked
One with the other even as spirits do,
None fawned, none trampled; hate, disdain, or fear,
Self-love or self-contempt, on human brows
No more inscribed, as o'er the gate of hell,
'All hope abandon ye who enter here;'
None frowned, none trembled, none with eager fear
Gazed on another's eye of cold command,
Until the subject of a tyrant's will
Became, worse fate, the abject of his own,
Which spurred him, like an outspent horse, to death.
None wrought his lips in truth-entangling lines
Which smiled the lie his tongue disdained to speak;
None, with firm sneer, trod out in his own heart
The sparks of love and hope till there remained

Those bitter ashes, a soul self-consumed,
And the wretch crept a vampire among men,
Infecting all with his own hideous ill;
None talked that common, false, cold, hollow talk
Which makes the heart deny the *yes* it breathes,
Yet question that unmeant hypocrisy
With such a self-mistrust as has no name.
And women, too, frank, beautiful, and kind
As the free heaven which rains fresh light and dew
On the wide earth, past; gentle radiant forms,
From custom's evil taint exempt and pure;
Speaking the wisdom once they could not think,
Looking emotions once they feared to feel,
And changed to all which once they dared not be,
Yet being now, made earth like heaven; nor pride,
Nor jealousy, nor envy, nor ill shame,
The bitterest of those drops of treasured gall,
Spoilt the sweet taste of the nepenthe, love.

Thrones, altars, judgement-seats, and prisons; wherein,
And beside which, by wretched men were borne
Sceptres, tiaras, swords, and chains, and tomes
Of reasoned wrong, glozed on by ignorance,
Were like those monstrous and barbaric shapes,
The ghosts of a no more remembered fame,
Which, from their unworn obelisks, look forth
In triumph o'er the palaces and tombs
Of those who were their conquerors, mouldering round.
These imaged, to the pride of kings and priests,
A dark yet mighty faith, a power as wide
As is the world it wasted, and are now
But an astonishment; even so the tools

And emblems of its last captivity,
Amid the dwellings of the peopled earth,
Stand, not o'erthrown, but unregarded now.
And those foul shapes, abhorred by god and man, –
Which, under many a name and many a form
Strange, savage, ghastly, dark and execrable,
Were Jupiter, the tyrant of the world;
And which the nations, panic-stricken, served
With blood, and hearts broken by long hope, and love
Dragged to his altars soiled and garlandless,
And slain amid men's unreclaiming tears,
Flattering the thing they feared, which fear was hate, –
Frown, mouldering fast, o'er their abandoned shrines:
The painted veil, by those who were, called life,
Which mimicked, as with colours idly spread,
All men believed or hoped, is torn aside;
The loathsome mask has fallen, the man remains
Sceptreless, free, uncircumscribed, but man
Equal, unclassed, tribeless, and nationless,
Exempt from awe, worship, degree, the king
Over himself; just, gentle, wise: but man
Passionless? – no, yet free from guilt or pain,
Which were, for his will made or suffered them,
Nor yet exempt, tho' ruling them like slaves,
From chance, and death, and mutability,
The clogs of that which else might oversoar
The loftiest star of unascended heaven,
Pinnacled dim in the intense inane.

END OF THE THIRD ACT

Act IV

SCENE: *A Part of the Forest near the Cave of* PROMETHEUS. PANTHEA *and* IONE *are sleeping: they awaken gradually during the first song.*

VOICE OF UNSEEN SPIRITS:

The pale stars are gone!
For the sun, their swift shepherd,
To their folds them compelling,
In the depths of the dawn,
Hastes, in meteor-eclipsing array, and they flee
Beyond his blue dwelling,
As fawns flee the leopard.
But where are ye?

A Train of dark FORMS *and* SHADOWS *passes by confusedly, singing:*

Here, oh, here:
We bear the bier
Of the Father of many a cancelled year!
Spectres we
Of the dead Hours be,
We bear Time to his tomb in eternity.

Strew, oh, strew
Hair, not yew!
Wet the dusty pall with tears, not dew!
Be the faded flowers
Of Death's bare bowers
Spread on the corpse of the King of Hours!

Haste, oh, haste!
As shades are chased,
Trembling, by day, from heaven's blue waste
We melt away,
Like dissolving spray,
From the children of a diviner day,
With the lullaby
Of winds that die
On the bosom of their own harmony!

IONE:

What dark forms were they?

PANTHEA:

The past Hours weak and grey,
With the spoil which their toil
Raked together
From the conquest but One could foil.

IONE:

Have they past?

PANTHEA:

They have past;
They outspeeded the blast,
While 'tis said, they are fled:

IONE:

Whither, oh, whither?

PANTHEA:

To the dark, to the past, to the dead.

VOICE OF UNSEEN SPIRITS:

Bright clouds float in heaven,
Dew-stars gleam on earth,
Waves assemble on ocean,
They are gathered and driven
By the storm of delight, by the panic of glee!
They shake with emotion,
They dance in their mirth.
But where are ye?

The pine boughs are singing
Old songs with new gladness,
The billows and fountains
Fresh music are flinging,
Like the notes of a spirit from land and from sea;
The storms mock the mountains
With the thunder of gladness.
But where are ye?

IONE: What charioteers are these?

PANTHEA: Where are their chariots?

SEMICHORUS OF HOURS:

The voice of the Spirits of Air and of Earth
Have drawn back the figured curtain of sleep
Which covered our being and darkened our birth
In the deep.

A VOICE:

In the deep?

SEMICHORUS II:

Oh, below the deep.

SEMICHORUS I:

An hundred ages we had been kept
  Cradled in visions of hate and care,
And each one who waked as his brother slept,
  Found the truth –

SEMICHORUS II:

Worse than his visions were!

SEMICHORUS I:

We have heard the lute of Hope in sleep;
  We have known the voice of Love in dreams,
We have felt the wand of Power, and leap –

SEMICHORUS II:

  As the billows leap in the morning beams!

CHORUS:

Weave the dance on the floor of the breeze,
  Pierce with song heaven's silent light,
Enchant the day that too swiftly flees,
  To check its flight ere the cave of night.

Once the hungry Hours were hounds
  Which chased the day like a bleeding deer,
And it limped and stumbled with many wounds
  Through the nightly dells of the desart year.

But now, oh weave the mystic measure
  Of music, and dance, and shapes of light,
Let the Hours, and the spirits of might and pleasure,
  Like the clouds and sunbeams, unite.

A VOICE:

Unite!

PANTHEA: See, where the Spirits of the human mind
Wrapt in sweet sounds, as in bright veils, approach.

CHORUS OF SPIRITS:

We join the throng
Of the dance and the song,
By the whirlwind of gladness borne along;
As the flying-fish leap
From the Indian deep,
And mix with the sea-birds half asleep.

CHORUS OF HOURS:

Whence come ye, so wild and so fleet,
For sandals of lightning are on your feet,
And your wings are soft and swift as thought,
And your eyes are as love which is veiled not?

CHORUS OF SPIRITS:

We come from the mind
Of human kind
Which was late so dusk, and obscene, and blind,
Now 'tis an ocean
Of clear emotion,
A heaven of serene and mighty motion.

From that deep abyss
Of wonder and bliss,
Whose caverns are crystal palaces;
From those skiey towers
Where Thought's crowned powers
Sit watching your dance, ye happy Hours!

From the dim recesses
Of woven caresses,
Where lovers catch ye by your loose tresses;
From the azure isles,
Where sweet Wisdom smiles,
Delaying your ships with her syren wiles.

From the temples high
Of Man's ear and eye,
Roofed over Sculpture and Poesy;
From the murmurings
Of the unsealed springs
Where Science bedews her Daedal wings.

Years after years,
Through blood, and tears,
And a thick hell of hatreds, and hopes, and fears;
We waded and flew,
And the islets were few
Where the bud-blighted flowers of happiness grew.

Our feet now, every palm,
Are sandalled with calm,
And the dew of our wings is a rain of balm;
And, beyond our eyes,
The human love lies
Which makes all its gazes on Paradise.

CHORUS OF SPIRITS AND HOURS:

Then weave the web of the mystic measure;
From the depths of the sky and the ends of the earth,
Come, swift Spirits of might and of pleasure,
Fill the dance and the music of mirth,
As the waves of a thousand streams rush by
To an ocean of splendour and harmony!

CHORUS OF SPIRITS:

Our spoil is won,
Our task is done,
We are free to dive, or soar, or run;
Beyond and around,
Or within the bound
Which clips the world with darkness round.

We'll pass the eyes
Of the starry skies
Into the hoar deep to colonize:
Death, Chaos, and Night,
From the sound of our flight,
Shall flee, like mist from a tempest's might.

And Earth, Air, and Light,
And the Spirit of Might,
Which drives round the stars in their fiery flight:
And Love, Thought, and Breath,
The powers that quell Death,
Wherever we soar shall assemble beneath.

And our singing shall build
In the void's loose field
A world for the Spirit of Wisdom to wield;
We will take our plan
From the new world of man,
And our work shall be called the Promethean.

CHORUS OF HOURS:

Break the dance, and scatter the song:
Let some depart, and some remain.

SEMICHORUS I:

We, beyond heaven, are driven along:

SEMICHORUS II:

Us the enchantments of earth retain:

SEMICHORUS I:

Ceaseless, and rapid, and fierce, and free,
With the Spirits which build a new earth and sea,
And a heaven where yet heaven could never be;

SEMICHORUS II:

Solemn, and slow, and serene, and bright,
Leading the Day and outspeeding the Night,
With the powers of a world of perfect light;

SEMICHORUS I:

We whirl, singing loud, round the gathering sphere,
Till the trees, and the beasts, and the clouds appear
From its chaos made calm by love, not fear.

SEMICHORUS II:

We encircle the ocean and mountains of earth,
And the happy forms of its death and birth
Change to the music of our sweet mirth.

CHORUS OF HOURS AND SPIRITS:

Break the dance, and scatter the song,
  Let some depart, and some remain,
Wherever we fly we lead along
In leashes, like starbeams, soft yet strong.
  The clouds that are heavy with love's sweet rain.

PANTHEA: Ha! they are gone!

IONE: Yet feel you no delight
From the past sweetness?
PANTHEA: As the bare green hill
When some soft cloud vanishes into rain,
Laughs with a thousand drops of sunny water
To the unpavilioned sky!
IONE: Even whilst we speak
New notes arise. What is that awful sound?
PANTHEA: 'Tis the deep music of the rolling world
Kindling within the strings of the waved air,
Aeolian modulations.
IONE: Listen too,
How every pause is filled with under-notes,
Clear, silver, icy, keen awakening tones,
Which pierce the sense, and live within the soul,
As the sharp stars pierce winter's crystal air
And gaze upon themselves within the sea.
PANTHEA: But see where through two openings in the forest
Which hanging branches overcanopy,
And where two runnels of a rivulet,
Between the close moss violet-inwoven,
Have made their path of melody, like sisters
Who part with sighs that they may meet in smiles,
Turning their dear disunion to an isle
Of lovely grief, a wood of sweet sad thoughts;
Two visions of strange radiance float upon
The ocean-like enchantment of strong sound,
Which flows intenser, keener, deeper yet
Under the ground and through the windless air.
IONE: I see a chariot like that thinnest boat,
In which the mother of the months is borne
By ebbing light into her western cave,
When she upsprings from interlunar dreams,
O'er which is curved an orblike canopy

Of gentle darkness, and the hills and woods
Distinctly seen through that dusk aery veil,
Regard like shapes in an enchanter's glass;
Its wheels are solid clouds, azure and gold,
Such as the genii of the thunder-storm,
Pile on the floor of the illumined sea
When the sun rushes under it; they roll
And move and grow as with an inward wind;
Within it sits a winged infant, white
Its countenance, like the whiteness of bright snow,
Its plumes are as feathers of sunny frost,
Its limbs gleam white, through the wind-flowing folds
Of its white robe, woof of aetherial pearl.
Its hair is white, the brightness of white light
Scattered in strings; yet its two eyes are heavens
Of liquid darkness, which the Deity
Within seems pouring, as a storm is poured
From jagged clouds, out of their arrowy lashes,
Tempering the cold and radiant air around,
With fire that is not brightness; in its hand
It sways a quivering moon-beam, from whose point
A guiding power directs the chariot's prow
Over its wheeled clouds, which as they roll
Over the grass, and flowers, and waves, wake sounds.
Sweet as a singing rain of silver dew.

PANTHEA: And from the other opening in the wood
Rushes, with loud and whirlwind harmony,
A sphere, which is as many thousand spheres,
Solid as chrystal, yet through all its mass
Flow, as through empty space, music and light:
Ten thousand orbs involving and involved,
Purple and azure, white, and green, and golden,
Sphere within sphere; and every space between
Peopled with unimaginable shapes,

Such as ghosts dream dwell in the lampless deep,
Yet each inter-transpicuous, and they whirl
Over each other with a thousand motions,
Upon a thousand sightless axles spinning.
And with the force of self-destroying swiftness,
Intensely, slowly, solemnly roll on,
Kindling with mingled sounds, and many tones,
Intelligible words and music wild.
With mighty whirl the multitudinous orb
Grinds the bright brook into an azure mist
Of elemental subtlety, like light;
And the wild odour of the forest flowers,
The music of the living grass and air,
The emerald light of leaf-entangled beams
Round its intense yet self-conflicting speed,
Seem kneaded into one aerial mass
Which drowns the sense. Within the orb itself,
Pillowed upon its alabaster arms,
Like to a child o'erwearied with sweet toil,
On its own folded wings, and wavy hair,
The Spirit of the Earth is laid asleep,
And you can see its little lips are moving,
Amid the changing light of their own smiles,
Like one who talks of what he loves in dream.

IONE: 'Tis only mocking the orb's harmony.

PANTHEA: And from a star upon its forehead, shoot,
Like swords of azure fire, or golden spears
With tyrant-quelling myrtle overtwined,
Embleming heaven and earth united now,
Vast beams like spokes of some invisible wheel
Which whirl as the orb whirls, swifter than thought,
Filling the abyss with sun-like lightenings,
And perpendicular now, and now transverse,
Pierce the dark soil, and as they pierce and pass,

Make bare the secrets of the earth's deep heart;
Infinite mines of adamant and gold,
Valueless stones, and unimagined gems,
And caverns on crystalline columns poised
With vegetable silver overspread;
Wells of unfathomed fire, and water springs
Whence the great sea, even as a child is fed,
Whose vapours clothe earth's monarch mountain-tops
With kingly, ermine snow. The beams flash on
And make appear the melancholy ruins
Of cancelled cycles; anchors, beaks of ships;
Planks turned to marble; quivers, helms, and spears,
And gorgon-headed targes, and the wheels
Of scythed chariots, and the emblazonry
Of trophies, standards, and armorial beasts,
Round which death laughed, sepulchred emblems
Of dead destruction, ruin within ruin!
The wrecks beside of many a city vast,
Whose population which the earth grew over
Was mortal, but not human; see, they lie
Their monstrous works, and uncouth skeletons,
Their statues, homes and fanes; prodigious shapes
Huddled in gray annihilation, split,
Jammed in the hard, black deep; and over these,
The anatomies of unknown winged things,
And fishes which were isles of living scale,
And serpents, bony chains, twisted around
The iron crags, or within heaps of dust
To which the tortuous strength of their last pangs
Had crushed the iron crags; and over these
The jagged alligator, and the might
Of earth-convulsing behemoth, which once
Were monarch beasts, and on the slimy shores,
And weed-overgrown continents of earth,

Increased and multiplied like summer worms
On an abandoned corpse, till the blue globe
Wrapped deluge round it like a cloke, and they
Yelled, gasped, and were abolished; or some God
Whose throne was in a comet, past, and cried,
'Be not!' And like my words they were no more.

THE EARTH:

The joy, the triumph, the delight, the madness!
The boundless, overflowing, bursting gladness,
The vapourous exultation not to be confined!
Ha! ha! the animation of delight
Which wraps me, like an atmosphere of light,
And bears me as a cloud is borne by its own wind.

THE MOON:

Brother mine, calm wanderer,
Happy globe of land and air,
Some Spirit is darted like a beam from thee,
Which penetrates my frozen frame,
And passes with the warmth of flame,
With love, and odour, and deep melody
Through me, through me!

THE EARTH:

Ha! ha! the caverns of my hollow mountains,
My cloven fire-crags, sound-exulting fountains
Laugh with a vast and inextinguishable laughter.
The oceans, and the desarts, and the abysses
Of the deep air's unmeasured wildernesses,
Answer from all their clouds and billows, echoing after.

They cry aloud as I do. Sceptred curse,
Who all our green and azure universe
Threatenedst to muffle round with black destruction,
sending
A solid cloud to rain hot thunder-stones,
And splinter and knead down my children's bones
All I bring forth, to one void mass battering and
blending.

Until each crag-like tower, and storied column,
Palace, and obelisk, and temple solemn,
My imperial mountains crowned with cloud, and snow,
and fire;
My sea-like forests, every blade and blossom
Which finds a grave or cradle in my bosom,
Were stamped by thy strong hate into a lifeless mire.

How art thou sunk, withdrawn, covered, drunk up
By thirsty nothing, as the brackish cup
Drained by a desart-troop, a little drop for all;
And from beneath, around, within, above,
Filling thy void annihilation, love
Bursts in like light on caves cloven by the thunder-ball.

THE MOON:

The snow upon my lifeless mountains
Is loosened into living fountains,
My solid oceans flow, and sing, and shine:
A spirit from my heart bursts forth,
It clothes with unexpected birth
My cold bare bosom: Oh! it must be thine
On mine, on mine!

Gazing on thee I feel, I know
Green stalks burst forth, and bright flowers grow,
And living shapes upon my bosom move:
Music is in the sea and air,
Winged clouds soar here and there,
Dark with the rain new buds are dreaming of:
'Tis love, all love!

THE EARTH:

It interpenetrates my granite mass,
Through tangled roots and trodden clay doth pass,
Into the utmost leaves and delicatest flowers;
Upon the winds, among the clouds 'tis spread.
It wakes a life in the forgotten dead,
They breathe a spirit up from their obscurest bowers.

And like a storm bursting its cloudy prison
With thunder, and with whirlwind, has arisen
Out of the lampless caves of unimagined being:
With earthquake shock and swiftness making shiver
Thought's stagnant chaos, unremoved for ever,
Till hate, and fear, and pain, light-vanquished shadows, fleeing,

Leave Man, who was a many sided mirror,
Which could distort to many a shape of error,
This true fair world of things, a sea reflecting love;
Which over all his kind as the sun's heaven
Gliding o'er ocean, smooth, serene, and even,
Darting from starry depths radiance and life, doth move.

Leave man, even as a leprous child is left,
Who follows a sick beast to some warm cleft
Of rocks, through which the might of healing springs is poured;
Then when it wanders home with rosy smile,
Unconscious, and its mother fears awhile
It is a spirit, then, weeps on her child restored.

Man, oh, not men! a chain of linked thought,
Of love and might to be divided not,
Compelling the elements with adamantine stress;
As the sun rules, even with a tyrant's gaze,
The unquiet republic of the maze
Of planets, struggling fierce towards heaven's free wilderness.

Man, one harmonious soul of many a soul,
Whose nature is its own divine controul,
Where all things flow to all, as rivers to the sea;
Familiar acts are beautiful through love;
Labour, and pain, and grief, in life's green grove
Sport like tame beasts, none knew how gentle they could be!

His will, with all mean passions, bad delights,
And selfish cares, its trembling satellites,
A spirit ill to guide, but mighty to obey,
Is as a tempest-winged ship, whose helm
Love rules, through waves which dare not overwhelm,
Forcing life's wildest shores to own its sovereign sway.

All things confess his strength. Through the cold
mass
Of marble and of colour his dreams pass;
Bright threads whence mothers weave the robes their
children wear;
Language is a perpetual Orphic song,
Which rules with Daedal harmony a throng
Of thoughts and forms, which else senseless and shape-
less were.

The lightning is his slave; heaven's utmost deep
Gives up her stars, and like a flock of sheep
They pass before his eye, are numbered, and roll on!
The tempest is his steed, he strides the air;
And the abyss shouts from her depth laid bare,
Heaven, hast thou secrets? Man unveils me; I have
none.

THE MOON:

The shadow of white death has past
From my path in heaven at last,
A clinging shroud of solid frost and sleep;
And through my newly-woven bowers,
Wander happy paramours,
Less mighty, but as mild as those who keep
Thy vales more deep.

THE EARTH:

As the dissolving warmth of dawn may fold
A half unfrozen dew-globe, green, and gold,
And crystalline, till it becomes a winged mist,
And wanders up the vault of the blue day,
Outlives the noon, and on the sun's last ray
Hangs o'er the sea, a fleece of fire and amethyst.

THE MOON:

Thou art folded, thou art lying
In the light which is undying
Of thine own joy, and heaven's smile divine;
All suns and constellations shower
On thee a light, a life, a power
Which doth array thy sphere; thou pourest thine
On mine, on mine!

THE EARTH:

I spin beneath my pyramid of night,
Which points into the heavens dreaming delight,
Murmuring victorious joy in my enchanted sleep;
As a youth lulled in love-dreams faintly sighing,
Under the shadow of his beauty lying,
Which round his rest a watch of light and warmth doth keep.

THE MOON:

As in the soft and sweet eclipse,
When soul meets soul on lovers' lips,
High hearts are calm, and brightest eyes are dull;
So when thy shadow falls on me,
Then am I mute and still, by thee
Covered; of thy love, Orb most beautiful,
Full, oh, too full!

Thou art speeding round the sun
Brightest world of many a one; –
Green and azure sphere which shinest
With a light which is divinest
Among all the lamps of Heaven
To whom life and light is given;
I, thy crystal paramour

Borne beside thee by a power
Like the polar Paradise,
Magnet-like of lovers' eyes;
I, a most enamoured maiden
Whose weak brain is overladen
With the pleasure of her love,
Maniac-like around thee move
Gazing, an insatiate bride,
On thy form from every side
Like a Maenad, round the cup
Which Agave lifted up
In the weird Cadmaean forest.
Brother, wheresoe'er thou soarest
I must hurry, whirl and follow
Through the heavens wide and hollow,
Sheltered by the warm embrace
Of thy soul from hungry space,
Drinking from thy sense and sight
Beauty, majesty, and might,
As a lover or a cameleon
Grows like what it looks upon,
As a violet's gentle eye
Gazes on the azure sky
Until its hue grows like what it beholds,
As a grey and watery mist
Glows like solid amethyst
Athwart the western mountain it enfolds,
When the sunset sleeps
Upon its snow –

THE EARTH:

And the weak day weeps
That it should be so.
Oh, gentle Moon, the voice of thy delight

Falls on me like thy clear and tender light
Soothing the seaman, borne the summer night,
  Through isles for ever calm;
Oh, gentle Moon, thy crystal accents pierce
The caverns of my pride's deep universe,
Charming the tiger joy, whose tramplings fierce
  Made wounds which need thy balm.

PANTHEA: I rise as from a bath of sparkling water,
A bath of azure light, among dark rocks,
Out of the stream of sound.

IONE: Ah me! sweet sister,
The stream of sound has ebbed away from us,
And you pretend to rise out of its wave,
Because your words fall like the clear, soft dew
Shaken from a bathing wood-nymph's limbs and hair.

PANTHEA: Peace! peace! A mighty Power, which is as darkness,
Is rising out of Earth, and from the sky
Is showered like night, and from within the air
Bursts, like eclipse which had been gathered up
Into the pores of sunlight: the bright visions,
Wherein the singing spirits rode and shone,
Gleam like pale meteors through a watery night.

IONE: There is a sense of words upon mine ear.

PANTHEA: An universal sound like words: Oh, list!

DEMOGORGON:

Thou, Earth, calm empire of a happy soul,
  Sphere of divinest shapes and harmonies,
Beautiful orb! gathering as thou dost roll
  The love which paves thy path along the skies:

THE EARTH:

  I hear: I am as a drop of dew that dies.

DEMOGORGON:

Thou, Moon, which gazest on the nightly Earth
  With wonder, as it gazes upon thee;
Whilst each to men, and beasts, and the swift birth
  Of birds, is beauty, love, calm, harmony:

THE MOON:

  I hear: I am a leaf shaken by thee!

DEMOGORGON:

Ye kings of suns and stars, Daemons and Gods,
  Aetherial Dominations, who possess
Elysian, windless, fortunate abodes
  Beyond Heaven's constellated wilderness:

A VOICE FROM ABOVE:

  Our great Republic hears, we are blest, and bless.

DEMOGORGON:

Ye happy dead, whom beams of brightest verse
  Are clouds to hide, not colours to pourtray,
Whether your nature is that universe
  Which once ye saw and suffered –

A VOICE FROM BENEATH:

Or as they
  Whom we have left, we change and pass away.

DEMOGORGON:

Ye elemental Genii, who have homes
  From man's high mind even to the central stone
Of sullen lead; from Heaven's star-fretted domes
  To the dull weed some sea-worm battens on:

A CONFUSED VOICE:

We hear: thy words waken Oblivion.

DEMOGORGON:

Spirits, whose homes are flesh: ye beasts and birds,
Ye worms, and fish; ye living leaves and buds;
Lightning and wind; and ye untameable herds,
Meteors and mists, which throng air's solitudes:

A VOICE:

Thy voice to us is wind among still woods.

DEMOGORGON:

Man, who wert once a despot and a slave;
A dupe and a deceiver; a decay;
A traveller from the cradle to the grave
Through the dim night of this immortal day:

ALL:

Speak: thy strong words may never pass away.

DEMOGORGON:

This is the day, which down the void abysm
At the Earth-born's spell yawns for Heaven's despotism,
And Conquest is dragged captive through the deep:
Love, from its awful throne of patient power
In the wise heart, from the last giddy hour
Of dread endurance, from the slippery, steep,
And narrow verge of crag-like agony, springs
And folds over the world its healing wings,

Gentleness, Virtue, Wisdom, and Endurance,
These are the seals of that most firm assurance
  Which bars the pit over Destruction's strength;
And if, with infirm hand, Eternity,
Mother of many acts and hours, should free
  The serpent that would clasp her with his length;
These are the spells by which to re-assume
An empire o'er the disentangled doom.

To suffer woes which Hope thinks infinite;
To forgive wrongs darker than death or night;
  To defy Power, which seems omnipotent;
To love, and bear; to hope till Hope creates
From its own wreck the thing it contemplates;
  Neither to change, nor faulter, nor repent;
This, like thy glory, Titan, is to be
Good, great and joyous, beautiful and free;
This is alone Life, Joy, Empire, and Victory.

Ode to the West Wind*

I

O, wild West Wind, thou breath of Autumn's being,
Thou, from whose unseen presence the leaves dead
Are driven, like ghosts from an enchanter fleeing,

Yellow, and black, and pale, and hectic red,
Pestilence-stricken multitudes: O, thou,
Who chariotest to their dark wintry bed

The winged seeds, where they lie cold and low,
Each like a corpse within its grave, until
Thine azure sister of the spring shall blow

Her clarion o'er the dreaming earth, and fill
(Driving sweet buds like flocks to feed in air)
With living hues and odours plain and hill:

Wild Spirit, which art moving every where;
Destroyer and preserver; hear, O, hear!

*This poem was conceived and chiefly written in a wood that skirts the Arno, near Florence, and on a day when that tempestuous wind, whose temperature is at once mild and animating, was collecting the vapours which pour down the autumnal rains. They began, as I foresaw, at sunset with a violent tempest of hail and rain, attended by that magnificent thunder and lightning peculiar to the Cisalpine regions.

The phenomenon alluded to at the conclusion of the third stanza is well known to naturalists. The vegetation at the bottom of the sea, of rivers, and of lakes, sympathises with that of the land in the change of seasons, and is consequently influenced by the winds which announce it [*Shelley's Note*].

II

Thou on whose stream, 'mid the steep sky's commotion,
Loose clouds like earth's decaying leaves are shed,
Shook from the tangled boughs of Heaven and Ocean,

Angels of rain and lightning: there are spread
On the blue surface of thine airy surge,
Like the bright hair uplifted from the head

Of some fierce Maenad, even from the dim verge
Of the horizon to the zenith's height
The locks of the approaching storm. Thou dirge

Of the dying year, to which this closing night
Will be the dome of a vast sepulchre,
Vaulted with all thy congregated might

Of vapours, from whose solid atmosphere
Black rain, and fire, and hail will burst: O, hear!

III

Thou who didst waken from his summer dreams
The blue Mediterranean, where he lay,
Lulled by the coil of his crystalline streams,

Beside a pumice isle in Baiae's bay,
And saw in sleep old palaces and towers
Quivering within the wave's intenser day,

All overgrown with azure moss and flowers
So sweet, the sense faints picturing them! Thou
For whose path the Atlantic's level powers

Cleave themselves into chasms, while far below
The sea-blooms and the oozy woods which wear
The sapless foliage of the ocean, know

Thy voice, and suddenly grow grey with fear,
And tremble and despoil themselves: O, hear!

IV

If I were a dead leaf thou mightest bear;
If I were a swift cloud to fly with thee;
A wave to pant beneath thy power, and share

The impulse of thy strength, only less free
Than thou, O, uncontroulable! If even
I were as in my boyhood, and could be

The comrade of thy wanderings over heaven
As then, when to outstrip thy skiey speed
Scarce seemed a vision; I would ne'er have striven

As thus with thee in prayer in my sore need.
Oh! lift me as a wave, a leaf, a cloud!
I fall upon the thorns of life! I bleed!

A heavy weight of hours has chained and bowed
One too like thee: tameless, and swift, and proud.

V

Make me thy lyre, even as the forest is:
What if my leaves are falling like its own!
The tumult of thy mighty harmonies

Will take from both a deep, autumnal tone,
Sweet though in sadness. Be thou, spirit fierce
My spirit! Be thou me, impetuous one!

Drive my dead thoughts over the universe
Like withered leaves to quicken a new birth!
And, by the incantation of this verse,

Scatter, as from an unextinguished hearth
Ashes and sparks, my words among mankind!
Be through my lips to unawakened earth

The trumpet of a prophecy! O Wind,
If Winter comes, can Spring be far behind?

On the Medusa of Leonardo da Vinci in the Florentine Gallery

I

It lieth, gazing on the midnight sky,
  Upon the cloudy mountain peak supine;
Below, far lands are seen tremblingly;
  Its horror and its beauty are divine.
Upon its lips and eyelids seems to lie
  Loveliness like a shadow, from which shine,
Fiery and lurid, struggling underneath,
The agonies of anguish and of death.

II

Yet it is less the horror than the grace
  Which turns the gazer's spirit into stone,
Whereon the lineaments of that dead face
  Are graven, till the characters be grown
Into itself, and thought no more can trace;
  'Tis the melodious hues of beauty thrown
Athwart the darkness and the glare of pain,
Which humanize and harmonize the strain.

III

And from its head as from one body grow,
  As   grass out of a watery rock,
Hairs which are vipers, and they curl and flow
  And their long tangles in each other lock,
And with unending involutions show
  Their mailed radiance, as it were to mock
The torture and the death within, and saw
The solid air with many a ragged jaw.

IV

And, from a stone beside, a poisonous eft
  Peeps idly into those Gorgonian eyes;
Whilst in the air a ghastly bat, bereft
  Of sense, has flitted with a mad surprise
Out of the cave this hideous light had cleft,
  And he comes hastening like a moth that hies
After a taper; and the midnight sky
Flares, a light more dread than obscurity.

V

'Tis the tempestuous loveliness of terror;
  For from the serpents gleams a brazen glare
Kindled by that inextricable error,
  Which makes a thrilling vapour of the air
Become a   and ever-shifting mirror
  Of all the beauty and the terror there –
A woman's countenance, with serpent-locks,
Gazing in death on heaven from those wet rocks.

Fragment

Ye gentle visitations of calm thought –
  Moods like the memories of happier earth,
  Which come arrayed in thoughts of little worth,
Like stars in clouds by the weak winds enwrought,
  But that the clouds depart and stars remain,
While they remain, and ye, alas, depart!

Fragment

Is it that in some brighter sphere
We part from friends we meet with here?
Or do we see the Future pass
Over the Present's dusky glass?

Or what is that that makes us seem
To patch up fragments of a dream,
Part of which comes true, and part
Beats and trembles in the heart?

The Sensitive Plant

PART FIRST

A Sensitive Plant in a garden grew,
And the young winds fed it with silver dew,
And it opened its fan-like leaves to the light,
And closed them beneath the kisses of night.

And the Spring arose on the garden fair,
Like the Spirit of Love felt every where;
And each flower and herb on Earth's dark breast
Rose from the dreams of its wintry rest. –

But none ever trembled and panted with bliss
In the garden, the field, or the wilderness,
Like a doe in the noon tide with love's sweet want,
As the companionless Sensitive Plant.

The snow-drop, and then the violet,
Arose from the ground with warm rain wet,
And their breath was mixed with fresh odour, sent
From the turf, like the voice and the instrument.

Then the pied wind-flowers and the tulip tall,
And narcissi, the fairest among them all,
Who gaze on their eyes in the stream's recess,
Till they die of their own dear loveliness;

And the Naiad-like lily of the vale,
Whom youth makes so fair and passion so pale,
That the light of its tremulous bells is seen
Through their pavilions of tender green;

And the hyacinth purple, and white, and blue,
Which flung from its bells a sweet peal anew
Of music so delicate, soft, and intense,
It was felt like an odour within the sense;

And the rose like a nymph to the bath addrest,
Which unveiled the depth of her glowing breast,
Till, fold after fold, to the fainting air
The soul of her beauty and love lay bare:

And the wand-like lily, which lifted up,
As a Maenad, its moonlight-coloured cup,
Till the fiery star, which is its eye,
Gazed through clear dew on the tender sky;

And the jessamine faint, and the sweet tuberose,
The sweetest flower for scent that blows;
And all rare blossoms from every clime
Grew in that garden in perfect prime.

And on the stream whose inconstant bosom
Was prankt under boughs of embowering blossom,
With golden and green light, slanting through
Their heaven of many a tangled hue,

Broad waterlilies lay tremulously,
And starry river-buds glimmered by,
And around them the soft stream did glide and dance
With a motion of sweet sound and radiance.

And the sinuous paths of lawn and of moss,
Which led through the garden along and across,
Some open at once to the sun and the breeze,
Some lost among bowers of blossoming trees,

Were all paved with daisies and delicate bells
As fair as the fabulous asphodels,
And flowrets which drooping as day drooped too
Fell into pavilions, white, purple, and blue,
To roof the glow-worm from the evening dew.

And from this undefiled Paradise
The flowers (as an infant's awakening eyes
Smile on its mother, whose singing sweet
Can first lull, and at last must awaken it.)

When Heaven's blithe winds had unfolded them,
As mine-lamps enkindle a hidden gem,
Shone smiling to Heaven, and every one
Shared joy in the light of the gentle sun;

For each one was interpenetrated
With the light and the odour its neighbour shed,
Like young lovers whom youth and love make dear
Wrapped and filled by their mutual atmosphere.

But the Sensitive Plant which could give small fruit
Of the love which it felt from the leaf to the root,
Received more than all, it loved more than ever,
Where none wanted but it, could belong to the giver,

For the sensitive plant has no bright flower;
Radiance and odour are not its dower;
It loves, even like Love, its deep heart is full,
It desires what it has not, the beautiful!

The light winds which from unsustaining wings
Shed the music of many murmurings;
The beams which dart from many a star
Of the flowers whose hues they bear afar;

The plumed insects swift and free,
Like golden boats on a sunny sea,
Laden with light and odour, which pass
Over the gleam of the living grass;

The unseen clouds of the dew, which lie
Like fire in the flowers till the sun rides high,
Then wander like spirits among the spheres,
Each cloud faint with the fragrance it bears;

The quivering vapours of dim noontide,
Which like a sea o'er the warm earth glide,
In which every sound, and odour, and beam,
Move, as reeds in a single stream;

Each and all like ministering angels were
For the sensitive plant sweet joy to bear,
Whilst the lagging hours of the day went by
Like windless clouds o'er a tender sky.

And when evening descended from heaven above,
And the Earth was all rest, and the air was all love,
And delight, tho' less bright, was far more deep,
And the day's veil fell from the world of sleep.

And the beasts, and the birds, and the insects were drowned
In an ocean of dreams without a sound;
Whose waves never mark, tho' they ever impress
The light sand which paves it, consciousness;

(Only overhead the sweet nightingale
Ever sang more sweet as the day might fail,
And snatches of its Elysian chant
Were mixed with the dreams of the Sensitive Plant.)

The sensitive plant was the earliest
Upgathered into the bosom of rest;
A sweet child weary of its delight,
The feeblest and yet the favourite,
Cradled within the embrace of night.

PART SECOND

There was a Power in this sweet place,
An Eve in this Eden; a ruling grace
Which to the flowers, did they waken or dream,
Was as God is to the starry scheme.

A Lady, the wonder of her kind,
Whose form was upborne by a lovely mind
Which, dilating, had moulded her mien and motion
Like a sea-flower unfolded beneath the ocean,

Tended the garden from morn to even:
And the meteors of that sublunar heaven,
Like the lamps of the air when night walks forth,
Laughed round her footsteps up from the Earth!

She had no companion of mortal race,
But her tremulous breath and her flushing face
Told, whilst the morn kissed the sleep from her eyes
That her dreams were less slumber than Paradise:

As if some bright Spirit for her sweet sake
Had deserted heaven while the stars were awake,
As if yet around her he lingering were,
Tho' the veil of daylight concealed him from her.

Her step seemed to pity the grass it prest;
You might hear by the heaving of her breast,
That the coming and going of the wind
Brought pleasure there and left passion behind.

And wherever her airy footstep trod,
Her trailing hair from the grassy sod
Erased its light vestige, with shadowy sweep,
Like a sunny storm o'er the dark green deep.

I doubt not the flowers of that garden sweet
Rejoiced in the sound of her gentle feet;
I doubt not they felt the spirit that came
From her glowing fingers thro' all their frame.

She sprinkled bright water from the stream
On those that were faint with the sunny beam;
And out of the cups of the heavy flowers
She emptied the rain of the thunder showers.

She lifted their heads with her tender hands,
And sustained them with rods and osier bands;
If the flowers had been her own infants, she
Could never have nursed them more tenderly.

And all killing insects and gnawing worms,
And things of obscene and unlovely forms,
She bore in a basket of Indian woof,
Into the rough woods far aloof,

In a basket, of grasses and wildflowers full,
The freshest her gentle hands could pull
For the poor banished insects, whose intent,
Although they did ill, was innocent.

But the bee and the beamlike ephemeris
Whose path is the lightning's, and soft moths that kiss
The sweet lips of the flowers, and harm not, did she
Make her attendant angels be.

And many an antenatal tomb,
Where butterflies dream of the life to come,
She left clinging round the smooth and dark
Edge of the odorous cedar bark.

This fairest creature from earliest spring
Thus moved through the garden ministering
All the sweet season of summertide,
And ere the first leaf looked brown – she died!

PART THIRD

Three days the flowers of the garden fair,
Like stars when the moon is awakened, were,
Or the waves of Baiae, ere luminous
She floats up through the smoke of Vesuvius.

And on the fourth, the Sensitive Plant
Felt the sound of the funeral chaunt,
And the steps of the bearers, heavy and slow,
And the sobs of the mourners deep and low;

The weary sound and the heavy breath,
And the silent motions of passing death,
And the smell, cold, oppressive, and dank,
Sent through the pores of the coffin plank;

The dark grass, and the flowers among the grass,
Were bright with tears as the crowd did pass;
From their sighs the wind caught a mournful tone,
And sate in the pines, and gave groan for groan.

The garden, once fair, became cold and foul,
Like the corpse of her who had been its soul,
Which at first was lovely as if in sleep,
Then slowly changed, till it grew a heap
To make men tremble who never weep.

Swift summer into the autumn flowed,
And frost in the mist of the morning rode,
Though the noonday sun looked clear and bright,
Mocking the spoil of the secret night.

The rose leaves, like flakes of crimson snow,
Paved the turf and the moss below.
The lilies were drooping, and white, and wan,
Like the head and the skin of a dying man.

And Indian plants, of scent and hue
The sweetest that ever were fed on dew,
Leaf by leaf, day after day,
Were massed into the common clay.

And the leaves, brown, yellow, and grey, and red,
And white with the whiteness of what is dead,
Like troops of ghosts on the dry wind past;
Their whistling noise made the birds aghast.

And the gusty winds waked the winged seeds,
Out of their birthplace of ugly weeds,
Till they clung round many a sweet flower's stem,
Which rotted into the earth with them.

The water-blooms under the rivulet
Fell from the stalks on which they were set;
And the eddies drove them here and there,
As the winds did those of the upper air.

Then the rain came down, and the broken stalks,
Were bent and tangled across the walks;
And the leafless net-work of parasite bowers
Massed into ruin; and all sweet flowers.

Between the time of the wind and the snow,
All loathliest weeds began to grow,
Whose coarse leaves were splashed with many a speck,
Like the water-snake's belly and the toad's back.

And thistles, and nettles, and darnels rank,
And the dock, and henbane, and hemlock dank,
Stretched out its long and hollow shank,
And stifled the air till the dead wind stank.

And plants, at whose names the verse feels loath,
Filled the place with a monstrous undergrowth,
Prickly, and pulpous, and blistering, and blue,
Livid, and starred with a lurid dew.

And agarics and fungi, with mildew and mould
Started like mist from the wet ground cold;
Pale, fleshy, as if the decaying dead
With a spirit of growth had been animated!

Spawn, weeds, and filth, a leprous scum,
Made the running rivulet thick and dumb
And at its outlet flags huge as stakes
Dammed it up with roots knotted like water snakes.

And hour by hour, when the air was still,
The vapours arose which have strength to kill:
At morn they were seen, at noon they were felt,
At night they were darkness no star could melt.

And unctuous meteors from spray to spray
Crept and flitted in broad noon-day
Unseen; every branch on which they alit
By a venomous blight was burned and bit.

The Sensitive Plant like one forbid
Wept, and the tears within each lid
Of its folded leaves which together grew,
Were changed to a blight of frozen glue.

For the leaves soon fell, and the branches soon
By the heavy axe of the blast were hewn;
The sap shrank to the root through every pore
As blood to a heart that will beat no more.

For Winter came: the wind was his whip:
One choppy finger was on his lip:
He had torn the cataracts from the hills
And they clanked at his girdle like manacles;

His breath was a chain which without a sound
The earth, and the air, and the water bound;
He came, fiercely driven, in his chariot-throne
By the tenfold blasts of the arctic zone.

Then the weeds which were forms of living death
Fled from the frost to the earth beneath.
Their decay and sudden flight from frost
Was but like the vanishing of a ghost!

And under the roots of the Sensitive Plant
The moles and the dormice died for want:
The birds dropped stiff from the frozen air
And were caught in the branches naked and bare.

First there came down a thawing rain
And its dull drops froze on the boughs again,
Then there steamed up a freezing dew
Which to the drops of the thaw-rain grew;

And a northern whirlwind, wandering about
Like a wolf that had smelt a dead child out,
Shook the boughs thus laden, and heavy and stiff,
And snapped them off with his rigid griff.

When winter had gone and spring came back
The Sensitive Plant was a leafless wreck;
But the mandrakes, and toadstools, and docks, and darnels,
Rose like the dead from their ruined charnels.

CONCLUSION

Whether the sensitive plant, or that
Which within its boughs like a spirit sat,
Ere its outward form had known decay,
Now felt this change, I cannot say.

Whether that lady's gentle mind,
No longer with the form combined
Which scattered love, as stars do light,
Found sadness, where it left delight,

I dare not guess; but in this life
Of error, ignorance, and strife,
Where nothing is, but all things seem,
And we the shadows of the dream,

It is a modest creed, and yet
Pleasant if one considers it,
To own that death itself must be,
Like all the rest, a mockery.

That garden sweet, that lady fair,
And all sweet shapes and odours there,
In truth have never passed away:
'Tis we, 'tis ours, are changed; not they.

For love, and beauty, and delight,
There is no death nor change: their might
Exceeds our organs, which endure
No light, being themselves obscure.

The Cloud

I bring fresh showers for the thirsting flowers,
From the seas and the streams;
I bear light shade for the leaves when laid
In their noon-day dreams.
From my wings are shaken the dews that waken
The sweet buds every one,
When rocked to rest on their mother's breast,
As she dances about the sun.
I wield the flail of the lashing hail,
And whiten the green plains under,
And then again I dissolve it in rain,
And laugh as I pass in thunder.

I sift the snow on the mountains below,
And their great pines groan aghast;
And all the night 'tis my pillow white,
While I sleep in the arms of the blast.
Sublime on the towers of my skiey bowers,
Lightning my pilot sits;
In a cavern under is fettered the thunder,
It struggles and howls at fits;
Over earth and ocean, with gentle motion,
This pilot is guiding me,
Lured by the love of the genii that move
In the depths of the purple sea;
Over the rills, and the crags, and the hills,
Over the lakes and the plains,
Wherever he dream, under mountain or stream,
The Spirit he loves remains;
And I all the while bask in heaven's blue smile,
Whilst he is dissolving in rains.

The sanguine sunrise, with his meteor eyes,
And his burning plumes outspread,
Leaps on the back of my sailing rack,
When the morning star shines dead.
As on the jag of a mountain crag,
Which an earthquake rocks and swings,
An eagle alit one moment may sit
In the light of its golden wings.
And when sunset may breathe, from the lit sea beneath,
Its ardours of rest and of love,
And the crimson pall of eve may fall
From the depth of heaven above,
With wings folded I rest, on mine airy nest,
As still as a brooding dove.

That orbed maiden with white fire laden,
Whom mortals call the moon,
Glides glimmering o'er my fleece-like floor,
By the midnight breezes strewn;
And wherever the beat of her unseen feet,
Which only the angels hear,
May have broken the woof of my tent's thin roof,
The stars peep behind her and peer;
And I laugh to see them whirl and flee,
Like a swarm of golden bees,
When I widen the rent in my wind-built tent,
Till the calm rivers, lakes, and seas,
Like strips of the sky fallen through me on high,
Are each paved with the moon and these.

I bind the sun's throne with a burning zone,
And the moon's with a girdle of pearl;
The volcanos are dim, and the stars reel and swim,
When the whirlwinds my banner unfurl.

From cape to cape, with a bridge-like shape,
    Over a torrent sea,
Sunbeam-proof, I hang like a roof,
    The mountains its columns be.
The triumphal arch through which I march
    With hurricane, fire, and snow,
When the powers of the air are chained to my chair,
    Is the million-coloured bow;
The sphere-fire above its soft colours wove,
    While the moist earth was laughing below.

I am the daughter of earth and water,
    And the nursling of the sky;
I pass through the pores of the ocean and shores;
    I change, but I cannot die.
For after the rain when with never a stain,
    The pavilion of heaven is bare,
And the winds and sunbeams with their convex gleams,
    Build up the blue dome of air,
I silently laugh at my own cenotaph,
    And out of the caverns of rain,
Like a child from the womb, like a ghost from the tomb,
    I arise and unbuild it again.

To a Skylark

Hail to thee, blithe spirit!
  Bird thou never wert,
That from heaven, or near it,
  Pourest thy full heart
In profuse strains of unpremeditated art.

Higher still and higher
  From the earth thou springest
Like a cloud of fire;
  The blue deep thou wingest,
And singing still dost soar, and soaring ever singest.

In the golden lightning
  Of the sunken sun,
O'er which clouds are brightning,
  Thou dost float and run;
Like an unbodied joy whose race is just begun.

The pale purple even
  Melts around thy flight;
Like a star of heaven,
  In the broad day-light
Thou art unseen, but yet I hear thy shrill delight,

Keen as are the arrows
  Of that silver sphere,
Whose intense lamp narrows
  In the white dawn clear,
Until we hardly see, we feel that it is there.

All the earth and air
  With thy voice is loud,
As, when night is bare,
  From one lonely cloud
The moon rains out her beams, and heaven is overflowed.

What thou art we know not;
  What is most like thee?
From rainbow clouds there flow not
  Drops so bright to see,
As from thy presence showers a rain of melody.

Like a poet hidden
  In the light of thought,
Singing hymns unbidden,
  Till the world is wrought
To sympathy with hopes and fears it heeded not:

Like a high-born maiden
  In a palace-tower,
Soothing her love-laden
  Soul in secret hour
With music sweet as love, which overflows her bower:

Like a glow-worm golden
  In a dell of dew,
Scattering unbeholden
  Its aerial hue
Among the flowers and grass, which screen it from the view:

Like a rose embowered
  In its own green leaves,
By warm winds deflowered,
  Till the scent it gives
Makes faint with too much sweet these heavy-wingèd thieves:

Sound of vernal showers
On the twinkling grass,
Rain-awakened flowers,
All that ever was
Joyous, and clear, and fresh, thy music doth surpass:

Teach us, sprite or bird,
What sweet thoughts are thine:
I have never heard
Praise of love or wine
That panted forth a flood of rapture so divine.

Chorus Hymenaeal,
Or triumphal chaunt,
Matched with thine would be all
But an empty vaunt,
A thing wherein we feel there is some hidden want.

What objects are the fountains
Of thy happy strain?
What fields, or waves, or mountains?
What shapes of sky or plain?
What love of thine own kind? what ignorance of pain?

With thy clear keen joyance
Languor cannot be:
Shadow of annoyance
Never came near thee:
Thou lovest; but ne'er knew love's sad satiety.

Waking or asleep,
Thou of death must deem
Things more true and deep
Than we mortals dream,
Or how could thy notes flow in such a crystal stream?

We look before and after,
  And pine for what is not:
Our sincerest laughter
  With some pain is fraught;
Our sweetest songs are those that tell of saddest thought.

Yet if we could scorn
  Hate, and pride, and fear;
If we were things born
  Not to shed a tear,
I know not how thy joy we ever should come near.

Better than all measures
  Of delightful sound,
Better than all treasures
  That in books are found,
Thy skill to poet were, thou scorner of the ground!

Teach me half the gladness
  That thy brain must know,
Such harmonious madness
  From my lips would flow,
The world should listen then, as I am listening now.

The Witch of Atlas

To Mary

(On her objecting to the following poem, upon the score of its containing no human interest.)

I

How, my dear Mary, are you critic-bitten,
  (For vipers kill, though dead,) by some review,
That you condemn these verses I have written,
  Because they tell no story, false or true!
What, though no mice are caught by a young kitten,
  May it not leap and play as grown cats do,
Till its claws come? Prithee, for this one time,
Content thee with a visionary rhyme.

II

What hand would crush the silken-winged fly,
  The youngest of inconstant April's minions,
Because it cannot climb the purest sky,
  Where the swan sings, amid the sun's dominions?
Not thine. Thou knowest 'tis its doom to die,
  When day shall hide within her twilight pinions,
The lucent eyes, and the eternal smile,
Serene as thine, which lent it life awhile.

III

To thy fair feet a winged Vision came,
  Whose date should have been longer than a day,
And o'er thy head did beat its wings for fame,
  And in thy sight its fading plumes display;

The watery bow burned in the evening flame,
But the shower fell, the swift sun went his way –
And that is dead. – O, let me not believe
That any thing of mine is fit to live!

IV

Wordsworth informs us he was nineteen years
  Considering and retouching Peter Bell;
Watering his laurels with the killing tears
  Of slow, dull care, so that their roots to hell
Might pierce, and their wide branches blot the spheres
  Of heaven, with dewy leaves and flowers; this well
May be, for Heaven and Earth conspire to foil
The over-busy gardener's blundering toil.

V

My Witch indeed is not so sweet a creature
  As Ruth or Lucy, whom his graceful praise
Clothes for our grandsons – but she matches Peter,
  Though he took nineteen years, and she three days
In dressing. Light the vest of flowing metre
  She wears; he, proud as dandy with his stays,
Has hung upon his wiry limbs a dress
Like King Lear's 'looped and windowed raggedness'.

VI

If you strip Peter, you will see a fellow,
  Scorched by Hell's hyperequatorial climate
Into a kind of a sulphureous yellow:

A lean mark, hardly fit to fling a rhyme at;
In shape a Scaramouch, in hue Othello,
If you unveil my Witch, no priest nor primate
Can shrive you of that sin, – if sin there be
In love, when it becomes idolatry.

The Witch of Atlas

I

Before those cruel Twins, whom at one birth
Incestuous Change bore to her father Time,
Error and Truth, had hunted from the Earth
All those bright natures which adorned its prime,
And left us nothing to believe in, worth
The pains of putting into learned rhyme,
A lady-witch there lived on Atlas' mountain
Within a cavern, by a secret fountain.

II

Her mother was one of the Atlantides:
The all-beholding Sun had ne'er beholden
In his wide voyage o'er continents and seas
So fair a creature, as she lay enfolden
In the warm shadow of her loveliness; –
He kissed her with his beams, and made all golden
The chamber of grey rock in which she lay –
She, in that dream of joy, dissolved away.

III

'Tis said, she first was changed into a vapour,
  And then into a cloud, such clouds as flit,
Like splendour-winged moths about a taper,
  Round the red west when the sun dies in it:
And then into a meteor, such as caper
  On hill-tops when the moon is in a fit:
Then, into one of those mysterious stars
Which hide themselves between the Earth and Mars.

IV

Ten times the Mother of the Months had bent
  Her bow beside the folding-star, and bidden
With that bright sign the billows to indent
  The sea-deserted sand – like children chidden,
At her command they ever came and went –
  Since in that cave a dewy splendour hidden
Took shape and motion: with the living form
Of this embodied Power, the cave grew warm.

V

A lovely lady garmented in light
  From her own beauty – deep her eyes, as are
Two openings of unfathomable night
  Seen through a Temple's cloven roof – her hair
Dark – the dim brain whirls dizzy with delight,
  Picturing her form; her soft smiles shone afar,
And her low voice was heard like love, and drew
All living things towards this wonder new.

VI

And first the spotted cameleopard came,
  And then the wise and fearless elephant;
Then the sly serpent, in the golden flame
  Of his own volumes intervolved; – all gaunt
And sanguine beasts her gentle looks made tame.
  They drank before her at her sacred fount;
And every beast of beating heart grew bold,
Such gentleness and power even to behold.

VII

The brinded lioness led forth her young,
  That she might teach them how they should forego
Their inborn thirst of death; the pard unstrung
  His sinews at her feet, and sought to know
With looks whose motions spoke without a tongue
  How he might be as gentle as the doe.
The magic circle of her voice and eyes
All savage natures did imparadise.

VIII

And old Silenus, shaking a green stick
  Of lilies, and the wood-gods in a crew
Came, blithe, as in the olive copses thick
  Cicadae are, drunk with the noonday dew:
And Dryope and Faunus followed quick,
  Teazing the God to sing them something new;
Till in this cave they found the lady lone,
Sitting upon a seat of emerald stone.

IX

And universal Pan, 'tis said, was there,
  And though none saw him, – through the adamant
Of the deep mountains, through the trackless air,
  And through those living spirits, like a want
He past out of his everlasting lair
  Where the quick heart of the great world doth pant,
And felt that wondrous lady all alone, –
And she felt him, upon her emerald throne.

X

And every nymph of stream and spreading tree,
  And every shepherdess of Ocean's flocks,
Who drives her white waves over the green sea,
  And Ocean with the brine on his grey locks,
And quaint Priapus with his company,
  All came, much wondering how the enwombed rocks
Could have brought forth so beautiful a birth; –
Her love subdued their wonder and their mirth.

XI

The herdsmen and the mountain maidens came,
  And the rude kings of pastoral Garamant –
Their spirits shook within them, as a flame
  Stirred by the air under a cavern gaunt:
Pigmies, and Polyphemes, by many a name,
  Centaurs and Satyrs, and such shapes as haunt
Wet clefts, – and lumps neither alive nor dead,
Dog-headed, bosom-eyed, and bird-footed.

XII

For she was beautiful – her beauty made
  The bright world dim, and every thing beside
Seemed like the fleeting image of a shade:
  No thought of living spirit could abide,
Which to her looks had ever been betrayed,
  On any object in the world so wide,
On any hope within the circling skies,
But on her form, and in her inmost eyes.

XIII

Which when the lady knew, she took her spindle
  And twined three threads of fleecy mist, and three
Long lines of light, such as the dawn may kindle
  The clouds and waves and mountains with; and she
As many star-beams, ere their lamps could dwindle
  In the belated moon, wound skilfully;
And with these threads a subtle veil she wove –
A shadow for the splendour of her love.

XIV

The deep recesses of her odorous dwelling
  Were stored with magic treasures – sounds of air,
Which had the power all spirits of compelling,
  Folded in cells of chrystal silence there;
Such as we hear in youth, and think the feeling
  Will never die – yet ere we are aware,
The feeling and the sound are fled and gone,
And the regret they leave remains alone.

XV

And there lay Visions swift, and sweet, and quaint,
  Each in its thin sheath, like a chrysalis,
Some eager to burst forth, some weak and faint
  With the soft burthen of intensest bliss;
It was its work to bear to many a saint
  Whose heart adores the shrine which holiest is,
Even Love's: – and others white, green, grey and black,
And of all shapes – and each was at her beck.

XVI

And odours in a kind of aviary
  Of ever-blooming Eden-trees she kept,
Clipt in a floating net, a love-sick Fairy
  Had woven from dew-beams while the moon yet slept;
As bats at the wired window of a dairy,
  They beat their vans; and each was an adept,
When loosed and missioned, making wings of winds,
To stir sweet thoughts or sad, in destined minds.

XVII

And liquors clear and sweet, whose healthful might
  Could medicine the sick soul to happy sleep,
And change eternal death into a night
  Of glorious dreams – or if eyes needs must weep,
Could make their tears all wonder and delight,
  She in her chrystal vials did closely keep:
If men could drink of those clear vials, 'tis said
The living were not envied of the dead.

XVIII

Her cave was stored with scrolls of strange device,
  The works of some Saturnian Archimage,
Which taught the expiations at whose price
  Men from the Gods might win that happy age
Too lightly lost, redeeming native vice;
  And which might quench the Earth-consuming rage
Of gold and blood – till men should live and move
Harmonious as the sacred stars above.

XIX

And how all things that seem untameable,
  Not to be checked and not to be confined,
Obey the spells of wisdom's wizard skill;
  Time, earth and fire – the ocean and the wind,
And all their shapes – and man's imperial will;
  And other scrolls whose writings did unbind
The inmost lore of Love – let the prophane
Tremble to ask what secrets they contain.

XX

And wondrous works of substances unknown,
  To which the enchantment of her father's power
Had changed those ragged blocks of savage stone,
  Were heaped in the recesses of her bower;
Carved lamps and chalices, and phials which shone
  In their own golden beams – each like a flower,
Out of whose depth a fire-fly shakes his light
Under a cypress in a starless night.

XXI

At first she lived alone in this wild home,
  And her own thoughts were each a minister,
Clothing themselves, or with the ocean foam,
  Or with the wind, or with the speed of fire,
To work whatever purposes might come
  Into her mind; such power her mighty Sire
Had girt them with, whether to fly or run,
Through all the regions which he shines upon.

XXII

The Ocean-nymphs and Hamadryades,
  Oreads and Naiads, with long weedy locks,
Offered to do her bidding through the seas,
  Under the earth, and in the hollow rocks,
And far beneath the matted roots of trees,
  And in the knarled heart of stubborn oaks.
So they might live for ever in the light
Of her sweet presence – each a satellite.

XXIII

'This may not be', the wizard maid replied;
  'The fountains where the Naiades bedew
'Their shining hair, at length are drained and dried;
  'The solid oaks forget their strength, and strew
'Their latest leaf upon the mountains wide;
  'The boundless ocean like a drop of dew
'Will be consumed – the stubborn centre must
'Be scattered, like a cloud of summer dust.

XXIV

'And ye with them will perish, one by one; –
  'If I must sigh to think that this shall be,
'If I must weep when the surviving Sun
  'Shall smile on your decay – Oh, ask not me
'To love you till your little race is run;
  'I cannot die as ye must – over me
'Your leaves shall glance – the streams in which ye dwell
'Shall be my paths henceforth, and so – farewell!'

XXV

She spoke and wept: – the dark and azure well
  Sparkled beneath the shower of her bright tears,
And every little circlet where they fell
  Flung to the cavern-roof inconstant spheres
And intertangled lines of light: – a knell
  Of sobbing voices came upon her ears
From those departing Forms, o'er the serene
Of the white streams and of the forest green.

XXVI

All day the wizard lady sate aloof,
  Spelling out scrolls of dread antiquity,
Under the cavern's fountain-lighted roof;
  Or broidering the pictured poesy
Of some high tale upon her growing woof,
  Which the sweet splendour of her smiles could dye
In hues outshining Heaven – and ever she
Added some grace to the wrought poesy.

XXVII

While on her hearth lay blazing many a piece
  Of sandal wood, rare gums and cinnamon;
Men scarcely know how beautiful fire is –
  Each flame of it is as a precious stone
Dissolved in ever-moving light, and this
  Belongs to each and all who gaze upon.
The Witch beheld it not, for in her hand
She held a woof that dimmed the burning brand.

XXVIII

This lady never slept, but lay in trance
  All night within the fountain – as in sleep.
Its emerald crags glowed in her beauty's glance;
  Through the green splendour of the water deep
She saw the constellations reel and dance
  Like fire-flies – and withal did ever keep
The tenour of her contemplations calm,
With open eyes, closed feet, and folded palm.

XXIX

And when the whirlwinds and the clouds descended
  From the white pinnacles of that cold hill,
She past at dewfall to a space extended,
  Where in a lawn of flowering asphodel
Amid a wood of pines and cedars blended,
  There yawned an inextinguishable well
Of crimson fire – full even to the brim,
And overflowing all the margin trim.

XXX

Within the which she lay when the fierce war
  Of wintry winds shook that innocuous liquor
In many a mimic moon and bearded star
  O'er woods and lawns; – the serpent heard it flicker
In sleep, and dreaming still, he crept afar –
  And when the windless snow descended thicker
Than autumn leaves, she watched it as it came
Melt on the surface of the level flame.

XXXI

She had a Boat, which some say Vulcan wrought
  For Venus, as the chariot of her star;
But it was found too feeble to be fraught
  With all the ardours in that sphere which are,
And so she sold it, and Apollo bought
  And gave it to this daughter: from a car
Changed to the fairest and the lightest boat
Which ever upon mortal stream did float.

XXXII

And others say, that, when but three hours old,
  The first-born Love out of his cradle leapt,
And clove dun Chaos with his wings of gold,
  And like an horticultural adept,
Stole a strange seed, and wrapt it up in mould,
  And sowed it in his mother's star, and kept
Watering it all the summer with sweet dew,
And with his wings fanning it as it grew.

XXXIII

The plant grew strong and green, the snowy flower
  Fell, and the long and gourd-like fruit began
To turn the light and dew by inward power
  To its own substance; woven tracery ran
Of light firm texture, ribbed and branching, o'er
  The solid rind, like a leaf's veined fan –
Of which Love scooped this boat – and with soft motion
Piloted it round the circumfluous ocean.

XXXIV

This boat she moored upon her fount, and lit
  A living spirit within all its frame,
Breathing the soul of swiftness into it.
  Couched on the fountain like a panther tame,
One of the twain at Evan's feet that sit –
  Or as on Vesta's sceptre a swift flame –
Or on blind Homer's heart a winged thought, –
In joyous expectation lay the boat.

XXXV

Then by strange art she kneaded fire and snow
  Together, tempering the repugnant mass
With liquid love – all things together grow
  Through which the harmony of love can pass;
And a fair Shape out of her hands did flow –
  A living Image, which did far surpass
In beauty that bright shape of vital stone
Which drew the heart out of Pygmalion.

XXXVI

A sexless thing it was, and in its growth
  It seemed to have developed no defect
Of either sex, yet all the grace of both, –
  In gentleness and strength its limbs were decked;
The bosom swelled lightly with its full youth,
  The countenance was such as might select
Some artist that his skill should never die,
Imaging forth such perfect purity.

XXXVII

From its smooth shoulders hung two rapid wings,
  Fit to have borne it to the seventh sphere,
Tipped with the speed of liquid lightenings,
  Dyed in the ardours of the atmosphere:
She led her creature to the boiling springs
  Where the light boat was moored, and said: 'Sit here!'
And pointed to the prow, and took her seat
Beside the rudder, with opposing feet.

XXXVIII

And down the streams which clove those mountains vast,
  Around their inland islets, and amid
The panther-peopled forests, whose shade cast
  Darkness and odours, and a pleasure hid
In melancholy gloom, the pinnace past;
  By many a star-surrounded pyramid
Of icy crag cleaving the purple sky,
And caverns yawning round unfathomably.

XXXIX

The silver noon into that winding dell,
  With slanted gleam athwart the forest tops,
Tempered like golden evening, feebly fell;
  A green and glowing light, like that which drops
From folded lilies in which glow-worms dwell,
  When earth over her face night's mantle wraps;
Between the severed mountains lay on high
Over the stream, a narrow rift of sky.

XL

And ever as she went, the Image lay
  With folded wings and unawakened eyes;
And o'er its gentle countenance did play
  The busy dreams, as thick as summer flies,
Chasing the rapid smiles that would not stay,
  And drinking the warm tears, and the sweet sighs
Inhaling, which, with busy murmur vain,
They had aroused from the full heart and brain.

XLI

And ever down the prone vale, like a cloud
  Upon a stream of wind, the pinnace went:
Now lingering on the pools, in which abode
  The calm and darkness of the deep content
In which they paused; now o'er the shallow road
  Of white and dancing waters, all besprent
With sand and polished pebbles: – mortal boat
In such a shallow rapid could not float.

XLII

And down the earthquaking cataracts which shiver
  Their snow-like waters into golden air,
Or under chasms unfathomable ever
  Sepulchre them, till in their rage they tear
A subterranean portal for the river,
  It fled – the circling sunbows did upbear
Its fall down the hoar precipice of spray,
Lighting it far upon its lampless way.

XLIII

And when the wizard lady would ascend
  The labyrinths of some many-winding vale,
Which to the inmost mountain upward tend –
  She called 'Hermaphroditus!' – and the pale
And heavy hue which slumber could extend
  Over its lips and eyes, as on the gale
A rapid shadow from a slope of grass,
Into the darkness of the stream did pass.

XLIV

And it unfurled its heaven-coloured pinions,
  With stars of fire spotting the stream below;
And from above into the Sun's dominions
  Flinging a glory, like the golden glow
In which spring clothes her emerald-winged minions,
  All interwoven with fine feathery snow
And moonlight splendour of intensest rime,
With which frost paints the pines in winter time.

XLV

And then it winnowed the Elysian air
  Which ever hung about that lady bright,
With its aetherial vans – and speeding there,
  Like a star up the torrent of the night,
Or a swift eagle in the morning glare
  Breasting the whirlwind with impetuous flight,
The pinnace, oared by those enchanted wings,
Clove the fierce streams towards their upper springs.

XLVI

The water flashed like sunlight, by the prow
  Of a noon-wandering meteor flung to Heaven;
The still air seemed as if its waves did flow
  In tempest down the mountains; loosely driven
The lady's radiant hair streamed to and fro:
  Beneath, the billows having vainly striven
Indignant and impetuous, roared to feel
The swift and steady motion of the keel.

XLVII

Or, when the weary moon was in the wane,
  Or in the noon of interlunar night,
The lady-witch in visions could not chain
  Her spirit; but sailed forth under the light
Of shooting stars, and bade extend amain
  Its storm-outspeeding wings, the Hermaphrodite;
She to the Austral waters took her way,
Beyond the fabulous Thamondocana.

XLVIII

Where, like a meadow which no scythe has shaven,
  Which rain could never bend, or whirl-blast shake
With the Antarctic constellations paven,
  Canopus and his crew, lay the Austral lake –
There she would build herself a windless haven
  Out of the clouds whose moving turrets make
The bastions of the storm, when through the sky
The spirits of the tempest thundered by:

XLIX

A haven beneath whose translucent floor
  The tremulous stars sparkled unfathomably,
And around which the solid vapours hoar,
  Based on the level waters, to the sky
Lifted their dreadful crags, and like a shore
  Of wintry mountains, inaccessibly
Hemmed in with rifts and precipices grey,
And hanging crags, many a cove and bay.

L

And whilst the outer lake beneath the lash
  Of the wind's scourge, foamed like a wounded thing;
And the incessant hail with stony clash
  Ploughed up the waters, and the flagging wing
Of the roused cormorant in the lightning flash
  Looked like the wreck of some wind-wandering
Fragment of inky thunder-smoke – this haven
Was as a gem to copy Heaven engraven.

LI

On which that lady played her many pranks,
  Circling the image of a shooting star,
Even as a tiger on Hydaspes' banks
  Outspeeds the antelopes which speediest are,
In her light boat; and many quips and cranks
  She played upon the water, till the car
Of the late moon, like a sick matron wan,
To journey from the misty east began.

LII

And then she called out of the hollow turrets
  Of those high clouds, white, golden and vermilion,
The armies of her ministering spirits –
  In mighty legions, million after million.
They came, each troop emblazoning its merits
  On meteor flags; and many a proud pavilion
Of the intertexture of the atmosphere
They pitched upon the plain of the calm mere.

LIII

They framed the imperial tent of their great Queen
  Of woven exhalations, underlaid
With lambent lightning-fire, as may be seen
  A dome of thin and open ivory inlaid
With crimson silk – cressets from the serene
  Hung there, and on the water for her tread
A tapestry of fleece-like mist was strewn,
Dyed in the beams of the ascending moon.

LIV

And on a throne o'erlaid with starlight, caught
  Upon those wandering isles of aëry dew,
Which highest shoals of mountain shipwreck not,
  She sate, and heard all that had happened new
Between the earth and moon, since they had brought
  The last intelligence – and now she grew
Pale as that moon, lost in the watery night –
And now she wept, and now she laughed outright.

LV

These were tame pleasures; she would often climb
  The steepest ladder of the crudded rack
Up to some beaked cape of cloud sublime,
  And like Arion on the dolphin's back
Ride singing through the shoreless air; – oft time
  Following the serpent lightning's winding track,
She ran upon the platforms of the wind,
And laughed to hear the fire-balls roar behind.

LVI

And sometimes to those streams of upper air
  Which whirl the earth in its diurnal round,
She would ascend, and win the spirits there
  To let her join their chorus. Mortals found
That on those days the sky was calm and fair,
  And mystic snatches of harmonious sound
Wandered upon the earth where'er she past,
And happy thoughts of hope, too sweet to last.

LVII

But her choice sport was, in the hours of sleep,
  To glide adown old Nilus, where he threads
Egypt and Aethiopia, from the steep
  Of utmost Axumè, until he spreads,
Like a calm flock of silver-fleeced sheep,
  His waters on the plain: and crested heads
Of cities and proud temples gleam amid,
And many a vapour-belted pyramid.

LVIII

By Moeris and the Mareotid lakes,
  Strewn with faint blooms like bridal chamber floors.
Where naked boys bridling tame water-snakes,
  Or charioteering ghastly alligators,
Had left on the sweet waters mighty wakes
  Of those huge forms – within the brazen doors
Of the great Labyrinth slept both boy and beast,
Tired with the pomp of their Osirian feast.

LIX

And where within the surface of the river
  The shadows of the massy temples lie,
And never are erased – but tremble ever
  Like things which every cloud can doom to die,
Through lotus-pav'n canals, and wheresoever
  The works of man pierced that serenest sky
With tombs, and towers, and fanes, 'twas her delight
To wander in the shadow of the night.

LX

With motion like the spirit of that wind
  Whose soft step deepens slumber, her light feet
Past through the peopled haunts of human kind,
  Scattering sweet visions from her presence sweet,
Through fane, and palace-court, and labyrinth mined
  With many a dark and subterranean street
Under the Nile, through chambers high and deep
She past, observing mortals in their sleep.

LXI

A pleasure sweet doubtless it was to see
  Mortals subdued in all the shapes of sleep.
Here lay two sister twins in infancy;
  There, a lone youth who in his dreams did weep;
Within, two lovers linked innocently
  In their loose locks which over both did creep
Like ivy from one stem; – and there lay calm
Old age with snow-bright hair and folded palm.

LXII

But other troubled forms of sleep she saw,
  Not to be mirrored in a holy song –
Distortions foul of supernatural awe,
  And pale imaginings of visioned wrong;
And all the code of custom's lawless law
  Written upon the brows of old and young:
'This', said the wizard maiden, 'is the strife
Which stirs the liquid surface of man's life.'

LXIII

And little did the sight disturb her soul. –
  We, the weak mariners of that wide lake
Where'er its shores extend or billows roll,
  Our course unpiloted and starless make
O'er its wild surface to an unknown goal: –
  But she in the calm depths her way could take,
Where in bright bowers immortal forms abide
Beneath the weltering of the restless tide.

LXIV

And she saw princes couched under the glow
  Of sunlike gems; and round each temple-court
In dormitories ranged, row after row,
  She saw the priests asleep – all of one sort –
For all were educated to be so. –
  The peasants in their huts, and in the port
The sailors she saw cradled on the waves,
And the dead lulled within their dreamless graves.

LXV

And all the forms in which those spirits lay
  Were in her sight like the diaphanous
Veils, in which those sweet ladies oft array
  Their delicate limbs, who would conceal from us
Only their scorn of all concealment: they
  Move in the light of their own beauty thus.
But these and all now lay with sleep upon them,
And little thought a Witch was looking on them.

LXVI

She, all those human figures breathing there,
  Beheld as living spirits – to her eyes
The naked beauty of the soul lay bare,
  And often through a rude and worn disguise
She saw the inner form most bright and fair –
  And then she had a charm of strange device,
Which, murmured on mute lips with tender tone,
Could make that spirit mingle with her own.

LXVII

Alas! Aurora, what wouldst thou have given
  For such a charm when Tithon became grey?
Or how much, Venus, of thy silver Heaven
  Wouldst thou have yielded, ere Proserpina
Had half (oh! why not all?) the debt forgiven
  Which dear Adonis had been doomed to pay,
To any witch who would have taught you it?
The Heliad doth not know its value yet.

LXVIII

'Tis said in after times her spirit free
  Knew what love was, and felt itself alone –
But holy Dian could not chaster be
  Before she stooped to kiss Endymion,
Than now this lady – like a sexless bee
  Tasting all blossoms, and confined to none,
Among those mortal forms, the wizard-maiden
Past with an eye serene and heart unladen.

LXIX

To those she saw most beautiful, she gave
  Strange panacea in a crystal bowl: –
They drank in their deep sleep of that sweet wave,
  And lived thenceforward as if some controul,
Mightier than life, were in them; and the grave
  Of such, when death oppressed the weary soul,
Was as a green and overarching bower
Lit by the gems of many a starry flower.

LXX

For on the night that they were buried, she
  Restored the embalmers' ruining, and shook
The light out of the funeral lamps, to be
  A mimic day within that deathy nook;
And she unwound the woven imagery
  Of second childhood's swaddling bands, and took
The coffin, its last cradle, from its niche,
And threw it with contempt into a ditch.

LXXI

And there the body lay, age after age,
  Mute, breathing, beating, warm, and undecaying,
Like one asleep in a green hermitage,
  With gentle smiles about its eyelids playing,
And living in its dreams beyond the rage
  Of death or life; while they were still arraying
In liveries ever new, the rapid, blind
And fleeting generations of mankind.

LXXII

And she would write strange dreams upon the brain
  Of those who were less beautiful, and make
All harsh and crooked purposes more vain
  Than in the desart is the serpent's wake
Which the sand covers, – all his evil gain
  The miser in such dreams would rise and shake
Into a beggar's lap; – the lying scribe
Would his own lies betray without a bribe.

LXXIII

The priests would write an explanation full,
  Translating hieroglyphics into Greek,
How the God Apis really was a bull,
  And nothing more; and bid the herald stick
The same against the temple doors, and pull
  The old cant down; they licensed all to speak
Whate'er they thought of hawks, and cats, and geese,
By pastoral letters to each diocese.

LXXIV

The king would dress an ape up in his crown
  And robes, and seat him on his glorious seat,
And on the right hand of the sunlike throne
  Would place a gaudy mock-bird to repeat
The chatterings of the monkey. – Every one
  Of the prone courtiers crawled to kiss the feet
Of their great Emperor, when the morning came,
And kissed – alas, how many kiss the same!

LXXV

The soldiers dreamed that they were blacksmiths, and
  Walked out of quarters in somnambulism;
Round the red anvils you might see them stand
  Like Cyclopses in Vulcan's sooty abysm,
Beating their swords to ploughshares; – in a band
  The gaolers sent those of the liberal schism
Free through the streets of Memphis, much, I wis
To the annoyance of king Amasis.

LXXVI

And timid lovers who had been so coy,
  They hardly knew whether they loved or not,
Would rise out of their rest, and take sweet joy,
  To the fulfilment of their inmost thought;
And when next day the maiden and the boy
  Met one another, both, like sinners caught,
Blushed at the thing which each believed was done
Only in fancy – till the tenth moon shone;

LXXVII

And then the Witch would let them take no ill:
  Of many thousand schemes which lovers find,
The Witch found one, – and so they took their fill
  Of happiness in marriage warm and kind.
Friends who, by practice of some envious skill,
  Were torn apart, a wide wound, mind from mind!
She did unite again with visions clear
Of deep affection and of truth sincere.

LXXVIII

These were the pranks she played among the cities
  Of mortal men, and what she did to sprites
And Gods, entangling them in her sweet ditties
  To do her will, and show their subtle sleights,
I will declare another time; for it is
  A tale more fit for the weird winter nights
Than for these garish summer days, when we
Scarcely believe much more than we can see.

Arethusa

I

Arethusa arose
From her couch of snows
In the Acroceraunian mountains, –
From cloud and from crag,
With many a jag,
Shepherding her bright fountains.
She leapt down the rocks,
With her rainbow locks
Streaming among the streams; –
Her steps paved with green
The downward ravine
Which slopes to the western gleams;
And gliding and springing
She went, ever singing,
In murmurs as soft as sleep;
The Earth seemed to love her,
And Heaven smiled above her,
As she lingered towards the deep.

II

Then Alpheus bold,
On his glacier cold,
With his trident the mountains strook;
And opened a chasm
In the rocks – with the spasm
All Erymanthus shook.
And the black south wind
It unsealed behind

The urns of the silent snow,
    And earthquake and thunder
    Did rend in sunder
The bars of the springs below.
    And the beard and the hair
    Of the River-god were
Seen through the torrent's sweep,
    As he followed the light
    Of the fleet nymph's flight
To the brink of the Dorian deep.

III

    'Oh, save me! Oh, guide me!
    And bid the deep hide me,
For he grasps me now by the hair!'
    The loud Ocean heard,
    To its blue depth stirred,
And divided at her prayer;
    And under the water
    The Earth's white daughter
Fled like a sunny beam;
    Behind her descended
    Her billows, unblended
With the brackish Dorian stream: –
    Like a gloomy stain
    On the emerald main
Alpheus rushed behind, –
    As an eagle pursuing
    A dove to its ruin
Down the streams of the cloudy wind.

IV

Under the bowers
Where the Ocean Powers
Sit on their pearlèd thrones;
Through the coral woods
Of the weltering floods,
Over heaps of unvalued stones;
Through the dim beams
Which amid the streams
Weave a network of coloured light;
And under the caves,
Where the shadowy waves
Are as green as the forest's night: –
Outspeeding the shark,
And the sword-fish dark,
Under the Ocean's foam,
And up through the rifts
Of the mountain clifts
They passed to their Dorian home.

V

And now from their fountains
In Enna's mountains,
Down one vale where the morning basks,
Like friends once parted
Grown single-hearted,
They ply their watery tasks.
At sunrise they leap
From their cradles steep
In the cave of the shelving hill;
At noontide they flow
Through the woods below

And the meadows of asphodel;
    And at night they sleep
    In the rocking deep
Beneath the Ortygian shore; –
    Like spirits that lie
    In the azure sky
When they love but live no more.

The Question

I

I dreamed that, as I wandered by the way,
  Bare winter suddenly was changed to spring,
And gentle odours led my steps astray,
  Mixed with a sound of waters murmuring
Along a shelving bank of turf, which lay
  Under a copse, and hardly dared to fling
Its green arms round the bosom of the stream,
But kissed it and then fled, as thou mightest in dream.

II

There grew pied wind-flowers and violets,
  Daisies, those pearled Arcturi of the earth,
The constellated flower that never sets;
  Faint oxlips; tender bluebells, at whose birth
The sod scarce heaved; and that tall flower that wets –
  Like a child, half in tenderness and mirth –
Its mother's face with Heaven's collected tears,
When the low wind, its playmate's voice, it hears.

III

And in the warm hedge grew lush eglantine,
  Green cowbind and the moonlight-coloured May,
And cherry-blossoms, and white cups, whose wine
  Was the bright dew yet drained not by the day;
And wild roses, and ivy serpentine,
  With its dark buds and leaves, wandering astray;
And flowers azure, black, and streaked with gold,
Fairer than any wakened eyes behold.

IV

And nearer to the river's trembling edge
  There grew broad flag-flowers, purple prankt with white,
And starry river buds among the sedge,
  And floating water-lilies, broad and bright,
Which lit the oak that overhung the hedge
  With moonlight beams of their own watery light;
And bulrushes, and reeds of such deep green
As soothed the dazzled eye with sober sheen.

V

Methought that of these visionary flowers
  I made a nosegay, bound in such a way
That the same hues, which in their natural bowers
  Were mingled or opposed, the like array
Kept these imprisoned children of the Hours
  Within my hand, – and then, elate and gay,
I hastened to the spot whence I had come,
That I might there present it! – Oh! to whom?

Epipsychidion

Verses Addressed to the Noble and Unfortunate Lady Emilia V—

NOW IMPRISONED IN THE CONVENT OF —

L'anima amante si slancia fuori del creato, e si crea nel infinito un Mondo tutto per essa, diverso assai da questo oscuro e pauroso baratro.*

Her own words

My Song, I fear that thou wilt find but few
Who fitly shall conceive thy reasoning,
Of such hard matter dost thou entertain;
Whence, if by misadventure, chance should bring
Thee to base company, (as chance may do)
Quite unaware of what thou dost contain,
I prithee, comfort thy sweet self again,
My last delight! tell them that they are dull,
And bid them own that thou art beautiful.

Advertisement

The writer of the following lines died at Florence, as he was preparing for a voyage to one of the wildest of the Sporades, which he had bought, and where he had fitted up the ruins of an old building, and where it was his hope to have realised a scheme of life, suited perhaps to that happier and better world of which he is now an inhabitant, but hardly practicable in this. His life was singular; less on account of the

*'The loving soul throws herself outside creation, and creates in the infinite a world all for herself, very different from this dark and fearful abyss.'

romantic vicissitudes which diversified it, than the ideal tinge which it received from his own character and feelings. The present Poem, like the Vita Nuova of Dante, is sufficiently intelligible to a certain class of readers without a matter-of-fact history of the circumstances to which it relates; and to a certain other class it must ever remain incomprehensible, from a defect of a common organ of perception for the ideas of which it treats. Not but that, *gran vergogna sarebbe a colui, che rimasse cosa sotto veste di figura, o di colore rettorico: e domandato non sapesse denudare le sue parole da cotal veste, in guisa che avessero verace intendimento.**

The present poem appears to have been intended by the Writer as the dedication to some longer one. The stanza on the opposite page is almost a literal translation from Dante's famous Canzone

Voi, ch' intendendo, il terzo ciel movete, &c.

The presumptuous application of the concluding lines to his own composition will raise a smile at the expense of my unfortunate friend: be it a smile not of contempt, but pity.

Sweet Spirit! Sister of that orphan one,
Whose empire is the name thou weepest on,
In my heart's temple I suspend to thee
These votive wreaths of withered memory.

Poor captive bird! who, from thy narrow cage,
Pourest such music, that it might assuage
The rugged hearts of those who prisoned thee,
Were they not deaf to all sweet melody;

*Not but that it would be extremely shameful if someone who had written [literally rhymed] under cover of a figure or of a rhetorical colour could not, when asked, strip his words bare of that colour so that they should have real meaning.

This song shall be thy rose: its petals pale
Are dead, indeed, my adored Nightingale!
But soft and fragrant is the faded blossom,
And it has no thorn left to wound thy bosom.

High, spirit-winged Heart! who dost for ever
Beat thine unfeeling bars with vain endeavour,
'Till those bright plumes of thought, in which arrayed
It over-soared this low and worldly shade,
Lie shattered; and thy panting, wounded breast
Stains with dear blood its unmaternal nest!
I weep vain tears; blood would less bitter be,
Yet poured forth gladlier, could it profit thee.

Seraph of Heaven! too gentle to be human,
Veiling beneath that radiant form of Woman
All that is insupportable in thee
Of light, and love, and immortality!
Sweet Benediction in the eternal Curse!
Veiled Glory of this lampless Universe!
Thou Moon beyond the clouds! Thou living Form
Among the Dead! Thou Star above the Storm!
Thou Wonder, and thou Beauty, and thou Terror!
Thou Harmony of Nature's art! Thou Mirror
In whom, as in the splendour of the Sun,
All shapes look glorious which thou gazest on!
Ay, even the dim words which obscure thee now
Flash, lightning-like, with unaccustomed glow;
I pray thee that thou blot from this sad song
All of its much mortality and wrong,
With those clear drops, which start like sacred dew
From the twin lights thy sweet soul darkens through,
Weeping, till sorrow becomes ecstasy:
Then smile on it, so that it may not die.

I never thought before my death to see
Youth's vision thus made perfect. Emily,
I love thee; though the world by no thin name
Will hide that love, from its unvalued shame.
Would we two had been twins of the same mother!
Or, that the name my heart lent to another
Could be a sister's bond for her and thee,
Blending two beams of one eternity!
Yet were one lawful and the other true,
These names, though dear, could paint not, as is due,
How beyond refuge I am thine. Ah me!
I am not thine: I am a part of *thee*.

Sweet Lamp! my moth-like Muse has burned its wings;
Or, like a dying swan who soars and sings,
Young Love should teach Time, in his own grey style,
All that thou art. Art thou not void of guile,
A lovely soul formed to be blest and bless?
A well of sealed and secret happiness,
Whose waters like blithe light and music are,
Vanquishing dissonance and gloom? A Star
Which moves not in the moving Heavens, alone?
A smile amid dark frowns? a gentle tone
Amid rude voices? a beloved light?
A Solitude, a Refuge, a Delight?
A Lute, which those whom love has taught to play
Make music on, to soothe the roughest day
And lull fond grief asleep? a buried treasure?
A cradle of young thoughts of wingless pleasure;
A violet-shrouded grave of Woe? – I measure
The world of fancies, seeking one like thee,
And find – alas! mine own infirmity.

She met me, Stranger, upon life's rough way,
And lured me towards sweet Death; as Night by Day,

Winter by Spring, or Sorrow by swift Hope,
Led into light, life, peace. An antelope,
In the suspended impulse of its lightness,
Were less ethereally light: the brightness
Of her divinest presence trembles through
Her limbs, as underneath a cloud of dew
Embodied in the windless Heaven of June
Amid the splendour-winged stars, the Moon
Burns, inextinguishably beautiful:
And from her lips, as from a hyacinth full
Of honey-dew, a liquid murmur drops,
Killing the sense with passion; sweet as stops
Of planetary music heard in trance.
In her mild lights the starry spirits dance,
The sun-beams of those wells which ever leap
Under the lightnings of the soul – too deep
For the brief fathom-line of thought or sense.
The glory of her being, issuing thence,
Stains the dead, blank, cold air with a warm shade
Of unentangled intermixture, made
By Love, of light and motion: one intense
Diffusion, one serene Omnipresence,
Whose flowing outlines mingle in their flowing.
Around her cheeks and utmost fingers glowing
With the unintermitted blood, which there
Quivers, (as in a fleece of snow-like air
The crimson pulse of living morning quiver,)
Continuously prolonged, and ending never,
Till they are lost, and in that Beauty furled
Which penetrates and clasps and fills the world;
Scarce visible from extreme loveliness.
Warm fragrance seems to fall from her light dress,
And her loose hair; and where some heavy tress
The air of her own speed has disentwined,

The sweetness seems to satiate the faint wind;
And in the soul a wild odour is felt,
Beyond the sense, like fiery dews that melt
Into the bosom of a frozen bud. –
See where she stands! a mortal shape indued
With love and life and light and deity,
And motion which may change but cannot die;
An image of some bright Eternity;
A shadow of some golden dream; a Splendour
Leaving the third sphere pilotless; a tender
Reflection of the eternal Moon of Love
Under whose motions life's dull billows move;
A Metaphor of Spring and Youth and Morning;
A Vision like incarnate April, warning,
With smiles and tears, Frost the Anatomy
Into his summer grave.
Ah, woe is me!
What have I dared? where am I lifted? how
Shall I descend, and perish not? I know
That Love makes all things equal: I have heard
By mine own heart this joyous truth averred:
The spirit of the worm beneath the sod
In love and worship, blends itself with God.

Spouse! Sister! Angel! Pilot of the Fate
Whose course has been so starless! O too late
Beloved! O too soon adored, by me!
For in the fields of immortality
My spirit should at first have worshipped thine,
A divine presence in a place divine;
Or should have moved beside it on this earth,
A shadow of that substance, from its birth;
But not as now: – I love thee; yes, I feel
That on the fountain of my heart a seal

Is set, to keep its waters pure and bright
For thee, since in those *tears* thou hast delight.
We – are we not formed, as notes of music are,
For one another, though dissimilar;
Such difference without discord, as can make
Those sweetest sounds, in which all spirits shake
As trembling leaves in a continuous air?

Thy wisdom speaks in me, and bids me dare
Beacon the rocks on which high hearts are wreckt.
I never was attached to that great sect,
Whose doctrine is, that each one should select
Out of the crowd a mistress or a friend,
And all the rest, though fair and wise, commend
To cold oblivion, though it is in the code
Of modern morals, and the beaten road
Which those poor slaves with weary footsteps tread,
Who travel to their home among the dead
By the broad highway of the world, and so
With one chained friend, perhaps a jealous foe,
The dreariest and the longest journey go.

True Love in this differs from gold and clay,
That to divide is not to take away.
Love is like understanding, that grows bright,
Gazing on many truths; 'tis like thy light,
Imagination! which from earth and sky,
And from the depths of human phantasy,
As from a thousand prisms and mirrors, fills
The Universe with glorious beams, and kills
Error, the worm, with many a sun-like arrow
Of its reverberated lightning. Narrow
The heart that loves, the brain that contemplates,
The life that wears, the spirit that creates

One object, and one form, and builds thereby
A sepulchre for its eternity.

Mind from its object differs most in this:
Evil from good; misery from happiness;
The baser from the nobler; the impure
And frail, from what is clear and must endure.
If you divide suffering and dross, you may
Diminish till it is consumed away;
If you divide pleasure and love and thought,
Each part exceeds the whole; and we know not
How much, while any yet remains unshared,
Of pleasure may be gained, of sorrow spared:
This truth is that deep well, whence sages draw
The unenvied light of hope; the eternal law
By which those live, to whom this world of life
Is as a garden ravaged, and whose strife
Tills for the promise of a later birth
The wilderness of this Elysian earth.

There was a Being whom my spirit oft
Met on its visioned wanderings, far aloft,
In the clear golden prime of my youth's dawn,
Upon the fairy isles of sunny lawn,
Amid the enchanted mountains, and the caves
Of divine sleep, and on the air-like waves
Of wonder-level dream, whose tremulous floor
Paved her light steps; – on an imagined shore,
Under the grey beak of some promontory
She met me, robed in such exceeding glory,
That I beheld her not. In solitudes
Her voice came to me through the whispering woods,
And from the fountains, and the odours deep
Of flowers, which, like lips murmuring in their sleep

Of the sweet kisses which had lulled them there,
Breathed but of *her* to the enamoured air;
And from the breezes whether low or loud,
And from the rain of every passing cloud,
And from the singing of the summer-birds,
And from all sounds, all silence. In the words
Of antique verse and high romance, – in form
Sound, colour – in whatever checks that Storm
Which with the shattered present chokes the past;
And in that best philosophy, whose taste
Makes this cold common hell, our life, a doom
As glorious as a fiery martyrdom;
Her Spirit was the harmony of truth. –

Then, from the caverns of my dreamy youth
I sprang, as one sandalled with plumes of fire,
And towards the loadstar of my one desire,
I flitted, like a dizzy moth, whose flight
Is as a dead leaf's in the owlet light,
When it would seek in Hesper's setting sphere
A radiant death, a fiery sepulchre,
As if it were a lamp of earthly flame. –
But She, whom prayers or tears then could not tame,
Passed, like a God throned on a winged planet,
Whose burning plumes to tenfold swiftness fan it,
Into the dreary cone of our life's shade;
And as a man with mighty loss dismayed,
I would have followed, though the grave between
Yawned like a gulf whose spectres are unseen:
When a voice said: – 'O thou of hearts the weakest,
'The phantom is beside thee whom thou seekest.'
Then I – 'where?' the world's echo answered 'where!'
And in that silence, and in my despair,
I questioned every tongueless wind that flew

Over my tower of mourning, if it knew
Whither 'twas fled, this soul out of my soul;
And murmured names and spells which have controul
Over the sightless tyrants of our fate;
But neither prayer nor verse could dissipate
The night which closed on her; nor uncreate
That world within this Chaos, mine and me,
Of which she was the veiled Divinity,
The world I say of thoughts that worshipped her:
And therefore I went forth, with hope and fear
And every gentle passion sick to death,
Feeding my course with expectation's breath,
Into the wintry forest of our life;
And struggling through its error with vain strife,
And stumbling in my weakness and my haste,
And half bewildered by new forms, I past
Seeking among those untaught foresters
If I could find one form resembling hers,
In which she might have masked herself from me.
There, – One, whose voice was venomed melody
Sate by a well, under blue night-shade bowers;
The breath of her false mouth was like faint flowers,
Her touch was as electric poison, – flame
Out of her looks into my vitals came,
And from her living cheeks and bosom flew
A killing air, which pierced like honey-dew
Into the core of my green heart, and lay
Upon its leaves; until, as hair grown grey
O'er a young brow, they hid its unblown prime
With ruins of unseasonable time.

In many mortal forms I rashly sought
The shadow of that idol of my thought.
And some were fair – but beauty dies away:

Others were wise – but honeyed words betray:
And One was true – oh! why not true to me?
Then, as a hunted deer that could not flee,
I turned upon my thoughts, and stood at bay,
Wounded and weak and panting; the cold day
Trembled, for pity of my strife and pain.
When, like a noon-day dawn, there shone again
Deliverance. One stood on my path who seemed
As like the glorious shape which I had dreamed,
As is the Moon, whose changes ever run
Into themselves, to the eternal Sun;
The cold chaste Moon, the Queen of Heaven's bright
 isles,
Who makes all beautiful on which she smiles.
That wandering shrine of soft yet icy flame
Which ever is transformed, yet still the same,
And warms not but illumines. Young and fair
As the descended Spirit of that sphere,
She hid me, as the Moon may hide the night
From its own darkness, until all was bright
Between the Heaven and Earth of my calm mind,
And, as a cloud charioted by the wind,
She led me to a cave in that wild place,
And sate beside me, with her downward face
Illumining my slumbers, like the Moon
Waxing and waning o'er Endymion.
And I was laid asleep, spirit and limb,
And all my being became bright or dim
As the Moon's image in a summer sea,
According as she smiled or frowned on me;
And there I lay, within a chaste cold bed:
Alas, I then was nor alive nor dead: –
For at her silver voice came Death and Life,
Unmindful each of their accustomed strife,

Masked like twin babes, a sister and a brother,
The wandering hopes of one abandoned mother,
And through the cavern without wings they flew,
And cried 'Away, he is not of our crew.'
I wept, and though it be a dream, I weep.

What storms then shook the ocean of my sleep,
Blotting that Moon, whose pale and waning lips
Then shrank as in the sickness of eclipse; –
And how my soul was as a lampless sea,
And who was then its Tempest; and when She,
The Planet of that hour was quenched, what frost
Crept o'er those waters, 'till from coast to coast
The moving billows of my being fell
Into a death of ice, immoveable; –
And then – what earthquakes made it gape and split,
The white Moon smiling all the while on it,
These words conceal: – If not, each word would be
The key of staunchless tears. Weep not for me!

At length, into the obscure Forest came
The Vision I had sought through grief and shame.
Athwart that wintry wilderness of thorns
Flashed from her motion splendour like the Morn's,
And from her presence life was radiated
Through the grey earth and branches bare and dead;
So that her way was paved, and roofed above
With flowers as soft as thoughts of budding love;
And music from her respiration spread
Like light, – all other sounds were penetrated
By the small, still, sweet spirit of that sound,
So that the savage winds hung mute around;
And odours warm and fresh fell from her hair
Dissolving the dull cold in the frore air:

Soft as an Incarnation of the Sun,
When light is changed to love, this glorious One
Floated into the cavern where I lay,
And called my Spirit, and the dreaming clay
Was lifted by the thing that dreamed below
As smoke by fire, and in her beauty's glow
I stood, and felt the dawn of my long night
Was penetrating me with living light:
I knew it was the Vision veiled from me
So many years – that it was Emily.

Twin Spheres of light who rule this passive Earth,
This world of love, this *me*; and into birth
Awaken all its fruits and flowers, and dart
Magnetic might into its central heart;
And lift its billows and its mists, and guide
By everlasting laws, each wind and tide
To its fit cloud, and its appointed cave;
And lull its storms, each in the craggy grave
Which was its cradle, luring to faint bowers
The armies of the rain-bow-winged showers;
And, as those married lights, which from the towers
Of Heaven look forth and fold the wandering globe
In liquid sleep and splendour, as a robe;
And all their many-mingled influence blend,
If equal, yet unlike, to one sweet end; –
So ye, bright regents, with alternate sway
Govern my sphere of being, night and day!
Thou, not disdaining even a borrowed might;
Thou, not eclipsing a remoter light;
And, through the shadow of the seasons three,
From Spring to Autumn's sere maturity,
Light it into the Winter of the tomb,
Where it may ripen to a brighter bloom.

Thou too, O Comet beautiful and fierce,
Who drew the heart of this frail Universe
Towards thine own; till, wreckt in that convulsion,
Alternating attraction and repulsion,
Thine went astray and that was rent in twain;
Oh, float into our azure heaven again!
Be there love's folding-star at thy return;
The living Sun will feed thee from its urn
Of golden fire; the Moon will veil her horn
In thy last smiles; adoring Even and Morn
Will worship thee with incense of calm breath
And lights and shadows; as the star of Death
And Birth is worshipped by those sisters wild
Called Hope and Fear – upon the heart are piled
Their offerings, – of this sacrifice divine
A World shall be the altar.
Lady mine,
Scorn not these flowers of thought, the fading birth
Which from its heart of hearts that plant puts forth
Whose fruit, made perfect by thy sunny eyes,
Will be as of the trees of Paradise.

The day is come, and thou wilt fly with me.
To whatsoe'er of dull mortality
Is mine, remain a vestal sister still;
To the intense, the deep, the imperishable,
Not mine but me, henceforth be thou united
Even as a bride, delighting and delighted.
The hour is come: – the destined Star has risen
Which shall descend upon a vacant prison.
The walls are high, the gates are strong, thick set
The sentinels – but true love never yet
Was thus constrained: it overleaps all fence:
Like lightning, with invisible violence

Piercing its continents; like Heaven's free breath,
Which he who grasps can hold not; liker Death,
Who rides upon a thought, and makes his way
Through temple, tower, and palace, and the array
Of arms: more strength has Love than he or they;
For it can burst his charnel, and make free
The limbs in chains, the heart in agony,
The soul in dust and chaos.

Emily,

A ship is floating in the harbour now,
A wind is hovering o'er the mountain's brow;
There is a path on the sea's azure floor,
No keel has ever ploughed that path before;
The halcyons brood around the foamless isles;
The treacherous Ocean has forsworn its wiles;
The merry mariners are bold and free:
Say, my heart's sister, wilt thou sail with me?
Our bark is as an albatross, whose nest
Is a far Eden of the purple East;
And we between her wings will sit, while Night
And Day, and Storm, and Calm, pursue their flight,
Our ministers, along the boundless Sea,
Treading each other's heels, unheededly.
It is an isle under Ionian skies,
Beautiful as a wreck of Paradise,
And, for the harbours are not safe and good,
This land would have remained a solitude
But for some pastoral people native there,
Who from the Elysian, clear, and golden air
Draw the last spirit of the age of gold,
Simple and spirited; innocent and bold.
The blue Aegean girds this chosen home,
With ever-changing sound and light and foam,
Kissing the sifted sands, and caverns hoar;

And all the winds wandering along the shore
Undulate with the undulating tide:
There are thick woods where sylvan forms abide;
And many a fountain, rivulet, and pond,
As clear as elemental diamond,
Or serene morning air; and far beyond,
The mossy tracks made by the goats and deer
(Which the rough shepherd treads but once a year,)
Pierce into glades, caverns, and bowers, and halls
Built round with ivy, which the waterfalls
Illumining, with sound that never fails
Accompany the noon-day nightingales;
And all the place is peopled with sweet airs;
The light clear element which the isle wears
Is heavy with the scent of lemon-flowers,
Which floats like mist laden with unseen showers,
And falls upon the eye-lids like faint sleep;
And from the moss violets and jonquils peep,
And dart their arrowy odour through the brain
Till you might faint with that delicious pain.
And every motion, odour, beam, and tone,
With that deep music is in unison:
Which is a soul within the soul – they seem
Like echoes of an antenatal dream. –
It is an isle 'twixt Heaven, Air, Earth, and Sea,
Cradled, and hung in clear tranquillity;
Bright as that wandering Eden Lucifer,
Washed by the soft blue Oceans of young air.
It is a favoured place. Famine or Blight,
Pestilence, War and Earthquake, never light
Upon its mountain-peaks; blind vultures, they
Sail onward far upon their fatal way:
The winged storms, chaunting their thunder-psalm
To other lands, leave azure chasms of calm

Over this isle, or weep themselves in dew,
From which its fields and woods ever renew
Their green and golden immortality.
And from the sea there rise, and from the sky
There fall, clear exhalations, soft and bright.
Veil after veil, each hiding some delight,
Which Sun or Moon or zephyr draw aside,
Till the isle's beauty, like a naked bride
Glowing at once with love and loveliness,
Blushes and trembles at its own excess:
Yet, like a buried lamp, a Soul no less
Burns in the heart of this delicious isle,
An atom of th' Eternal, whose own smile
Unfolds itself, and may be felt not seen
O'er the grey rocks, blue waves, and forests green,
Filling their bare and void interstices. –
But the chief marvel of the wilderness
Is a lone dwelling, built by whom or how
None of the rustic island-people know:
'Tis not a tower of strength, though with its height
It overtops the woods; but, for delight,
Some wise and tender Ocean-King, ere crime
Had been invented, in the world's young prime,
Reared it, a wonder of that simple time,
An envy of the isles, a pleasure-house
Made sacred to his sister and his spouse.
It scarce seems now a wreck of human art,
But, as it were Titanic; in the heart
Of Earth having assumed its form, then grown
Out of the mountains, from the living stone,
Lifting itself in caverns light and high:
For all the antique and learned imagery
Has been erased, and in the place of it
The ivy and the wild-vine interknit

The volumes of their many twining stems;
Parasite flowers illume with dewy gems
The lampless halls, and when they fade, the sky
Peeps through their winter-woof of tracery
With Moon-light patches, or star atoms keen,
Or fragments of the day's intense serene; –
Working mosaic on their Parian floors.
And, day and night, aloof, from the high towers
And terraces, the Earth and Ocean seem
To sleep in one another's arms, and dream
Of waves, flowers, clouds, woods, rocks, and all that
    we
Read in their smiles, and call reality.

This isle and house are mine, and I have vowed
Thee to be lady of the solitude. –
And I have fitted up some chambers there
Looking towards the golden Eastern air,
And level with the living winds, which flow
Like waves above the living waves below. –
I have sent books and music there, and all
Those instruments with which high spirits call
The future from its cradle, and the past
Out of its grave, and make the present last
In thoughts and joys which sleep, but cannot die,
Folded within their own eternity.
Our simple life wants little, and true taste
Hires not the pale drudge Luxury, to waste
The scent it would adorn, and therefore still,
Nature with all her children, haunts the hill.
The ring-dove, in the embowering ivy, yet
Keeps up her love-lament, and the owls flit
Round the evening tower, and the young stars glance
Between the quick bats in their twilight dance;

The spotted deer bask in the fresh moon-light
Before our gate, and the slow, silent night
Is measured by the pants of their calm sleep.
Be this our home in life, and when years heap
Their withered hours, like leaves, on our decay,
Let us become the over-hanging day,
The living soul of this Elysian isle,
Conscious, inseparable, one. Meanwhile
We two will rise, and sit, and walk together,
Under the roof of blue Ionian weather,
And wander in the meadows, or ascend
The mossy mountains, where the blue heavens bend
With lightest winds, to touch their paramour;
Or linger, where the pebble-paven shore,
Under the quick, faint kisses of the sea
Trembles and sparkles as with ecstasy, –
Possessing and possest by all that is
Within that calm circumference of bliss,
And by each other, till to love and live
Be one: – or, at the noontide hour, arrive
Where some old cavern hoar seems yet to keep
The moonlight of the expired night asleep,
Through which the awakened day can never peep;
A veil for our seclusion, close as Night's,
Where secure sleep may kill thine innocent lights;
Sleep, the fresh dew of languid love, the rain
Whose drops quench kisses till they burn again.
And we will talk, until thought's melody
Become too sweet for utterance, and it die
In words, to live again in looks, which dart
With thrilling tone into the voiceless heart,
Harmonizing silence without a sound.
Our breath shall intermix, our bosoms bound,
And our veins beat together; and our lips

With other eloquence than words, eclipse
The soul that burns between them, and the wells
Which boil under our being's inmost cells,
The fountains of our deepest life, shall be
Confused in passion's golden purity,
As mountain-springs under the morning Sun.
We shall become the same, we shall be one
Spirit within two frames, oh! wherefore two?
One passion in twin-hearts, which grows and grew,
'Till like two meteors of expanding flame,
Those spheres instinct with it become the same,
Touch, mingle, are transfigured; ever still
Burning, yet ever inconsumable:
In one another's substance finding food,
Like flames too pure and light and unimbued
To nourish their bright lives with baser prey,
Which point to Heaven and cannot pass away:
One hope within two wills, one will beneath
Two overshadowing minds, one life, one death,
One Heaven, one Hell, one immortality,
And one annihilation. Woe is me!
The winged words on which my soul would pierce
Into the height of Love's rare Universe,
Are chains of lead around its flight of fire. –
I pant, I sink, I tremble, I expire!

Weak Verses, go, kneel at your Sovereign's feet,
And say: – 'We are the masters of thy slave;
'What wouldest thou with us and ours and thine?'
Then call your sisters from Oblivion's cave,
All singing loud: 'Love's very pain is sweet,
'But its reward is in the world divine
'Which, if not here, it builds beyond the grave.'
So shall ye live when I am there. Then haste

Over the hearts of men, until ye meet
Marina, Vanna, Primus, and the rest,
And bid them love each other and be blest:
And leave the troop which errs, and which reproves,
And come and be my guest, – for I am Love's.

Adonais

An Elegy on the Death of John Keats, Author of Endymion, Hyperion etc.

Ἀστὴρ πρὶν μὲν ἔλαμπες ἐνὶ ζωοῖσιν Ἑῷος·
*νῦν δὲ θανὼν λάμπεις Ἕσπερος ἐν φθιμένοις**
Plato

Preface

Φάρμακον ἦλθε, Βίων, ποτὶ σὸν στόμα, φάρμακον εἶδες.
πῶς τεν τοῖς χείλεσσι ποτέδραμε, κοὐκ ἐγλυκάνθη;
τίς δὲ βροτὸς τοσσοῦτον ἀνάμερος, ἢ κεράσαι τοι,
ἢ δοῦναι λαλέοντι τὸ φάρμακον; ἔκφυγεν ᾠδάν.†
Moschus, Epitaph. Bion.

It is my intention to subjoin to the London edition of this poem, a criticism upon the claims of its lamented object to be classed among the writers of the highest genius who have adorned our age. My known repugnance to the narrow principles of taste on which several of his earlier compositions were modelled, prove at least that I am an impartial judge. I consider the fragment of Hyperion, as second to nothing that was ever produced by a writer of the same years.

John Keats died at Rome of a consumption, in his twenty-fourth year, on the — of — 1821; and was buried in the romantic and lonely cemetery of the protestants in that city, under the pyramid which is the tomb of Cestius, and the massy walls and towers, now mouldering and desolate, which formed the circuit of ancient Rome. The cemetery is an open space among the ruins covered in winter with violets and

*'You shone before, the star of morn among the living; now in death you shine, the star of eve among the dead.'

†'Poison came, Bion, to your mouth, you ate poison – how could it come to such lips and not be sweetened? And what mortal man is there so savage as to mix it for you or give it to you at your call? And song went cold' (Moschus, 'Lament for Bion').

daisies. It might make one in love with death, to think that one should be buried in so sweet a place.

The genius of the lamented person to whose memory I have dedicated these unworthy verses, was not less delicate and fragile than it was beautiful; and where cankerworms abound, what wonder, if it's young flower was blighted in the bud? The savage criticism on his Endymion, which appeared in the Quarterly Review, produced the most violent effect on his susceptible mind; the agitation thus originated ended in the rupture of a blood-vessel in the lungs; a rapid consumption ensued, and the succeeding acknowledgments from more candid critics, of the true greatness of his powers, were ineffectual to heal the wound thus wantonly inflicted.

It may be well said, that these wretched men know not what they do. They scatter their insults and their slanders without heed as to whether the poisoned shaft lights on a heart made callous by many blows, or one, like Keats's composed of more penetrable stuff. One of their associates, is, to my knowledge, a most base and unprincipled calumniator. As to 'Endymion;' was it a poem, whatever might be it's defects, to be treated contemptuously by those who had celebrated with various degrees of complacency and panegyric, 'Paris,' and 'Woman,' and a 'Syrian Tale,' and Mrs Lefanu, and Mr Barrett, and Mr Howard Payne, and a long list of the illustrious obscure? Are these the men, who in their venal good nature, presumed to draw a parallel between the Rev. Mr Milman and Lord Byron? What gnat did they strain at here, after having swallowed all those camels? Against what woman taken in adultery, dares the foremost of these literary prostitutes to cast his opprobrious stone? Miserable man! you, one of the meanest, have wantonly defaced one of the noblest specimens of the workmanship of God. Nor shall it be your excuse, that, murderer as you are, you have spoken daggers, but used none.

The circumstances of the closing scene of poor Keats's life

were not made known to me until the Elegy was ready for the press. I am given to understand that the wound which his sensitive spirit had received from the criticism of Endymion, was exasperated by the bitter sense of unrequited benefits; the poor fellow seems to have been hooted from the stage of life, no less by those on whom he had wasted the promise of his genius, than those on whom he had lavished his fortune and his care. He was accompanied to Rome, and attended in his last illness by Mr Severn, a young artist of the highest promise, who, I have been informed 'almost risked his own life, and sacrificed every prospect to unwearied attendance upon his dying friend.' Had I known these circumstances before the completion of my poem, I should have been tempted to add my feeble tribute of applause to the more solid recompense which the virtuous man finds in the recollection of his own motives. Mr Severn can dispense with a reward from 'such stuff as dreams are made of.' His conduct is a golden augury of the success of his future career – may the unextinguished Spirit of his illustrious friend animate the creations of his pencil, and plead against Oblivion for his name!

Adonais

I

I weep for Adonais – he is dead!
O, weep for Adonais! though our tears
Thaw not the frost which binds so dear a head!
And thou, sad Hour, selected from all years
To mourn our loss, rouse thy obscure compeers,
And teach them thine own sorrow, say: with me
Died Adonais; till the Future dares
Forget the Past, his fate and fame shall be
An echo and a light unto eternity!

II

Where wert thou mighty Mother, when he lay,
When thy Son lay, pierced by the shaft which flies
In darkness? where was lorn Urania
When Adonais died? With veiled eyes,
'Mid listening Echoes, in her Paradise
She sate, while one, with soft enamoured breath,
Rekindled all the fading melodies,
With which, like flowers that mock the corse beneath,
He had adorned and hid the coming bulk of death.

III

O weep for Adonais – he is dead!
Wake, melancholy Mother, wake and weep!
Yet wherefore? Quench within their burning bed
Thy fiery tears, and let thy loud heart keep
Like his, a mute and uncomplaining sleep;
For he is gone, where all things wise and fair
Descend; – oh, dream not that the amorous Deep
Will yet restore him to the vital air;
Death feeds on his mute voice, and laughs at our despair.

IV

Most musical of mourners, weep again!
Lament anew, Urania! – He died,
Who was the Sire of an immortal strain,
Blind, old, and lonely, when his country's pride,
The priest, the slave, and the liberticide,
Trampled and mocked with many a loathed rite
Of lust and blood; he went, unterrified,
Into the gulf of death; but his clear Sprite
Yet reigns o'er earth; the third among the sons of light.

V

Most musical of mourners, weep anew!
Not all to that bright station dared to climb;
And happier they their happiness who knew,
Whose tapers yet burn through that night of time
In which suns perished; others more sublime,
Struck by the envious wrath of man or God,
Have sunk, extinct in their refulgent prime;
And some yet live, treading the thorny road,
Which leads, through toil and hate, to Fame's serene abode.

VI

But now, thy youngest, dearest one, has perished –
The nursling of thy widowhood, who grew,
Like a pale flower by some sad maiden cherished,
And fed with true love tears, instead of dew;
Most musical of mourners, weep anew!
Thy extreme hope, the loveliest and the last,
The bloom, whose petals nipt before they blew
Died on the promise of the fruit, is waste;
The broken lily lies – the storm is overpast.

VII

To that high Capital, where kingly Death
Keeps his pale court in beauty and decay,
He came; and bought, with price of purest breath,
A grave among the eternal. – Come away!
Haste, while the vault of blue Italian day
Is yet his fitting charnel-roof! while still
He lies, as if in dewy sleep he lay;
Awake him not! surely he takes his fill
Of deep and liquid rest, forgetful of all ill.

VIII

He will awake no more, oh, never more! –
Within the twilight chamber spreads apace,
The shadow of white Death, and at the door
Invisible Corruption waits to trace
His extreme way to her dim dwelling-place;
The eternal Hunger sits, but pity and awe
Soothe her pale rage, nor dares she to deface
So fair a prey, till darkness, and the law
Of change, shall o'er his sleep the mortal curtain draw.

IX

O weep for Adonais! – The quick Dreams,
The passion-winged Ministers of thought,
Who were his flocks, whom near the living streams
Of his young spirit he fed, and whom he taught
The love which was its music, wander not, –
Wander no more, from kindling brain to brain,
But droop there, whence they sprung; and mourn their lot
Round the cold heart, where, after their sweet pain,
They ne'er will gather strength, or find a home again.

X

And one with trembling hands clasps his cold head,
And fans him with her moonlight wings, and cries;
'Our love, our hope, our sorrow, is not dead;
'See, on the silken fringe of his faint eyes,
'Like dew upon a sleeping flower, there lies
'A tear some Dream has loosened from his brain.'
Lost Angel of a ruined Paradise!
She knew not 'twas her own; as with no stain
She faded, like a cloud which had outwept its rain.

XI

One from a lucid urn of starry dew
Washed his light limbs as if embalming them;
Another clipt her profuse locks, and threw
The wreath upon him, like an anadem,
Which frozen tears instead of pearls begem;
Another in her wilful grief would break
Her bow and winged reeds, as if to stem
A greater loss with one which was more weak;
And dull the barbed fire against his frozen cheek.

XII

Another Splendour on his mouth alit,
That mouth, whence it was wont to draw the breath
Which gave it strength to pierce the guarded wit,
And pass into the panting heart beneath
With lightning and with music: the damp death
Quenched its caress upon his icy lips;
And, as a dying meteor stains a wreath
Of moonlight vapour, which the cold night clips,
It flushed through his pale limbs, and past to its eclipse.

XIII

And others came ... Desires and Adorations,
Winged Persuasions and veiled Destinies,
Splendours, and Glooms, and glimmering Incarnations
Of hopes and fears, and twilight Phantasies;
And Sorrow, with her family of Sighs,
And Pleasure, blind with tears, led by the gleam
Of her own dying smile instead of eyes,
Came in slow pomp; – the moving pomp might seem
Like pageantry of mist on an autumnal stream.

XIV

All he had loved, and moulded into thought,
From shape, and hue, and odour, and sweet sound,
Lamented Adonais. Morning sought
Her eastern watch tower, and her hair unbound,
Wet with the tears which should adorn the ground,
Dimmed the aërial eyes that kindle day;
Afar the melancholy thunder moaned,
Pale Ocean in unquiet slumber lay,
And the wild Winds flew round, sobbing in their dismay.

XV

Lost Echo sits amid the voiceless mountains,
And feeds her grief with his remembered lay,
And will no more reply to winds or fountains,
Or amorous birds perched on the young green spray,
Or herdsman's horn, or bell at closing day;
Since she can mimic not his lips, more dear
Than those for whose disdain she pined away
Into a shadow of all sounds: – a drear
Murmur, between their songs, is all the woodmen hear.

XVI

Grief made the young Spring wild, and she threw down
Her kindling buds, as if she Autumn were,
Or they dead leaves; since her delight is flown,
For whom should she have waked the sullen year?
To Phoebus was not Hyacinth so dear
Nor to himself Narcissus, as to both
Thou Adonais: wan they stand and sere
Amid the drooping comrades of their youth,
With dew all turned to tears; odour, to sighing ruth.

XVII

Thy spirit's sister, the lorn nightingale
Mourns not her mate with such melodious pain;
Not so the eagle, who like thee could scale
Heaven, and could nourish in the sun's domain
Her mighty youth with morning, doth complain,
Soaring and screaming round her empty nest,
As Albion wails for thee: the curse of Cain
Light on his head who pierced thy innocent breast,
And scared the angel soul that was its earthly guest!

XVIII

Ah woe is me! Winter is come and gone,
But grief returns with the revolving year;
The airs and streams renew their joyous tone;
The ants, the bees, the swallows reappear;
Fresh leaves and flowers deck the dead Seasons' bier;
The amorous birds now pair in every brake,
And build their mossy homes in field and brere;
And the green lizard, and the golden snake,
Like unimprisoned flames, out of their trance awake.

XIX

Through wood and stream and field and hill and Ocean
A quickening life from the Earth's heart has burst
As it has ever done, with change and motion,
From the great morning of the world when first
God dawned on Chaos; in its stream immersed
The lamps of Heaven flash with a softer light;
All baser things pant with life's sacred thirst;
Diffuse themselves; and spend in love's delight,
The beauty and the joy of their renewed might.

XX

The leprous corpse touched by this spirit tender
Exhales itself in flowers of gentle breath;
Like incarnations of the stars, when splendour
Is changed to fragrance, they illumine death
And mock the merry worm that wakes beneath;
Nought we know, dies. Shall that alone which knows
Be as a sword consumed before the sheath
By sightless lightning? – th' intense atom glows
A moment, then is quenched in a most cold repose.

XXI

Alas! that all we loved of him should be,
But for our grief, as if it had not been,
And grief itself be mortal! Woe is me!
Whence are we, and why are we? of what scene
The actors or spectators? Great and mean
Meet massed in death, who lends what life must borrow.
As long as skies are blue, and fields are green,
Evening must usher night, night urge the morrow,
Month follow month with woe, and year wake year to sorrow.

XXII

He will awake no more, oh, never more!
'Wake thou,' cried Misery, 'childless Mother, rise
'Out of thy sleep, and slake, in thy heart's core,
'A wound more fierce than his with tears and sighs.'
And all the Dreams that watched Urania's eyes,
And all the Echoes whom their sister's song
Had held in holy silence, cried: 'Arise!'
Swift as a Thought by the snake Memory stung,
From her ambrosial rest the fading Splendour sprung.

XXIII

She rose like an autumnal Night, that springs
Out of the East, and follows wild and drear
The golden Day, which, on eternal wings,
Even as a ghost abandoning a bier,
Had left the Earth a corpse. Sorrow and fear
So struck, so roused, so rapt Urania;
So saddened round her like an atmosphere
Of stormy mist; so swept her on her way
Even to the mournful place where Adonais lay.

XXIV

Out of her secret Paradise she sped,
Through camps and cities rough with stone, and steel,
And human hearts, which to her aery tread
Yielding not, wounded the invisible
Palms of her tender feet where'er they fell:
And barbed tongues, and thoughts more sharp than they
Rent the soft Form they never could repel,
Whose sacred blood, like the young tears of May,
Paved with eternal flowers that undeserving way.

XXV

In the death chamber for a moment Death
Shamed by the presence of that living Might
Blushed to annihilation, and the breath
Revisited those lips, and life's pale light
Flashed through those limbs, so late her dear delight.
'Leave me not wild and drear and comfortless,
'As silent lightning leaves the starless night!
'Leave me not!' cried Urania; her distress
Roused Death: Death rose and smiled, and met her vain caress.

XXVI

'Stay yet awhile! speak to me once again;
'Kiss me, so long but as a kiss may live;
'And in my heartless breast and burning brain
'That word, that kiss shall all thoughts else survive,
'With food of saddest memory kept alive,
'Now thou art dead, as if it were a part
'Of thee, my Adonais! I would give
'All that I am to be as thou now art!
'But I am chained to Time, and cannot thence depart!

XXVII

'Oh gentle child, beautiful as thou wert,
'Why didst thou leave the trodden paths of men
'Too soon, and with weak hands though mighty heart
'Dare the unpastured dragon in his den?
'Defenceless as thou wert, oh, where was then
'Wisdom the mirrored shield, or scorn the spear?
'Or hadst thou waited the full cycle, when
'Thy spirit should have filled its crescent sphere,
'The monsters of life's waste had fled from thee like deer.

XXVIII

'The herded wolves, bold only to pursue;
'The obscene ravens, clamorous oer the dead;
'The vultures to the conqueror's banner true
'Who feed where Desolation first has fed,
'And whose wings rain contagion; – how they fled,
'When like Apollo, from his golden bow,
'The Pythian of the age one arrow sped
'And smiled! – The spoilers tempt no second blow,
'They fawn on the proud feet that spurn them as they go.

XXIX

'The sun comes forth, and many reptiles spawn;
'He sets, and each ephemeral insect then
'Is gathered into death without a dawn,
'And the immortal stars awake again;
'So is it in the world of living men:
'A godlike mind soars forth, in its delight
'Making earth bare and veiling heaven, and when
'It sinks, the swarms that dimmed or shared its light
'Leave to its kindred lamps the spirit's awful night.'

XXX

Thus ceased she: and the mountain shepherds came
Their garlands sere, their magic mantles rent;
The Pilgrim of Eternity, whose fame
Over his living head like Heaven is bent,
An early but enduring monument,
Came, veiling all the lightnings of his song
In sorrow; from her wilds Ierne sent
The sweetest lyrist of her saddest wrong,
And love taught grief to fall like music from his tongue.

XXXI

Midst others of less note, came one frail Form,
A phantom among men; companionless
As the last cloud of an expiring storm
Whose thunder is its knell; he, as I guess,
Had gazed on Nature's naked loveliness,
Actaeon-like, and now he fled astray
With feeble steps o'er the world's wilderness,
And his own thoughts, along that rugged way,
Pursued, like raging hounds, their father and their prey.

XXXII

A pardlike Spirit beautiful and swift –
A Love in desolation masked; – a Power
Girt round with weakness; – it can scarce uplift
The weight of the superincumbent hour;
It is a dying lamp, a falling shower,
A breaking billow; – even whilst we speak
Is it not broken? On the withering flower
The killing sun smiles brightly: on a cheek
The life can burn in blood, even while the heart may break.

XXXIII

His head was bound with pansies overblown,
And faded violets, white, and pied, and blue;
And a light spear topped with a cypress cone,
Round whose rude shaft dark ivy tresses grew
Yet dripping with the forest's noonday dew,
Vibrated, as the ever-beating heart
Shook the weak hand that grasped it; of that crew
He came the last, neglected and apart;
A herd-abandoned deer struck by the hunter's dart.

XXXIV

All stood aloof, and at his partial moan
Smiled through their tears; well knew that gentle band
Who in another's fate now wept his own,
As in the accents of an unknown land
He sung new sorrow; sad Urania scanned
The Stranger's mien, and murmured: 'who art thou?'
He answered not, but with a sudden hand
Made bare his branded and ensanguined brow,
Which was like Cain's or Christ's – oh! that it should be so!

XXXV

What softer voice is hushed over the dead?
Athwart what brow is that dark mantle thrown?
What form leans sadly o'er the white death-bed,
In mockery of monumental stone,
The heavy heart heaving without a moan?
If it be He, who, gentlest of the wise,
Taught, soothed, loved, honoured the departed one;
Let me not vex, with inharmonious sighs
The silence of that heart's accepted sacrifice.

XXXVI

Our Adonais has drunk poison – oh!
What deaf and viperous murderer could crown
Life's early cup with such a draught of woe?
The nameless worm would now itself disown:
It felt, yet could escape the magic tone
Whose prelude held all envy, hate, and wrong,
But what was howling in one breast alone,
Silent with expectation of the song,
Whose master's hand is cold, whose silver lyre unstrung.

XXXVII

Live thou, whose infamy is not thy fame!
Live! fear no heavier chastisement from me,
Thou noteless blot on a remembered name!
But be thyself, and know thyself to be!
And ever at thy season be thou free
To spill the venom when thy fangs o'erflow:
Remorse and Self-contempt shall cling to thee;
Hot Shame shall burn upon thy secret brow,
And like a beaten hound tremble thou shalt – as now.

XXXVIII

Nor let us weep that our delight is fled
Far from these carrion kites that scream below;
He wakes or sleeps with the enduring dead;
Thou canst not soar where he is sitting now. –
Dust to the dust! but the pure spirit shall flow
Back to the burning fountain whence it came,
A portion of the Eternal, which must glow
Through time and change, unquenchably the same,
Whilst thy cold embers choke the sordid hearth of shame.

XXXIX

Peace, peace! he is not dead, he doth not sleep –
He hath awakened from the dream of life –
'Tis we, who lost in stormy visions, keep
With phantoms an unprofitable strife,
And in mad trance, strike with our spirit's knife
Invulnerable nothings. – *We* decay
Like corpses in a charnel; fear and grief
Convulse us and consume us day by day,
And cold hopes swarm like worms within our living clay.

XL

He has outsoared the shadow of our night;
Envy and calumny and hate and pain,
And that unrest which men miscall delight,
Can touch him not and torture not again;
From the contagion of the world's slow stain
He is secure, and now can never mourn
A heart grown cold, a head grown grey in vain;
Nor, when the spirit's self has ceased to burn,
With sparkless ashes load an unlamented urn.

XLI

He lives, he wakes – 'tis Death is dead, not he;
Mourn not for Adonais. – Thou young Dawn
Turn all thy dew to splendour, for from thee
The spirit thou lamentest is not gone;
Ye caverns and ye forests, cease to moan!
Cease ye faint flowers and fountains, and thou Air
Which like a mourning veil thy scarf hadst thrown
O'er the abandoned Earth, now leave it bare
Even to the joyous stars which smile on it's despair!

XLII

He is made one with Nature: there is heard
His voice in all her music, from the moan
Of thunder, to the song of night's sweet bird;
He is a presence to be felt and known
In darkness and in light, from herb and stone,
Spreading itself where'er that Power may move
Which has withdrawn his being to its own;
Which wields the world with never-wearied love,
Sustains it from beneath, and kindles it above.

XLIII

He is a portion of the loveliness
Which once he made more lovely: he doth bear
His part, while the one Spirit's plastic stress
Sweeps through the dull dense world, compelling there,
All new successions to the forms they wear;
Torturing th' unwilling dross that checks its flight
To it's own likeness, as each mass may bear;
And bursting in it's beauty and it's might
From trees and beasts and men into the Heaven's light.

XLIV

The splendours of the firmament of time
May be eclipsed, but are extinguished not;
Like stars to their appointed height they climb
And death is a low mist which cannot blot
The brightness it may veil. When lofty thought
Lifts a young heart above its mortal lair,
And love and life contend in it, for what
Shall be its earthly doom, the dead live there
And move like winds of light on dark and stormy air.

XLV

The inheritors of unfulfilled renown
Rose from their thrones, built beyond mortal thought,
Far in the Unapparent. Chatterton
Rose pale, his solemn agony had not
Yet faded from him; Sidney, as he fought
And as he fell and as he lived and loved
Sublimely mild, a Spirit without spot,
Arose; and Lucan, by his death approved:
Oblivion as they rose shrank like a thing reproved.

XLVI

And many more, whose names on Earth are dark
But whose transmitted effluence cannot die
So long as fire outlives the parent spark,
Rose, robed in dazzling immortality.
'Thou art become as one of us,' they cry,
'It was for thee yon kingless sphere has long
'Swung blind in unascended majesty,
'Silent alone amid an Heaven of Song.
'Assume thy winged throne, thou Vesper of our throng!'

XLVII

Who mourns for Adonais? Oh come forth
Fond wretch! and know thyself and him aright.
Clasp with thy panting soul the pendulous Earth;
As from a centre, dart thy spirit's light
Beyond all worlds, until its spacious might
Satiate the void circumference: then shrink
Even to a point within our day and night;
And keep thy heart light lest it make thee sink
When hope has kindled hope, and lured thee to the brink.

XLVIII

Or go to Rome, which is the sepulchre,
O, not of him, but of our joy; 'tis nought
That ages, empires, and religions there
Lie buried in the ravage they have wrought;
For such as he can lend, – they borrow not
Glory from those who made the world their prey;
And he is gathered to the kings of thought
Who waged contention with their time's decay,
And of the past are all that cannot pass away.

XLIX

Go thou to Rome, – at once the Paradise,
The grave, the city, and the wilderness;
And where its wrecks like shattered mountains rise,
And flowering weeds, and fragrant copses dress
The bones of Desolation's nakedness
Pass, till the spirit of the spot shall lead
Thy footsteps to a slope of green access
Where, like an infant's smile, over the dead,
A light of laughing flowers along the grass is spread.

L

And gray walls moulder round, on which dull Time
Feeds, like slow fire upon a hoary brand;
And one keen pyramid with wedge sublime,
Pavilioning the dust of him who planned
This refuge for his memory, doth stand
Like flame transformed to marble; and beneath,
A field is spread, on which a newer band
Have pitched in Heaven's smile their camp of death
Welcoming him we lose with scarce extinguished breath.

LI

Here pause: these graves are all too young as yet
To have outgrown the sorrow which consigned
Its charge to each; and if the seal is set,
Here, on one fountain of a mourning mind,
Break it not thou! too surely shalt thou find
Thine own well full, if thou returnest home,
Of tears and gall. From the world's bitter wind
Seek shelter in the shadow of the tomb.
What Adonais is, why fear we to become?

LII

The One remains, the many change and pass;
Heaven's light forever shines, Earth's shadows fly;
Life, like a dome of many-coloured glass,
Stains the white radiance of Eternity,
Until Death tramples it to fragments. – Die,
If thou wouldst be with that which thou dost seek!
Follow where all is fled! – Rome's azure sky,
Flowers, ruins, statues, music, words, are weak
The glory they transfuse with fitting truth to speak.

LIII

Why linger, why turn back, why shrink, my Heart?
Thy hopes are gone before: from all things here
They have departed; thou shouldst now depart!
A light is past from the revolving year,
And man, and woman; and what still is dear
Attracts to crush, repels to make thee wither.
The soft sky smiles, – the low wind whispers near:
'Tis Adonais calls! oh, hasten thither,
No more let Life divide what Death can join together.

LIV

That Light whose smile kindles the Universe,
That Beauty in which all things work and move,
That Benediction which the eclipsing Curse
Of birth can quench not, that sustaining Love
Which through the web of being blindly wove
By man and beast and earth and air and sea,
Burns bright or dim, as each are mirrors of
The fire for which all thirst; now beams on me,
Consuming the last clouds of cold mortality.

LV

The breath whose might I have invoked in song
Descends on me; my spirit's bark is driven,
Far from the shore, far from the trembling throng
Whose sails were never to the tempest given;
The massy earth and sphered skies are riven!
I am borne darkly, fearfully, afar;
Whilst burning through the inmost veil of Heaven,
The soul of Adonais, like a star,
Beacons from the abode where the Eternal are.

Fragment on Keats

Who desired that on his tomb should be inscribed –

'Here lieth One whose name was writ on water.'
But, ere the breath that could erase it blew,
Death, in remorse for that fell slaughter,
Death, the immortalizing winter, flew
Athwart the stream, and time's printless torrent grew
A scroll of crystal, blazoning the name
Of Adonais.

Hellas

A Lyrical Drama

Μαντις εἰμ' ἐσθλων ἀγωνων* – *Oedip. Colon.*

To His Excellency

Prince Alexander Mavrocordato

Late Secretary for Foreign Affairs to the Hospodar of Wallachia
The drama of Hellas is inscribed as an imperfect token of the admiration, sympathy, and friendship of the author

PISA, *November* 1, 1821.

Preface

The poem of *Hellas*, written at the suggestion of the events of the moment, is a mere improvise, and derives its interest (should it be found to possess any) solely from the intense sympathy which the Author feels with the cause he would celebrate.

The subject, in its present state, is insusceptible of being treated otherwise than lyrically, and if I have called this poem a drama from the circumstance of its being composed in dialogue, the licence is not greater than that which has been assumed by other poets who have called their productions epics, only because they have been divided into twelve or twenty-four books.

The Persae of Aeschylus afforded me the first model of my conception, although the decision of the glorious contest now waging in Greece being yet suspended forbids a catastrophe

*'I am the prophet of noble struggles' (*Oedipus at Colonus*).

parallel to the return of Xerxes and the desolation of the Persians. I have, therefore, contented myself with exhibiting a series of lyric pictures, and with having wrought upon the curtain of futurity, which falls upon the unfinished scene, such figures of indistinct and visionary delineation as suggest the final triumph of the Greek cause as a portion of the cause of civilization and social improvement.

The drama (if drama it must be called) is, however, so inartificial that I doubt whether, if recited on the Thespian waggon to an Athenian village at the Dionysiaca, it would have obtained the prize of the goat. I shall bear with equanimity any punishment, greater than the loss of such a reward which the Aristarchi of the hour may think fit to inflict.

The only *goat-song* which I have yet attempted has, I confess, in spite of the unfavourable nature of the subject, received a greater and a more valuable portion of applause than I expected or than it deserved.

Common fame is the only authority which I can allege for the details which form the basis of the poem, and I must trespass upon the forgiveness of my readers for the display of newspaper erudition to which I have been reduced. Undoubtedly, until the conclusion of the war, it will be impossible to obtain an account of it sufficiently authentic for historical materials; but poets have their privilege, and it is unquestionable that actions of the most exalted courage have been performed by the Greeks – that they have gained more than one naval victory, and that their defeat in Wallachia was signalized by circumstances of heroism more glorious even than victory.

The apathy of the rulers of the civilized world to the astonishing circumstance of the descendants of that nation to which they owe their civilisation – rising as it were from the ashes of their ruin, is something perfectly inexplicable to a mere spectator of the shews of this mortal scene. We are all

Greeks. Our laws, our literature, our religion, our arts, have their root in Greece. But for Greece – Rome, the instructor, the conqueror, or the metropolis of our ancestors, would have spread no illumination with her arms, and we might still have been savages and idolaters; or, what is worse, might have arrived at such a stagnant and miserable state of social institution as China and Japan possess.

The human form and the human mind attained to a perfection in Greece which has impressed its image on those faultless productions, whose many fragments are the despair of modern art, and has propagated impulses which cannot cease, through a thousand channels of manifest or imperceptible operation, to ennoble and delight mankind until the extinction of the race.

The modern Greek is the descendant of those glorious beings whom the imagination almost refuses to figure to itself as belonging to our kind, and he inherits much of their sensibility, their rapidity of conception, their enthusiasm, and their courage. If in many instances he is degraded, by moral and political slavery to the practice of the basest vices it engenders, and that below the level of ordinary degradation; let us reflect that the corruption of the best produces the worst, and that habits which subsist only in relation to a peculiar state of social institution may be expected to cease as soon as that relation is dissolved. In fact, the Greeks, since the admirable novel of 'Anastasius' could have been a faithful picture of their manners, have undergone most important changes; the flower of their youth returning to their country from the universities of Italy, Germany, and France, have communicated to their fellow-citizens the latest results of that social perfection of which their ancestors were the original source. The university of Chios contained before the breaking out of the revolution eight hundred students, and among them several Germans and Americans. The munificence and energy of many of the Greek princes and merchants, directed to the renovation of their country with a spirit and a wisdom which has few examples, is above all praise.

The English permit their own oppressors to act according to their natural sympathy with the Turkish tyrant, and to brand upon their name the indelible blot of an alliance with the enemies of domestic happiness, of Christianity and civilisation.

Russia desires to possess, not to liberate Greece; and is contented to see the Turks, its natural enemies, and the Greeks, its intended slaves, enfeeble each other until one or both fall into its net. The wise and generous policy of England would have consisted in establishing the independence of Greece, and in maintaining it both against Russia and the Turk; – but when was the oppressor generous or just?

Should the English people ever become free, they will reflect upon the part which those who presume to represent their will have played in the great drama of the revival of liberty, with feelings which it would become them to anticipate. This is the age of the war of the oppressed against the oppressors, and every one of those ringleaders of the privileged gangs of murderers and swindlers, called Sovereigns, look to each other for aid against the common enemy, and suspend their mutual jealousies in the presence of a mightier fear. Of this holy alliance all the despots of the earth are virtual members. But a new race has arisen throughout Europe, nursed in the abhorrence of the opinions which are its chains, and she will continue to produce fresh generations to accomplish that destiny which tyrants foresee and dread.

The Spanish Peninsula is already free. France is tranquil in the enjoyment of a partial exemption from the abuses which its unnatural and feeble government are vainly attempting to revive. The seed of blood and misery has been sown in Italy, and a more vigorous race is arising to go forth to the harvest.

The world waits only the news of a revolution of Germany to see the tyrants who have pinnacled themselves on its supineness precipitated into the ruin from which they shall never arise. Well do these destroyers of mankind know their enemy, when they impute the insurrection in Greece to the same spirit before which they tremble throughout the rest of Europe, and that enemy well knows the power and the cunning of its opponents, and watches the moment of their approaching weakness and inevitable division to wrest the bloody sceptres from their grasp.

Hellas

Dramatis Personae

MAHMUD.
HASSAN.
CHORUS *of Greek Captive Women.*
Messengers, Slaves, and Attendants.
DAOOD.
AHASUERUS, *a Jew.*
The Phantom of Mahomet II.
SCENE, *Constantinople.*
TIME, *Sunset.*

SCENE: *A Terrace on the Seraglio.* MAHMUD (*sleeping*), *an Indian Slave sitting beside his Couch.*

CHORUS OF GREEK CAPTIVE WOMEN:

We strew these opiate flowers
On thy restless pillow, –
They were stript from Orient bowers,
By the Indian billow.
Be thy sleep
Calm and deep,
Like their's who fell – not our's who weep!

INDIAN:

Away, unlovely dreams!
Away, false shapes of sleep!
Be his, as Heaven seems,
Clear, and bright, and deep!
Soft as love, and calm as death,
Sweet as a summer night without a breath.

CHORUS:

Sleep! sleep! our song is laden
With the soul of slumber;
It was sung by a Samian maiden,
Whose lover was of the number
Who now keep
That calm sleep
Whence none may wake, where none shall weep.

INDIAN:

I touch thy temples pale!
I breathe my soul on thee!
And could my prayers avail,
All my joy should be
Dead, and I would live to weep,
So thou might'st win one hour of quiet sleep.

CHORUS:

Breathe low, low
The spell of the mighty mistress now!
When Conscience lulls her sated snake,
And Tyrants sleep, let Freedom wake.
Breathe low – low
The words which, like secret fire, shall flow
Through the veins of the frozen earth – low, low!

SEMICHORUS I:

Life may change, but it may fly not;
Hope may vanish, but can die not;
Truth be veiled, but still it burneth;
Love repulsed, – but it returneth!

SEMICHORUS II:

Yet were life a charnel where
Hope lay coffined with Despair;
Yet were truth a sacred lie,
Love were lust –

SEMICHORUS I:

If Liberty
Lent not life its soul of light,
Hope its iris of delight,
Truth its prophet's robe to wear,
Love its power to give and bear.

CHORUS:

In the great morning of the world,
The Spirit of God with might unfurled
The flag of Freedom over Chaos,
And all its banded anarchs fled,
Like vultures frighted from Imaus,
Before an earthquake's tread. –
So from Time's tempestuous dawn
Freedom's splendour burst and shone: –
Thermopylae and Marathon
Caught, like mountains beacon-lighted,
The springing Fire. – The winged glory
On Philippi half-alighted,

Like an eagle on a promontory.
Its unwearied wings could fan
The quenchless ashes of Milan.
From age to age, from man to man,
It lived; and lit from land to land,
Florence, Albion, Switzerland.

Then night fell; and, as from night,
Re-assuming fiery flight,
From the West swift Freedom came,
Against the course of Heaven and doom,
A second sun arrayed in flame,
To burn, to kindle, to illume.
From far Atlantis its young beams
Chased the shadows and the dreams.
France, with all her sanguine streams,
Hid, but quenched it not; again
Through clouds its shafts of glory rain
From utmost Germany to Spain.
As an eagle fed with morning
Scorns the embattled tempests warning,
When she seeks her aiëry hanging
In the mountain-cedar's hair,
And her brood expect the clanging
Of her wings through the wild air,
Sick with famine: – Freedom, so
To what of Greece remaineth now
Returns; her hoary ruins glow
Like Orient mountains lost in day;
Beneath the safety of her wings
Her renovated nurselings prey,
And in the naked lightnings
Of truth they purge their dazzled eyes.
Let Freedom leave – where'er she flies,

A Desart, or a Paradise:
Let the beautiful and the brave
Share her glory, or a grave.

SEMICHORUS I:

With the gifts of gladness
Greece did thy cradle strew;

SEMICHORUS II:

With the tears of sadness
Greece did thy shroud bedew!

SEMICHORUS I:

With an orphan's affection
She followed thy bier through Time;

SEMICHORUS II:

And at thy resurrection
Re-appeareth, like thou, sublime!

SEMICHORUS I:

If Heaven should resume thee,
To Heaven shall her spirit ascend;

SEMICHORUS II:

If Hell should entomb thee,
To Hell shall her high hearts bend.

SEMICHORUS I:

If Annihilation –

SEMICHORUS II:

Dust let her glories be!
And a name and a nation
Be forgotten, Freedom, with thee!

INDIAN:

His brow grows darker – breathe not – move not!
He starts – he shudders – ye that love not,
With your panting loud and fast,
Have awakened him at last.

MAHMUD (*starting from his sleep*): Man the Seraglio-guard! make fast the gate.
What! from a cannonade of three short hours?
'Tis false! that breach towards the Bosphorus
Cannot be practicable yet – who stirs?
Stand to the match; that when the foe prevails
One spark may mix in reconciling ruin
The conqueror and the conquered! Heave the tower
Into the gap – wrench off the roof!
[*Enter* HASSAN.] Ha! what!
The truth of day lightens upon my dream
And I am Mahmud still.

HASSAN: Your Sublime Highness
Is strangely moved.

MAHMUD: The times do cast strange shadows
On those who watch and who must rule their course,
Lest they, being first in peril as in glory,
Be whelmed in the fierce ebb: – and these are of them.
Thrice has a gloomy vision hunted me
As thus from sleep into the troubled day;
It shakes me as the tempest shakes the sea,
Leaving no figure upon memory's glass.
Would that – no matter. Thou didst say thou knewest

A Jew, whose spirit is a chronicle
Of strange and secret and forgotten things.
I bade thee summon him: – 'tis said his tribe
Dream, and are wise interpreters of dreams.

HASSAN: The Jew of whom I spake is old, – so old
He seems to have outlived a world's decay;
The hoary mountains and the wrinkled ocean
Seem younger still than he; – his hair and beard
Are whiter than the tempest-sifted snow;
His cold pale limbs and pulseless arteries
Are like the fibres of a cloud instinct
With light, and to the soul that quickens them
Are as the atoms of the mountain-drift
To the winter wind: – but from his eye looks forth
A life of unconsumed thought which pierces
The present, and the past, and the to-come.
Some say that this is he whom the great prophet
Jesus, the son of Joseph, for his mockery
Mocked with the curse of immortality.
Some feign that he is Enoch: others dream
He was pre-adamite and has survived
Cycles of generation and of ruin.
The sage, in truth, by dreadful abstinence
And conquering penance of the mutinous flesh,
Deep contemplation, and unwearied study,
In years outstretched beyond the date of man,
May have attained to sovereignty and science
Over those strong and secret things and thoughts
Which others fear and know not.

MAHMUD: I would talk
With this old Jew.

HASSAN: Thy will is even now
Made known to him, where he dwells in a sea-cavern
'Mid the Demonesi less accessible

Than thou or God! He who would question him
Must sail alone at sunset, where the stream
Of Ocean sleeps around those foamless isles,
When the young moon is westering as now,
And evening airs wander upon the wave;
And when the pines of that bee-pasturing isle,
Green Erebinthus, quench the fiery shadow
Of his gilt prow within the sapphire water,
Then must the lonely helmsman cry aloud
'Ahasuerus!' and the caverns round
Will answer 'Ahasuerus!' If his prayer
Be granted, a faint meteor will arise
Lighting him over Marmora, and a wind
Will rush out of the sighing pine-forest,
And with the wind a storm of harmony
Unutterably sweet, and pilot him
Through the soft twilight to the Bosphorus:
Thence at the hour and place and circumstance
Fit for the matter of their conference
The Jew appears. Few dare, and few who dare
Win the desired communion – but that shout
Bodes –

[*A shout within.*]

MAHMUD: Evil, doubtless; like all human sounds.
Let me converse with spirits.

HASSAN: That shout again.

MAHMUD: This Jew whom thou hast summoned –

HASSAN: Will be here –

MAHMUD: When the omnipotent hour to which are yoked
He, I, and all things shall compel – enough!
Silence those mutineers – that drunken crew,
That crowd about the pilot in the storm.
Ay! strike the foremost shorter by a head!
They weary me, and I have need of rest.

Kings are like stars – they rise and set, they have
The worship of the world, but no repose.
[*Exeunt severally.*]

CHORUS:

Worlds on worlds are rolling ever
From creation to decay,
Like the bubbles on a river
Sparkling, bursting, borne away.
But they are still immortal
Who, through birth's orient portal
And death's dark chasm hurrying to and fro,
Clothe their unceasing flight
In the brief dust and light
Gathered around their chariots as they go;
New shapes they still may weave,
New gods, new laws receive,
Bright or dim are they as the robes they last
On Death's bare ribs had cast.

A power from the unknown God,
A Promethean conqueror came;
Like a triumphal path he trod
The thorns of death and shame.
A mortal shape to him
Was like the vapour dim
Which the orient planet animates with light;
Hell, Sin, and Slavery came,
Like blood-hounds mild and tame,
Nor preyed, until their Lord had taken flight;
The moon of Mahomet
Arose, and it shall set:
While blazoned as on heaven's immortal noon
The cross leads generations on.

Swift as the radiant shapes of sleep
From one whose dreams are Paradise
Fly, when the fond wretch wakes to weep,
And day peers forth with her blank eyes;
So fleet, so faint, so fair,
The Powers of earth and air
Fled from the folding star of Bethlehem:
Apollo, Pan, and Love,
And even Olympian Jove
Grew weak, for killing Truth had glared on them;
Our hills and seas and streams
Dispeopled of their dreams,
Their waters turned to blood, their dew to tears,
Wailed for the golden years.

[*Enter* MAHMUD, HASSAN, DAOOD, *and others.*]

MAHMUD: More gold? our ancestors bought gold with victory,
And shall I sell it for defeat?

DAOOD: The Janizars
Clamour for pay.

MAHMUD: Go! bid them pay themselves
With Christian blood! Are there no Grecian virgins
Whose shrieks and spasms and tears they may enjoy?
No infidel children to impale on spears?
No hoary priests after that Patriarch
Who bent the curse against his country's heart,
Which clove his own at last? Go! bid them kill,
Blood is the seed of gold.

DAOOD: It has been sown,
And yet the harvest to the sicklemen
Is as a grain to each.

MAHMUD: Then, take this signet,
Unlock the seventh chamber in which lie

The treasures of victorious Solyman.
An empire's spoil stored for a day of ruin.
O spirit of my sires! is it not come?
The prey-birds and the wolves are gorged and sleep;
But these, who spread their feast on the red earth,
Hunger for gold, which fills not. – See them fed;
Then, lead them to the rivers of fresh death.
[*Exit* DAOOD.]
O! miserable dawn, after a night
More glorious than the day which it usurped!
O, faith in God! O, power on earth! O, word
Of the great prophet, whose o'ershadowing wings
Darkened the thrones and idols of the West,
Now bright! – For thy sake cursed be the hour,
Even as a father by an evil child,
When the Orient moon of Islam rolled in triumph
From Caucasus to White Ceraunia!
Ruin above, and anarchy below;
Terror without, and treachery within;
The Chalice of destruction full, and all
Thirsting to drink; and who among us dares
To dash it from his lips? and where is Hope?
HASSAN: The lamp of our dominion still rides high;
One God is God – Mahomet is his prophet.
Four hundred thousand Moslems from the limits
Of utmost Asia, irresistibly
Throng, like full clouds at the Sirocco's cry;
But not like them to weep their strength in tears:
They bear destroying lightning, and their step
Wakes earthquake to consume and overwhelm,
And reign in ruin. Phrygian Olympus,
Tmolus, and Latmos, and Mycale, roughen
With horrent arms; and lofty ships even now,

Like vapours anchored to a mountain's edge,
Freighted with fire and whirlwind, wait at Scala
The convoy of the ever-veering wind.
Samos is drunk with blood; – the Greek has paid
Brief victory with swift loss and long despair.
The false Moldavian serfs fled fast and far.
When the fierce shout of 'Allah-illa-Allah!'
Rose like the war-cry of the northern wind
Which kills the sluggish clouds, and leaves a flock
Of wild swans struggling with the naked storm.
So were the lost Greeks on the Danube's day!
If night is mute, yet the returning sun
Kindles the voices of the morning birds;
Nor at thy bidding less exultingly
Than birds rejoicing in the golden day.
The Anarchies of Africa unleash
Their tempest-winged cities of the sea,
To speak in thunder to the rebel world.
Like sulphurous clouds, half-shattered by the storm,
They sweep the pale Aegean, while the Queen
Of Ocean, bound upon her island-throne,
Far in the West sits mourning that her sons
Who frown on Freedom spare a smile for thee:
Russia still hovers, as an eagle might
Within a cloud, near which a kite and crane
Hang tangled in inextricable fight,
To stoop upon the victor; – for she fears
The name of Freedom, even as she hates thine.
But recreant Austria loves thee as the Grave
Loves Pestilence, and her slow dogs of war,
Fleshed with the chase, come up from Italy,
And howl upon their limits; for they see
The panther, Freedom, fled to her old cover,

Amid seas and mountains, and a mightier brood
Crouch round. What Anarch wears a crown or mitre,
Or bears the sword, or grasps the key of gold,
Whose friends are not thy friends, whose foes thy foes?
Our arsenals and our armories are full;
Our forts defy assault; ten thousand cannon
Lie ranged upon the beach, and hour by hour
Their earth-convulsing wheels affright the city;
The galloping of fiery steeds makes pale
The Christian merchant; and the yellow Jew
Hides his hoard deeper in the faithless earth.
Like clouds, and like the shadows of the clouds,
Over the hills of Anatolia,
Swift in wide troops the Tartar chivalry
Sweep; – the far flashing of their starry lances
Reverberates the dying light of day.
We have one God, one King, one Hope, one Law;
But many-headed Insurrection stands
Divided in itself, and soon must fall.

MAHMUD: Proud words, when deeds come short, are seasonable:
Look, Hassan, on yon crescent moon, emblazoned
Upon that shattered flag of fiery cloud
Which leads the rear of the departing day;
Wan emblem of an empire fading now!
See how it trembles in the blood-red air,
And like a mighty lamp whose oil is spent
Shrinks on the horizon's edge, while, from above,
One star with insolent and victorious light
Hovers above its fall, and with keen beams,
Like arrows through a fainting antelope,
Strikes its weak form to death.

HASSAN: Even as that moon,
Renews itself –

MAHMUD: Shall we be not renewed!
Far other bark than our's were needed now
To stem the torrent of descending time:
The spirit that lifts the slave before his lord
Stalks through the capitals of armed kings,
And spreads his ensign in the wilderness:
Exults in chains; and, when the rebel falls,
Cries like the blood of Abel from the dust;
And the inheritors of the earth, like beasts
When earthquake is unleashed, with ideot fear
Cower in their kingly dens – as I do now.
What were Defeat when Victory must appal?
Or Danger, when Security looks pale? –
How said the messenger – who, from the fort
Islanded in the Danube, saw the battle
Of Bucharest? – that –
HASSAN: Ibrahim's scymitar
Drew with its gleam swift victory from heaven,
To burn before him in the night of battle –
A light and a destruction.
MAHMUD: Ay! the day
Was our's: but how? –
HASSAN: The light Wallachians,
The Arnaut, Servian, and Albanian allies
Fled from the glance of our artillery
Almost before the thunderstone alit.
One half the Grecian army made a bridge
Of safe and slow retreat, with Moslem dead;
The other –
MAHMUD: Speak – tremble not. –
HASSAN: Islanded
By victor myriads, formed in hollow square
With rough and steadfast front, and thrice flung back
The deluge of our foaming cavalry;

Thrice their keen wedge of battle pierced our lines.
Our baffled army trembled like one man
Before a host, and gave them space; but soon,
From the surrounding hills, the batteries blazed,
Kneading them down with fire and iron rain:
Yet none approached; till, like a field of corn
Under the hook of the swart sickleman,
The band, intrenched in mounds of Turkish dead,
Grew weak and few. – Then said the Pacha, 'Slaves,
Render yourselves – they have abandoned you –
What hope of refuge, or retreat, or aid?
We grant your lives.' 'Grant that which is thine own!'
Cried one, and fell upon his sword and died!
Another – 'God, and man, and hope abandon me;
But I to them, and to myself, remain
Constant:' – he bowed his head, and his heart burst.
A third exclaimed, 'There is a refuge, tyrant,
Where thou darest not pursue, and canst not harm,
Should'st thou pursue; there we shall meet again.'
Then held his breath, and, after a brief spasm,
The indignant spirit cast its mortal garment
Among the slain – dead earth upon the earth!
So these survivors, each by different ways,
Some strange, all sudden, none dishonourable,
Met in triumphant death; and when our army
Closed in, while yet wonder, and awe, and shame,
Held back the base hyenas of the battle
That feed upon the dead and fly the living,
One rose out of the chaos of the slain:
And if it were a corpse which some dread spirit
Of the old saviours of the land we rule
Had lifted in its anger wandering by; –
Or if there burned within the dying man
Unquenchable disdain of death, and faith

Creating what it feigned; – I cannot tell –
But he cried, 'Phantoms of the free, we come!
Armies of the Eternal, ye who strike
To dust the citadels of sanguine kings,
And shake the souls throned on their stony hearts,
And thaw their frostwork diadems like dew; –
O ye who float around this clime, and weave
The garment of the glory which it wears,
Whose fame, though earth betray the dust it clasped,
Lies sepulchred in monumental thought; –
Progenitors of all that yet is great,
Ascribe to your bright senate, O accept
In your high ministrations, us, your sons –
Us first, and the more glorious yet to come!
And ye, weak conquerors! giants who look pale
When the crushed worm rebels beneath your tread,
The vultures and the dogs, your pensioners tame,
Are overgorged; but, like oppressors, still
They crave the relic of Destruction's feast.
The exhalations and the thirsty winds
Are sick with blood; the dew is foul with death;
Heaven's light is quenched in slaughter: thus, where'er
Upon your camps, cities, or towers, or fleets,
The obscene birds the reeking remnants cast
Of these dead limbs, – upon your streams and mountains,
Upon your fields, your gardens, and your house-tops,
Where'er the winds shall creep, or the clouds fly,
Or the dews fall, or the angry sun look down
With poisoned light – Famine and Pestilence,
And Panic, shall wage war upon our side!
Nature from all her boundaries is moved
Against ye: Time has found ye light as foam.
The Earth rebels; and Good and Evil stake
Their empire o'er the unborn world of men

On this one cast; – but ere the die be thrown
The renovated genius of our race,
Proud umpire of the impious game, descends
A seraph-winged Victory, bestriding
The tempest of the Omnipotence of God,
Which sweeps all things to their appointed doom,
And you to oblivion!' – More he would have said,
But –

MAHMUD: Died – as thou shouldst ere thy lips had painted
Their ruin in the hues of our success.
A rebel's crime gilt with a rebel's tongue!
Your heart is Greek, Hassan.

HASSAN: It may be so:
A spirit not my own wrenched me within,
And I have spoken words I fear and hate;
Yet would I die for –

MAHMUD: Live! O live! outlive
Me and this sinking empire. But the fleet –

HASSAN: Alas! –

MAHMUD: The fleet which, like a flock of clouds
Chased by the wind, flies the insurgent banner.
Our winged castles from their merchant ships!
Our myriads before their weak pirate bands!
Our arms before their chains! our years of empire
Before their centuries of servile fear!
Death is awake! Repulse is on the waters!
They own no more the thunder-bearing banner
Of Mahmud; but, like hounds of a base breed,
Gorge from a stranger's hand, and rend their master.

HASSAN: Latmos, and Ampelos, and Phanae, saw
The wreck –

MAHMUD: The caves of the Icarian isles
Told each to the other in loud mockery,
And with the tongue as of a thousand echoes,

First of the sea-convulsing fight – and, then, –
Thou darest to speak – senseless are the mountains:
Interpret thou their voice!

HASSAN: My presence bore
A part in that day's shame. The Grecian fleet
Bore down at day-break from the North, and hung
As multitudinous on the ocean line,
As cranes upon the cloudless Thracian wind.
Our squadron, convoying ten thousand men,
Was stretching towards Nauplia when the battle
Was kindled. –
First through the hail of our artillery
The agile Hydriote barks with press of sail
Dashed: – ship to ship, cannon to cannon, man
To man were grappled in the embrace of war,
Inextricable but by death or victory.
The tempest of the raging fight convulsed
To its chrystalline depths that stainless sea,
And shook Heaven's roof of golden morning clouds,
Poised on an hundred azure mountain-isles.
In the brief trances of the artillery
One cry from the destroyed and the destroyer
Rose, and a cloud of desolation wrapt
The unforeseen event, till the north wind
Sprung from the sea, lifting the heavy veil
Of battle-smoke – then victory – victory!
For, as we thought, three frigates from Algiers
Bore down from Naxos to our aid, but soon
The abhorred cross glimmered behind, before,
Among, around us; and that fatal sign
Dried with its beams the strength in Moslem hearts,
As the sun drinks the dew. – What more? We fled! –
Our noonday path over the sanguine foam
Was beaconed, – and the glare struck the sun pale, –

By our consuming transports: the fierce light
Made all the shadows of our sails blood-red,
And every countenance blank. Some ships lay feeding
The ravening fire, even to the water's level;
Some were blown up; some, settling heavily,
Sunk; and the shrieks of our companions died
Upon the wind, that bore us fast and far,
Even after they were dead. Nine thousand perished!
We met the vultures legioned in the air
Stemming the torrent of the tainted wind;
They, screaming from their cloudy mountain peaks,
Stooped through the sulphurous battle-smoke and perched
Each on the weltering carcase that we loved,
Like its ill angel or its damned soul,
Riding upon the bosom of the sea.
We saw the dog-fish hastening to their feast.
Joy waked the voiceless people of the sea,
And ravening Famine left his ocean cave
To dwell with war, with us, and with despair.
We met night three hours to the west of Patmos,
And with night, tempest –

MAHMUD: Cease!

[*Enter a Messenger*.]

MESSENGER: Your Sublime Highness,
That Christian hound, the Muscovite Ambassador
Has left the city. – If the rebel fleet
Had anchored in the port, had victory
Crowned the Greek legions in the Hippodrome,
Panic were tamer. – Obedience and Mutiny,
Like giants in contention planet-struck,
Stand gazing on each other. – There is peace
In Stamboul. –

MAHMUD: Is the grave not calmer still?
Its ruins shall be mine.

HASSAN: Fear not the Russian:
The tiger leagues not with the stag at bay
Against the hunter. – Cunning, base, and cruel,
He crouches, watching till the spoil be won,
And must be paid for his reserve in blood.
After the war is fought, yield the sleek Russian
That which thou can'st not keep, his deserved portion
Of blood, which shall not flow through streets and fields,
Rivers and seas, like that which we may win,
But stagnate in the veins of Christian slaves!
[*Enter second Messenger.*]
SECOND MESSENGER: Nauplia, Tripolizza, Mothon, Athens,
Navarin, Artas, Monembasia,
Corinth and Thebes are carried by assault,
And every Islamite who made his dogs
Fat with the flesh of Galilean slaves
Passed at the edge of the sword: the lust of blood
Which made our warriors drunk, is quenched in death;
But like a fiery plague breaks out anew
In deeds which make the Christian cause look pale
In its own light. The garrison of Patras
Has store but for ten days, nor is there hope
But from the Briton: at once slave and tyrant
His wishes still are weaker than his fears,
Or he would sell what faith may yet remain
From the oaths broke in Genoa and in Norway;
And if you buy him not, your treasury
Is empty even of promises – his own coin.
The freedman of a western poet chief
Holds Attica with seven thousand rebels,
And has beat back the Pacha of Negropont:
The aged Ali sits in Yanina
A crownless metaphor of empire:
His name, that shadow of his withered might,

Holds our besieging army like a spell
In prey to famine, pest, and mutiny;
He, bastioned in his citadel, looks forth
Joyless upon the sapphire lake that mirrors
The ruins of the city where he reigned
Childless and sceptreless. The Greek has reaped
The costly harvest his own blood matured,
Not the sower, Ali – who has bought a truce
From Ypsilanti with ten camel loads
Of Indian gold.

[*Enter a third Messenger.*]

MAHMUD: What more?

THIRD MESSENGER: The Christian tribes
Of Lebanon and the Syrian wilderness
Are in revolt; – Damascus, Hems, Aleppo
Tremble; – the Arab menaces Medina,
The Ethiop has intrenched himself in Sennaar,
And keeps the Egyptian rebel well employed,
Who denies homage, claims investiture
As price of tardy aid. Persia demands
The cities on the Tigris, and the Georgians
Refuse their living tribute. Crete and Cyprus,
Like mountain-twins that from each other's veins
Catch the volcano-fire and earthquake-spasm,
Shake in the general fever. Through the city,
Like birds before a storm, the Santons shriek,
And prophecyings horrible and new
Are heard among the crowd: that sea of men
Sleeps on the wrecks it made, breathless and still.
A Dervise, learned on the Koran, preaches
That it is written how the sins of Islam
Must raise up a destroyer even now.
The Greeks expect a Saviour from the west,
Who shall not come, men say, in clouds and glory,

But in the omnipresence of that spirit
In which all live and are. Ominous signs
Are blazoned broadly on the noon-day sky:
One saw a red cross stamped upon the sun;
It has rained blood; and monstrous births declare
The secret wrath of Nature and her Lord.
The army encamped upon the Cydaris,
Was roused last night by the alarm of battle,
And saw two hosts conflicting in the air,
The shadows doubtless of the unborn time
Cast on the mirror of the night. While yet
The fight hung balanced, there arose a storm
Which swept the phantoms from among the stars.
At the third watch the spirit of the plague
Was heard abroad flapping among the tents;
Those who relieved watch found the sentinels dead.
The last news from the camp is, that a thousand
Have sickened, and –
[*Enter a fourth Messenger*.]

MAHMUD: And thou, pale ghost, dim shadow
Of some untimely rumour, speak!

FOURTH MESSENGER: One comes
Fainting with toil, covered with foam and blood:
He stood, he says, upon Chelonites'
Promontory, which o'erlooks the isles that groan
Under the Briton's frown, and all their waters
Then trembling in the splendour of the moon,
When as the wandering clouds unveiled or hid
Her boundless light, he saw two adverse fleets
Stalk through the night in the horizon's glimmer,
Mingling fierce thunders and sulphureous gleams,
And smoke which strangled every infant wind
That soothed the silver clouds through the deep air.
At length the battle slept, but the Sirocco

Awoke, and drove his flock of thunder-clouds
Over the sea-horizon, blotting out
All objects – save that in the faint moon-glimpse
He saw, or dreamed he saw, the Turkish admiral
And two the loftiest of our ships of war,
With the bright image of that Queen of Heaven
Who hid, perhaps, her face for grief, reversed;
And the abhorred cross –
[*Enter an Attendant.*]

ATTENDANT: Your Sublime Highness
The Jew, who –

MAHMUD: Could not come more seasonably:
Bid him attend. I'll hear no more! too long
We gaze on danger through the mist of fear,
And multiply upon our shattered hopes
The images of ruin. Come what will!
To-morrow and to-morrow are as lamps
Set in our path to light us to the edge
Through rough and smooth, nor can we suffer aught
Which he inflicts not in whose hand we are.
[*Exeunt.*]

SEMICHORUS I:

Would I were the winged cloud
Of a tempest swift and loud!
I would scorn
The smile of morn
And the wave where the moon rise is born!
I would leave
The spirits of eve
A shroud for the corpse of the day to weave
From other threads than mine!
Bask in the deep blue noon divine.
Who would? Not I.

SEMICHORUS II:

Whither to fly?

SEMICHORUS I:

Where the rocks that gird th' Aegean
Echo to the battle paean
Of the free –
I would flee
A tempestuous herald of victory!
My golden rain
For the Grecian slain
Should mingle in tears with the bloody main,
And my solemn thunder knell
Should ring to the world the passing bell
Of Tyranny!

SEMICHORUS II:

Ah king! wilt thou chain
The rack and the rain?
Wilt thou fetter the lightning and hurricane?
The storms are free,
But we –

CHORUS:

O Slavery! thou frost of the world's prime,
Killing its flowers and leaving its thorns bare!
Thy touch has stamped these limbs with crime,
These brows thy branding garland bear,
But the free heart, the impassive soul
Scorn thy control!

SEMICHORUS I:

Let there be light! said Liberty,
And like sunrise from the sea,
Athens arose! – Around her born,
Shone like mountains in the morn
Glorious states; – and are they now
Ashes, wrecks, oblivion?

SEMICHORUS II:

Go,
Where Thermae and Asopus swallowed
  Persia, as the sand does foam.
Deluge upon deluge followed,
  Discord, Macedon, and Rome:
And lastly thou!

SEMICHORUS I:

Temples and towers,
  Citadels and marts, and they
Who live and die there, have been ours,
  And may be thine, and must decay;
But Greece and her foundations are
Built below the tide of war,
Based on the crystalline sea
Of thought and its eternity;
Her citizens, imperial spirits,
  Rule the present from the past,
On all this world of men inherits
  Their seal is set.

SEMICHORUS II:

Hear ye the blast,
Whose Orphic thunder thrilling calls
From ruin her Titanian walls?
Whose spirit shakes the sapless bones
Of Slavery? Argos, Corinth, Crete
Hear, and from their mountain thrones
The daemons and the nymphs repeat
The harmony.

SEMICHORUS I:

I hear! I hear!

SEMICHORUS II:

The world's eyeless charioteer,
Destiny, is hurrying by!
What faith is crushed, what empire bleeds
Beneath her earthquake-footed steeds?
What eagle-winged victory sits
At her right hand? what shadow flits
Before? what splendour rolls behind?
Ruin and renovation cry
'Who but We?'

SEMICHORUS I:

I hear! I hear!
The hiss as of a rushing wind,
The roar as of an ocean foaming,
The thunder as of earthquake coming.
I hear! I hear!
The crash as of an empire falling,
The shrieks as of a people calling

Mercy! mercy! – How they thrill!
Then a shout of 'kill! kill! kill!'
And then a small still voice, thus –

SEMICHORUS II:

For
Revenge and Wrong bring forth their kind,
  The foul cubs like their parents are,
Their den is in the guilty mind
  And Conscience feeds them with despair.

SEMICHORUS I:

In sacred Athens, near the fane
  Of Wisdom, Pity's altar stood:
Serve not the unknown God in vain,
But pay that broken shrine again,
  Love for hate and tears for blood.

[*Enter* MAHMUD *and* AHASUERUS.]

MAHMUD: Thou art a man, thou sayest, even as we.
AHASUERUS: No more!
MAHMUD: But raised above thy fellow men
  By thought, as I by power.
AHASUERUS: Thou sayest so.
MAHMUD: Thou art an adept in the difficult lore
  Of Greek and Frank philosophy; thou numberest
  The flowers, and thou measurest the stars;
  Thou severest element from element;
  Thy spirit is present in the past, and sees
  The birth of this old world through all its cycles
  Of desolation and of loveliness,

And when man was not, and how man became
The monarch and the slave of this low sphere,
And all its narrow circles – it is much –
I honour thee, and would be what thou art
Were I not what I am; but the unborn hour,
Cradled in fear and hope, conflicting storms,
Who shall unveil? Nor thou, nor I, nor any
Mighty or wise. I apprehended not
What thou hast taught me, but I now perceive
That thou art no interpreter of dreams;
Thou dost not own that art, device, or God,
Can make the future present – let it come!
Moreover thou disdainest us and ours;
Thou art as God, whom thou contemplatest.

AHASUERUS: Disdain thee? – not the worm beneath thy feet!
The Fathomless has care for meaner things
Than thou canst dream, and has made pride for those
Who would be what they may not, or would seem
That which they are not. Sultan! talk no more
Of thee and me, the future and the past;
But look on that which cannot change – the One
The unborn and the undying. Earth and ocean,
Space, and the isles of life or light that gem
The sapphire floods of interstellar air,
This firmament pavilioned upon chaos,
With all its cressets of immortal fire,
Whose outwall, bastioned impregnably
Against the escape of boldest thoughts, repels them
As Calpe the Atlantic clouds – this Whole
Of suns, and worlds, and men, and beasts, and flowers,
With all the silent or tempestuous workings
By which they have been, are, or cease to be,
Is but a vision: – all that it inherits

Are motes of a sick eye, bubbles and dreams;
Thought is its cradle and its grave, nor less
The future and the past are idle shadows
Of thought's eternal flight – they have no being:
Nought is but that which feels itself to be.

MAHMUD: What meanest thou? Thy words stream like a tempest
Of dazzling mist within my brain – they shake
The earth on which I stand, and hang like night
On Heaven above me. What can they avail?
They cast on all things surest, brightest, best,
Doubt, insecurity, astonishment.

AHASUERUS: Mistake me not! All is contained in each.
Dodona's forest to an acorn's cup
Is that which has been, or will be, to that
Which is – the absent to the present. Thought
Alone, and its quick elements, Will, Passion,
Reason, Imagination, cannot die;
They are, what that which they regard appears,
The stuff whence mutability can weave
All that it hath dominion o'er, worlds, worms,
Empires, and superstitions. What has thought
To do with time, or place, or circumstance?
Would'st thou behold the future? – ask and have!
Knock and it shall be opened – look, and lo!
The coming age is shadowed on the past
As on a glass.

MAHMUD: Wild, wilder thoughts convulse
My spirit – Did not Mahomet the Second
Win Stamboul?

AHASUERUS: Thou would'st ask that giant spirit
The written fortunes of thy house and faith.
Thou would'st cite one out of the grave to tell
How what was born in blood must die.

MAHMUD: Thy words
Have power on me! I see –
AHASUERUS: What hearest thou?
MAHMUD: A far whisper –
Terrible silence.
AHASUERUS: What succeeds?
MAHMUD: The sound
As of the assault of an imperial city,
The hiss of inextinguishable fire,
The roar of giant cannon: the earthquaking
Fall of vast bastions and precipitous towers,
The shock of crags shot from strange engin'ry,
The clash of wheels, and clang of armed hoofs,
And crash of brazen mail as of the wreck
Of adamantine mountains – the mad blast
Of trumpets, and the neigh of raging steeds,
The shrieks of women whose thrill jars the blood,
And one sweet laugh, most horrible to hear,
As of a joyous infant waked and playing
With its dead mother's breast, and now more loud
The mingled battle-cry, – ha! hear I not
'Εν τούτῳ νίκη!* 'Allah-illa-Allah!?'
AHASUERUS: The sulphurous mist is raised – thou see'st –
MAHMUD: A chasm,
As of two mountains in the wall of Stamboul;
And in that ghastly breach the Islamites,
Like giants on the ruins of a world,
Stand in the light of sunrise. In the dust
Glimmers a kingless diadem, and one
Of regal port has cast himself beneath

*'In this sign victory.' The difference from the words attributed to Constantine the Great is only in the last word. Constantine's instructions read, 'In this sign conquer' (the sign referred to is the sign of the cross) which Shelley seems to have modified.

The stream of war. Another proudly clad
In golden arms spurs a Tartarian barb
Into the gap, and with his iron mace
Directs the torrent of that tide of men,
And seems – he is – Mahomet!

AHASUERUS: What thou see'st
Is but the ghost of thy forgotten dream.
A dream itself, yet less, perhaps, than that
Thou call'st reality. Thou may'st behold
How cities, on which Empire sleeps enthroned,
Bow their towered crests to mutability.
Poised by the flood, e'en on the height thou holdest,
Thou may'st now learn how the full tide of power
Ebbs to its depths. – Inheritor of glory,
Conceived in darkness, born in blood, and nourished
With tears and toil, thou see'st the mortal throes
Of that whose birth was but the same. The Past
Now stands before thee like an Incarnation
Of the To-come; yet would'st thou commune with
That portion of thyself which was ere thou
Didst start for this brief race whose crown is death,
Dissolve with that strong faith and fervent passion
Which called it from the uncreated deep,
Yon cloud of war, with its tempestuous phantoms
Of raging death; and draw with mighty will
The imperial shade hither.

[*Exit* AHASUERUS. *The Phantom of* MAHOMET THE SECOND *appears*.]

MAHMUD: Approach!

PHANTOM: I come
Thence whither thou must go! The grave is fitter
To take the living than give up the dead;
Yet has thy faith prevailed, and I am here.
The heavy fragments of the power which fell

When I arose, like shapeless crags and clouds,
Hang round my throne on the abyss, and voices
Of strange lament soothe my supreme repose,
Wailing for glory never to return. –
  A later Empire nods in its decay:
The autumn of a greener faith is come,
And wolfish change, like winter, howls to strip
The foliage in which Fame, the eagle, built
Her aiëry, while Dominion whelped below.
The storm is in its branches, and the frost
Is on its leaves, and the blank deep expects
Oblivion on oblivion, spoil on spoil,
Ruin on ruin: – Thou art slow, my son;
The Anarchs of the world of darkness keep
A throne for thee, round which thine empire lies
Boundless and mute; and for thy subjects thou,
Like us, shalt rule the ghosts of murdered life,
The phantoms of the powers who rule thee now –
Mutinous passions, and conflicting fears,
And hopes that sate themselves on dust and die! –
Stript of their mortal strength, as thou of thine.
Islam must fall, but we will reign together
Over its ruins in the world of death: –
And if the trunk be dry, yet shall the seed
Unfold itself even in the shape of that
Which gathers birth in its decay. Woe! woe!
To the weak people tangled in the grasp
Of its last spasms.

MAHMUD: Spirit, woe to all!
Woe to the wronged and the avenger! Woe
To the destroyer, woe to the destroyed!
Woe to the dupe, and woe to the deceiver!
Woe to the oppressed, and woe to the oppressor!
Woe both to those that suffer and inflict;

Those who are born and those who die! but say,
Imperial shadow of the thing I am,
When, how, by whom, Destruction must accomplish
Her consummation?

PHANTOM: Ask the cold pale Hour,
Rich in reversion of impending death,
When *he* shall fall upon whose ripe grey hairs
Sit Care, and Sorrow, and Infirmity –
The weight which Crime, whose wings are plumed with years,
Leaves in his flight from ravaged heart to heart
Over the heads of men, under which burthen
They bow themselves unto the grave: fond wretch!
He leans upon his crutch, and talks of years
To come, and how in hours of youth renewed
He will renew lost joys, and –

VOICE WITHOUT: Victory! Victory!

[*The Phantom vanishes.*]

MAHMUD: What sound of the importunate earth has broken
My mighty trance?

VOICE WITHOUT: Victory! Victory!

MAHMUD: Weak lightning before darkness! poor faint smile
Of dying Islam! Voice which art the response
Of hollow weakness! Do I wake and live?
Were there such things, or may the unquiet brain,
Vexed by the wise mad talk of the old Jew,
Have shaped itself these shadows of its fear?
It matters not! – for nought we see or dream
Possess, or lose, or grasp at, can be worth
More than it gives or teaches. Come what may
The future must become the past, and I
As they were to whom once this present hour,
This gloomy crag of time to which I cling,

Seemed an Elysian isle of peace and joy
Never to be attained. – I must rebuke
This drunkenness of triumph ere it die,
And dying, bring despair. Victory! poor slaves! [*Exit* MAHMUD.]

VOICE WITHOUT: Shout in the jubilee of death! The Greeks
Are as a brood of lions in the net
Round which the kingly hunters of the earth
Stand smiling. Anarchs, ye whose daily food
Are curses, groans, and gold, the fruit of death
From Thule to the girdle of the world,
Come, feast! the board groans with the flesh of men:
The cup is foaming with a nation's blood,
Famine and Thirst await! eat, drink, and die!

SEMICHORUS I:

Victorious Wrong, with vulture scream,
Salutes the rising sun, pursues the flying day!
I saw her, ghastly as a tyrant's dream,
Perch on the trembling pyramid of night,
Beneath which earth and all her realms pavilioned lay
In visions of the dawning undelight.
Who shall impede her flight?
Who rob her of her prey?

VOICE WITHOUT: Victory! Victory! Russia's famished eagles
Dare not to prey beneath the crescent's light.
Impale the remnant of the Greeks! despoil!
Violate! make their flesh cheaper than dust!

SEMICHORUS II:

Thou voice which art
The herald of the ill in splendour hid!
Thou echo of the hollow heart
Of monarchy, bear me to thine abode
When desolation flashes o'er a world destroyed:
Oh, bear me to those isles of jagged cloud
Which float like mountains on the earthquake, mid
The momentary oceans of the lightning,
Or to some toppling promontory proud
Of solid tempest whose black pyramid,
Riven, overhangs the founts intensely brightning
Of those dawn-tinted deluges of fire
Before their waves expire,
When heaven and earth are light, and only light
In the thunder night!

VOICE WITHOUT: Victory! Victory! Austria, Russia, England,
And that tame serpent, that poor shadow, France,
Cry peace, and that means death when monarchs speak.
Ho, there! bring torches, sharpen those red stakes,
These chains are light, fitter for slaves and poisoners
Than Greeks. Kill! plunder! burn! let none remain.

SEMICHORUS I:

Alas! for Liberty!
If numbers, wealth, or unfulfilling years,
Or fate, can quell the free!
Alas! for Virtue, when
Torments, or contumely, or the sneers
Of erring judging men
Can break the heart where it abides.

Alas! if Love, whose smile makes this obscure world
splendid,
Can change with its false times and tides,
Like hope and terror, –
Alas for Love!
And Truth, who wanderest lone and unbefriended,
If thou canst veil thy lie-consuming mirror
Before the dazzled eyes of Error,
Alas for thee! Image of the Above.

SEMICHORUS II:

Repulse, with plumes from conquest torn,
Led the ten thousand from the limits of the morn
Through many an hostile Anarchy!
At length they wept aloud, and cried, 'the Sea! the Sea!'
Through exile, persecution, and despair,
Rome was, and young Atlantis shall become
The wonder, or the terror, or the tomb
Of all whose step wakes power lulled in her savage lair:
But Greece was as a hermit-child,
Whose fairest thoughts and limbs were built
To woman's growth, by dreams so mild,
She knew not pain or guilt;
And now, O Victory, blush! and Empire tremble
When ye desert the free –
If Greece must be
A wreck, yet shall its fragments re-assemble,
And build themselves again impregnably
In a diviner clime.
To Amphionic music on some Cape sublime,
Which frowns above the idle foam of Time.

SEMICHORUS I:

Let the tyrants rule the desert they have made;
  Let the free possess the paradise they claim;
Be the fortune of our fierce oppressors weighed
  With our ruin, our resistance, and our name!

SEMICHORUS II:

Our dead shall be the seed of their decay,
  Our survivors be the shadow of their pride,
Our adversity a dream to pass away –
  Their dishonour a remembrance to abide!

VOICE WITHOUT: Victory! Victory! The bought Briton sends
The keys of ocean to the Islamite. –
Now shall the blazon of the cross be veiled,
And British skill directing Othman might,
Thunder-strike rebel victory. O keep holy
This jubilee of unrevenged blood –
Kill! crush! despoil! Let not a Greek escape!

SEMICHORUS I:

Darkness has dawned in the East
    On the noon of time:
The death-birds descend to their feast,
    From the hungry clime.
Let Freedom and Peace flee far
    To a sunnier strand,
And follow Love's folding star
    To the Evening land!

SEMICHORUS II:

The young moon has fed
Her exhausted horn,
With the sunset's fire:
The weak day is dead,
But the night is not born;
And, like loveliness panting with wild desire
While it trembles with fear and delight,
Hesperus flies from awakening night,
And pants in its beauty and speed with light
Fast flashing, soft, and bright.
Thou beacon of love! thou lamp of the free!
Guide us far, far away,
To climes where now veiled by the ardour of day
Thou art hidden
From waves on which weary noon,
Faints in her summer swoon,
Between Kingless continents sinless as Eden,
Around mountains and islands inviolably
Prankt on the sapphire sea.

SEMICHORUS I:

Through the sunset of hope,
Like the shapes of a dream,
What Paradise islands of glory gleam!
Beneath Heaven's cope,
Their shadows more clear float by –
The sound of their oceans, the light of their sky,
The music and fragrance their solitudes breathe
Burst, like morning on dream, or like Heaven on death
Through the walls of our prison;
And Greece, which was dead, is arisen!

CHORUS:

The world's great age begins anew,
  The golden years return,
The earth doth like a snake renew
  Her winter weeds outworn:
Heaven smiles, and faiths and empires gleam,
Like wrecks of a dissolving dream.

A brighter Hellas rears its mountains
  From waves serener far;
A new Peneus rolls his fountains
  Against the morning-star.
Where fairer Tempes bloom, there sleep
Young Cyclads on a sunnier deep.

A loftier Argo cleaves the main,
  Fraught with a later prize;
Another Orpheus sings again,
  And loves, and weeps, and dies.
A new Ulysses leaves once more
Calypso for his native shore.

O, write no more the tale of Troy,
  If earth Death's scroll must be!
Nor mix with Laian rage the joy
  Which dawns upon the free:
Although a subtler Sphinx renew
Riddles of death Thebes never knew.

Another Athens shall arise,
  And to remoter time

Bequeath, like sunset to the skies,
The splendour of its prime.
And leave, if nought so bright may live,
All earth can take or Heaven can give.

Saturn and Love their long repose
Shall burst, more bright and good
Than all who fell, than One who rose,
Than many unsubdued:
Not gold, not blood, their altar dowers
But votive tears and symbol flowers.

O cease! must hate and death return?
Cease! must men kill and die?
Cease! drain not to its dregs the urn
Of bitter prophecy.
The world is weary of the past,
O might it die or rest at last!

Notes

The quenchless ashes of Milan (page 299, line 3): Milan was the centre of the resistance of the Lombard league against the Austrian tyrant. Frederic Barbarossa burnt the city to the ground, but liberty lived in its ashes, and it rose like an exhalation from its ruin. See Sismondi's *Histoire des Républiques Italiennes*, a book which has done much towards awakening the Italians to an imitation of their great ancestors. *The Chorus* (page 301): The popular notions of Christianity are represented in this chorus as true in their relation to the worship they superseded, and that which in all probability they will supersede, without considering their merits in a relation more universal. The first stanza contrasts the immortality of the living and thinking beings which inhabit the planets, and to use a common and inadequate phrase, *clothe themselves in matter* with the transience of the noblest manifestations of the external world.

The concluding verses indicate a progressive state of more or less exalted existence, according to the degree of perfection which every distinct intelligence may have attained. Let it not be supposed that I mean to dogmatise upon a subject, concerning which all men are equally ignorant, or that I think the Gordian knot of the origin of evil can be disentangled by that or any similar assertions. The received hypothesis of a Being resembling men in the moral attributes of his nature, having called us out of non-existence, and after inflicting on us the misery of the commission of error, should superadd that of the punishment and the privations consequent upon it, still would remain inexplicable and incredible. That there is a true solution of the riddle, and that in our present state that solution is unattainable by us, are propositions which may be regarded as equally certain: meanwhile, as it is the province of the poet to attach himself to those ideas which exalt and ennoble humanity, let him be permitted to have conjectured the condition of that futurity towards which we are all impelled by an inextinguishable thirst for immortality. Until better arguments can be produced than sophisms which disgrace the cause, this desire itself must remain the strongest and the only presumption that eternity is the inheritance of every thinking being.

No hoary priest[*s*] *after that Patriarch* (page 305, line 24): The Greek Patriarch after having been compelled to fulminate an anathema against the insurgents was put to death by the Turks.

Fortunately the Greeks have been taught that they cannot buy security by degradation, and the Turks, though equally

cruel, are less cunning than the smooth-faced tyrants of Europe. As to the anathema, his Holiness might as well have thrown his mitre at Mount Athos for any effect that it produced. The chiefs of the Greeks are almost all men of comprehension and enlightened views on religion and politics.
The freedman of a western poet chief (page 315, line 28): A Greek who had been Lord Byron's servant commands the insurgents in Attica. This Greek, Lord Byron informs me, though a poet and an enthusiastic patriot, gave him rather the idea of a timid and unenterprising person. It appears that circumstances make men what they are, and that we all contain the germ of a degree of degradation or of greatness whose connexion with our character is determined by events.
The Greeks expect a Saviour from the west (page 316, line 32): It is reported that this Messiah had arrived at a seaport near Lacedaemon in an American brig. The association of names and ideas is irresistibly ludicrous, but the prevalence of such a rumour strongly marks the state of popular enthusiasm in Greece.
The sound as of an assault [sic] *of an imperial city* (page 325, lines 7–8): For the vision of Mahmud, of the taking of Constantinople in 1445 [*sic*], see Gibbon's *Decline and Fall of the Roman Empire*, vol. xii, p. 223.

The manner of the invocation of the spirit of Mahomet the Second will be censured as over subtle. I could easily have made the Jew a regular conjuror, and the Phantom an ordinary ghost. I have preferred to represent the Jew as disclaiming all pretension, or even belief, in supernatural agency, and as tempting Mahmud to that state of mind in which ideas may be supposed to assume the force of sensations through the confusion of thought with the objects of thought, and the excess of passion animating the creations of imagination.

It is a sort of natural magic, susceptible of being exercised in a degree by any one who should have made himself master of the secret associations of another's thoughts.

The Chorus (page 334): The final chorus is indistinct and obscure, as the event of the living drama whose arrival it foretells. Prophecies of wars, and rumours of wars, &c., may safely be made by poet or prophet in any age, but to anticipate however darkly a period of regeneration and happiness is a more hazardous exercise of the faculty which bards possess or feign. It will remind the reader 'magno *nec* proximus intervallo' of Isaiah and Virgil, whose ardent spirits overleaping the actual reign of evil which we endure and bewail, already saw the possible and perhaps approaching state of society in which the '*lion shall lie down with the lamb*' and 'omnis feret omnia tellus.' Let these great names be my authority and my excuse.

Saturn and Love their long repose shall burst (page 335, lines 5–6): Saturn and Love were among the deities of a real or imaginary state of innocence and happiness. *All* those *who fell*, or the Gods of Greece, Asia, and Egypt; [the *One who rose*, or Jesus Christ, at whose appearance the idols of the Pagan World were amerced of their worship;] and *the many unsubdued*, or the monstrous objects of the idolatry of China, India, the Antarctic islands, and the native tribes of America, certainly have reigned over the understandings of men in conjunction or in succession, during periods in which all we know of evil has been in a state of portentous, and, until the revival of learning and the arts, perpetually increasing activity. The Grecian gods seem indeed to have been personally more innocent, although it cannot be said, that as far as temperance and chastity are concerned, they gave so edifying an example as their successor. The sublime human character of Jesus Christ was deformed by an imputed identification with a power, who tempted, betrayed, and punished the innocent beings who were called into existence by his sole will; and for the period of a thousand years, the spirit of this most just, wise, and benevolent of men, has been propitiated with myriads of hecatombs of those who approached the nearest to his innocence and wisdom, sacrificed under every aggravation of atrocity and variety of torture. The horrors of the Mexican, the Peruvian, and the Indian superstitions are well known.

To Night

I

Swiftly walk o'er the western wave,
Spirit of Night!
Out of the misty eastern cave,
Where, all the long and lone daylight,
Thou wovest dreams of joy and fear,
Which make thee terrible and dear, –
Swift be thy flight!

II

Wrap thy form in a mantle grey,
Star-inwrought!
Blind with thine hair the eyes of Day;
Kiss her until she be wearied out,
Then wander o'er city, and sea, and land,
Touching all with thine opiate wand –
Come, long sought!

III

When I arose and saw the dawn,
I sighed for thee;
When light rode high, and the dew was gone,
And noon lay heavy on flower and tree,
And the weary Day turned to his rest,
Lingering like an unloved guest,
I sighed for thee.

IV

Thy brother Death came, and cried,
Wouldst thou me?
Thy sweet child Sleep, the filmy-eyed,
Murmured like a noon-tide bee,
Shall I nestle near thy side?
Wouldst thou me? – And I replied,
No, not thee!

V

Death will come when thou art dead,
Soon, too soon –
Sleep will come when thou art fled;
Of neither would I ask the boon
I ask of thee, beloved Night –
Swift be thine approaching flight,
Come soon, soon!

Time

Unfathomable Sea! whose waves are years,
   Ocean of Time, whose waters of deep woe
Are brackish with the salt of human tears!
   Thou shoreless flood, which in thy ebb and flow
Claspest the limits of mortality,
And sick of prey, yet howling on for more,
Vomitest thy wrecks on its inhospitable shore;
Treacherous in calm, and terrible in storm,
   Who shall put forth on thee,
   Unfathomable Sea?

To —

I

One word is too often profaned
    For me to profane it,
One feeling too falsely disdained
    For thee to disdain it.
One hope is too like despair
    For prudence to smother,
And pity from thee more dear
    Than that from another.

II

I can give not what men call love,
    But wilt thou accept not
The worship the heart lifts above
    And the Heavens reject not,
The desire of the moth for the star,
    Of the night for the morrow,
The devotion to something afar
    From the sphere of our sorrow?

To —

Music, when soft voices die,
Vibrates in the memory –
Odours, when sweet violets sicken,
Live within the sense they quicken.

Rose leaves, when the rose is dead,
Are heaped for the beloved's bed;
And so thy thoughts, when thou art gone,
Love itself shall slumber on.

To Jane: The Invitation

Best and brightest, come away!
Fairer far than this fair Day,
Which, like thee to those in sorrow,
Comes to bid a sweet good-morrow
To the rough Year just awake
In its cradle on the brake.

The brightest hour of unborn Spring,
Through the winter wandering,
Found, it seems, the halcyon Morn
To hoar February born;
Bending from Heaven, in azure mirth,
It kissed the forehead of the Earth,
And smiled upon the silent sea,
And bade the frozen streams be free,
And waked to music all their fountains,
And breathed upon the frozen mountains,
And like a prophetess of May
Strewed flowers upon the barren way,
Making the wintry world appear
Like one on whom thou smilest, dear.

Away, away, from men and towns,
To the wild wood and the downs –
To the silent wilderness
Where the soul need not repress
Its music lest it should not find
An echo in another's mind,
While the touch of Nature's art
Harmonizes heart to heart.
I leave this notice on my door

For each accustomed visitor: –
'I am gone into the fields
To take what this sweet hour yields; –
Reflection, you may come to-morrow,
Sit by the fireside with Sorrow. –
You with the unpaid bill, Despair, –
You, tiresome verse-reciter, Care, –
I will pay you in the grave, –
Death will listen to your stave.
Expectation too, be off!
To-day is for itself enough;
Hope, in pity mock not Woe
With smiles, nor follow where I go;
Long having lived on thy sweet food,
At length I find one moment's good
After long pain – with all your love,
This you never told me of.'

Radiant Sister of the Day,
Awake! arise! and come away!
To the wild woods and the plains,
And the pools where winter rains
Image all their roof of leaves,
Where the pine its garland weaves
Of sapless green and ivy dun
Round stems that never kiss the sun;
Where the lawns and pastures be,
And the sandhills of the sea; –
Where the melting hoar-frost wets
The daisy-star that never sets,
And wind-flowers, and violets,
Which yet join not scent to hue,
Crown the pale year weak and new;
When the night is left behind

In the deep east, dun and blind,
And the blue noon is over us,
And the multitudinous
Billows murmur at our feet,
Where the earth and ocean meet,
And all things seem only one
In the universal sun.

To Jane: The Recollection

I

Now the last day of many days,
  All beautiful and bright as thou,
    The loveliest and the last, is dead,
Rise, Memory, and write its praise!
  Up, – to thy wonted work! come, trace
    The epitaph of glory fled, –
For now the Earth has changed its face,
  A frown is on the Heaven's brow.

II

We wandered to the Pine Forest
  That skirts the Ocean's foam,
The lightest wind was in its nest,
  The tempest in its home.
The whispering waves were half asleep,
  The clouds were gone to play,
And on the bosom of the deep,
  The smile of Heaven lay;
It seemed as if the hour were one
  Sent from beyond the skies,
Which scattered from above the sun
  A light of Paradise.

III

We paused amid the pines that stood
  The giants of the waste,
Tortured by storms to shapes as rude
  As serpents interlaced,
And soothed by every azure breath,
  That under heaven is blown,
To harmonies and hues beneath,
  As tender as its own;
Now all the tree-tops lay asleep,
  Like green waves on the sea,
As still as in the silent deep
  The ocean woods may be.

IV

How calm it was! – the silence there
  By such a chain was bound
That even the busy woodpecker
  Made stiller by her sound
The inviolable quietness;
  The breath of peace we drew
With its soft motion made not less
  The calm that round us grew.
There seemed from the remotest seat
  Of the white mountain waste,
To the soft flower beneath our feet,
  A magic circle traced, –
A spirit interfused around,
  A thrilling silent life, –
To momentary peace it bound
  Our mortal nature's strife; –

And still I felt the centre of
  The magic circle there,
Was one fair form that filled with love
  The lifeless atmosphere.

V

We paused beside the pools that lie
  Under the forest bough,
Each seemed as 'twere a little sky
  Gulphed in a world below;
A firmament of purple light,
  Which in the dark earth lay,
More boundless than the depth of night,
  And purer than the day –
In which the lovely forests grew
  As in the upper air,
More perfect both in shape and hue
  Than any spreading there.
There lay the glade and neighbouring lawn,
  And through the dark green wood
The white sun twinkling like the dawn
  Out of a speckled cloud.
Sweet views which in our world above
  Can never well be seen,
Were imaged by the water's love
  Of that fair forest green.
And all was interfused beneath
  With an Elysian glow,
An atmosphere without a breath,
  A softer day below.
Like one beloved the scene had lent
  To the dark water's breast,

Its every leaf and lineament
  With more than truth exprest;
Until an envious wind crept by,
  Like an unwelcome thought,
Which from the mind's too faithful eye
  Blots one dear image out.
Though thou art ever fair and kind,
  The forests ever green,
Less oft is peace in Shelley's mind,
  Than calm in waters seen.

With a Guitar, To Jane

Ariel to Miranda: – Take
This slave of Music, for the sake
Of him who is the slave of thee,
And teach it all the harmony
In which thou canst, and only thou,
Make the delighted spirit glow,
Till joy denies itself again,
And, too intense, is turned to pain;
For by permission and command
Of thine own Prince Ferdinand,
Poor Ariel sends this silent token
Of more than ever can be spoken;
Your guardian spirit, Ariel, who,
From life to life, must still pursue
Your happiness; – for thus alone
Can Ariel ever find his own.
From Prospero's inchanted cell,
As the mighty verses tell,
To the throne of Naples, he
Lit you o'er the trackless sea,
Flitting on, your prow before,
Like a living meteor.
When you die, the silent Moon,
In her interlunar swoon,
Is not sadder in her cell
Than deserted Ariel.
When you live again on earth,
Like an unseen star of birth,
Ariel guides you o'er the sea
Of life from your nativity.
Many changes have been run,

Since Ferdinand and you begun
Your course of love, and Ariel still
Has tracked your steps, and served your will;
Now, in humbler, happier lot,
This is all remembered not;
And now, alas! the poor sprite is
Imprisoned, for some fault of his,
In a body like a grave; –
From you he only dares to crave,
For his service and his sorrow,
A smile to-day, a song to-morrow.

The artist who this idol wrought,
To echo all harmonious thought,
Felled a tree, while on the steep
The woods were in their winter sleep,
Rocked in that repose divine
On the wind-swept Apennine;
And dreaming, some of Autumn past,
And some of Spring approaching fast,
And some of April buds and showers,
And some of songs in July bowers,
And all of love; and so this tree, –
O that such our death may be! –
Died in sleep, and felt no pain,
To live in happier form again:
From which, beneath Heaven's fairest star,
The artist wrought this loved Guitar,
And taught it justly to reply,
To all who question skilfully,
In language gentle as thine own;
Whispering in enamoured tone
Sweet oracles of woods and dells,
And summer winds in sylvan cells;

For it had learnt all harmonies
Of the plains and of the skies,
Of the forests and the mountains,
And the many-voiced fountains;
The clearest echoes of the hills,
The softest notes of falling rills,
The melodies of birds and bees,
The murmuring of summer seas,
And pattering rain, and breathing dew,
And airs of evening; and it knew
That seldom-heard mysterious sound,
Which, driven on its diurnal round,
As it floats through boundless day,
Our world enkindles on its way –
All this it knows, but will not tell
To those who cannot question well
The spirit that inhabits it;
It talks according to the wit
Of its companions; and no more
Is heard than has been felt before,
By those who tempt it to betray
These secrets of an elder day:
But sweetly as its answers will
Flatter hands of perfect skill,
It keeps its highest, holiest tone
For our beloved Jane alone.

To Jane

I

The keen stars were twinkling,
And the fair moon was rising among them,
Dear Jane!
The guitar was tinkling,
But the notes were not sweet till you sung them
Again.

II

As the moon's soft splendour
O'er the faint cold starlight of Heaven
Is thrown,
So your voice most tender
To the strings without soul had then given
Its own.

III

The stars will awaken,
Though the moon sleep a full hour later,
To-night;
No leaf will be shaken
Whilst the dews of your melody scatter
Delight.

IV

Though the sound overpowers,
Sing again, with your dear voice revealing
A tone
Of some world far from ours,
Where music and moonlight and feeling
Are one.

Lines Written in the Bay of Lerici

She left me at the silent time
When the moon had ceased to climb
The azure path of Heaven's steep,
And, like an albatross asleep,
Balanced on her wings of light,
Hovered in the purple night,
Ere she sought her ocean nest
In the chambers of the west.
She left me, and I staid alone,
Thinking over every tone,
Which, though silent to the ear,
The inchanted heart could hear,
Like notes which die when born, but still
Haunt the echoes of the hill;
And feeling ever – O too much! –
The soft vibration of her touch,
As if her gentle hand even now
Lightly trembled on my brow;
And thus, although she absent were,
Memory gave me all of her
That even Fancy dares to claim: –
Her presence had made weak and tame
All passions, and I lived alone
In the time which is our own;
The past and future were forgot,
As they had been, and would be, not.
But soon, the guardian angel gone,
The daemon re-assumed his throne
In my faint heart. I dare not speak
My thoughts, but thus disturbed and weak;
I sat, and saw the vessels glide

Over the ocean bright and wide,
Like spirit-winged chariots sent
O'er some serenest element
For ministrations strange and far;
As if to some Elysian star
Sailed for drink to medicine
Such sweet and bitter pain as mine.
And the wind that winged their flight
From the land came fresh and light;
And the scent of winged flowers,
And the coolness of the hours
Of dew, and sweet warmth left by day,
Were scattered o'er the twinkling bay;
And the fisher, with his lamp
And spear, about the low rocks damp
Crept, and struck the fish which came
To worship the delusive flame.
Too happy they, whose pleasure sought
Extinguishes all sense and thought
Of the regret that pleasure leaves,
Destroying life alone, not peace!

The Isle

There was a little lawny islet
By anemone and violet,
  Like mosaic, paven:
And its roof was flowers and leaves
Which the summer's breath enweaves,
Where nor sun nor showers nor breeze
Pierce the pines and tallest trees,
  Each a gem engraven; –
Girt by many an azure wave
With which the clouds and mountains pave
  A lake's blue chasm.

The Triumph of Life

Swift as a spirit hastening to his task
Of glory and of good, the Sun sprang forth
Rejoicing in his splendour, and the mask

Of darkness fell from the awakened Earth –
The smokeless altars of the mountain snows
Flamed above crimson clouds, and at the birth

Of light, the Ocean's orison arose,
To which the birds tempered their matin lay.
All flowers in field or forest which unclose

Their trembling eyelids to the kiss of day,
Swinging their censers in the element,
With orient incense lit by the new ray

Burned slow and inconsumably, and sent
Their odorous sighs up to the smiling air;
And, in succession due, did continent,

Isle, ocean, and all things that in them wear
The form and character of mortal mould,
Rise as the sun their father rose, to bear

Their portion of the toil, which he of old
Took as his own, and then imposed on them:
But I, whom thoughts which must remain untold

Had kept as wakeful as the stars that gem
The cone of night, now they were laid asleep
Stretched my faint limbs beneath the hoary stem

Which an old chesnut flung athwart the steep
Of a green Apennine: before me fled
The night; behind me rose the day; the deep

Was at my feet, and Heaven above my head,
When a strange trance over my fancy grew
Which was not slumber, for the shade it spread

Was so transparent, that the scene came through
As clear as when a veil of light is drawn
O'er evening hills they glimmer; and I knew

That I had felt the freshness of that dawn
Bathed in the same cold dew my brow and hair,
And sate as thus upon that slope of lawn

Under the self-same bough, and heard as there
The birds, the fountains and the ocean hold
Sweet talk in music through the enamoured air,
And then a vision on my brain was rolled.

*

As in that trance of wondrous thought I lay,
This was the tenour of my waking dream: –
Methought I sate beside a public way

Thick strewn with summer dust, and a great stream
Of people there was hurrying to and fro,
Numerous as gnats upon the evening gleam,

All hastening onward, yet none seemed to know
Whither he went, or whence he came, or why
He made one of the multitude, and so

Was borne amid the crowd, as through the sky
One of the million leaves of summer's bier;
Old age and youth, manhood and infancy,

Mixed in one mighty torrent did appear,
Some flying from the thing they feared, and some
Seeking the object of another's fear;

And others as with steps towards the tomb,
Pored on the trodden worms that crawled beneath,
And others mournfully within the gloom

Of their own shadow walked and called it death;
And some fled from it as it were a ghost,
Half fainting in the affliction of vain breath:

But more, with motions which each other crost,
Pursued or shunned the shadows the clouds threw,
Or birds within the noonday ether lost,

Upon that path where flowers never grew, –
And, weary with vain toil and faint for thirst,
Heard not the fountains, whose melodious dew

Out of their mossy cells for ever burst;
Nor felt the breeze which from the forest told
Of grassy paths and wood-lawns interspersed

With overarching elms and caverns cold,
And violet banks where sweet dreams brood, but they
Pursued their serious folly as of old.

And as I gazed, methought that in the way
The throng grew wilder, as the woods of June
When the south wind shakes the extinguished day,

And a cold glare, intenser than the noon,
But icy cold, obscured with blinding light
The sun, as he the stars. Like the young moon

When on the sunlit limits of the night
Her white shell trembles amid crimson air,
And whilst the sleeping tempest gathers might,

Doth, as the herald of its coming, bear
The ghost of its dead mother, whose dim form
Bends in dark ether from her infant's chair, –

So came a chariot on the silent storm
Of its own rushing splendour, and a Shape
So sate within, as one whom years deform,

Beneath a dusky hood and double cape,
Crouching within the shadow of a tomb;
And o'er what seemed the head a cloud-like crape

Was bent, a dun and faint ethereal gloom
Tempering the light. Upon the chariot beam
A Janus-visaged Shadow did assume

The guidance of that wonder-winged team;
The shapes which drew it in thick lightenings
Were lost: – I heard alone on the air's soft stream

The music of their ever-moving wings.
All the four faces of that charioteer
Had their eyes banded; little profit brings

Speed in the van and blindness in the rear,
Nor then avail the beams that quench the sun
Or that with banded eyes could pierce the sphere

Of all that is, has been or will be done;
So ill was the car guided – but it past
With solemn speed majestically on.

The crowd gave way, and I arose aghast,
Or seemed to rise, so mighty was the trance,
And saw, like clouds upon the thunder blast,

The million with fierce song and maniac dance
Raging around – such seemed the jubilee
As when to greet some conqueror's advance

Imperial Rome poured forth her living sea
From senate-house, and forum, and theatre,
When   upon the free

Had bound a yoke, which soon they stooped to bear.
Nor wanted here the just similitude
Of a triumphal pageant, for where'er

The chariot rolled, a captive multitude
Was driven; – all those who had grown old in power
Or misery, – all who had their age subdued

By action or by suffering, and whose hour
Was drained to its last sand in weal or woe,
So that the trunk survived both fruit and flower; –

All those whose fame or infamy must grow
Till the great winter lay the form and name
Of this green earth with them for ever low; –

All but the sacred few who could not tame
Their spirits to the conqueror – but as soon
As they had touched the world with living flame,

Fled back like eagles to their native noon,
Or those who put aside the diadem
Of earthly thrones or gems . . .

Were there, of Athens or Jerusalem,
Were neither mid the mighty captives seen,
Nor mid the ribald crowd that followed them,

Nor those who went before fierce and obscene.
The wild dance maddens in the van, and those
Who lead it – fleet as shadows on the green,

Outspeed the chariot, and without repose
Mix with each other in tempestuous measure
To savage music, wilder as it grows,

They, tortured by their agonizing pleasure,
Convulsed and on the rapid whirlwinds spun
Of that fierce spirit, whose unholy leisure

Was soothed by mischief since the world begun,
Throw back their heads and loose their streaming hair;
And in their dance round her who dims the sun,

Maidens and youths fling their wild arms in air
As their feet twinkle; they recede, and now
Bending within each other's atmosphere,

Kindle invisibly – and as they glow,
Like moths by light attracted and repelled,
Oft to their bright destruction come and go,

Till like two clouds into one vale impelled
That shake the mountains when their lightnings mingle
And die in rain – the fiery band which held

Their natures, snaps – while the shock still may tingle
One falls and then another in the path
Senseless – nor is the desolation single,

Yet ere I can say *where* – the chariot hath
Past over them – nor other trace I find
But as of foam after the ocean's wrath

Is spent upon the desart shore; – behind,
Old men and women foully disarrayed,
Shake their gray hairs in the insulting wind,

And follow in the dance, with limbs decayed,
Seeking to reach the light which leaves them still
Farther behind and deeper in the shade.

But not the less with impotence of will
They wheel, though ghastly shadows interpose
Round them and round each other, and fulfil

Their work, and in the dust from whence they rose
Sink, and corruption veils them as they lie,
And past in these performs what   in those.

Struck to the heart by this sad pageantry,
Half to myself I said – 'And what is this?
Whose shape is that within the car? And why –'

I would have added – 'is all here amiss?' –
But a voice answered – 'Life!' – I turned, and knew
(O Heaven, have mercy on such wretchedness!)

That what I thought was an old root which grew
To strange distortion out of the hill side,
Was indeed one of those deluded crew,

And that the grass, which methought hung so wide
And white, was but his thin discoloured hair
And that the holes it vainly sought to hide,

Were or had been eyes: – 'If thou canst, forbear
To join the dance, which I had well forborne,'
Said the grim Feature, of my thought aware.

'I will unfold that which to this deep scorn
Led me and my companions, and relate
The progress of the pageant since the morn;

'If thirst of knowledge shall not then abate,
Follow it thou even to the night, but I
Am weary.' – Then like one who with the weight

Of his own words is staggered, wearily
He paused; and ere he could resume, I cried:
'First, who art thou?' – 'Before thy memory,

'I feared, loved, hated, suffered, did and died,
And if the spark with which Heaven lit my spirit
Had been with purer nutriment supplied,

'Corruption would not now thus much inherit
Of what was once Rousseau, – nor this disguise
Stain that which ought to have disdained to wear it;

'If I have been extinguished, yet there rise
A thousand beacons from the spark I bore' –
'And who are those chained to the car?' – 'The wise,

'The great, the unforgotten, – they who wore
Mitres and helms and crowns, or wreaths of light,
Signs of thought's empire over thought – their lore

'Taught them not this, to know themselves; their might
Could not repress the mystery within,
And for the morn of truth they feigned, deep night

'Caught them ere evening.' – 'Who is he with chin
Upon his breast, and hands crost on his chain?' –
'The Child of a fierce hour; he sought to win

'The world, and lost all that it did contain
Of greatness, in its hope destroyed; and more
Of fame and peace than virtue's self can gain

'Without the opportunity which bore
Him on its eagle pinions to the peak
From which a thousand climbers have before

'Fallen, as Napoleon fell.' – I felt my cheek
Alter, to see the shadow pass away,
Whose grasp had left the giant world so weak,

That every pigmy kicked it as it lay;
And much I grieved to think how power and will
In opposition rule our mortal day,

And why God made irreconcilable
Good and the means of good; and for despair
I half disdained mine eyes' desire to fill

With the spent vision of the times that were
And scarce have ceased to be. – 'Dost thou behold,'
Said my guide, 'those spoilers spoiled, Voltaire,

'Frederick, and Paul, Catherine, and Leopold,
And hoary anarchs, demagogues, and sage –
        names which the world thinks always old,

'For in the battle life and they did wage,
She remained conqueror. I was overcome
By my own heart alone, which neither age,

'Nor tears, nor infamy, nor now the tomb
Could temper to its object.' – 'Let them pass',
I cried, 'the world and its mysterious doom

'Is not so much more glorious than it was,
That I desire to worship those who drew
New figures on its false and fragile glass

'As the old faded.' – 'Figures ever new
Rise on the bubble, paint them as you may;
We have but thrown, as those before us threw,

'Our shadows on it as it past away.
But mark how chained to the triumphal chair
The mighty phantoms of an elder day;

'All that is mortal of great Plato there
Expiates the joy and woe his master knew not;
The star that ruled his doom was far too fair,

'And life, where long that flower of Heaven grew not,
Conquered that heart by love, which gold, or pain,
Or age, or sloth, or slavery could subdue not.

'And near him walk the   twain,
The tutor and his pupil, whom Dominion
Followed as tame as vulture in a chain.

'The world was darkened beneath either pinion
Of him whom from the flock of conquerors
Fame singled out for her thunder-bearing minion;

'The other long outlived both woes and wars,
Throned in the thoughts of men, and still had kept
The jealous key of Truth's eternal doors,

'If Bacon's eagle spirit had not leapt
Like lightning out of darkness – he compelled
The Proteus shape of Nature as it slept

'To wake, and lead him to the caves that held
The treasure of the secrets of its reign.
See the great bards of elder time, who quelled

'The passions which they sung, as by their strain
May well be known: their living melody
Tempers its own contagion to the vein

'Of those who are infected with it – I
Have suffered what I wrote, or viler pain!
And so my words have seeds of misery –

'Even as the deeds of others, not as theirs.'
And then he pointed to a company,

'Midst whom I quickly recognized the heirs
Of Caesar's crime, from him to Constantine;
The anarch chiefs, whose force and murderous snares

Had founded many a sceptre-bearing line,
And spread the plague of gold and blood abroad:
And Gregory and John, and men divine,

Who rose like shadows between man and God;
Till that eclipse, still hanging over heaven,
Was worshipped by the world o'er which they strode,

For the true sun it quenched – 'Their power was given
But to destroy,' replied the leader: – 'I
Am one of those who have created, even

'If it be but a world of agony.' –
'Whence camest thou? and whither goest thou?
How did thy course begin?' I said, 'and why?

'Mine eyes are sick of this perpetual flow
Of people, and my heart sick of one sad thought –
Speak!' – 'Whence I am, I partly seem to know,

'And how and by what paths I have been brought
To this dread pass, methinks even thou mayst guess; –
Why this should be, my mind can compass not;

'Whither the conqueror hurries me, still less; –
But follow thou, and from spectator turn
Actor or victim in this wretchedness,

'And what thou wouldst be taught I then may learn
From thee. Now listen: – In the April prime,
When all the forest tips began to burn

'With kindling green, touched by the azure clime
Of the young season, I was laid asleep
Under a mountain, which from unknown time

'Had yawned into a cavern, high and deep;
And from it came a gentle rivulet,
Whose water, like clear air, in its calm sweep

'Bent the soft grass, and kept for ever wet
The stems of the sweet flowers, and filled the grove
With sounds, which whoso hears must needs forget

'All pleasure and all pain, all hate and love,
Which they had known before that hour of rest;
A sleeping mother then would dream not of

'Her only child who died upon the breast
At eventide – a king would mourn no more
The crown of which his brows were dispossest

'When the sun lingered o'er his ocean floor,
To gild his rival's new prosperity.
Thou wouldst forget thus vainly to deplore

'Ills, which if ills can find no cure from thee,
The thought of which no other sleep will quell,
Nor other music blot from memory,

'So sweet and deep is the oblivious spell;
And whether life had been before that sleep
The Heaven which I imagine, or a Hell

'Like this harsh world in which I wake to weep,
I know not. I arose, and for a space
The scene of woods and waters seemed to keep,

'Though it was now broad day, a gentle trace
Of light diviner than the common sun
Sheds on the common earth, and all the place

'Was filled with magic sounds woven into one
Oblivious melody, confusing sense
Amid the gliding waves and shadows dun;

'And, as I looked, the bright omnipresence
Of morning through the orient cavern flowed,
And the sun's image radiantly intense

'Burned on the waters of the well that glowed
Like gold, and threaded all the forest's maze
With winding paths of emerald fire; there stood

'Amid the sun, as he amid the blaze
Of his own glory, on the vibrating
Floor of the fountain, paved with flashing rays,

'A Shape all light, which with one hand did fling
Dew on the earth, as if she were the dawn,
And the invisible rain did ever sing

'A silver music on the mossy lawn;
And still before me on the dusky grass,
Iris her many-coloured scarf had drawn:

'In her right hand she bore a crystal glass,
Mantling with bright Nepenthe; the fierce splendour
Fell from her as she moved under the mass

'Of the deep cavern, and with palms so tender,
Their tread broke not the mirror of its billow,
Glided along the river, and did bend her

'Head under the dark boughs, till like a willow
Her fair hair swept the bosom of the stream
That whispered with delight to be its pillow.

'As one enamoured is upborne in dream
O'er lily-paven lakes 'mid silver mist,
To wondrous music, so this shape might seem

'Partly to tread the waves with feet which kissed
The dancing foam; partly to glide along
The air which roughened the moist amethyst,

'Or the faint morning beams that fell among
The trees, or the soft shadows of the trees;
And her feet, ever to the ceaseless song

'Of leaves, and winds, and waves, and birds, and bees,
And falling drops, moved in a measure new
Yet sweet, as on the summer evening breeze,

'Up from the lake a shape of golden dew
Between two rocks, athwart the rising moon,
Dances i' the wind, where never eagle flew;

'And still her feet, no less than the sweet tune
To which they moved, seemed as they moved to blot
The thoughts of him who gazed on them; and soon

'All that was, seemed as if it had been not;
And all the gazer's mind was strewn beneath
Her feet like embers; and she, thought by thought,

'Trampled its sparks into the dust of death;
As day upon the threshold of the east
Treads out the lamps of night, until the breath

'Of darkness re-illumine even the least
Of heaven's living eyes – like day she came,
Making the night a dream; and ere she ceased

'To move, as one between desire and shame
Suspended, I said – If, as it doth seem,
Thou comest from the realm without a name,

'Into this valley of perpetual dream,
Show whence I came, and where I am, and why –
Pass not away upon the passing stream.

'Arise and quench thy thirst, was her reply.
And as a shut lily stricken by the wand
Of dewy morning's vital alchemy,

'I rose; and, bending at her sweet command,
Touched with faint lips the cup she raised,
And suddenly my brain became as sand

'Where the first wave had more than half erased
The track of deer on desert Labrador;
Whilst the wolf, from which they fled amazed,

'Leaves his stamp visibly upon the shore,
Until the second bursts; – so on my sight
Burst a new vision, never seen before,

'And the fair shape waned in the coming light,
As veil by veil the silent splendour drops
From Lucifer, amid the chrysolite

'Of sun-rise, ere it tinge the mountain tops;
And as the presence of that fairest planet,
Although unseen, is felt by one who hopes

'That his day's path may end as be began it,
In that star's smile, whose light is like the scent
Of a jonquil when evening breezes fan it,

'Or the soft note in which his dear lament
The Brescian shepherd breathes, or the caress
That turned his weary slumber to content;

'So knew I in that light's severe excess
The presence of that shape which on the stream
Moved, as I moved along the wilderness,

'More dimly than a day-appearing dream,
The ghost of a forgotten form of sleep;
A light of heaven, whose half-extinguished beam

'Through the sick day in which we wake to weep,
Glimmers, for ever sought, for ever lost;
So did that shape its obscure tenour keep

'Beside my path, as silent as a ghost;
But the new Vision, and the cold bright car,
With solemn speed and stunning music, crost

'The forest, and as if from some dread war
Triumphantly returning, the loud million
Fiercely extolled the fortune of her star.

'A moving arch of victory, the vermilion
And green and azure plumes of Iris had
Built high over her wind-winged pavilion,

'And underneath etherial glory clad
The wilderness, and far before her flew
The tempest of the splendour, which forbade

'Shadow to fall from leaf and stone; the crew
Seemed in that light, like atomies to dance
Within a sunbeam; – some upon the new

'Embroidery of flowers, that did enhance
The grassy vesture of the desert, played,
Forgetful of the chariot's swift advance;

'Others stood gazing, till within the shade
Of the great mountain its light left them dim;
Others outspeeded it; and others made

'Circles around it, like the clouds that swim
Round the high moon in a bright sea of air;
And more did follow, with exulting hymn,

'The chariot and the captives fettered there: –
But all like bubbles on an eddying flood
Fell into the same track at last, and were

'Borne onward. – I among the multitude
Was swept – me, sweetest flowers delayed not long;
Me, not the shadow nor the solitude;

'Me, not that falling stream's Lethean song;
Me, not the phantom of that early Form
Which moved upon its motion – but among

'The thickest billows of that living storm
I plunged, and bared my bosom to the clime
Of that cold light, whose airs too soon deform.

'Before the chariot had begun to climb
The opposing steep of that mysterious dell,
Behold a wonder worthy of the rhyme

'Of him who from the lowest depths of hell,
Through every paradise and through all glory,
Love led serene, and who returned to tell

'In words of hate and awe; the wondrous story
How all things are transfigured except Love;
For deaf as is a sea, which wrath makes hoary,

'The world can hear not the sweet notes that move
The sphere whose light is melody to lovers –
A wonder worthy of his rhyme – the grove

'Grew dense with shadows to its inmost covers,
The earth was grey with phantoms, and the air
Was peopled with dim forms, as when there hovers

'A flock of vampire-bats before the glare
Of the tropic sun, bringing, ere evening,
Strange night upon some Indian isle; – thus were

'Phantoms diffused around; and some did fling
Shadows of shadows, yet unlike themselves,
Behind them; some like eaglets on the wing

'Were lost in the white day; others like elves
Danced in a thousand unimagined shapes
Upon the sunny streams and grassy shelves;

'And others sate chattering like restless apes
On vulgar hands, . . .
Some made a cradle of the ermined capes

'Of kingly mantles; some across the tire
Of pontiffs sate like vultures; others played
Under the crown which girt with empire

'A baby's or an ideot's brow, and made
Their nests in it. The old anatomies
Sate hatching their bare broods under the shade

'Of demon wings, and laughed from their dead eyes
To re-assume the delegated power,
Arrayed in which those worms did monarchize,

'Who made this earth their charnel. Others more
Humble, like falcons, sate upon the fist
Of common men, and round their heads did soar;

'Or like small gnats and flies, as thick as mist
On evening marshes, thronged about the brow
Of lawyers, statesmen, priest and theorist; –

'And others, like discoloured flakes of snow
On fairest bosoms and the sunniest hair,
Fell, and were melted by the youthful glow

'Which they extinguished; and, like tears, they were
A vein to those from whose faint lids they rained
In drops of sorrow. I became aware

'Of whence those forms proceeded which thus stained
The track in which we moved. After brief space,
From every form the beauty slowly waned;

'From every firmest limb and fairest face
The strength and freshness fell like dust, and left
The action and the shape without the grace

'Of life. The marble brow of youth was cleft
With care; and in those eyes where once hope shone,
Desire, like a lioness bereft

'Of her last cub, glared ere it died; each one
Of that great crowd sent forth incessantly
These shadows, numerous as the dead leaves blown

'In autumn evening from a poplar tree.
Each like himself and like each other were
At first; but some distorted seemed to be

'Obscure clouds, moulded by the casual air;
And of this stuff the car's creative ray
Wrought all the busy phantoms that were there,

'As the sun shapes the clouds; thus on the way
Mask after mask fell from the countenance
And form of all; and long before the day

'Was old, the joy which waked like heaven's glance
The sleepers in the oblivious valley, died;
And some grew weary of the ghastly dance,

'And fell, as I have fallen, by the way-side; –
Those soonest from whose forms most shadows past,
And least of strength and beauty did abide.

'Then, what is life? I cried.' –

MORE ABOUT PENGUINS AND PELICANS

Penguinews, which appears every month, contains details of all the new books issued by Penguins as they are published. From time to time it is supplemented by *Penguins in Print*, which is a complete list of all available books published by Penguins. (There are well over four thousand of these.)

A specimen copy of *Penguinews* will be sent to you free on request. For a year's issues (including the complete lists) please send 30p if you live in the United Kingdom, or 60p if you live elsewhere. Just write to Dept EP, Penguin Books Ltd, Harmondsworth, Middlesex, enclosing a cheque or postal order, and your name will be added to the mailing list.

Note: *Penguinews* and *Penguins in Print* are not available in the U.S.A. or Canada

PENGUIN MODERN POETS

1* Lawrence Durrell Elizabeth Jennings R. S. Thomas
2* Kingsley Amis Dom Moraes Peter Porter
3* George Barker Martin Bell Charles Causley
4* David Holbrook Christopher Middleton David Wevill
5† Gregory Corso Lawrence Ferlinghetti Allen Ginsberg
6 George MacBeth Edward Lucie-Smith Jack Clemo
7* Richard Murphy Jon Silkin Nathaniel Tarn
8* Edwin Brock Geoffrey Hill Stevie Smith
9† Denise Levertov Kenneth Rexroth William Carlos Williams
10 Adrian Henri Roger McGough Brian Patten
11 D. M. Black Peter Redgrove D. M. Thomas
12* Alan Jackson Jeff Nuttall William Wantling
13 Charles Bukowski Philip Lamantia Harold Norse
14 Alan Brownjohn Michael Hamburger Charles Tomlinson
15 Alan Bold Edward Brathwaite Edwin Morgan
16 Jack Beeching Harry Guest Matthew Mead
17 W. S. Graham Kathleen Raine David Gascoyne
18 A. Alvarez Roy Fuller Anthony Thwaite
19 John Ashbery Lee Harwood Tom Raworth
20 John Heath-Stubbs F. T. Prince Stephen Spender
21* George Mackay Brown Norman MacCaig Iain Crichton Smith
22* John Fuller Peter Levi Adrian Mitchell
23 Geoffrey Grigson Edwin Muir Adrian Stokes
24 Kenward Elmslie Kenneth Koch James Schuyler

* *Not for sale in the U.S.A.*
† *Not for sale in the U.S.A. or Canada*

POET TO POET

In the introductions to their personal selections from the work of poets they have admired, the individual editors write as follows:

Crabbe Selected by C. Day Lewis

As his poetry displays a balance and decorum in its versification, so his moral ideal is a kind of normality to which every civilized being should aspire. This, when one looks at the desperate expedients and experiments of poets (and others) today, is at least refreshing.'

Wordsworth Selected by Lawrence Durrell

'Wordsworth almost more than any other English poet enjoyed a sense of inner confirmation – the mysterious sense of election to poetry as a whole way of life. He realized too that one cannot condescend to nature – one must work for it like a monk over a missal which he will not live to see finished.'

Tennyson Selected by Kingsley Amis

'England notoriously had its doubts as well as its certainties, its neuroses as well as its moral health, its fits of gloom and frustration and panic as well as its complacency. Tennyson is the voice of those doubts and their accompaniments, and his genius enabled him to communicate them in such a way that we can understand them and feel them as our own. In short we know from experience just what he means. Eliot called him the saddest of all English poets, and I cannot improve on that judgement.'

Also available

Henryson *Selected by Hugh MacDiarmid*
Herbert *Selected by W. H. Auden*
Whitman *Selected by Robert Creeley*
Cotton *Selected by Geoffrey Grigson*
Jonson *Selected by Thomas Gunn*
Pope *Selected by Peter Levi*